HOLLYWOOD
LOST

Center Point
Large Print

Also by Ace Collins and available from
Center Point Large Print:

Yellow Packard
Darkness Before Dawn
Cutting Edge

HOLLYWOOD LOST

Ace Collins

CENTER POINT LARGE PRINT
THORNDIKE, MAINE

This Center Point Large Print edition is published
in the year 2015 by arrangement with Abingdon Press.

The text of this Large Print edition is unabridged.
In other aspects, this book may vary
from the original edition.
Printed in the United States of America
on permanent paper.
Set in 16-point Times New Roman type.

ISBN: 978-1-62899-586-2

Library of Congress Cataloging-in-Publication Data

Collins, Ace.
  Hollywood lost / Ace Collins. — Center Point Large Print edition.
    pages cm
  Summary: "A small-town girl is used as bait to uncover the identity of
a serial killer in this romantic suspense novel where separating reality
from fantasy is all but impossible, where love is rare, life is cheap, and
values are lost in pursuit of fame and fortune"—Provided by publisher.
  ISBN 978-1-62899-586-2 (library binding : alk. paper)
  1. Large type books. I. Title.
  PS3553.O47475H65 2015b
  813'.54—dc23
                                                              2015007340

To Shelby Rebekah Seabaugh,
whose spirit lit up every room she entered
and who positively changed every life
she touched. No one defined joy
as completely as she did.

Acknowledgments

I would like to thank my Abingdon team:
Ramona Richards, Susan Cornell,
and Cat Hoort; my agent, Joyce Hart;
and Barrett Gay.

1

June 5, 1936

"Why can't people get murdered in the day-time?"

Bill Barrister glanced over to his young sergeant, Barry Jenkins, frowned, and said, "Why do they have to get killed at all?" The captain then looked back at the body sprawled on the ground beneath the Hollywoodland sign and sighed. She looked to be about twenty, her hair was platinum, though he figured it was dyed. She was dressed in a torn ice-blue evening gown and high heels. Her nails were polished and manicured, her skin almost ivory, and her lips painted deep red. She was way too young to be dead.

"We can't find any identification," a uniformed cop called out from down the hill. "There's no purse or anything else within twenty feet of the body no matter what direction I search."

Barrister didn't figure there would be. After all, when you are the head of the Los Angeles homicide division nothing ever comes easy. So he had to scratch and claw for every clue and there were never any movie detectives like Philo Vance or Nick Charles trying to help him. Crouching beside the body, the heavyset Barrister took a closer look

7

and shook his head. "She must have been pretty before someone strangled her."

"Hard to tell now," Jenkins chimed in. The twenty-eight-year old lanky investigator stuck his hands into his gray suit slacks, looked away from the victim toward the city, and asked, "How long you been on the force, Cap?"

"Too long," came the abrupt response. Pulling off his hat and running his short, thick fingers over his bald head, Barrister studied the body more closely. After his eyes roamed from her head to her feet, he finally answered his partner's question. "Barry, it has been twenty-one years." He pushed his short body upright and glanced over to the other man. "Tonight, I wish I was back on a beat. When I get cases like this, I hate this job. This was personal. This wasn't some random robbery or domestic squabble; this was a crime of passion. Someone wanted to not just kill this girl; they wanted her to watch them as they squeezed the life from her body. What kind of monster does this?"

"Just like the other three," Jenkins suggested.

"Yeah," Barrister admitted, "just like the other three."

The captain loosened his tie. Even on this cool night he was sweating. Death did that to him. It made his insides burn and his head pound and left a foul taste as his stomach churned like a Kansas twister. And most of all it made him want to race home and hug his wife and two children and then walk away from this job forever. And yet, he couldn't do that. That wasn't his nature. Like a hound with his nose to the ground, he had to doggedly stay on the trail until he treed or killed the man who did this.

"Do you think it's the same guy?" Jenkins asked.

Barrister, his gaze once more falling on the body, didn't reply. And there was a good reason too. Before he connected the cases, he had to put them into some kind of context that allowed him to view them logically and unemotionally. After all, a dozen people were strangled in his city last year, and he knew for a fact not all of them were killed by the same person. What did these four have in common? Were they looking at random acts of violence or was there a madman on the loose? His gut assured him it was the latter, but logic begged him to consider the former.

"Barry," the captain explained as he did a mental inventory, "we've caught and convicted four stranglers this year. Two were husbands, another escaped from prison and was after the guy who set him up, and the other one was a jealous boy-friend. Who is to say this one doesn't fall into one of those categories? Before I determine anything that might give the press something to sensa-tionalize and scare the citizens of our city half to death, I need to be sure. Right now, you and I are the only people who think this one might be connected to the others. For the moment, that's how I want to keep it. So put your flashlight beam back on the body and let's take another look and without allowing past prejudices to influence us, let's see what this one body and single crime scene tell us."

With the body now bathed in the yellow glow of the flashlight, Barrister mentally put the unsolved but similar cases side by side. Judging by how this girl was dressed, she had likely been to a party. At least one of the other victims had been dressed for a fancy or formal social gathering. But where did she go, and was it the same location as this woman? Could the murderer seek women out at a nightclub or on the party scene? It might be a possibility and something he needed to consider.

Victim #2 was tossed in a vacant lot in Beverly Hills about nine months ago . . . September 15, 1935. The brunette was tall, attractive, and wearing a dress that matched the California sky on a summer day. As they'd never found out that woman's name, there was no way for Barrister to know what she might have had in common with the blonde lying at his feet. So was there something else tying the two women together and was it hiding in plain sight right in front of him? If it was, he didn't see it, so it was time to move on to another victim of strangulation.

The first one was discovered a year ago, June 3,

1935, on a beach outside of Malibu. She was dressed in a light blue bathing suit. Maggie Reason was a brunette, twenty-three, and lived on the West Coast for five months. Like so many others she was trying to make it in the movie business, but only managed a couple of walk-on roles before she was killed. She had grown up in Illinois and, when the medical examiner finished with her, she'd been shipped back there. Beyond having someone wrap their fingers around her throat, what did she have in common with the dead woman they found tonight? On the surface it looked like nothing.

In December they'd found victim #3. She was a brunette, beautiful, and athletic. She was raised in Los Angeles and was a freshman at UCLA. Her last night was spent at a movie in Beverly Hills before her body was dumped in an alley behind the restaurant of the stars—Musso and Frank. She'd been wearing a navy sweater and light blue skirt when she was found. She'd been strangled too, but did that tie her murder to any of the other three?

"It just doesn't add up," Barrister grumbled turning to look at his partner. "Where is the connection? The two we identified didn't know each other and had far different backgrounds. And, in each case, the bodies were found in much different locations."

Barrister studied the dead woman again and mumbled, "Why not dump them in a canyon or someplace few people ever visit? That's what smart killers do. Each time we've found young strangulation victims, the bodies have been dropped in places people pass by all the time."

"Maybe he's dumped others in out-of-the-way spots," Jenkins suggested. "Maybe these aren't the only ones."

As if trying to deal with four dead women was not enough, now Barrister had something even more sobering to consider. What if there *were* more?

Leaning back over the body, the captain took a final look at the victim. Just like the other three, her face was forever frozen in terror. He therefore figured the attacker or attackers had to be people who felt a sense of great power from their actions. And if these four were all murdered by the same man, then this was an urge he probably had to satisfy on a regular basis. And it would likely not end until he was either caught or dead. It looked more and more like there was a deranged killer on the loose in Los Angeles.

"What's that by her right hand?" Jenkins asked, pointing a flashlight's beam to a place two feet from the dead woman.

The captain stepped over the body to the area where the light had spotlighted something in the grass. "It's a kitchen match," Barrister noted. "Look, it's been broken in two." He picked up the pieces and placed them in the palm of his hand.

He studied them for a moment before looking back to his partner, "Didn't we spot a match on the beach beside the first victim?"

"Yeah." Jenkins replied, "but a lot of folks use matches on beaches."

Barrister stood, "Was that one used?"

"I don't think so," the younger man replied.

"We need to examine the crime scene photos," Barrister suggested. "This might be nothing more than just a coincidence, but I need to find out for sure. If there is an unused, broken match at each crime scene, it could be our first break."

"If there was a broken kitchen match at each scene," Jenkins asked, "what do you think it means?"

"It could be a signature," Barrister explained. The fact he might have uncovered his first real clue caused the captain's heart to race, but that excitement was tempered with the knowledge that a clever madman was much more difficult to find than any other kind of killer. He could literally be anybody. By day, he might be a respected businessman, doctor, preacher, or actor, but for an hour or two every few months he might become something much more evil than any fictional character ever dreamed up by Hollywood script-writers. And the only clue he possessed was the broken match he held in his hand.

"Barry," Barrister suggested, "this might just be our murderer's way of signing his work. Based on how and where he lays out his victims, I'm guessing he thinks of himself as an artist too. He wants these women to be found. He wants to know there are others admiring his work. He might even be looking at us right now." Barrister stopped, looked back into his hand, and sighed, "Or it could be nothing at all."

2

June 6, 1936

Filled with grief, her deep blue eyes were drawn to the small, three-room farmhouse that had been her home since birth. It wasn't much to look at, the Oklahoma wind had pretty much stripped away the peeling white paint, and the sagging tin roof was patched in four different places with old rusty metal signs, but that didn't matter. She belonged there or at least always thought she did.

To the young woman's right, an early twenties Model T Ford roadster, half buried by drifting dirt, sat beside a small, almost roofless, plank barn that, from constantly being pushed by a relentless south wind, was leaning at a twenty-degree angle in a northerly direction. To her left, a circular stone wall surrounded the opening to a well that had gone dry the previous summer. Just beyond that was a garden spot filled with little more than brown, stiff, and broken weeds holding a sad vigil where vegetables had once thrived. But it was still home.

For twenty-one years, this now depressing patch of land just outside of Cordell, Oklahoma, was the place she'd learned to walk, read, sew, and cook. During those years she'd spent hours on the front porch and, while washing clothes in an old tub, she thought about the future. And in those modest musings the future was bright and joyful filled with a happy marriage, a small neat home, and lots of children. And those simple ponderings were so unlike the reality of what her life and prospects had become.

Five miles down the dirt road running in front of her home, she'd gone to school, sitting day after day and year after year at old desks with scores of names that generations of students had carved deep into the tops. In poorly lit classrooms, she learned to read, write, spell, and add as well as made scores of friends. There had been dances and hayrides, ice cream socials, and band concerts, and each of those events was now etched deeply into her soul's fabric and was seeping from places in her mind that had been dormant. And right now, she didn't want those memories in her life because they brought far more pain than joy.

In Cordell, just off the town square, the community church might have been just a

15

simple, plank-board building, but it was where she'd learned about values and faith as well as where God tugged at her heart and led her to trust Him. In hard pews holding shaped-note, canvas-backed hymnals, she'd sung and prayed and even suffered during long, loud sermons. And though it had often been a struggle to get out of bed and get there on Sunday mornings, it, along with her family, was her anchor.

Then there were the fields her father had farmed. The sunny days she'd walked barefoot beside the mule as her dad, always outfitted in a straw hat, white shirt, and bib overalls, plowed. How she relished the feel of the warm soil between her toes, how she'd loved to listen to his stories, been captivated by the tunes he'd whistled, and taken in by the smell of the Prince Albert tobacco he always smoked in his pipe. When the hard times hit, it was the tobacco that went first. Her dad gave up smoking to save a few cents a day. Later, Jasper, the old mule was sold and the stories and whistling stopped. Then her mother, who'd always sewn their clothes, started patching them instead. And that meant fewer trips to the general store where the young woman had once bought orange sodas, looked at dolls, and read movie magazines. She treasured those bitter-sweet recollections even more than the cameo her grandmother had given her for her sixteenth birthday.

For the past three years it had been her pay-check that had kept the hounds from the door. She'd worked at Maybelle's Dress Shop. For a time her skills as a seamstress had given her value. She'd altered dresses and even sewn original outfits. Then the Depression had deepened to the point where Maybelle Johnson no longer sold enough stock to keep the doors open. And that was the real beginning of the end.

The sound of a screen door slamming shut yanked her from sad reminiscing to the even sadder reality of what life had become. Lifting her large, expressive eyes, Shelby dejectedly watched as her mother, wearing a faded, long blue dress stepped out onto the porch for a final time. Looking far older than her forty-one years, the frail woman, her straw-colored hair pushed under a bonnet, wiped tears from her eyes as she patted the porch railing and gazed out on what had once been fertile farmland. Finally, she turned to once more study the foreclosure notice tacked to the wooden entry. Rather than see her mother's sagging shoulders tremble and her eyes explode with tears, twenty-one-year-old Shelby pushed her eyes back to a blue 1932 Ford truck. Her father, a short, thin man stood beside it inspecting the family's meager possessions. He was just another Okie who had run out of luck, but in his eyes Shelby could see he felt as though he'd failed as a farmer, husband, and father. Giving up and moving was breaking both his spirit and his heart but there were no other options. So, surviving the June 3 auction that stripped him of every vestige of how he'd once fed his family, he'd spent the last two days packing everything the family kept into the vehicle's six-foot bed.

Her eyes misting, Shelby smoothed her washed-out green dress and turned her gaze to Rex. The old collie/shepherd mix jumped into the truck's bed and found a place on an oak rocking chair. If the dog regretted leaving the farm, he didn't show it. His eyes were bright and his expression filled with a mixture of joy and curiosity. The black and tan mutt, the only animal that hadn't been sold or given away, seemed more than ready to make the trip that everyone else was dreading. He had no regrets about what he was leaving behind and no fears of what was ahead. If only she had the old dog's blissful, optimistic faith.

The July wind stirred up dirt that hadn't seen rain in months and sent it swirling by the house and barn and down the long straight road. It seemed that even the wind and the dust that had choked the life out of the farm were now urging the family to move on.

"Time to get going," John announced, his voice cracking with emotion.

"I know," Mary answered, her words barely carrying the twenty feet from the porch to the truck. Shaking her head, she stepped onto the

18

ground before adding, "It ain't going to be easy, Pa."

"Can't be any worse than here," he assured her. "We didn't have nothing twenty-three years ago when we got hitched. So we'll be fine. Cousin Stew assured me there was work in California. You read his letter a dozen times. You just got to have faith."

"Not sure I know what that is anymore," the woman admitted as she opened the passenger door and placed her foot on the running board. "Pa, you get everything on the truck?"

"Everything but our troubles and problems," he assured her. "Hopefully, I'm leaving those here."

The sound of a car motoring up the road caused Shelby to turn her eyes away from her parents and to the road. She immediately recognized the black Model A coupe stirring up the dust as belonging to Calvin Kelly. They'd graduated high school together and, thanks to the fact that his family owned a couple of the stores in town, the tall, dark-headed young man was attending the University of Oklahoma studying business. In a state filled with sad and suffering people, Kelly was one of the lucky ones.

Pulling up behind the Beckett's truck, Calvin switched off the four-cylinder motor, swung the door open, jumped out, and quickly covered the thirty feet between him and Shelby. After smoothing his light blue shirt, he pushed his hair out of his eyes and announced, "I had to catch you before you left."

Shelby forced a smile and nodded as the visitor fidgeted in front of her. Looking over her shoulder, Kelly pushed his hands into the pockets of his black pants and nodded to her parents.

"Good to see you, Calvin," Mary called out.

The young man politely smiled and then turned to once more face Shelby. "I came out here to tell you, well . . ."He paused, licked his lips, and finally stammered, "I guess I love you."

Her blue eyes catching the morning sun, Shelby smiled, "Calvin Kelly, you've never even kissed me; you have no idea what love is."

"But," he argued, "if you'd just stay, we could get married and . . ."

"And you wouldn't go back to Norman and finish college," she quickly chimed in. "You've only got one year left. You can't quit now."

"But . . ."

"No buts," Shelby announced placing her finger to his lips. "Your world's not lost. You get to live your dreams. Don't trade all of that just because you feel sorry for me. I'll do fine." She forced a smile and then lied, "It will be kind of fun seeing someplace new for the first time in my life. You know I've never even been out of Oklahoma."

"This isn't about charity," he argued, his dark eyes showing a mixture of hope and pain. "I've loved you since our first day in grade school.

There's not another girl like you in these parts. I can't let you get away."

His offer was tempting. After all, she didn't want to leave, her whole life was here and her folks would look at her marrying Calvin as a blessing from heaven. But that wasn't the best thing for Calvin and likely not the best for her either.

"When you get your degree," she assured him, "if you haven't found some cute girl at school, you can come look for me. I'll write and tell you where I am. After all, if you keep your nose to the grindstone that is only a year away. Now, we have to get on the road. We have a long way to go."

"But . . ."

"Quit that," she whispered.

"Can I at least have a good-bye kiss?" he begged, his face framed in a hopeful expression usually reserved for small children sitting on Santa's lap.

Shelby smiled, "You should have asked for that a long time ago, like after the junior dance or during the hayride our sophomore year."

"Guess I should have," he admitted. "Guess I should have said and done a lot of things. I just always figured there'd be time."

She heard her father step into the truck and close the door. This was it, her last moment standing on the soil that had embraced her, defined her, and was now rejecting her. With a million memories fighting for space in her head, she leaned her face toward his until her lips met his. In the brief seconds they touched, Shelby was overcome with a sense of sadness and loss, of things that might have been and now could not be, of the security of the past and the insecurity of what lay ahead. And, even when the gentle kiss ended, those feelings still demanded her attention, tugging at her with the strength of the winter's north wind.

"That was nice," he whispered, their faces still close. "I'll miss you."

She nodded, stepped back, and moved to the truck. Grabbing hold of the tied-down rocking chair, she pulled herself onto the truck bed's floor, turned and sat down, her legs dangling over the open tailgate. After taking a final look at Calvin, she moved her eyes once more to the only home she'd ever known. As she studied the house, her father started the motor, the gearbox groaning as he slid the transmission into first gear, and, a moment later, the heavily loaded Ford lurched forward.

"Good-bye, Shelby," the young man sadly called out.

Pulling her knees up to her chest, she wrapped her arms around the dress that covered her legs and nodded. The truck was heading west, her eyes were looking east and everything that had been was now quickly fading away behind her.

3

June 10, 1936

Galaxy Studios, with more than forty sound-stages and a three hundred-acre back lot, was the crown jewel of the movie industry. Headed by Jacob Yates, a small, balding man with a huge ego and an even larger appetite for cash, the studio claimed to have more stars than those in the night sky above Hollywood. And though an exaggeration of the greatest magnitude, there was no doubt Galaxy had the top talent in the industry, headed by the king of the box office, Flynn Sparks.

Sparks, who'd grown up in Gary, Indiana, and migrated to California in his late teens, first found work as a stunt man with the Roach Studios. After a few minor roles at MGM, in which he never spoke a single line, Sparks, who was then using his given name of Hamilton, was spotted by Yates. What everyone but Galaxy's boss missed was that when the young man strolled through a door every other person in the room disappeared. With his dark, almost black eyes, his wavy brown hair, square jaw, broad shoulders and deep baritone voice, the six-footer was the dream catch of females from ten to ninety and he was made to order for this new era of talking motion pictures. Who cared if he couldn't act; Galaxy had people who could teach him enough skills to get by.

Hamilton jumped at Yates's offer of seventy-five dollars a week, and with the young man under contract, the studio's publicity team rewrote his history. Bill Hamilton disappeared as Yates invented Flynn Sparks. With a biography that included growing up in Montana and time spent looking for gold in South Africa, Hollywood introduced a new actor to the world who was an adventurer living for thrills and excitement. Above all other American males, Sparks was a man who grabbed life and squeezed every moment of pleasure from it. He lived on the edge and had no fear of death. It was an image Sparks loved almost as much as he did his new name.

First cast opposite Dalton Andrews, who was then Galaxy's top draw, in a crime picture, Sparks charmed fans even as he was panned by critics as nothing more than an empty package with a nice face used as wrapping. His acting improved marginally when he played a New York lawyer who spent as much time captivating his costar, Betty Foster, as he did working on a capital case. In the next three years, Sparks made a dozen more films and his image graced more magazine covers than any actor in the world. While critics still wrote him off as nothing more than set decoration, Sparks made millions for Galaxy, and Yates rewarded the actor with a series of raises and showered him with tens of thousands of dollars in gifts.

As hot as he was at the theaters, the young man was even more combustible off the set. Because of his fame, money, and charm, scores of women constantly hovered in his shadow and he took full advantage of everything they offered. His night-life, complete with parties, drinking, and even fistfights, was written about in every newspaper in the country. And rather than hurt his career, it enhanced it. Soon known as Hollywood's Rogue, Sparks's popularity was only exceeded by his thirst for life. And while his fans loved his smug confidence, his ever-growing arrogance soon turned off most of the film community.

On the set of *Born To Lead*, a formula picture with Sparks playing a young officer in World War I, the actor smoked a cigarette and impatiently waited for director Charles Holcomb to call the crew back into action. Leaning against a long bar, built as a part of a set representing a café in Paris, the actor studied a nervous but beautiful brunette sitting at a table about twenty feet in front of him. With her huge brown eyes, full lips and nice figure, she appeared to have everything needed to make a big splash in Tinseltown. And none of that was lost on the actor now on the prowl for a new conquest.

"She's a real doll," Dalton Andrews announced

as he took his place beside Sparks. "I understand she's from Missouri."

"The Show Me State," Sparks laughed as he turned to face the tall, thin, blond actor.

"Yates just signed her," Andrews continued, "She's eighteen, green, and innocent. I doubt if alcohol has ever touched her lips."

"What's her name?" Sparks asked, his eyes moving once more to the woman on the far side of the soundstage.

"Don't know what it was when she was born," Andrews said with a shrug, "but it's Leslie Bryant now."

"Miss Bryant," Sparks announced. "I like that. It suits her. I wonder what she'll think of the view from my new home?"

"Your ten-room shack up in the hills?"

"Yeah," Sparks laughed. "And it's fifteen."

"She'll never see it," Andrews quipped. "I spent some time with her yesterday and she is as cold as a January wind in Canada. She's not the kind of girl who would give you the time of day. She has something foreign to you. It's called morals."

Sparks looked back to the studio's second highest-paid actor and said, "Want to bet?"

"What do you have in mind?"

"How about my blue Auburn against your Packard? I know you love my car."

"How do we determine the winner?" Andrews asked.

"Miss Bryant takes in the view from my house on our first date and spends the night."

"That's like taking candy from a baby," Andrews laughed. "She's straighter than the arrows the Indians shot at Custer. You're on."

As the two actors shook hands, a short, stout man, about forty, waved his arms and announced, "Let's film this fight scene and wrap things up for the day."

"Looks like Holcomb is ready for you," Andrews noted. "I just stopped by to see if you wanted to go with me to Santa Catalina this weekend, but it appears you have something else on your mind." He paused and gazed back at the actress before adding, "You have one week. If, you've not worked your magic by then, the Auburn is mine."

"Too easy," Sparks shot back. "Let's make it four days."

"My word, you are sure of yourself."

"I've got nothing to doubt," Sparks laughed. "I'm completely irresistible."

"Mr. Sparks," the director called out. "Are you ready?"

"And willing," the actor assured Holcomb and moved quickly toward the center of the stage.

It was time for action, and hopefully that action would set in motion a way for him to be introduced to Leslie Bryant. He was sure that once they met, he would have her under his control.

4

June 10, 1936

It was just past five in the afternoon when Ellen Rains waltzed into the office of Jacob Yates. Rains was in her fifties, plump but stylish, and wore a dark blue suit, large matching hat and carried a handbag that could have doubled for a suitcase. Though she called herself a journalist, she was in truth nothing more than a gossip scribe. She got the dope on the stars and splashed the information to the world via daily columns in newspapers, monthly stories in magazines, and her own radio show. With a single word, she could make or break an actor or actress and, like a heavy club, she held that power over men like Yates.

"Jacob," Rains sang the man's name as if getting ready to launch into an opera.

Looking up from his desk, Yates forced a smile. "Ellen, to what do I owe this extreme pleasure? It always makes my day to have you come into my office."

"You know you don't mean that," she snapped. "My being hit by a train would give you more reason to celebrate than having a best picture winner. You likely pray for my death and look forward to the day you can dance on my grave."

"I wouldn't say that," he quickly replied.

"Of course you wouldn't," she grinned as she took a seat in front of his massive walnut desk, "but I know that's what you are thinking. Now, let's forget this pretending we still like each other —those days passed a long time ago—and let's get down to brass tacks."

Yates frowned, "Who did you catch doing what and how much is it going to cost me?"

"I have several things on my list," she admitted, and, after slipping off her hat and setting it on the studio boss's desk, she continued, "but those will keep. Today, my inside information comes from a contact down at the DA's office. Did you hear about the woman they found last week by the Hollywoodland sign?"

Yates nodded as he opened up the wooden box on his desk and pulled out a cigar. Leaning back in his chair, he propped his feet on his desk, retrieved a match from his pocket, struck it against the arm of his chair, and lit up.

Rains frowned, "Must you smoke those things? Everyone in town knows when I've come to your office, because for the rest of the day I smell like the inside of a men's club."

Yates blew smoke towards the woman and smiled, "My wife spends my money as if I was richer than William Randolph Hearst. My three adult children refuse to get real jobs and still live at my house. I have distant relatives that come and visit me for weeks at a time and every actor and actress in this studio thinks they are not making enough money. The cigars are about the only pleasure I have left."

"I'm so sorry for your horrible life," she groaned. "Anyway, back to the reason I came. Did you know the dead girl was one of the young women Galaxy signed to a contract last month?"

Yanking his feet from the desk, Yates rolled his chair forward, leaned over the desk and barked, "What?"

"Her name was Linda Watkins," Rains announced in a deliberate and emotionless manner. "She appeared in a couple of your recent films. She even had a line in the Flynn Sparks' movie that's shooting now. What's that one called again?"

"*Born To Lead*," Yates said.

"Well, she's the one who took her swan song at the sign we all love. Who knows, Sparks might have been the last man she kissed."

"I didn't see anything in the paper about her being identified," the studio boss noted as he dropped his still-burning cigar into a large ashtray. "Last thing I read, she was an unknown."

"It hasn't been released yet," she explained. "Unable to dig up anything on their own, the cops played a hunch . . . a smart one even if I do say so myself . . . that she might be a starlet. So naturally they called me in to see if I recognized the body. Just last week your public relations people sent me photos of the young woman along with her biography. I believe, according to what I read, she was a former Miss Alabama."

"You know we make that stuff up," Yates answered.

"Of course I know that," Rains replied. "I also know that you were the reason she was signed. A certain source informed me that you personally auditioned her."

"So how are you going to play this in the press?" the studio head demanded. "I've got a marriage to protect and a name that means something in the community. I don't need any press linking me to a dead girl. Especially a young, attractive dead girl."

"I'm not out to hurt you or the studio," she assured him. "If I'd wanted to reveal the person you really are, I could have done it years ago. You and I need each other, so all your skeletons will remain in the closet."

His dark eyes glowing, Yates leaned forward and growled, "Ellen, you always have an angle. If you didn't want to hold my feet over the fire, you wouldn't be here. So what hoop do you want me to jump through?"

"No hoops," Rains answered. Crossing her legs and letting her high heel dangle from her right foot, she continued, "And no fires either. Here is the story you need to hear and we need to discuss. The homicide chief, Bill Barrister, seems to think this murder is tied to three other murders. At least one of those other victims had appeared as an extra in a Galaxy film as well. Her name was Maggie Reason. Per chance did you also get to know her too well?"

"I don't remember the name," he admitted. "What did she look like?"

"She was brunette, well-built, and about five-five."

"We have dozens on the lot who fit that description," Yates noted.

"She never got an actual credit on a film at Galaxy," Rains explained. "So her connection won't be obvious. She was also a freelancer who did work at Columbia and a couple of the poverty row studios as well. Unlike Watkins, Reason shouldn't haunt you. But the truth is, the latest victim might."

"I can see you playing this for a while," he grumbled. "What's it going to cost us to bury the connection?"

"Nothing," she assured him. "The police don't want to sensationalize this story. They are not even officially connecting the cases. They're afraid that once the word gets out it might cause a panic and the press would go into a frenzy playing it for all it's worth and more. That would make solving the case almost impossible. But that is why I'm here. If we play this the right way, it can be dynamite for us."

"What are you talking about?" Yates asked. "We need to stay as far away from this as possible. I wouldn't touch it with a ten-foot pole."

"Listen, Jacob, I have a source who can give me all the evidence in this case as it comes in. In other words, I will know about the details almost as soon as Barrister. And best of all, the cops will never know I have it."

"Until you go to press," Yates barked as he picked up his cigar. "Then my studio gets hit with more black eyes than you see in a Three Stooges film."

"The story's not worth that much," Rains assured him. "Starlets get killed all the time. But this thing does have box office potential written all over it."

"What are you yapping about now?" the studio boss demanded.

"Jacob, think of this, the public loves crime movies. Well, why not give them one based on something lurid and real?"

Yates's dark eyes lit up just a bit and he seemed to catch at least a part of the woman's vision. Leaning forward he waited with bated breath for her to continue.

"Imagine," she smiled, "a movie based on a true-life case the cops are trying to keep quiet."

"It might work," he admitted. "Let me think

about it." He paused and looked toward the ceiling. "The legal issues are troubling. We might be sued."

She raised her eyebrows, "You have a law degree; do you think Galaxy would lose if that happened?"

He shook his head, "This would be factual stuff, nothing would be made up and we'd be safe."

"So," she added, "any lawsuits would actually generate more ticket sales. Because you would be the only one getting the real police information and because you would have information the newspapers didn't have access to, you would have the inside track to providing the public with the only real story almost as it happens."

Yates leaned back in his chair and put his feet back on his desk. After taking another puff from his cigar, he looked back to his guest. "Let's say I agree to do the movie and you pump the information to me, what's your price? You don't do anything for free, not even for an old friend like me."

"We are much more than just old friends," Rains noted, "And don't you ever forget that."

"How can I?" he grumbled.

"I want to make some money," she admitted, "and it won't be chump change. But I don't want my name on the project."

"Why not?" he demanded. "Not taking credit for something is not like you at all."

"In this case," she smiled, "it means I put more money in my pocket."

"How's that?"

"I want 10 percent of the action," Rains explained. "Beyond the information I can get you on the case, I will also feed the public the noble reasons you're making the movie. I will make you sound so good that, if you'd switch your faith, a certain church leader might make you a saint."

"How are you going to do that?" Yates asked. "Right now, I'm ahead of Jack Warner and Louis B. Mayer in the race for Hollywood's top tyrant."

The woman smiled, "You are making this flick in order to properly remember the women killed by the Hollywood Madman."

"The Hollywood Madman?"

"That's what I'm going to call the murderer."

"A bit gruesome," Yates suggested, "but it does have box office appeal." He put the cigar down, pulled his feet to the floor, leaned forward and placed his elbows on the desk. "I'm guessing that if I don't go along with this, you will tie the murders to the studio every day for weeks."

"For years," she replied as she picked up her hat and set it atop her auburn hair. "Do we have a deal?"

"You didn't have to blackmail me to get it," he added. "This really is a can't-miss project."

"I know," she gleefully announced as she grabbed her purse and stood. "But doing it this way was so much more fun." She grinned, "Now, I'll have copies of all of the case files in a couple of days and get them over to you. Good-bye, Jacob." She was almost to the door when Yates's voice stopped her.

"Ellen, do you have any information that someone from my studio might be this Hollywood Madman?"

She turned and slyly smiled, "No, darling, do you?" She didn't wait for an answer before waltzing out the door.

5

June 12, 1936

"What do you think?" Mary Beckett asked as she moved the last box of possessions off their truck and into the tiny house. Her daughter could tell the woman was trying hard to be positive, though the lilt in her voice proved she was anything but. She didn't want to be in Los Angeles and she was already homesick for Oklahoma.

From her place in the back of the truck, Shelby had seen prairies, mountains, and deserts. Now the young woman who'd always lived in the country was surrounded by a city too large for her to even comprehend and the neighbors were so close she could almost reach out and touch them.

The sounds of nature had been replaced by man-made noise. Yet as loud as Los Angeles seemed, she was sure she could still hear her mother's heart breaking.

"It's nice, Mom," Shelby lied.

It was small, only about eight hundred square feet, with a bedroom, combined kitchen and living area, and bath. It certainly beat living in a tent along the side of the road as they had since leaving their Oklahoma farm, but, in truth, it was only a modest step up. And with twenty other similar bungalows stacked all around them, it was going to be difficult for folks used to the wide-open spaces to adjust to the lack of privacy. Still, Mary did her best to spin things in a bright light.

"I mean, we can walk to a market, and Shelby, you won't have to chop wood for the stove, this one plugs right in. And it has two burners!"

"It's wonderful, Mom; things will be just fine."

Mary nervously smiled as she looked around the tiny home, "I know we don't really know any-body here, but folks are folks and we'll find friends." She paused, her eyes misting, "You know, I've never lived someplace where everyone didn't know me. Might be nice to make new friends." She picked a towel out of a box and began to fold it. "I'm sorry you don't have a room of your own."

"We'll get something bigger down the road," her father chimed in as he stepped through the entry. "And it shouldn't take long either. My cousin Stew just stopped by and he got me that job in the woodworking shop at . . ."He paused, "What did they call that business where he works, Mom? It is kind of important I know that. Let me see . . ."

"Galaxy," she reminded him. "It was Galaxy Studios. It's the place they make all those moving pictures that folks talk about. Maybe, with you now making regular money, we can go to them again. It's been three years since we saw a movie."

"Sure, we'll be able to," John chimed in. "We'll see as many as we want. As we drove into the city it seemed to me like they had a picture house on every block. Once, at a stop sign, I even smelled the popcorn. There's nothing like popcorn at a movie."

The woman used the towel to dab at her eye. "Must have some dust in it. When do you start, Pa?"

"Monday," he answered, his voice filled with obviously false enthusiasm. "Good pay too. I'll be pulling down seven dollars a day. I wasn't making that in a week back home."

"That's good, Pa," Shelby assured him. "You deserve that and a lot more. You'll be running that place before you know it."

John forced a smile and put his hands onto the straps of his bib overalls, "When I told Stew you were the best seamstress in your homemaking class and how you'd worked for three years doing that at Maybelle's, he suggested I take you along on Monday too. They're looking for folks to create costumes in the wardrobe department. They're making so many pictures they just can't keep up."

"I'd like that," Shelby assured him. "I want to pull my weight."

Mary looked from her daughter to her husband, "She should be going to college, John. It'd be a crying shame if she didn't use those brains of hers."

He shrugged, "I know, but that will have to come a bit later. Got to get on our feet first." The man glanced around the home and nodded, "For the moment, we have to concentrate on the good news. We have a way to make a living here; we didn't have that back in Oklahoma. And we have a roof over our heads and we were about to lose ours back home."

"Let's finish unpacking these boxes," Mary suggested, "and then I'll make some supper. Been a long day!"

Shelby picked up a box of dishes and cookware and headed for the cabinets by the sink. As she opened the lid and reached in to fish out a plate, her mother sidled up beside her.

"What are you thinking about?" Mary softly asked.

"Nothing."

As her mother opened a cabinet and placed glasses and cups on shelves, she mused, "Guess every girl in the country dreams about coming to Hollywood. And as pretty as you are and as good as you were in those high-school plays, you might just find a place for yourself out here. You might be discovered and be somebody those magazines write about."

"Mom, I'd rather just be in Oklahoma."

"Don't let your father hear that," Mary warned. "He already feels like a failure. So we have to act like we are happy to be here, even if we aren't. We can't show we're homesick. We just can't."

"I know," Shelby quietly replied. "But I don't want to be a star. I never dreamed about that."

"What did you dream about?" the woman asked. "Until now I never thought to ask you that."

Shelby put another plate in place and looked out the small window over the sink. She studied two boys kicking a tin can back and forth before looking down the street toward a billboard advertising a movie starring Clark Gable, Myrna Loy, and Jean Harlow.

"I never dreamed I'd be here," Shelby sighed. "Guess I just thought I'd get married and raise a family. Maybe live in a small town, clean, cook, sing in the church choir, and sit by the radio with a family around me listening to music."

"Those aren't dreams," Mary cut in. "That's reality, except for the radio part. We've never had one of those." She paused, holding a cup in her hand and shook her head, "Maybe it's my fault you never dreamed big. I never encouraged it. I pretty much taught you to just do your best and let the chips fall where they may. Guess I was just too caught up in living to encourage you to dream."

"It's not your fault," Shelby assured her, "I was born a realist. I knew what I had and I was smart enough to realize what I could never have."

"Shelby, it doesn't hurt to dream. Sometimes that's all that keeps us from choking on reality." The woman sadly glanced to the other side of the room; as she did, Shelby continued to look at the billboard. Mary sighed, "Even when our life was crumbling, I kept dreaming we'd strike oil and we'd be rich. I dreamed of building a huge mansion on the place and of having a big car. I dreamed about getting our own radio and maybe a record player too. I kept dreaming that until the day the bank foreclosed on us."

"But," Shelby pointed out, "didn't it hurt even more when the dream didn't happen? Shouldn't we just accept who we are and where we came from and live in that world?"

"I don't know," Mary admitted as she walked back to the other side of the room to get another box.

Shelby looked down at Rex who was now sitting at her feet. If he missed the fields to run in or the familiarity of the dirt roads around the old place, he didn't show it. So maybe things would be better here. Maybe there was a chance in California for her to be more than she ever thought possible. Maybe she'd get that job at the studio and some producers would see her working on a dress and make her the next big star. And maybe, just maybe, writers like Ellen Rains would be penning stories about Shelby Beckett. But no matter what happened she was still going to be the same girl she'd always been. She'd be honest, straightforward, and direct. She'd be true to herself no matter what. Nothing and no one was going to change her.

6

June 12, 1936

"Cut! That's a wrap."

Because of lighting issues the day ran long. It was past seven and the cast and crew were more than ready to call it a week. As most hurriedly headed for the exits, Flynn Sparks casually stepped between a beautiful, dark-haired actress and the door.

"You've got something," Sparks announced. He smiled and leaned closer before adding, "You're a cut above most of the actresses who roll in here. You're not going to be playing background parts for long. Within no time, the newspapers will be writing about you."

The shy, doe-eyed actress grinned, "Thank you, Mr. Sparks."

"Call me Flynn."

Her eyes lit up as if she'd just been given a new car, "OK, Flynn."

Placing his right hand gently on Leslie Bryant's shoulder he locked his almost black eyes onto hers and posed the question of the moment. "What are you doing this evening? As I'm sure you and I are going to be working together often, I thought it would be nice if we got to know each other over dinner. There's a place just off the strip where the prime rib just melts in your mouth and the orchestra plays romantic tunes that will make your heart flutter."

"It sounds awfully nice," she replied, her large, brown eyes still looking into his, "but I'm supposed to eat with my mother tonight."

"I bet you've had a thousand meals with your mother," he whispered, his lips now just inches from hers, "and there will likely be a thousand more, but you've never eaten with me and having missed out sharing a dinner with you is one of my life's greatest regrets. Don't you think you could alter your plans?"

She stepped back, took a deep breath, and shook her head, "I'd really rather be with you than doing anything else. But it's Mom's birthday and I couldn't cancel. I'm all she's got. So, I'm sorry."

Sparks took his hand from her shoulder, pushed his fists into his pants' pockets and cracked a smile. With his eyes still locked firmly on to hers, he allowed the petite woman to bask in that moment, sure that his good looks and charm were working their magic, before breaking the silence.

"We're the only two left on the set."

"I guess we are," she whispered. "It's kind of scary."

Sparks brought his hands from his pockets to her arms as an already nervous Bryant glanced to the left and right. He could feel her tense as his fingers gently squeezed.

"Leslie," he more breathed than said, "we will always remember our first time alone. Maybe it's the way you fill out that dress or perhaps it's the melody that springs from your lips when you speak, but my heart's trying to run up my chest and push into my throat. My brain is alive too. It's telling me that if I'm not careful I could drown in those eyes of yours. I sure hope you're ready to save me."

Simply by quoting lines taken from one of his movies, he had her exactly where he wanted. The actress went limp in his grasp. Now it was time to stray from Hollywood scripts and try something he'd written and used so many times he had these lines memorized as well. "Leslie, there is a view from my patio of the whole city. At night, the lights look like stars. It is almost magical. But I don't even see it when I'm alone. I have to share it to really enjoy it, and I only share that view with someone whose heart beats as one with mine. And I can feel ours beating together right now."

"I'll bet it's wonderful," she whispered. "The view, that is. And I never knew that hearts could beat in time with each other."

He grinned as he realized her resolve was melting. Dalton Andrews's Packard was almost his. So he leaned closer and said, "I'll admit to being a bit selfish. You see, with the little free time I have, I rarely share my life, much less my home, with anyone. But they say tonight is going to be clear, and it would be a crime if I didn't introduce that view to you. I don't think I could ever forgive myself for not giving you that scene as a gift." He pulled to within an inch of her face, "So, won't you reconsider?"

"I want to," she admitted. "I really do, but I planned the party for my mom. She rode a train clear from Alabama to visit me. This is her last night in California. She goes back east tomorrow. I couldn't desert her on her last night here. I might not see her again for who knows how long. But I do hope you will forgive me."

"On one condition," Sparks replied.

"What?"

"That you let me take you to dinner tomorrow night and we end the evening by taking in the view."

"I guess I could do that," she whispered. "I mean, if it means that much to you."

Sparks leaned forward and brought his lips to her. She melted into his arms. By the time he ended the kiss and broke the embrace Bryant's legs were so wobbly she could barely stand. While she breathlessly swayed, her feet glued to the floor, he smiled, turned, and walked toward the door. He stopped as he neared the exit and slowly spun around. "I'll need your address."

She nodded, "Hollywood Arms Apartments—number eight."

"I'll pick you up at seven," he assured her. "Have fun at your party tonight."

The trap was set and he was confident Leslie Bryant would take the bait. So before the sun set on Sunday, Dalton Andrews's V-12 Packard would be his. And while the car was nice, watching Andrews's expression as he handed over the keys would be even sweeter.

7

June 13, 1936

There were plenty of unsolved murders in Los Angeles, the homicide files were overflowing with them, but the quartet of women who had been so cruelly strangled set them above all the others on the bureau's priority list. In fact, these four crimes were so disturbing that they kept Bill Barrister awake at night and gave him indigestion during the day. It had been a year since the first one, and he was no closer to identifying who was responsible. So even though he was dog-tired and normally spent Saturdays with his kids, today the cop was working unpaid overtime in the police lab. Somewhere in what they knew about the murders there had to be a clue they were missing.

"What's going on, Cap?"

Barrister lifted his nose from the file long enough to nod toward a smiling cop. Yancey Caldwell was a tall, blocky, thirty-year vet who'd never wanted anything more than to wear a uniform and be a regular policeman. Maybe it was this lack of ambition that was the secret to the sparkle in his brown eyes and that perpetual smile framing his face.

"Yance," Barrister wearily asked, "are you ever unhappy?"

"Bill, I've got the best reason in the world to be happy."

"What's that?"

"You're not investigating my death," he quipped. "Now that makes me a lot luckier than some folks. And besides, no one is afraid of me. I'm just the harmless kind of cop, the old Joe who works the same streets each day, who passes out a few parking tickets, jokes with shop owners and pets the horses that pull the milk wagon. I'm folks' friend and the guy they tell their troubles to and share the news of graduations, weddings, and grandkids. That makes me kind of related to all the people I serve and that makes me pretty lucky, too."

Barrister nodded while setting a file down on the table. "Not a bad life, Yancey. Wish I loved my job as much as you do."

"There's lots of murders," Caldwell noted, the grin momentarily fading from his lips, "I've seen you handle them through the years. But your eyes are different today and the lines in your forehead are deeper than normal. So I'm guessing this case must be one of those that doesn't leave you alone. It stays with you even after you go to bed and close your eyes."

"Kind of like old Miss Taylor's terrier," Barrister noted with a smile.

"I'd forgotten about him," Caldwell laughed. "We were both beat cops back then. What was that old mutt's name?"

"Benny."

"Yeah, he didn't like me a bit. Always nipping at my heels."

"You griped a lot about Benny," the captain teased. "You tried every day to kick him."

"Then I found the secret to winning him over."

"What was that?" Barrister asked.

"Just a wee bit of ham was all it took to win him over to my side," Caldwell paused, his smile turning down a bit, "I cried a bit when Benny finally died."

"We all did," the captain agreed. Dramatically altering the direction of the conversation, Barrister said, "I read a book once, and when I got to the end, the last chapter was missing. That was twenty years ago and I still wonder if it was the butler or the maid who poisoned the old woman's soup. Do you know what that says about me?"

"You like to have pat endings," Caldwell chimed in. "But, Bill, life's not that way. Everything doesn't tie up in a neat bow. Sometimes there are questions that can't be answered and crimes that aren't solved."

"And that's what bugs me."

"What's this one about?" Caldwell asked.

Barrister got up from the table and strolled over to a window. He looked out on a street busy with afternoon traffic. "One of those people out there might well be the guy I'm looking for," he explained. Without turning to face his old friend, he continued, "Four young women have been strangled, and there is no connection between them." He turned, "Well, there is actually one. There was a broken, unburned kitchen match left at the place where each body was dumped. But what does that give us?"

"The potential for some light," Caldwell

suggested. "You strike a match and things get brighter."

Barrister crossed his arms just above his bulging stomach and smiled grimly, "And sometimes a match tip breaks off and you strike out."

"Bill," Barry Jenkins barked as he rushed by Caldwell into the captain's office. "We have another body, and it fits with the four others in almost every way."

"Where?"

"In a park off Sunset. Except this one has been there for a long time. Based on a newspaper found underneath the body—looks like thirteen months. Shultze, a beat cop, is on the line, you want to talk to him?"

"Yeah," Barrister groaned.

"Pick up your phone," Jenkins suggested, "I've already had it transferred."

Ambling over to the phone, the captain picked up the receiver and announced his name. He then pulled himself up onto the corner of his desk and waited for a response.

"Captain, this is Rick Schultze. A dog walker found the body today. It seems his hound got off the leash and went racing into some brush."

"What did you observe about the body?" Barrister asked.

"By the clothes it was obviously a woman, but she is pretty much just bones. I can see a lot of the skull. There's no purse, so no way to identify her."

"Any idea what killed her?"

"Nothing obvious," Schultze replied, "guess the ME will have to tell us that. He should have her body by now. They took it away a couple of hours ago. I didn't think it was any big deal until I told Jenkins at lunch. He kind of went crazy over it and wanted me to talk to you."

"Thanks," Barrister replied. "I'll check with the medical examiner and see if it connects to anything we are working on." Setting the receiver back into the phone's black cradle, the captain pushed off his desk and headed to the door.

"I've been there," Jenkins announced.

Barrister turned, "And?"

"She was strangled," he explained. "And I went back to the scene, too, but this time I didn't find a match. It's been a long time, it could have been washed away by rain and wind."

The homicide chief solemnly nodded. If this murder was connected to the others, then that made five. How many more were there left waiting to be found, and how many more would there be before they identified the person or persons responsible?

"Bill," Caldwell asked, "does this give you a hint as to what's in the missing chapter of your book?"

"Yancey, I don't think so."

"Too bad," the uniformed cop said, "but still try to find something to smile about anyway. Maybe you need to just go home, kiss the wife, and spend some time talking to your kids. You have a boy and girl, don't you?"

"Yeah, Mike and Molly, both in high school."

"The case will be here for a while," Caldwell suggested, "but your kids will be gone before you know it."

"I know," Barrister agreed, "but the dead girls were somebody's kids too. I can't walk away from them anymore than I can quit loving my own."

8

June 13, 1936

"So are you impressed?" Flynn Sparks asked as he moved near enough to smell his date's perfume. "Is it everything I told you it would be?"

"More," Leslie Bryant announced with a hint of awe in her voice. "It's like I can see the whole world."

"Only the parts that matter," he corrected her. "And right now the only two people that matter are you and me."

He smiled his million-dollar smile, the same one that made women swoon as they watched his films, stepped away from the woman and slowly removed his white dinner jacket. After signaling with his head and eyes that it was time to move inside, he led the way from the patio and back into his five-thousand-square-foot, white, rock home. After tossing his coat onto a brown overstuffed chair, Sparks reached up to his neck, removed his tie, and unfastened the top button on his white shirt. Only then did he glance back to the woman who was shyly admiring him from the door.

Bryant was dressed in a dark blue form-fitting dress that embraced her curves like a road hugs a mountain. Her short brunette bob framed her high cheekbones and deep, dark eyes. If she could just learn to act a little, that look would make her a star. What she principally lacked was confidence. Even dressed to the nines and looking every bit the glamour queen, she couldn't completely hide the awkward and insecure country girl lurking behind the makeup. And it was her lack of confidence that opened the door for Sparks to have his way with her. Within minutes he was sure she'd be putty in his hands.

"I hope the party was fun," he said.

"What party?" she asked, confusion showing on her face.

"Your mother's birthday."

"Oh," Bryant smiled, balling her hands up at her waist, "it was nice. Mainly it was just the two of us. I told her I was going out with you tonight."

He cocked his eyebrow, "And what did she say?"

The woman giggled, "That by going out with you I'd be the envy of all the girls I went to high school with. She also suggested that I'd better latch onto you when I had a chance."

Sparks shook his head, "She's wrong about your friends envying you."

"What?" she asked. "I'm sure they will when they find out. I'll bet even my friends that are married will be jealous."

"Come here," he suggested. After she slowly and nervously closed the ten feet between them and he'd put his arms around her back and pulled her close, he explained, "It's not just the girls in your high school class; right now you're the envy of every woman in the country." He leaned closer to her ear, "Do you know how many women would pay to be where you are right now?"

Bryant nodded, "I guess a lot."

"More than you know," he laughed.

"I'm lucky to be here right now," she whispered.

"And," he continued, "you really want to see this view in the morning as the sun comes up, don't you?"

"Yes," she hesitantly replied.

"And you know what that means?" he asked a bit louder.

"I think so," she whispered.

Sparks smiled; Andrews was stupid to make that bet, the Packard was going to be his. Life was so easy.

9

June 14, 1936

It wasn't like the country church that had once been her spiritual home in Oklahoma. This was no drafty clapboard building with handmade pews and well-worn songbooks. This church was constructed of rock-solid brick, the windows were stained glass, the hymnals had round notes instead of shaped notes and the pews sported maroon cushions. And because of all those first-rate appointments and a thousand other things, Shelby, dressed in her faded green dress, felt as out of place at the Beverly Hills Christian Church as a bullfrog in the desert. Yet, as the Bible was the same and the message on hope offered a bit of comfort for the homesick girl, the solitary five-block walk produced a little something of value. She was sure that God was here too; he was evidently just a bit better dressed.

After the benediction, and as the organ played "Rock of Ages," she made her way quickly to the aisle. Her goal was to get through the exit without talking to anyone. And she would have made it if a finely dressed couple, likely in their fifties, hadn't stepped in out of the back pew and beat her to the door. The woman was short, stout, wore a yellow silk suit, pearls, a fox wrap and carried a large black purse. The man had a thin, gray mustache and was tall, lean, balding, and wearing an obviously tailored blue pinstriped suit. His outfit was completed with a white shirt, yellow silk tie, and shiny leather shoes.

"Thank you so much for visiting us today," the tall, white-haired, robed pastor announced as they exited. "I am Milton Green."

A serious expression on her round pale face, the woman looked the pastor in the eye, set her jaw, and proudly announced in a loud, booming voice that could be heard for blocks, "We are the Chattingtons of Sacramento, and we are here visiting the Warner family who run a studio you no doubt are familiar with."

The preacher gently took her gloved hand and smiled, "Nice to meet you, Mrs. Chattington. And I think I've seen a picture or two the Warners have made."

"I'm sure," she immediately replied. "This is my husband, Basil."

"Nice to have you in our church," the pastor said as he shook the man's hand. "Always good to have friends of the Warners."

The man leaned close and whispered, "We aren't *that good* friends."

"I understand," the amused pastor replied as he watched the couple make their way down the six steps to the sidewalk. Only when the Chattingtons were halfway across the lawn did he turn to Shelby. "And it is nice to have you with us as well. And you are?"

"I'm Shelby Beckett of the Cordell Becketts," she announced as she extended her ungloved right hand. "I'm here because the state of Oklahoma no longer wanted us. And, just so you can be profoundly unimpressed, my family doesn't know the Warners."

Green smiled, "Always an honor to have a member of the esteemed Beckett family with us. Are you by yourself?"

"My parents are still getting our house set up," Shelby explained. "I'm sure they'll come next Sunday."

"So you are new to this area?" he queried.

"Just came in from the country, and besides being new, I think we are kind of green too. This is a lot different place than our old farm and the country church where we went, but I did recognize a couple of the hymns."

"There're a lot of Okies and Arkies out here," he assured her as he took her hand. "But I will say this, there aren't many your age who'd find a church when coming to Los Angeles. Most young women who arrive here are looking for a party and for stardom."

"I'm not here to act," she explained.

"That'll save you some disappointment and heartache," he replied. "But your natural beauty was not lost on a number of the men in the congregation. They spent far more time finding excuses to crane their necks and glance your way than they did mine. I saw one teenager drop his bulletin at least a half dozen times, just so he could steal a look at you."

She blushed, "I'm just a country girl, they were probably looking because they saw me as some kind of freak."

"I doubt that," he said. "Now, is there anything the church can do for you or your family to help get you settled?"

"If you're asking if we have something to eat, we do. We brought enough canned goods with us to last a while. And my dad's got a job. But a prayer or two wouldn't hurt."

"I'll put the Becketts of Cordell on my prayer list."

"Thank you."

As she walked down the steps, Shelby looked up into the clear, California sky and sighed. The preacher might have quoted familiar verses, a couple of the hymns were the same, and the God the congregation worshipped was one she'd met, but it still wasn't home. It became more obvious with every passing moment that home was a long way away. Maybe she should have taken Calvin Kelly up on his proposal. If she had, she likely wouldn't feel so out of place and lonely now.

Frowning, she made her way past the chatting

and happy church members gathered on the lawn to the sidewalk. As she strolled by a drugstore she heard a paperboy calling out, "Cops release name of murdered woman." The kid, dressed in jeans and white shirt, rushed up to Shelby and asked, "You want a paper, lady?"

She barely finished her, "No, thank you," when he spotted the Chattingtons and moved on. Shelby watched the old man purchase a copy of *The Los Angeles Times* before stepping into his black Cadillac sedan. Murders, newsboys, wealthy folks, and a church with both a piano and an organ—she was definitely out of her element.

10

June 14, 1936

Dressed in gray slacks and a light blue dress shirt, Dalton Andrews knocked on the door of the swanky, hilltop bachelor's hideaway and waited for a response. A few seconds later, the entry swung open to reveal his grinning host. Flynn Sparks was outfitted in red silk pajamas that were almost as bright as his sparkling smile.

"You look like the cat that ate the canary," Andrews observed as he strolled into the home.

After closing the door behind his guest, the barefooted host chuckled, "I didn't eat the yellow bird, but I hope you have cab fare home. That Packard's staying here."

"You don't mean . . ."

Sparks put his finger over his lips before signaling with his dancing eyes for his friend to walk down the hall and look in the bedroom. Andrews frowned before strolling to the open door and glancing in. In the middle of the bed, covered by a white sheet, was a still sleeping Leslie Bryant. Shaking his head, the guest retraced his steps.

"I can't believe it," he griped.

"Shah," Sparks whispered, "no reason to wake her. Let's go out on the patio and continue this delightful conversation." They'd no more than stepped outside when the host noted, "Guess you'll be car shopping. Shame there's no dealerships open until tomorrow."

Andrews glared at his friend, "I can't believe you managed to take advantage of that innocent girl. You have no sense of decency."

"What my charms can't accomplish my liquor can," Sparks laughed. "Where are the keys to the maroon beast?"

Andrews reached into his pocket, yanked them out, and tossed them to the other man. "I knew you were out with Leslie, just didn't figure you'd get her to come up here. I just don't get how anyone could not get their fill of you within an hour."

Sparks grinned, "News gets around so quickly in this town. How'd you know we were out together?"

"Ellen Rains wrote about it in her column in this morning's *Times*," the guest explained. "Even had a picture of the two of you at a table at the Cocoanut Grove. I just can't believe she's still here this morning. I had her figured all wrong."

"Dalton, you had her figured just right. She's every bit as sweet and innocent as you guessed. Your problem is that you always underestimate me."

"No," Andrews spat, "I never underestimate you, I just always overestimate your character. I seem to forget you have none."

"Now, now, now, jealousy will get you nowhere."

"Flynn," Andrews announced as he folded his arms across his chest, "that's where you got me wrong. I'm not jealous, not in the least. I don't care if it meant more money and more fame, I wouldn't trade places with you even for all that you have right at this moment." Andrews stuffed his hands into his pocket, turned, walked over to the edge of the patio and looked down on the city. "Flynn, the view you have here is amazing. Not only can you see everything, but everyone can look up here and see you. A lot of those folks might point and whisper, 'Can you imagine what it's like to be Flynn Sparks?' But they don't see your soul." Andrews whirled back to face the other man, "In fact, I'm not sure you have a soul. Flynn, how many people have you used and how many hearts have you broken?"

Sparks shrugged, "They don't see it that way. It might hurt a bit when I move on, but I give them something to remember. I give them something no one else can. One night with me makes them legends in their worlds. They have stories they can tell their grandkids."

Andrews shook his head in disgust, "Grandmothers don't share stories like that with anyone. In fact, they try to bury them . . . the stories, not the kids. Let's face facts! You've taken advantage of more women than you can count. You likely don't even remember all of their faces, much less their names."

"Dalton," the host grinned, "I think you're jealous."

"Flynn, I have to look in the mirror every morning, and I want to respect the man who stares back at me. So I don't want to be a part of that."

"It's so easy for you to sound noble," Sparks chirped as he pushed his index finger into his guest's chest, "but if you had what I have, you'd do the same thing."

Andrews shook his head, "What do you have?"

"Women can't resist me," came the quick reply. "And I just give them what they want."

"Actually," Andrews countered, "women want

the same thing men want—respect. How long are you going to keep Leslie on your string?"

"She's not on a string," Sparks said with a grin. "She was just a means to getting your car. And really the car means nothing to me. It was just my way of winning the bet. You see that's what I really wanted. I wanted to watch your face when you found out I always win."

"So you're just cutting her loose after she spent the night here?"

"She's boring," Sparks laughed. "It was all I could do to stay awake during dinner. I'll tell you what. Tomorrow you can go back to her dressing room and soothe her broken heart. I'm sure she will need a shoulder to cry on, and I'm always pleased to give you my rejects." He chuckled, "Now, how are you getting home?"

"I'll walk," Andrews replied. "It's only five miles, and I need the exercise." He moved back into the house and to the front door. As he was about to twist the knob, Leslie Bryant, wrapped in a sheet, stumbled out of the bedroom and down the hall. When she saw Andrews, she blushed and froze.

"It's not what it seems," she softly announced.

"In this town it never is," Andrews shot back, his tone cold and uncaring. After shaking his head, he opened the door and hurriedly strolled out.

11

June 15, 1936

Jacob Yates had been fuming ever since he read the story in the *Los Angeles Times*. He was so upset he didn't bother touching his breakfast of coffee and toast. His biggest box office draw was in hot water again. A woman in Santa Monica was claiming Flynn Sparks was the father of her six-month old baby. Every paper in town was running with the story. Alongside the page one features, each had a picture of the woman and her child, as well as a headshot of the actor. As he frantically paced in his office, the intercom buzzed. Stomping to his desk, he pushed down a button and barked, "What is it?"

"Mr. Sparks is here to see you."

"About time, get him in here now!"

Yates watched the door open and a seemingly carefree Sparks waltzed in. After grabbing a donut from a silver platter resting on the studio mogul's side table, the actor plopped down into a large brown leather chair and put his feet on the desk.

"You seem happy this morning," Yates growled.

"I had a good weekend J. Y. I hope you did as well." He pushed his fist into the chair's bottom cushion, "I need one of these at home. Where can I get one like it?"

"I don't remember where I bought the chair and, to answer your other question, my weekend was fine until it was ruined by my reading this morning's papers. Have you seen the stories that feature a Mr. Flynn Sparks and a Miss Caroline Watson?"

"Actually," Sparks admitted between bites, "I have. I thought *The Times* piece was pretty well written, though I do wish they'd used a newer picture of me. I look like such a kid in that shot. By the way, do you have any coffee or juice?"

Yates's cheeks went purple as he screamed, "You're looking at a paternity suit and you want something to drink?"

"I'm thirsty," the actor replied with a shrug, "and no, I'm not worried about a suit."

"And why not?" Yates demanded.

"Because," Sparks explained, "I don't know this woman. I've never met her, much less kissed her. And, if you'd check your calendar, you'd realize that you sent me to Europe during the time she claimed we had the affair. I was making a picture in London and doing a publicity tour after that in Germany and France."

Yates sat down at his desk and picked up his massive appointment book. Glancing back through the pages confirmed Sparks was right. At least this fire could be put out. His people could wreck this woman's story and reputation within twenty-four hours.

"OK," the mogul barked, "fine, this is nothing more than a woman wanting some publicity and a payoff, but your little affairs have cost us more than fifty thousand dollars in hush money over the past two years. I can't deal with this anymore." Yates pounded his fist on his desk, "There was a story in the Sunday *Times* that claims Leslie Bryant spent the night at your home on Saturday night."

"She did," Sparks admitted.

"So you admit it?"

"Of course. Why wouldn't I? After all, she's beautiful!"

"Flynn, the government, the churches, and the fans all expect you and the others at this studio to at least give the appearances of being moral."

"Why lie?"

"Because bad publicity can ruin you. It's that simple."

Like a mother scolding her child, Sparks shook his finger toward his boss. "My wild ways have done nothing but enhance my box office appeal. Every time one of those so-called lurid stories runs, it means more people come to see my pictures. In other words, I'm worth more now than I was yesterday. And the next time I embrace the role of a playboy it will mean even more box office. If you reshape my image into that of a gentleman, then I'll become like Dalton Andrews —respectable and bland. And you have enough actors who fit that bill right now."

"I don't like and won't accept that attitude," Yates barked. "You don't run this studio, I do. In fact, I own it lock, stock, and barrel. And that means I own you too."

"Fine," the actor defiantly announced, "if I'm not living up to your expectations, then tear up my contract and fire me. The other studios would have an immediate bidding war for my services, and I'd be under contract by sundown. Wouldn't you love to watch me make the cash registers ring for Warner Brothers or MGM? And don't think I couldn't do it."

Yates shook his head but didn't answer. He couldn't respond because Sparks was right. The debate was over, and he'd lost. Jumping up, he moved back to the window, looked out of the Galaxy lot and folded his arms over his chest. Everything he saw was his and yet he had no more control over it at this moment than he did over his wife and children. After his blood pressure dropped twenty points, and he regained a small bit of his composure, he hissed, "Get back to wardrobe. You're late for a fitting." He continued to study the world he'd built until he was sure Sparks was long gone. It was a voice he respected that finally put a cap on his anger.

"I've got a message for you."

Yates turned and studied the woman standing in the entry to his office. His secretary, Eve Walen, was fifty-eight, plump and dressed like a school-teacher in mourning. This mother of three and a grandmother to four never complained, was always on time, and worked late if asked. If only all the people in his world had her character.

"What is it, Eve?" His tone showed his respect and admiration.

"One of our new actresses didn't make it to work today."

"Did you call her at home, maybe she's sick?"

The woman nodded, "I made the call, but there was no answer."

"What's her name?"

"Leslie Bryant."

"Great," Yates moaned. "Just wonderful. The curse of Flynn Sparks strikes again."

"What do you mean?" Walen asked.

"Nothing. Thanks for the information. Just please close the door on your way out and let me suffer in solitude."

Somewhere in Los Angeles there was a young, broken-hearted woman who had been taken advantage of by his biggest star. That meant Yates was going to have to track Bryant down, tend to her wounds, and likely pay out a few thousand to make sure she never said a word about this to any member of the press.

12

June 15, 1936

Coming through the ornate gates to Galaxy Studios was overwhelming. There were buildings and people everywhere! This was a city unto itself. As Shelby's eyes flashed from place to place, she recognized famous actors, saw huge trucks filled with props, observed countless extras dressed like everything from pioneers to gangsters to African natives and even spotted auburn-haired beauty Betty Foster wearing slacks and riding a bicycle. And while all of it looked so real, in truth, beyond the actress on the bike, it was nothing more than a grown-up version of playing make-believe. Of course, this playground cost tens of millions of dollars to keep running.

A slightly built male page escorted Shelby along narrow streets to a building housing the wardrobe department. Once inside the massive brick structure, she was taken to a large, noisy room filled with more than a hundred people working at electric sewing machines. They were making everything from ballroom gowns to Civil War uniforms.

After a brief meeting with Betsy Minser, a sixty-year-old, severe-looking woman who supervised the crew and ran everything in the three-story building, Shelby was given a dress pattern, material, thread, and told to go to work. For a half an hour, the visitor cut and stitched as she'd been taught by Maybelle, carefully making each element of the peasant dress fit together perfectly. She was just about to attach the buttons when the gray-headed supervisor stepped in.

"Miss Beckett," Minser growled, her piercing brown eyes seemingly searing Shelby's skin, "we are a motion picture studio, not a boutique. We don't need these outfits to be perfect; we just need for them to look good on film. You're putting far too much effort into things. This is a factory, we do it the tried and true American way and make it just good enough to last a scene or two and give the illusion it is complete. Do you understand?"

Shelby had always been taught to put everything she had into each task. At home, school, and the dress shop, she'd never been allowed to embrace the concept of "that will do." Just quickly piecing something together was completely foreign to her. And yet that seemed to be exactly what Minser wanted.

"Come here," the supervisor ordered.

A few moments later, the two stood next to a rack filled with clothes representing several different historical eras. Minser grabbed a scarlet velvet dress that, on first glance, appeared like something from a high-end New York shop.

"Look at this gown. If you just give it a casual

glance it appears perfect, but when you take a closer look you see it is unlined, the minimal stitching that is there is loose and the bow is barely attached. When an extra wears this it will look perfect, but it is not. For everyone but the stars, we don't have the time to make it perfect, we only take the time to make sure it looks that way for the camera."

The woman hung the dress back up and pointed to the scores of people behind her working at the sewing machines. "I can already tell that you are far better than most of my crew. Right now, you're likely good enough to work with me creating the wardrobe for the big stars. But, if you want this job, there will be times you'll be stitching things together for extras. That doesn't require focus, it doesn't mean you have to pay attention to detail, it doesn't matter if the buttons only stay on for one wearing, it just means you have to work at lightning speed. Now, can you do that?"

"Yes," Shelby assured her.

"Good, because I will also find a way to use your real talents where needed." She paused and glanced across the room where a powerful man dressed in a black suit was waving. "In fact," she continued, "if you can start now, I have something for you to do and I just don't have the time to do it myself."

"I can start now," Shelby eagerly explained.

"Then follow me, young woman."

As if navigating a maze, the two walked between and behind long rows of sewing machines and tables stacked with material before coming to a door at the far back of the huge room. Minser opened it and stepped into a forty-by-forty-foot area with a half dozen more machines and several hundred costumes hanging on movable racks. Standing in the center of the room, with a small woman pulling at his suit coat, was Flynn Sparks. Once his eyes locked onto Shelby, they didn't let go. His unrelenting stare followed her from the point she entered the room until she and Minser stopped directly in front of the actor.

"The sleeves are a bit long," one of Minser's assistants noted.

"Pin them where they need to be," the supervisor ordered, "then give it to the new girl. She can fix it. You can go back outside and get on your machine there." After taking another look at the jacket, Minser turned to Shelby, "Do this job as if you were doing it for yourself. This coat will be used several times and be subject to a slew of close-ups, so it needs to be perfect. That's basically the rule whenever you are assigned to create something for a star, and when you are not, forget everything I just said."

As Shelby nodded, Sparks spoke, "Betsy, who is this young woman? I'm sure I'd have remembered her if we'd met."

"She's new, Flynn. Her name is Miss Beckett."

"Is there a first name that goes with it?" he jibed more than asked.

"Shelby," Minser answered. "But you may call her Miss Beckett."

"Well, Shelby," the man sang out, ignoring the woman's advice, "I'm Flynn Sparks, and I do hope to be seeing much more of you in the future." After fully apprising himself of all of the new girl's charms, he turned his gaze back to Minser, "See that Shelby is assigned to do all my alterations."

The supervisor smiled, "If she proves herself capable, I can arrange that. But first, she has to prove herself. Take the coat off and give it to her."

Sparks nodded and eased the jacket from his shoulders and down his arms. He then held it to his body forcing Shelby to step so close she could smell his cologne. As she took the jacket from his right arm, he lifted his left hand and traced the skin along her cheek forcing her to look into his smoldering eyes.

"You are beautiful," he noted.

She nervously nodded as she turned back to Minser. The supervisor pointed to a workstation on the far side of the room and announced in an unyielding voice, "You will find all you need there."

"Thank you, ma'am." Moving to her station, Shelby still felt Sparks's gaze. It was almost as if he were trying to see through her dress.

"Don't you need to be on the set?" Minser asked the star. "We don't like loitering at this studio, not even from someone like you."

He nodded and then smoothly ordered, "Send Shelby with the coat when it is finished." He then turned and walked out of the room.

After Sparks was gone, Minser looked back to her new employee, "The first thing you do when you get something a star has worn and has to be mended or altered is go through the pockets. You'd be surprised what you will find."

Shelby nodded and ran her hand into the three outside pockets. In the third one, she found a fountain pen. "Got this, what do I do with it?"

"That would have made a mess," the supervisor griped. "If that thing had leaked we'd have had to make a whole new jacket." She frowned, "Put it in a sack. There are a stack of them at the end of each table. Write whose jacket it is, describe it, date, and then sign it. Roll the top over and staple it. Then place it on the shelf beside the coat rack on the wall. Oh, and Shelby, on Sparks, you'll have to deal with him, that will be part of your job, but keep it in the studio. Don't let him take you out. He has a way of spoiling all the good stuff he touches." She took a deep breath before adding, "Let me put it another way. Flynn Sparks treats women like a newspaper. He reads them from front to back and then throws them in the nearest trashcan."

13

June 15, 1936

As she finished the jacket sleeves, Shelby stood, stretched, and looked for her supervisor. Betsy Minser was nowhere to be seen. Unsure as to what she was to do next, she hung the coat on a wooden hanger and placed it on the rack nearest the table.

"You do really nice work."

Startled, Shelby whipped around to find a powerfully built, smiling man standing about ten feet behind her. His face was broad, his eyes deep and brooding, and there was a scar running from just above his left eye across his forehead before it disappeared in his dark chestnut hair. He was dressed in tweed pants, a black pullover, turtle-neck cotton shirt. He must have sensed he frightened her, because the first thing he did was apologize.

"I'm sorry," his voice was a register higher than most men his size and he spoke very slowly. His words were paced much like a mule's slow walk across a field when plowing. "I thought you knew I was organizing clothes on the racks in the corner. Getting them ready to move to stage 7. They're doing a Western saloon scene over there today and tomorrow. My name is Willard Mace. I'm kind of the go-to guy here. That means if they need some-thing taken someplace, they go to me."

"I'm Shelby," she announced as her heart fell out of her throat. "I guess I was so focused on doing a good job, that I didn't notice anything or anyone. What should I do with the coat?"

"I'm going that direction when I fill up this rack," he politely explained, "I can drop it off for you."

"But Mr. Sparks told me to take it to him," Shelby argued.

"No," Mace corrected her, "he told Betsy to have you bring it to him. She would never send you on that errand. She protects her girls as if she was a shepherd guarding a flock." He paused as if searching for words before adding, "And Flynn Sparks is the wolf she protects them from."

"I see," the young woman replied. "He did come on a bit strong."

Mace hung up a shirt and then, his stride powerful but deliberate, closed the distance between them. "Are you kidding? What you saw was the man at his mildest. He was only in first gear when he was talking to you. Most times, he has the shifter in high and literally runs you over. And you know what, most women love it."

"Really?"

"In Hollywood," Mace frowned, "you are either fast or last. Sparks will never be last. His kind makes me sick." The man looked past Shelby to a clock on the far wall. "If you have any questions, feel free to ask me. I can tell you how to stay out of trouble and keep on Betsy's good side. She's tough but fair. You do what she asks you to do and you'll have a job for as long as the studio's gates keep opening. And you really are an answered prayer for her."

"How's that?" Shelby asked, more than a bit confused by the man's unusual observation. "I'm just a country girl who needs a job."

"She is in desperate need of someone with your skills," he explained. "None of the women out in the big room can do much more than shoddy work. The two women who did most of the detail sewing were real pros, but Maud Haus died last week and Martha Noon just had a baby." He paused and looked around the room before adding, "If she comes back to work it won't be for a while. Betsy was starting to feel the heat. So, while you might be out there in what we call the factory from time to time, I'll bet most hours you'll be in here. At least I hope so. And if you prove to be as good as I think you are, you'll get a raise in no time."

Shelby grinned, "Thanks for the heads up. Anything else I need to know?"

"Yeah," he announced as he sat down behind a new Singer sewing machine. "Don't act star-struck. Betsy doesn't like girls who bow down to the actors and actresses. She'll want you to show some moxie. She wants you to see yourself as being just as good as they are."

"That's pretty much the way I am anyway."

"Then you'll be fine." Mace checked his watch, stood, strolled over, and grabbed Sparks's jacket. "OK, Shelby, I've got to deliver that rack of stuff, and I'll see that the spoiled jerk gets this coat too. While you wait for Betsy to get back, you should look around this room and get a handle on where things are and how we organize them. Start by looking on the racks, each will have the name of the film and the stage where it is being shot. For the stars' costumes, if you open them up and look inside you will find their name and the name of the picture pinned inside. In the files over there are patterns and notes with all the actors' measurements."

"Thanks again," Shelby said with a smile. "You better get moving and I'll do my homework until our boss returns."

"Nice meeting you," Mace said as he pushed the rack toward the door. "And Sparks was right about one thing. You are beautiful."

As the man went out one door, Minser marched in the other, her arms loaded with patterns. After setting them on a table, she looked toward her newest employee. "Where's the jacket?"

"Willard took it," she answered. "I hope that is all right."

"Perfect," came the quick reply. "Willie is a strange egg, a thirty-year-old mama's boy who's likely never had a date and seems to lose his train of thought, but even though he messes up and goofs off more than I like, I'd rather be around him than guys like Sparks." Minser looked down at the table, sorted through several envelopes before picking up the one she wanted. "Betty Foster will be wearing this suit in a film that starts shooting next week. This pattern was custom-made for her. You grab this and head over to that machine on the far wall. As you familiarize yourself with it, I'll get the material you need to make Miss Foster's costume."

"Yes, Miss Minser," Shelby answered as she took the pattern.

"Call me Betsy or go home," she snapped. "Now, let's see how good you are! You might just advance from the sewing factory room to the finishing room faster than anyone in history."

14

June 15, 1936

Bill Barrister stood on the vacant lot less than a block from Galaxy Studios and pulled a pack of cigarettes from his inside coat pocket. He tapped one out into his left hand, watched it fall into his right, then slipped it between his fingers, put it to his lips, replaced the pack, and retrieved a lighter. Popping the top on the Zippo brought the flame and a second later, the cop inhaled. Looking toward his partner, he pushed the smoke from his lungs and said, "Do you suppose these things are good for you?"

"You mean the smokes?" Jenkins asked.

"Yeah, the radio ad says they calm your nerves and clear your mind. The print ads have doctors endorsing them. They make them sound like vitamins. There are times when I wonder if they're selling us a bill of goods. After all, they are now costing almost fifteen cents a pack or two for twenty-five. I could have five bottles of pop for that."

"Who knows what's good or not?" the plain-clothes cop answered. "I mean, the smokes aren't making you any fatter, and five Cokes would likely add some weight."

"So you think I'm fat?" Barrister asked.

"I was speaking in general terms, Cap. I can say this for sure, what I'm looking at now is anything but good for someone's health."

"Yeah," Barrister agreed as he studied a woman's body lying in the weeds. "Who found her?"

"Mr. Nick Powell was sitting on his fourth floor balcony," Jenkins explained, "took a break to read his paper. Looked down and saw the body.

He has problems walking—hurt his leg in the Great War—so rather than come down and check it out in person he gave us a call. Jim Wright got here first, and he kept everyone away until we arrived. So far there's not any members of the press who have picked up on it."

"Jim's a good cop," Barrister noted. "And let's hope none of the scribes hear about this until we have processed the scene. Do we have an ID?"

"Cap, there's nothing here that gives us a clue as to who she is."

The homicide chief took another deep draw from his cigarette before tossing it on the ground and snuffing it out with the toe of his heavily scuffed right shoe. He then stepped forward and crouched beside the body. The young woman had apparently been strangled. He studied the bruising on her neck before turning his attention to her clothing. She was dressed as if for a date, wearing a high-dollar gown and pumps. At first glance, it seemed to be just like the other four cases he'd tied together. But on this one something didn't ring true.

"Barry, take a look at her and tell me what doesn't add up?"

Jenkins leaned over and studied the woman, "Other than the fact she's dead, what are you driving at?"

"Look at her makeup," Barrister suggested. "What does it tell you?"

"Well, Cap, I don't know much about the war paint women use, but this looks a bit subdued for a gal who'd spent a night out on the town. And that dress was not made for church or grocery shopping. So she had to be going to a social event or a club."

"That's it," Barrister replied, "on the other strangulation victims their makeup looked fresh, but on this girl it appears as it was applied well before she died. In several places, it's smeared and the lipstick is almost all gone."

A crew of four men drove up in a Ford sedan that the crime scene boys called the wagon, parked the vehicle at the curb, and hopped out. As the doors banged shut, Barrister briefly glanced that way before once more turning his attention to the woman. Just like the others she wore no jewelry, not even earrings. That confused him. Robbers might kill their victims but not like this. They'd use something clean and quick, like a knife. So was the guy behind these murders mixing passion with work, or did he take their valuables and identification as some kind of grisly souvenirs? Was his motive robbery or just the thrill of the kill? They needed a big break to find out.

"You ready for us, Captain?"

With some effort, Barrister pushed himself upright and looked toward the quartet of suited men. "I want lots of pictures from every angle.

And Johnson, as soon as you can, get me a time of death."

"You going back to the office?" Collins asked.

The captain looked at the sixty-year-old crime photographer, "Not yet, I want the photos shot and that body moved before I take off."

"You looking for something?" Collins asked.

"A kitchen match," came the quick reply.

The now confused photographer raised the camera and focused, but rather than begin shooting, he stopped and leaned closer to the body.

"Something wrong?" Jenkins asked.

"I know this woman." Collins declared. "Or at least I've seen her photograph."

"Who is she?" Barrister demanded.

"I don't remember the name," came the explanation, "but I'm sure I saw her picture in yesterday's *Times*. She was out on a date with some actor Saturday night."

"Jenkins," Barrister barked, "isn't there a newsstand a block down the street?"

"Yeah, I remember us passing it."

"Run down there and get me a copy of yesterday's paper. They're bound to have one left. If they don't, find one somewhere! I don't care if you have to knock on doors or go through trash."

"Got it," the man replied as he turned and jogged off.

"Now," the captain ordered, "You guys get to work and don't miss anything!"

As Barrister watched, the crime scene crew meticulously went about their varied duties. As they worked, their impatient boss smoked three cigarettes. Finally, with his anxious eyes following their every move, the quartet lifted the woman's body. Under her right shoulder was a broken, unused kitchen match.

"This what you wanted?" Collins asked.

"Bag it as evidence," came the solemn reply.

"Cap," Jenkins called out as he ran up. "Got the papers. The photo is in the third section, first page."

Barrister seized the newspaper, quickly discarding everything but the needed section. His eyes went from the image to the body now resting on a stretcher and then back.

"Was I right?" Collins asked.

The captain nodded, "The girl's name is Leslie Bryant. She is . . . or should I say . . . was an actress at Galaxy Studios." After folding the newspaper and slipping it into the side pocket of his suit jacket, he turned and began to resolutely stroll back to his car. His partner didn't catch up until Barrister was opening the 1935 Ford's passenger door.

"Are we going to the studio?" Jenkins asked.

"Not yet," the captain shot back, "I want to have copies of the crime scene photos to show Flynn

Sparks first. Then we'll see how the actor does without a script. Also, I want you to go to the *Times* and see if there are any old stories connecting the actor to our other victims."

15

June 15, 1936

It was just past five when Barrister and Jenkins walked into the ornate offices of Jacob Yates. Yates, dressed in gray slacks, a white shirt, and a blue double-breasted blazer with brass buttons, was on the phone. Waving toward two empty chairs in front of his desk, he finished his conversation and put the receiver of one of his three desk phones back into the empty cradle.

As Barrister sized up his host, Jenkins, his eyes all but popping from his head, made an observation, "This is some kind of office!"

Yates pointed toward the walls with seemingly condescending pride. "The wood paneling comes from an English castle, the light fixtures from Paris, all the furniture including my desk was made in Austria more than a century ago. The oil paintings are originals, the one on the far right is a Monet, the other two, hanging on each side of the bookshelf, are originals from Velázquez and

De Goya. The carpet is obviously Persian, but I'm sure you knew that."

"I'm just as sure he didn't know that," the older cop cut in. He pushed his hat back on his head and explained, "You see we don't spend much time around folks who have any type of culture in their lives. I'm Bill Barrister, the head of the homicide division of the Los Angeles Police Department"—he paused and glanced toward his immediate left before picking up his explanation—"and the young man who is so impressed with your office is my partner, Barry Jenkins. We are sorry to take some of your time, we know you must be busy, but this is a rather sensitive and urgent matter. Therefore, we need to speak with you privately and we didn't figure you'd want the press to see you coming to our modest offices."

"No problem," Yates assured them. "I want you to know that I always give a large gift to the police widows and orphans fund. I say this and I say it honestly: I admire your work so much that I make sure it is the focal point of many of our films."

"I've seen a few of those," the captain observed with a wry grin, "and it seems the head of homicide is never portrayed as being as smart as the newspaper reporters or the private investigators."

"I see," the studio head said, "I'll make a note to talk to our writers about that. Now, what can I do for you?"

Barrister wasted no time charging forward. "We need to visit with Flynn Sparks about a rather sensitive matter, and I'd would rather do that here in your office than on the set with a lot of curious eyes and sharp ears watching and hearing what we say."

"Let me say this up front," the studio boss cut in, "I know that Flynn can be a problem for you all. I mean, he's been in his share of fights, and there have been those times when he was driving drunk, but all things considered, he's pretty harmless; just a man who never grew up. And that report about his having fathered that child that ran in this morning's paper, I can prove there is nothing to that. The woman is a wacko trying to squeeze some money out of the studio and grab a bit of unearned fame for herself. So, I can pretty much guarantee the man has not done anything horrible. I just wish he'd grow up."

The captain smiled, "For a man who is so positive Mr. Flynn is not someone that we should be interested in, you sure began your defense with a long list of things he's done and," Barrister paused before adding, "that you feel don't amount to a hill of beans. Just based on your words he sounds pretty out of control to me."

"Not," Yates cut in, "in a way that would seriously harm anyone. Contrary to his screen image, he's as gentle as a lamb."

"We hope you're right," the captain calmly

87

replied, "but could you get him up here so that we could actually get his thoughts on a case we're working. This might sound strange, but I've found it never hurts to actually talk to a person who has some connection to a crime or a victim. It seems your script writers use that ploy all the time in movies. And, in your films, it seems that this . . . what can I call him? Let's go with . . . person of interest. I like that, I might use it again in the future. Anyway, this person of interest is never really very interesting in your films."

Yates nodded, pushed down the button on his intercom and said, "Eve."

"Yes, sir."

"Get Flynn up here as soon as possible." He let the button go. "You know, you've said a lot of words since you got in here that don't add up to much. Now it might be time to open up a bit. Why don't you tell me what this is all about?"

"Obviously murder," Barrister solemnly explained. "For some reason the department doesn't get us involved in stuff like traffic tickets or robberies."

"You don't think . . ."Yates asked.

Barrister waved his hand, "Are we here to accuse or arrest your actor? No. But as he might have been one of the last people to see the victim alive, we do need to find out where and when that meeting happened and what she was doing when they parted."

88

The studio boss leaned over his desk and lowered his voice, "Listen, we have had a long-standing arrangement with the police in this area. They understand we take care of our own. Remember that Fatty Arbuckle thing? The court let him go, but he never worked again."

The captain nodded in agreement, "There is an unwritten agreement in place, but I don't think it covers murder."

Yates pointed his finger at Barrister, "Listen, Pop, my studio employs more people than any business in town. In case you haven't looked, there's a depression going on. If anything happens to hurt our business then a lot of people—you know, just common workers, those with families and mortgages—they lose their jobs. So unless the person murdered was the president of the United States, then you're treading on ground that could be quicksand for you. If you play this the wrong way I can make one call and have both of you pounding a beat in some town that's not even on the map in Mississippi."

"That sounds like a threat," Barrister noted.

"It was one," Yates hissed. "And if you don't think I have the power to pull it off, you're crazy."

A knock caused all three men to redirect their attention to the door. A second later, Sparks, wearing a dark suit and white turtleneck sweater, casually walked in.

"I understand someone wanted to see me," he

announced as if he didn't have a care in the world.

Yates, his face stern, nodded, "These men are from homicide. They need to ask you a few questions."

"I've got nothing to hide," Sparks assured his boss as he made his way across the room and placed his rump on the corner of the man's desk. "Fire away, gentlemen."

Barrister looked to Jenkins and nodded. The younger man opened a folder sitting on his lap and pulled out a newspaper. With no explanation, he handed it to the actor. As Sparks looked at the picture on page 1C, the lead officer posed a question.

"I believe that is a photograph taken of you at a nightclub on Saturday evening."

"I don't remember it being taken," Sparks retorted, "but it must have been snapped at the Grove. I had supper there with my date that evening. Tommy Dorsey's band was playing, and, if you want, I can list a dozen people who know when I arrived and when I left. For your information, my bill was twenty-two dollars and I left a ten for a tip."

"And that is your date?" Barrister asked.

"Yes," Sparks replied, "that's Leslie Bryant. She hails from The Show Me State and is real proud of that fact."

"And what did you do after you left the club?"

The actor, his manner still relaxed, smiled,

"We went back to my place to check out the view."

"And when did you take her home?" Barrister asked.

"The next afternoon," he said unapologetically.

"So she spent the night in your home?"

"We're all adults here." Sparks looked over to his boss before bragging, "Most women who come home with me do spend the night. It might be immoral in your world, but the last time I checked it's no crime. At least not in this state."

Barrister looked to Jenkins and nodded. The cop once more opened the folder this time retrieving an eight by ten photograph. After holding it to where only Barrister could preview it, he handed it to Sparks. As the actor studied the image all the color drained from his face. Getting up from his seat, Yates looked over his biggest star's shoulder and shook his head.

"Mr. Sparks," Barrister began, his tone as deep as the ocean and as dark as midnight, "do you know where that picture was taken?"

The actor shook his head, "How could I?"

The cop continued, "Sometime yesterday or last night Leslie Bryant was strangled. She was then dumped in a vacant lot. And, as she was still wearing the same clothes she wore on your date and her makeup had evidently not been touched up, there seems to be a direct link to her time with you. I suggest you give us the whole story as to what happened this weekend. If I hear it all, perhaps you'll find a way to convince me why I should not book you on suspicion of having murdered this young woman."

"You shouldn't book me, because I didn't do it," Sparks, his voice now low and measured, explained.

"Then give me some reasons," Barrister calmly demanded. "I want to know why I should believe you."

"We had a good time on our date," the actor admitted. After folding his arms he added, "She came to my place and spent the night. The next morning, as a way of thanking me for the evening, she cooked me breakfast. We talked for a while, and we admired a car that my friend Dalton Andrews had given me. I even took her for a ride in it."

"Andrews gave you a car?" the captain asked. "That's awfully generous. You must have done something really nice for him."

"Actually, I won it in a bet. He bet me his V-12 Packard against my V-12 Auburn that I couldn't get Leslie to spend the night with me. When I got up that morning, I called and told him he'd lost and I wanted the car. He brought it over and then walked the five miles back to his place."

"Did he talk to Miss Bryant?" Barrister asked.

"Not really, but he saw her sleeping in my bed and later in the living room."

"Where did you and Miss Bryant go after you left your house?"

"To her apartment," Sparks quickly assured the cop. "I had a tennis game with Clark Gable at three, so I got her home around two. I took her to the Hollywood Arms Apartments in the Packard."

"What did you do last night?" Barrister demanded.

"I grabbed a bite with Clark, went home, and read over a script. We are finishing shooting a movie this week, and I had some lines I needed to learn."

"Was anyone with you?"

Sparks shrugged, "Sally Glenn called about nine. She's got a small part in the film. We talked for a while, and then she drove over and ran lines with me. She left about midnight. That's when I went to bed."

Yates chimed in, "Glenn works for us. If she's on the lot, I can call her in to confirm that."

"For the moment," Barrister explained, "that won't be necessary. But we will likely check it out down the line." He turned back to his suspect, "How long were you home alone last night before that call?"

"About two hours. Once I finished the match, Clark and I ate at the Derby, and then I drove up to my place."

"I'd stake my life," Yates chimed in, "that Flynn might be a bit of a character, but he'd never hurt anyone. It's just not something he's capable of doing."

Barrister grimly smiled, "If your word was all it took then we'd drop this matter right now, but the law requires a bit more than just having someone vouch for you. We need facts that can be substantiated. I'll admit, at this moment I can't put Mr. Sparks where we found the body, though, when the story runs tomorrow, we are hoping for witnesses to step forward, but I suggest that it would behoove him to make sure he isn't holding anything back. After all, until I find something that says otherwise, I'm thinking he was the last one to see Miss Bryant alive." The cop looked back toward the actor, "And usually the last one to see someone alive is the first person to see them dead. You figure out what I mean by that."

The policemen got up and moved toward the door. Just as Jenkins turned the knob, Yates called out to them. "You forgot something."

Barrister frowned, "No, I want you to keep the newspaper and the photo. Maybe they will stir something inside you that will prove there are some things more important in this town than Galaxy Studios and the movie business. In my mind, one of them is a young woman's life."

16

June 15, 1936

"What in the name of all that is holy did you do?" Yates demanded.

Sparks slipped off the desk and into a chair. Picking up the black-and-white photo, he studied the image and shook his head. Leslie Bryant's body was twisted in such a way that she could have been sleeping, but no one slept with their eyes open and with their mouth twisted in such a grotesque manner. At least no one he'd ever known.

"Flynn," Yates pleaded, "what did you do?"

The actor dropped the photo back on his boss's desk and ran his hand through his wavy hair. "I didn't do anything I don't always do."

"Well, that sure says a lot," the studio head cracked. "This might surprise you, but I try to keep from knowing what it is you do when you aren't at the studio. And you know why?"

"I'm sure you're going to tell me."

"Because your stunts have cost me thousands. And they've been the fodder for more news stories than I care to list. And there would have been even more if Ellen Rains hadn't worked with me to kill some of them. This morning you told me all your stunts just drummed up box office. Well, let me tell you something, murder doesn't do that."

Flynn balled his hands to fists, looked up, fire in his eyes, and shouted, "So you think I killed her. You think I put my hands around that woman's throat and watched the life drain slowly from her body."

"I didn't say that," Yates said, "but those cops might just be thinking that, and you are going to be in their sights. They'll be watching you day and night waiting until you slip up. And the reporters will be tagging along after you as well. You'll be under a microscope. You won't be able to go anywhere without a thousand eyes following your every move."

Flynn pulled himself out of the chair, his mind whirling, and walked over to the window that looked out on the back lot. He studied the activity below until he remembered a courtroom drama he'd made two years before. Turning, he set his jaw and pointed toward his boss.

"You get your legal team on this now. You pay them big bucks to keep you out of trouble with everyone from the censors to the White House. Now it's time you make them work harder than they've ever worked before."

"You don't order me around," Yates shouted. "I made you."

"But I can unmake you," Sparks said with a

droll smile. "If I get tagged for murdering Leslie Bryant, then the publicity that comes with it will take your whole studio down. Jacob, you make this go away. I don't care if you have to frame your son for this crime, you just make it go away."

Yates frowned, "I don't like this."

"You knew what you were getting when you signed me," Sparks stressed. "Now it's time to save both me and your legacy. You see, from this moment on Flynn Sparks and Galaxy Studios are tied together at the hip."

"OK, Flynn," the mogul growled, "you win. I'll get my lawyers at work on it today. I'll bring in more if I need to. The cops won't be able to touch you. And I'll make sure Ellen Rains is working on our side as well. But it's not going to be easy. Look at that picture, this is pure TNT."

"My survival means your survival"—the actor announced as he walked toward the door—"and I want both of us to live a long time. Now, I'm going back to the soundstage and going to work. And tonight I'm going to rest easy because you aren't going to let anything happen to me."

17

June 15, 1936

Jacob Yates sat on a bench just beyond a formation of giant boulders in a deserted section of Los Angeles' famed Griffith Park. The normally energetic and impatient man was uncharacteristically quiet and patient. Though there were the sights and sounds of nature all around him, he saw and heard nothing. Still wearing the dark blue suit he had put on at six this morning, he leaned forward with his elbows on his knees, seemingly staring into a small pond. His mind was so locked in on his suddenly overwhelming problems that he failed to even notice his appointment walk up the paved path on his left.

"Why meet here?" Ellen Rains grumbled as she took a seat beside the studio mogul. "I'm not a big fan of nature."

"For a couple of reasons," Jacob Yates cracked, "the first is symbolic. A man who, just a few years later, shot his wife gave this land to the city, and then he spent time in prison for the crime. He was wealthy and respected until one stupid move ruined him. Kind of reminds me of myself. My dumb move might have been signing an unknown hick, changing his name to Flynn Sparks and making him an American icon. Of course, now that I think about it, giving a guy a name like Sparks and have him burn down my studio might have been foreshadowing on my part. Now that is irony on a large scale."

"I'm sure," Rains shot back sarcastically, "if I wait long enough, you'll explain that to me in words that make sense. History lesson or not, I still don't like having to hike down a trail for a half mile just to meet with you or anyone else for that matter. As you can see I'm wearing heels. In fact, have you ever seen me when I didn't wear high heels? And Jacob, heels are made for looks, not exercise!"

He ignored Rains complaints as he continued his lecture, "Before this was a park it was an ostrich farm. I figured out today that I've spent two years emulating that species of bird. No matter what crazy or outlandish thing Sparks did, I just ignored it or I paid a few bucks and tried to make it go away. So I've had my head in the sand."

"Glad you figured yourself out," the woman shot back, "but you were doing that long before you discovered Sparks. Besides, I've always thought you were more like a turkey than an ostrich."

Jacob Yates frowned, turned his gaze from the boulders and looked the woman squarely in the eye. "The other reason we are meeting in the middle of nowhere is that I'm not a big fan of folks knowing you and I are spending time together. It reeks of disaster, especially now."

"Who put a tack in your chair?" Rains demanded. "Why all this gloom and doom? You didn't mind meeting me in your office the other day. In fact, the last time you and I tiptoed around and hid in the shadows was thirty years ago when I was a college student and you were trying to make it as a photographer."

"I'd rather not remember those days," he hissed. "I hated winters in New York. In fact, I hated everything about that city."

"Fine. Now what's got your feathers ruffled? Now you've got me talking about birds."

He frowned before charging forward. "Here's the bad news, and I mean really bad news. It seems your Hollywood Madman has struck again. Or did you already know about that?"

"I had no idea," she replied, her eyes suddenly alive with interest.

"Then let me spell it out; another woman's been strangled."

"I should have been told," she complained. "Of course, I've been on the MGM lot all day, maybe there's a message waiting at the office."

"I'm glad you didn't know," Yates barked. "I was beginning to think I was the last person to find out anything important in this whole blasted town. Imagine that, I got the scoop on Ellen Rains."

"Did you get the details?" she breathlessly asked.

"This is not something to be excited about," he scolded the writer. "A woman died, shouldn't we have a moment of silence or say a prayer or something?"

"Let the dead take care of the dead," Rains mockingly suggested. "I have readers that want ripe information. So did they tell you any good details? I need to know everything."

"The cops didn't want to share much with me, but they did demand to question Flynn Sparks. Seems he was the last person to see the woman alive."

"Who was it that got killed?" Rains demanded. "They obviously know. And why has the press not gotten the information yet?"

"Crime beat reporters," Yates explained, "are probably getting the story now. The victim was one of our recently signed actresses—Leslie Bryant."

The woman's eyes almost fell out of her head, "My word, she spent the night at Sparks's house on Saturday."

"And thanks to you, the whole world knows that," the studio boss quipped. "Now that I think about it, you were the one who created this whole mess. If you hadn't run that photo and blurb in your column no one would have likely connected Sparks to the girl. Or if they had, it would have been much, much later. You set my guy up."

"How was I supposed to know the girl was going to get murdered?"

Both went mute. Yates's eyes locked on a robin building a nest in a fruit tree while Rains followed the antics of a squirrel as it bounced up and down on the lawn. It was the still-shocked woman who finally broke the silence.

"Wish someone would invent a phone a person could carry in a purse. I'd sure like to break this story."

"I'd like to bury it," he snapped.

"Not if you're smart," she reasoned. "This could be a huge break for the movie concept I gave you. And, speaking of that, how are your people coming along with a script?"

"It's a little weak," he pointed out. "In a whodunit, it helps to know who did it. Until the case wraps up we can't make a movie."

"If you wait until that happens it will be too late," she corrected him. "Let's beat the cops at their own game. You take all the information that I give you, then you figure out who did it even before they do."

"I'm not Sherlock Holmes, Philo Vance, or Nick Charles," he assured her.

"Never thought you were."

Yates looked at the woman as if she were crazy, "You mean release a movie and frame someone for the crimes?"

"No," she smiled, "I don't want to hang this on

102

anyone who is innocent. I might be a bit cutthroat, but I do have some standards." She tapped her foot for a few seconds before posing a question. "Who has the best mystery and crime writers in the business?"

"My studio, but what difference does that make now?"

"Then put them to work solving this mess," she suggested. "They're smarter than Bill Barrister and his team. So just keep pushing them. Give them the budget to dig deep and get more leads. Right now you've got enough information to shoot the first third to half of the picture. Put that into motion. You can even create the posters and ads now."

"It hasn't even been cast," he whined.

"What is Dalton Andrews working on right now?" she demanded.

"Nothing except for a couple of retakes. He has a few weeks off."

"Give him the role as Barrister."

"He looks nothing like him," Yates pointed out.

"Yeah," she admitted, "but Barrister will love having folks think he's handsome and thin. I wish I could remember his partner's name?"

"He was in my office today," the studio boss announced, "I remember it well—Barry Jenkins."

"Sparks is the right age and build," Rains slyly offered.

"The cops have a frame around him for killing

Bryant," Yates noted. "Your column pretty much puts his hands around the woman's neck."

"That makes it all the better," she chuckled. "It will be perfect for publicity. I can't wait to write a bit in my column about the man the police suspect as the Hollywood Madman actually playing the cop trying to catch and convict him."

"You're actually serious," he whispered.

"Of course," she replied. "I have a piece of this picture, and I want it to be huge box office. Sparks and this real-life murder mystery will bring in the fans, and the media will love it. When can you start filming?"

"I guess next week."

"Good," she smiled, "wardrobe and sets will be easy. You can even shoot some things on location. Now get to work, Jacob, and I'll go back to my office and start writing a dynamite story on Leslie Bryant's murder. I can almost read it now . . . a star on the rise snuffed out and police suspect America's greatest actor. Wow!"

"I hope you know what you're doing," he sighed. "Right now, as I look into the future, I just see my studio being sold off piece by piece on an auction block. Then you can write a story with the headline, 'Sparks Destroys Galaxy.' "

"Not bad," she laughed, "but I won't have to use it. Sparks and this case are not going to ruin you, they will make you even more powerful. I know what I'm doing. Just make sure your writers figure out who the real murderer is before we film that last scene. If they beat the cops to that we'll have a movie people will be talking about fifty years from now. Got to get back to the office. Bye-bye, love!"

Yates watched the woman awkwardly trot off toward her car before once again turning his attention to the scene before him. The squirrel that had seemingly been observing the meeting was sitting on its back haunches staring at the man. The studio head smiled and chortled, "You must think I'm nuts too."

18

June 16, 1936

It was just past six, and Shelby Beckett was still working on altering a coat that was needed first thing in the morning. As she hand-stitched a sleeve, Betsy Minser walked in from the now quiet sewing factory.

"It has to look perfect," the supervisor reminded her newest employee. "They are shooting retakes for a movie that wrapped last week. It seems the film from one scene was overexposed and thus it forced the reshoot. So this jacket will be seen in close-ups from a lot of angles and that tear has to be patched so no one will notice it.

That's why you are doing it too. You're just that good. I got lucky when they brought you in here."

"I had a great home economics teacher," Shelby explained. "Mrs. Booth could teach anyone how to sew."

"Well," Minser noted, "you have some talent too. By the way, who is the man sitting in the corner and why is he in here?"

"My dad, he's my ride home."

"Hope he doesn't mind waiting," the supervisor whispered.

"I could give you a ride home," a hopeful Willard Mace chimed in. "I've got a nice Buick sedan."

"Where'd you come from?" Minser asked.

"I was behind the racks," he explained. "And I could give you a ride, Shelby. I'm a safe driver, and I would love to do that for you."

"You don't have to," Shelby replied between stitches. "Dad doesn't mind waiting. Besides I spent most of my life waiting for him to finish his work at the farm so we could eat supper, so this seems fair."

"Who's waiting?" Dalton Andrews asked as he flew into the room through an open side door.

"My father. He works on the lot too. We share rides. Some of us folks only have one car for the whole family."

"I see," the actor replied. "Well, is the jacket ready to try on?"

"It will be in another twenty minutes," came the reply.

"Then I'll wait. And I don't think we've met. My name's Dalton Andrews. That's my jacket you are working on."

"I'm Shelby, and I know who you are."

The handsome man grinned, "Now that is an unusual name. I've never met a Shelby before."

"Most people haven't," she assured him. "And before you ask, I was named after my mother. Her maiden name was Shelby."

"I like that," he chimed in, "a family that embraces its roots. Do you have a last name? I mean, you don't have to tell me if you don't want to."

"Beckett."

"Shelby Beckett," he almost sang the name out, "that's better than the ones the studio picks out for most of us. I used to be Jasper Rooks." He paused and grinned, "I can't believe I told you that."

Shelby looked up, "Really, that was your name?"

"Sadly, yes! I was named for my father who was named for his father. We had a lot of Jaspers in our family. It's a tradition that ended when Jacob Yates gave me a new name."

She smiled, "We once had a mule named Jasper back in Oklahoma."

"Shelby," Minser broke in, as she stepped

between her worker and Andrews, "I hate to interrupt this fascinating bit of family history, but I need to take a few dresses over to stage 6, are you clear on what you need to do?"

"No problem," the young woman assured her boss.

Shelby looked up from her work to observe Minser's exit. As she did Andrews walked across the room to where John Beckett was sitting. Shelby watched the two shake hands and exchange words before her father nodded, picked up his coat, and walked out a far door to the street that ran by the building. After the exit closed, the actor casually strolled back her way, dug his hands into his pockets and watched Shelby work.

"Where did Dad go?" she asked as she continued her tedious labor on the dark blue coat.

"He's headed home," Andrews explained. "I told him it was my fault you were working late and as my way of apologizing I'd take you out to eat and then drop you off at your house."

Shelby looked up, raised her left eyebrow, and frowned. "You didn't bother asking me about this."

"Did you want your father to be stuck waiting here?"

"No."

"Well," Andrews smiled, "that's taken care of then. So rather than be upset about it, you should be thanking me."

Shelby completed the stitching on the tear in the right sleeve and then studied a rip in the left one. Folding the wool fabric to where she needed it to be, she went back to work. As she did, she explained, "I usually make up my own mind on accepting a date or not. I don't remember you asking."

"OK," he laughed, "what if I had asked you if could I take you out to eat and then home? What would you have said?"

"No," came the derisive reply. "I don't go out with strange men."

"Now you see how smart I am," Andrews quipped. "I guessed how you'd respond and removed that option. So you have no choice."

"It's only a mile," she explained as she continued her work, "I can walk."

"It's raining," he announced. "So, I think you might want to reconsider."

"I don't even know you," Shelby chimed in.

"Are you kidding," he laughed, "you're one of a handful of people in this whole town that knows my real name."

"Not sure that counts much when it comes to judging your character." She tied off the thread and turned the coat right side out. She examined it closely before handing it to the actor. "Try it on. See what you think."

Andrews slipped into the jacket and walked over to the mirror. He turned and stretched, looking at it from several angles before nodding. After removing it, he walked back to her and gave it back. "Thanks."

"You're welcome," she replied as she placed the jacket on a wooden hanger and slipped it back on the rack. When she turned back the actor's way, he grinned.

"Miss Beckett, here's the deal. It was presumptuous on my part to just assume you'd let me take you out to eat and escort you home, but it really is raining. So, as a compromise, we can go over to the commissary, and then I can call you a cab."

"My name is Shelby," she grinned, "and no one has ever called me Cab before."

Andrews looked momentarily confused before locking onto her play on his words. "I guess I need a script to say things clearly. I meant that I would pay for a taxi to take you home."

She grinned, "Rather than the commissary, could you take me someplace that doesn't cost much?"

"I've got lots of money," he argued. "In case you hadn't figured this out . . . I'm a movie star."

"I know," she assured him, "before we got too poor to go to the movies I saw you in *East Of Tulsa*, *River's End*, and *Tried and True*. But I'm just off the truck from Oklahoma and I mean that literally. The dress I'm wearing is one I made from material that was left over at a secondhand store and that was two years and a hundred washings ago. The soles of my shoes have been lined with cardboard to cover the holes. So I'd be embarrassed to go anywhere really nice."

"I don't care," he argued.

"Maybe you don't," she softly replied, "but I do. So, if you will take me someplace where a quarter can buy a meal, I'll go with you."

"Wait right here," Andrews pleaded as he looked down at his wool slacks, shiny black leather shoes and silk shirt. "Give me five minutes."

Racing through a side door the actor disappeared. Completely baffled, Shelby, now realizing how tired she was, sat back down in a chair, closed her eyes, and dozed off. When she heard the clicking of shoes on the wooden floor she lifted her head and looked to the door. As it swung open, Dalton Andrews, now dressed in dungarees, a faded blue cotton shirt and scuffed brown shoes stepped into the room.

"Where'd you steal that getup?" she asked.

"My dressing room," he explained. "These were the clothes I was wearing when I came into town six years ago from Kentucky. In fact, they were the only ones I owned then. I look at them each day to remind myself just how fortunate I am to be where I am now. And, if dressing like this gets you to join me for dinner, then I'd say they are worth a lot more than the dozen silk suits that hang in that same closet."

"Jasper," Shelby laughed as she stood and

smoothed her faded, pink dress, "I'd be happy to accompany you to the nearest roadhouse and share a blue plate special."

"I could take you," Mace again offered as he looked on from where he was pressing suits. "It's out of Mr. Andrews's way. I saw your address on your job application, and I go by your house each morning and each night. So it'd be easy for me."

"That's OK," Andrews said with a grin. "You go ahead and finish up. I don't mind spending a bit of time with the woman who fixed my coat. After all, she's the reason I will look good tomorrow."

19

June 16, 1936

The City Diner was so off the beaten path it almost took a guide to find it. With a dozen tables, six well-worn booths and a twelve-stool counter all crowded into an adobe building a half-mile from the Pacific, it shouted, "Catering to those with almost empty pockets." The food was cheap, the plates chipped, the glasses mismatched and most of the forks bent. It appeared those folks who made their way out of the rain and into the place were largely solitary men dressed in greasy clothes and had likely spent a long day doing manual labor. They looked tired, beaten, and worn.

"Is this cheap enough for you?" Andrews asked while pulling out a chair for Shelby. After she was seated, he grabbed a seat across from her. He'd just gotten comfortable when she rewarded him with a smile and an observation.

"We've got a lot of places like this back home. The Bakers have a café in downtown Cordell that reminds me of this one. Except none of their chairs actually match. Here a few of them do."

"Has to be a mistake," Andrews laughed. "It seems there are no menus, so I guess we just read the chalkboard behind the counter and make our choices. What looks good to you?"

She scanned the offerings before landing on one near the bottom, "The ham sandwich fits my bill."

"I think I'll get the same." As a small, thin, middle-aged woman wearing a heavily stained, once-white apron strolled up, Andrews smiled and announced, "We'll each have a ham sandwich and a Coke."

The obviously tired waitress nodded, "You got it, Buster. And you only get one napkin each so don't get too messy. I'm the only one working, so I'll bring your drinks with your meal."

"She's a friendly sort," the actor noted after she was out of earshot.

"Probably has had a tough life," a suddenly saddened Shelby observed. "In truth, of those I saw on the road from Oklahoma, she would have been one of the happy ones. What I've discovered on our trip is there are a lot of people in this country who are more dead than alive. They've quit believing in things. When you quit believing, you might as well quit living."

A sad look replaced the smile on the actor's face as he noted, "When I convinced you to go out with me, that's not the direction I wanted to take this conversation. I was hoping we'd discuss things that make us smile, not make us cry. Right now, I feel like I need to sing a chorus of 'Nobody Knows The Trouble I've Seen' and was hoping we'd close tonight with 'Happy Days Are Here Again.' "

"Sorry," she replied. "I guess it's hard for you to identify with those of us who sometimes went to bed wondering if we'd eat the next day." She studied the people who were sitting around her in the café. "I'm betting some of these people know what that's like. For the past two years, money and even food has been harder to find than hen's teeth. And even now with Dad and me having jobs, it's still not easy. We live in a three-room flat, and I sleep on a couch. We have one tiny closest in the whole place and, sadly, we have plenty of room for everything we own. Don't get me wrong, I'm not feeling sorry for myself, I just don't guess you can imagine what life is like for the folks we are sharing this diner with tonight."

Andrews's eyes scanned the clientele before he

turned back to his date, "Look at these clothes. I was raised poor. For most of my life, we couldn't put two dimes together. So I take nothing I have now for granted. And because I know all about being poor and hungry, I know what being poor does to people. It either breaks their spirits or makes them so angry inside they boil up and explode."

"Broke my people," Shelby cut in. "My dad and mom never got mad, not even the day the bank foreclosed on our house. They just got sadder each day. It was like every new sunup brought a new funeral into our lives."

"My mom was that way," he chimed in, "but I was more the other way."

Shelby nodded, "Want to tell me about what life was like before you became Dalton Andrews, or is that something you'd rather leave buried in the past . . . like your real name?"

With a faraway look accompanied by a sober expression, he shrugged. "My story is not very interesting and not much different than any other poor person's. I grew up in a town in Kentucky that was so small it wasn't on a map. We were about sixty miles from Louisville, but we might as well have been a million. My dad worked on the railroad. He was killed in an accident when I was eight. I don't remember much about him. After that, my mother took in washing to make enough to keep food on the table for my sister and me.

Still, even with her working from sunup until sundown we were forced to move a half dozen times until we finally found a shack we shared with a thriving family of mice. From there, it just got worse."

"How could it get worse?" she asked.

He looked at the top of the wooden table and sighed, "My sister, Shirley, was four years older than me. She waited tables at a place not much different than this. One night she didn't come home. At first, that wasn't a big deal as there were a lot of nights she didn't come home until about sunup. But this time she didn't come home even then. We thought she might have run away until two days later, when they found her body down by the river. Someone strangled her. I was twelve, and I don't ever remember my mother smiling again. Five years later I buried Mom, but she really died when she saw Shirley wearing a blue dress and lying in the mud . . . dead."

Shelby nodded, now sad she'd asked Andrews to share his life. She fumbled for words before finally just admitting, "I have had it easy compared to you."

"Lots of folks have had it tougher," he quietly suggested. "Anyway, when Mom died I started west. A year and a hundred odd jobs later, Jacob Yates saw me unloading fruit at a grocery store and put me in the movies. I haven't been hungry since."

Shelby shook her head, "That's terrible about your sister. Did they ever find who did it?"

"No," the weight of his sadness carried in each word, "it could have been anyone. Shelby, Shirley wasn't a good girl. From the time she was fifteen, there were men in her life . . . a long list of them. It's not easy to have a sister who sells herself. I don't know if Mom was aware of it, but I knew the men she was with. They were low and dirty. And I came to hate her for being with them. On the night she died, Shirley likely went home with someone who wanted more than even she would give." He took a deep breath before mournfully adding, "In a sense she likely got what she deserved. What does the Bible say . . . sow the wind and reap the whirlwind?"

"No one deserves what happened to her," Shelby argued. "Just like that actress at the studio didn't deserve to be murdered."

"What actress?"

"Didn't you hear that Leslie Bryant was strangled?"

"No," he assured her. "I spent the day in my dressing room answering fan mail. When did you hear about it?"

"It was on the radio a few minutes before you came into wardrobe. It made Betsy so sick she turned it off. She'd worked with Miss Bryant at a fitting last week."

Andrews once more got a faraway look in his

117

eyes before quietly noting, "I guess she should have gone out with me."

"What?" Shelby asked. "I don't understand."

He forced a grim smile, "She picked the wrong man to go out with. She was a lamb and she opted to run with a wolf."

"Dalton, what are you talking about?"

"It's just this town, Shelby. You can't let your guard down. This place uses people and then throws them away. You have to be suspicious of everyone and trust no one. Leslie was a sweet girl who is now going to be remembered not for what she was, but for how she died. And just watch, people will make up lies and report them as news, and the lies will be believed long after the truth is just a memory."

"That's pretty harsh," Shelby noted.

"Shelby you're the real deal," he said with a smile, "while I'm a lie. My name is false, the bio they wrote up on me is fiction, and now, the parts I play on the screen become the parts I play in real life."

"You're real now," she argued.

"Yes, and I'm thankful for that. But tomorrow Jasper will disappear, and I'll once more be Dalton Andrews. Dalton has money and fame and his supposed best friend, at least according to studio publicity, is the biggest star in Tinseltown."

"You mean Flynn Sparks?" she cut in.

"Yeah," he shook his head, "and I don't even

like him. In fact at this moment, I hate him."

"Why?"

"It doesn't matter," Andrews shrugged.

"Dalton," she gently said, "my world has turned upside-down in the past few years. In the past few weeks it has gotten even stranger. I live in a world a million miles away from the girl I was but that change in location hasn't changed who I really am. I kind of think your name might have changed but you still are the same guy you were."

"Don't be like Leslie," he warned.

"What do you mean?"

"Don't have faith in other people," Andrews continued. "That kind of innocent thinking opens the gates for you to be taken advantage of."

"You wouldn't do that," she assured him. "I can see that in your eyes."

"Shelby, I'm an actor, my job is to play a character. But this town's also made me a user and even an abuser. If you give me your trust, I'll find a way to work it to my advantage. And when I or someone like me does that . . . when we steal your innocence . . . then we make you one of us. You see, misery loves company." He looked over to the counter, "Just like that menu board, my life can be erased and rewritten in the matter of a few minutes. Today, I played a part to get you to go out with me tonight. It's what I do. I can't turn it off. You can't be sure of who I am, because I can't be sure of it either."

"I don't believe that," she argued.

"And that's the first sign to my having played my part to perfection. You see me tonight as charming and sincere, but how do you know that, behind my green eyes and perfectly capped teeth, I might really be hiding an evil so dark you can't imagine it? You can't know because even I don't know who I really am."

Shelby didn't know how to respond. She fumbled for words before finally asking something she immediately wished she'd kept to herself. "So did you really have a sister who was murdered?"

He sadly nodded, "That was true, and it really did destroy my mother. But for years Shirley had really been killing Mom a piece at a time with her wild lifestyle. What my sister was I won't say in front of you, and the censors won't let me say it on the screen, but I can tell you this . . . I hated her for hurting Mom, and I didn't cry at her funeral. And even today, when I see a woman using her beauty and her body to get something she wants, it is like Shirley is once more alive and hurting more people. And all the rage comes back again."

"I'm sorry," Shelby whispered.

"Hey," he said with a smile as he looked back toward the kitchen, "our food is on the way. Let's quit this journey into my sad past and pretend the biography Galaxy Studios wrote for me is really true."

"What's that?" she asked.

"That I'm from North Carolina, raised on a tobacco farm and educated at elite private schools."

"I'm not buying it," she announced as the waitress set their food and drinks on the table. "At least, not like you're dressed right now. And I'm not buying you are what you said you are. I think there's a lot more good than evil in you."

"Shelby," Andrews's expression and tone were suddenly very serious, "please don't let your guard down, and don't give up being the sweet kid you are. If you do either of those things, someone like me will hurt you. Now, enough talk, let's eat."

20

June 16, 1936

It was just past nine when Andrews drove Shelby up to the small bungalow her family called home. He didn't bother turning off the car's motor, just slid it into neutral, and set the emergency brake. As he fiddled with the radio, she turned sideways in the seat and leaned against the passenger door.

"That's a nice song," she said as he adjusted the tuning.

Andrews, his face illuminated by the instrument

lights, grinned, "I've met the guy who cut that record. His name is Fats Waller and the song is 'All My Life.' That tune is on top of half the charts in the nation right now."

"It's a great song," Shelby noted. "I think it should be number one everywhere."

"Can't be," Andrews explained. "Fats is a Negro, and a lot of stations won't play his music because of the color of his skin."

"They are the ones who are missing out," she suggested.

"Guess you're right," he agreed. "Fats plays jazz, and I like it almost as much as I like swing music. How about you? What kind of music do you play most?"

She shrugged, "I couldn't answer that. You see we don't have a radio in our house, much less our truck. About all I get to hear at home is my mom singing, and she really can't carry a tune. I guess the only music I know much about is what I've heard and sung in church."

"Well," he smiled, "that's something. What was your favorite song from church?"

Her eyes lit up, "There were so many it would be hard to pick just one."

He turned off the radio and looked her way, "Give it a try. It's been a long time since I've been in church, but I remember a few hymns from my days in Kentucky."

Shelby leaned her head against the door glass

and took an unplanned trip through her memories. She bounced from one song to another, letting them play out in her head, before landing on one that demanded to be clung to like a child's teddy bear.

She hummed a few lines before saying, " 'Love Will Roll the Clouds Away.' "

He smiled, "I don't know that one. Why don't you sing a few lines?"

"I couldn't do that," she shyly answered.

"I know you can sing," he pointed out, "I just heard you hum. So please sing a verse. I want to know what makes it your favorite."

She bashfully nodded, took a deep breath and softly sang.

As along life's way you go,
Clouds may hide the light of day.
Have no fear for well you know,
Love will roll the clouds away.

When the road is rough and long,
And the world is cold and gray.
Lift your voice in happy song,
Love will roll the clouds away.

"Shelby, that was nice. I kind of needed to hear those words too."

She dipped her head and looked out the windshield. He wasn't the only one who needed to be reminded of those words from time to time. They were often a crutch for her. In fact, she'd sung them a hundred times as she rode in their old truck along Route 66 heading west. At times, it was singing old hymns that kept her from crying.

"You know," Andrews said softly, "I'd go crazy without music in my life. Whenever I'm depressed or really angry, if I turn on the radio or play a record it calms me down."

Her grandmother had told Shelby many times that music healed more wounds than any medicine ever invented, and time had proven her right. And, after listening to Andrews, she now figured music worked the same way for the rich as it did for the poor. But along with music, there was something else the rich and poor needed equally and that was sleep. It was late and she had a long day ahead of her tomorrow. She still had a lot to prove to Betsy Minser.

"Dalton," Shelby noted, "I want you to know this has been my best evening since we got to California, but I really need to go in now."

"Of course," he answered, "and as the rain has stopped you won't have to worry about getting wet. Let me walk you to the door."

"You don't have to," she insisted, "I'm a big girl."

"And Dalton Andrews might just take you up on that and drop you off and drive away. But you've been out with Jasper Rooks, and he's kind of old-fashioned. You wait there, and I'll run around and open your door."

Shelby watched him slide out from behind the wheel and walk in front of the car. She smiled at him through the glass as he came up to her door and twisted the handle. As it opened, she stepped out and led him up to the bungalow's front door. A bit embarrassed and unsure of what to do next, she demurely looked into his eyes, hoping he'd make the next move.

"May I?" he asked.

She nodded. An instant later, his lips were on hers. It lasted only a second, but in that time her body warmed and her head seemed to float. She stood frozen in the damp night air as he wordlessly turned and walked back to his car. She watched him get in, put the Hudson sedan into first, and drive away. Shelby didn't go inside until the taillights disappeared into the night. If only the kids back home could somehow find out that a real movie star had kissed her.

21

June 16, 1936

With his hands clasped behind him, Bill Barrister looked out his second floor window at the morning traffic and marveled at the strange nature of the city he called home. Rumbling by his windows were beat-up Model T Fords and ancient, dented, and rusting Chevrolets, and right next to them were two Lincoln K limousines and a block-long supercharged Duesenberg J cabriolet. The destitute and the elite, the poor and the rich, all sharing the same street equally while living lives that were barely connected. In the movie capital of the world perhaps the incongruity of what was Los Angeles was somehow lost on seemingly everyone but the police. But the fact was the hidden class structure in the city influenced every element of life including where people lived, their social opportunities, and even the way justice was dealt out. In each of those situations, the rich seemed to get all the breaks. A knock turned the man's attention to the frosted-glass door separating him from the noise of a police station at work.

"Come in!"

"Cap," Barry Jenkins announced as he opened

the door and quickly moved toward his partner, "what are we doing about the Bryant case?"

"Very little," came the honest reply.

"But we have tied Sparks to the woman," the younger cop argued. "He couldn't give any reason for us not to believe he might be guilty. We likely have a case. We should at least be searching his home, cars, and dressing room."

"Barry, you are exactly right. We should be searching his house right now."

"Then why aren't we?"

The older man frowned, "Because unwritten laws are often much more powerful than the written ones."

"I don't get it," Jenkins replied.

"Sit down," Barrister suggested. "Smoke if you want, and I'll explain how working in the City of Angels is much different than being a cop in Chicago or Cleveland." Only after both men were seated did the captain continue. "If Flynn Sparks was a banker, teacher, or garbage truck driver, we would have been all over him the moment we found the connection between Leslie Bryant and him. But Sparks is an actor—and not just any actor—he's the country's top box office draw. And he works for a studio that employs more people than any other business in this city. For those reasons and a few dozen more, no judge will give us a search warrant in this case. And that is the way it is."

"But . . ." With a wave of the hand, Barrister cut his partner off.

"Barry, the movie business is really a new-comer to this area. It has only been here a generation, but it has more power to impede law enforcement than Al Capone during his days of dominating Chicago. Why do you suppose no one ever was tried for the deaths of William Desmond Taylor or Thelma Todd? In both cases, we were blocked from doing the kind of investigation we would have normally done. And how many actors, directors, and producers in this town have been charged for anything from drunken driving to fatal car accidents to rape?"

"I can remember only a couple," Jenkins admitted.

"And how many have been convicted once charged?" Barrister asked.

"I can't name any," the younger man admitted.

"It is hard for me to think of anyone either," he announced while pointing to a stack of news-papers on the corner of his desk. "Have you read the news today?"

"No, I haven't had time."

"Well, at the same time the police chief and the district attorney are calling me and telling me to lay off Sparks, the *Times* and other rags are demanding I do something about Leslie Bryant's tragic death. It seems I am caught between a rock and hard place, and I've got no wiggle room at all."

"But," Jenkins argued, "Why isn't Galaxy Studios shutting the newspapers up? Why are they allowing them to put this thing all over the front pages?"

"Because," Barrister explained, "even bad publicity is good publicity when it comes to a man like Sparks. Simply by his being linked to the dead actress, the public's fascination with him will grow and the studio will make even more money off his films. In her column today, Ellen Rains even suggested that Bryant was the true love Sparks had been looking for. She hinted they were about to be engaged. I would bet money that is nothing but hogwash, but as Mark Twain said, lies, told over and over again, will become the truth."

Jenkins shifted uncomfortably in his chair, "So the five girls who've been strangled will be pushed aside just so Hollywood can continue to make movies about men who murder women?"

"Ironic isn't it?" The captain grinned, "But rather than fight a battle I can't win, I'm going to pull a few pages from a Hollywood script."

"What do you mean?"

"I still have some things to work out," Barrister confessed, "but let's just say I'm going to use a Model T to stop a Cadillac. For the time being, I need you to find out what matches were left at the scene. I want to know who made them and where they were sold."

"There are a lot of match companies out there," Jenkins argued. "How can I narrow it down?"

"Work with the lab boys," Barrister suggested. "And time doesn't matter. With our path to potential evidence blocked, about all we have is time."

As Jenkins got up and left, closing the door behind him, the homicide captain returned to the window and studied the traffic. If Sparks wasn't the killer then someone out there was. How was he going to find him with the power of Galaxy Studio blocking his every move?

22

June 18, 1936

The news of Leslie Bryant's death drained all the energy and life of everyone from the maintenance crews to the top-of-the-line actors. As work started, no one even exchanged greetings. It was as if the clock had been turned back to the days of silent film. During the day, except for the noise of the sewing machines, even the wardrobe department was quieter than an Ivy League class-room during final exams. When time came to leave, a few folks mumbled words, but most just silently walked to their cars and drove off the lot.

It was the same with Shelby and her father. They

were mute on the short ride home and stayed that way until they arrived at their rented home. After the young woman took a deep breath and sighed, John finally spoke.

"What are you thinking about?"

"This is a strange place, Dad. Every day at that studio where we work, a few hundred people die. They are taken down by bullets, arrows, and even poison. People stand over them and say words that are supposed to evoke some kind of explanation as to why what happened happened. And then someone calls cut and those dead folks get up, laugh, and walk away. Then today one of those that probably spent her whole life hoping to act out a death scene on that lot gets killed and reality moves into the place fantasy calls home. Suddenly there is no cut and the dead person stays dead. And no one knows what to say or do."

"It hasn't taken me long," the man sighed, "to get lost in that world. Sometimes I even forget what's real and what's not."

"Not today," she sighed. "Today it wasn't hard to separate the two." She shook her head, "It was easy back home. Everything in life was real. We quit pretending about the age we started school."

"Let's go inside," he suggested, "Mom's probably got supper ready."

Shelby stepped out of the truck, closed the door, and wearily walked to the door. She was about to twist the knob when she noted something that didn't make any sense. "Dad, do you hear that?"

He pulled his hat back and scratched his head, "Sounds like music."

"And it's coming from our house," she pointed out.

Pushing the door open, she looked across the room to where her mother sat by a large wooden cabinet with a round black dial located in the center. The box sported a half a dozen different types of wood inlays and was at least three feet tall. And the Benny Goodman music floating from its speaker sounded like it had been recorded in heaven.

"What's this all about?" John asked.

"It came today," Mary explained. "I was doing some mending about two and a truck pulled up. Two men got out and brought this thing up to the door. I tried to tell them they'd made some kind of mistake and that we couldn't afford a radio, and they just told me it was already paid for. They set it up, plugged it in, made sure it worked, and then left. I've been listening to it ever since."

He ambled over to the radio and nodded, "If that's not the strangest thing. Are you sure it was meant for us?"

Mary nodded, "I asked them if the radio was intended for the Beckett family, and they assured me it was. Even gave me a piece of paper proving it. It's amazing, Pa. It gets all kinds of stations, and I've listened to everything from quiz shows to something they call soap operas and even to the news and weather. And the music that comes out of this thing makes it sound like you are right there on the first row of a concert."

John twisted the center button and switched to a station playing some kind of comedy program. He listened to a joke about a man trying to please his mother-in-law and laughed out loud.

"I didn't think it was that funny," his wife scolded him. "My mom was always pretty good to you."

He grinned, "She's an even better mother-in-law now than ever."

"Why, thank you," Mary said.

"Yep, with her in Oklahoma and us in California, I've become quite fond of her."

"Pa!"

He wiped the grin from his face and looked back at the radio. "It's a Zenith! That's a real high-dollar brand. How did we end up with it?"

A still mystified Shelby walked across the room. She reached down to the tuning knob and looked to her dad, "Can I?"

"Sure."

She slowly twisted the dark brown bakelite knob to the right until she came across a song she heard the night before. Moving to another knob, she adjusted the volume.

"That's nice," Mary said.

Shelby nodded, "It's by a man named Fats Waller. It's called 'All My Life.' "

As the song slowly played, Shelby laid her hand across the top of the radio. She could feel the tune's beat in the wood. As she danced in place, her hand moved and neared the right edge, and something hit the tips of her fingers. Stepping closer, she looked over the top between the Zenith and the wall.

"There's something taped on the back," she noted.

"Probably an instruction booklet," John guessed.

"No," Shelby corrected her father, "it's an envelope." She pulled it loose. Not bothering to ask, she tore it open. Inside was a note.

"What's it say?" Mary asked.

Shelby's blue eyes lit up as she scanned the message. "All it says is this . . . 'It's time for some music in your life.' "

"Is it signed?" John asked.

"No, Dad, but I've got an idea who sent it to us."

"Who?" Mary demanded.

Shelby drew the unsigned letter to her heart and grinned, "A lonely guy from Kentucky named Jasper."

23

June 19, 1936

Due to the shadow cast over the lot by Leslie Bryant's murder, the first four days of the week had dragged by, but, as she had spent the last two days working on costumes for extras, Shelby had not been challenged on the job. In fact, she got so far ahead that her boss gave her an extra hour for lunch, and, as a bonus, the money for a meal in the commissary. Dressed in a two-year-old red, flower print house frock, white socks, and black flats, the woman took a seat in a back booth and scanned the menu. As she studied the wide variety of offerings a waitress brought her a glass of water. Shelby was just about to take a sip when a familiar voice posed a much overused line.

"Is this seat taken?"

Shelby looked up into the face of Mr. Flynn Sparks and smiled, "No, but something tells me it is about to be."

He grinned, "Just my luck to walk in when you did."

"Mr. Sparks, I might be just a country girl who knows very little, but I question your choice of tables. Wouldn't it be better for your image to eat with Eilene Waters?" Shelby pointed to the

135

actress. "She's all by herself just three tables over, and the gossip magazines seem to believe she is the next hot thing in Hollywood. You would look good with her."

"Actually," he corrected her as he slid onto the bench, "she would look good with me. Now let's move on to important news." He lifted his eyebrows and noted, "Talk around the lot is that you went out with Mr. Boring earlier this week."

She shook her head, "I've never met a Mr. Boring. Now what do you think I should order?"

"The roast beef with vegetables," he suggested, before continuing his earlier observation. "You know I'm talking about Dalton. Seems he took you to a dive. That is hardly surprising; he doesn't like to spend his money. He probably has the first dollar he ever made. Now a real gentleman would have taken you to a club and introduced you to Hollywood royalty instead of forcing you to rub elbows with the city's peasants."

A waitress waltzing up to the table halted what was about to become a verbal sparring match. "What would you like?"

Shelby glanced across to her uninvited guest, "Mr. Sparks suggested the roast beef plate."

"It is very good," she announced.

"Well, as Mr. Sparks suggested it, I'll have the turkey dinner."

The woman wrote down the order on her pad and then looked to the actor, "Do you want the usual?"

"No, I'll have what she's having." He handed the menu back to the waitress before picking up where the conversation had been interrupted. "I really could introduce you to Hollywood's blue-bloods. And I'd love that opportunity."

"I'll have you know," Shelby announced with a certain degree of pride, "that I was the home-coming queen at Cordell High School. We couldn't afford a crown, but I do have the sash to prove it. So, even if my dress is a bit tattered and my shoes scuffed, you are in the midst of royalty."

"You've got spunk," Sparks laughed. "I will give you that."

"I've wrestled hogs," she explained, "and more often than not I managed to win those battles too. I've hunted and fished and can throw a curve ball as good as most boys. Those experiences will give you spunk in pretty large doses. Oh," she sneered, more than smiled, "and even though this might strike a bit close to home, I've killed a lot of snakes too."

"You went out with Andrews," the actor said with a knowing grin, "and he crawls a lot. If you will go out to a dump with him, why not go out to eat with me and have a real meal?"

"In about ten minutes," she shot back, "I will be eating with you. So you're about to have your date. I suggest you pay attention, so you don't miss it."

"I'm serious," he whined.

"Let me explain something," Shelby announced as she placed her elbows on the table and leaned a bit closer to the other side of the booth, "Where you want to take me, I can't go."

"You're old enough," he assured her.

"I'm old enough," she agreed with a smirk, and then added, "to know better. But I also don't have a dress for a night with royalty. Dalton and I went to the so-called dive because I fit in there. Those people didn't look at my clothes and wonder what truck I just climbed off of."

"Listen Miss Beckett, you're the most beautiful woman in this room. Lots of men look at you. It happens all the time. It doesn't matter what you're wearing. But I want to do more than look. If it takes laying out some cash I will. I'll buy you a dress. Heck, I'll buy you a closet full of gowns and shoes. I'll make you feel like Cinderella if it means you'll go out with me."

"You're a strange-looking fairy godmother," she cracked.

"I'm serious," he said, his face moving closer to hers.

"You want to take me out?" she asked.

"Yes!" His reply was adamant.

"Do I get to pick the time and place?"

"Yes!"

She pulled her purse from the bench, opened it, took out a pencil and piece of paper and jotted down a note. After dropping everything but the note back into her purse, she handed what she'd written to Sparks.

"That's my address. Pick me up Sunday morning at fifteen before eleven and take me to church."

"But . . ."

"You said I got to pick," she replied with a smile. "If you want to pass then I'll bet Dalton would take me out. He's supposed to come by for a fitting this afternoon. I can ask him then."

"I'll do it," Sparks grumbled. "Besides, with the bad publicity I'm getting right now, the studio would love to have someone see me in a church."

"Here comes our waitress with our food," Shelby noted, "I hope you enjoy the turkey as much as I'm sure I will."

24

June 20, 1936

Bill Barrister paused outside the frosted-glass door that read "Arnold Forrest, Medical Examiner." Though he was a seasoned cop and had seen a great deal of death in his days on the force, this was not a place he ever got used to visiting. After rapping on the wooden entry, Barrister finally strolled into what for many was the last stop before the funeral home.

To Barrister, every body was almost sacred. When a person died, it was as if a part of him died as well. But to Forrest, a body was little more than a science experiment. The short, skinny, bespectacled forty-year veteran treated the remains with little more respect than he did an old newspaper. Forrest was standing over the body of a large man likely in his forties. The body's chest was open and the ME was lifting the skin and muscle to study the vital organs. With only a glance in the visitor's direction, the examiner noted, "Interesting case. Mr. Mills' wife got tired of living with him and pumped him full of lead. Three of the six shots she fired would have been fatal, so I can't determine which one killed him. I can tell you this, and it comes with a heavy dose of irony, she'll likely get life or go to death row, and it was all for nothing."

"What do you mean?" the suddenly interested cop asked.

After letting the muscle and skin drop back into place, Forrest smiled, "This guy is covered up with cancer. He had less than six months to live. If she'd have been patient, she could have had her wish come true and not forfeited her life in the process. It was just a matter of time."

"Impatience is the nature of this town," Barrister sadly noted. "People are in such a hurry to get things they want or think they need, they literally climb all over each other scrambling to grab it."

He paused, took another look at the body, and then chimed in with the reason for his visit. "You called me about my strangler case?"

"The second victim," Forrest explained, "or at least the woman we thought was the second victim before you found that bag of bones off Sunset. Anyway, I was finally able to match her dental work to dental x-rays of a woman who'd been reported missing about that same time." Forrest stepped around the table holding the body and strolled over to his desk. Shuffling through a pile of loose papers, he yanked a yellow one from the stack and continued, "Her name was Janet Sykes. She was a local girl, grew up in the valley, and had been working at Galaxy Studios for two months when she went missing."

"What was her job?" the captain asked.

"She was a page." He picked up a file, dropped the notes he'd taken into it before handing it to his guest. "If you look in there at the photo, you will see that she was a beautiful girl."

"Does she have family?" Barrister asked as he opened the file and studied the eight by ten.

"The address is in the folder," Forrest explained. "Both her parents are alive, and she has a young brother and sister. At least, that is what the report from Missing Persons says. And, before you ask, no one has told the family that her body has been identified."

The head of homicide nodded, "Says here that

her father's a Lutheran pastor. I see from the report her family called her Jan."

"Isn't that your daughter's name?"

"Her middle name." The admission was followed by a long sigh.

"You going to let Missing Persons know we found this girl, or do you want me to? They will need to notify the family before the press goes public with this."

"I'll drive over to West Los Angeles myself and tell the family," Barrister gloomily announced. "Janet Sykes has moved from being a missing person to being a victim of homicide, and that makes her a part of my family."

"Let's hope I never join your family," Forrest cracked.

"Yeah, if you do, I wouldn't have anyone here who could give me your cause of death." As the captain placed his hand on the doorknob, he solemnly said, "Thanks, Arnie. Do let Jack in Missing Persons know that, as far as he is concerned, the case is closed."

25

June 20, 1936

It was just past five when Barrister twisted the doorbell chime on the neat, white cottage at 1613 Cypress Street. A tall, thin woman, her dark hair streaked with gray, attractive in a down-home sort of way, answered.

"May I help you?" Her accent indicated her roots were likely from the Midwest.

The visitor reached into his suit pocket and produced his badge and credentials. "My name's Bill Barrister, I'm with the Los Angeles police," he paused, before almost apologetically adding, "homicide division. Are you Mrs. Sykes?"

As tears welled up in her emerald green eyes, she brought her hand to her mouth and took a shallow gasp of air. After gaining a bit of composure, she nervously glanced over her shoulder before once more turning her face back to her uninvited guest.

"Is this about Jan?"

Barrister avoided the question with a polite request, "May I come in?"

She nodded and moved away from the entry. As the cop stepped into the house, the woman called out, "Lucas, there is a policeman here to see us."

She pointed down the narrow hall, "It's the last door on the right."

"Thank you," the captain replied softly. With the woman leading the way, he made the short trek to where the father waited. During that walk, he saw a dozen framed photos. At least three of them were of Janet; the last one obviously from her high school graduation. This was not going to be easy. Stepping through the door into the home's quaintly furnished living room, Barrister noted a slightly built man with small dark eyes and a receding hairline standing beside a far window. As their gaze met the cop announced, "I'm Captain Bill Barrister. I'm with homicide."

The man nodded, "I think 'it's nice to meet you' is the proper term to use at times like this. I say that to every guest who comes into my church. But, if you will allow me to be honest, somehow I think when this visit is over I'd likely wish we'd never met." He took an awkward breath before quietly adding, "I'm Lucas Sykes, but I guess you already knew that. Why don't you take a seat on the couch, and I'll just ease back down in the chair by the window and pretend for a few more precious moments that this is about a parking ticket or expired driver's license." He forced a smile, "Or maybe you are looking for a pastor to visit with a condemned killer. Ironic, I'm the person who likely needs a clergyman right now."

"I wish any of those other options you

mentioned would have been the reason for my visit," Barrister replied, "I really do." After he eased down on the dark green divan, the cop looked over to the woman. He was fumbling for words when she beat him to the punch.

"Did you say you are a captain?" she asked.

"Yes."

"Captain, would you like something to drink? We have a few bottles of Coca-Cola, and I can put on some tea or coffee."

"No, thank you, ma'am."

Seemingly at a loss as to what to do next, the woman eased down onto the arm of the large chair that matched the couch, balled her hands in her lap and stared at the hardwood floor. Like her husband, she was buying time. She wanted a few more minutes before having to face the truth that, in fact, she already knew.

"My wife's name is Judy," the man interjected. "A . . . I was reading before you arrived." He picked up a book and laid it in his lap. Like his wife, Lucas Sykes was searching for ways to put off hearing what Barrister had come to say. "Captain Barrister," he continued while tapping the book's cover, "This is a fascinating novel about a family who lives back east. It's strange, it is such a dynamic story, and I have been lost in it for most of the afternoon, but now I can't even remember the book's title."

Watching the family go through this exercise

suddenly seemed cruel. It needed to stop. They had to hear what they already knew. So Barrister nodded, before quietly announcing, "You know why I'm here."

The woman looked up. "We do. You know, when you were at the door, I could read it in your eyes. But I didn't want to actually have you say the words. But putting them off is not going to make the truth go away, so won't you please say what you came to say. I need to hear it to really believe Jan is never going to stroll up that sidewalk and open that door again. If I don't hear it from you, then I will always be looking for her to come home."

Barrister seized the moment and wasted no more time. "She died," those two short words catching in his throat before finally tumbling out. After taking a deep breath, "We are guessing she died about the same time she disappeared. Probably the same day."

The woman nodded and buried her face in her hands. The man shook his head and glanced out the window toward the street. With the couple caught up in a flood of painful memories, the room was bathed in profound silence. The only sound was a clock ticking on a bookshelf. That timepiece chimed the half hour before the preacher finally brought the sound of the human voice back into this very sad corner of the world.

"The fact you are here indicates she didn't die in an accident."

"That's right," Barrister answered earnestly. "She was found in a park. This will be hard to say and even harder to hear, but she'd been strangled."

"Like that actress?" Mrs. Sykes gasped.

"Yes, ma'am. Pretty much like Miss Bryant. We think the same person murdered both women."

With tears streaming down her face she whispered, "But you don't know who it is that did it. He's still out there somewhere?"

Barrister nodded. "We don't have much to go on yet. It can help me do my job and bring the person who did this to justice if you will let me ask you few questions."

Mrs. Sykes violently shook her head. "Questions, you want to ask us questions? What good will that do Jan? What good will it do that actress who died? They'll both still be dead. Nothing's going to change! Catching the guy won't bring either one of them back."

"No, ma'am," the cop sadly agreed, "it won't. But the answers might stop him from taking another girl's life and having her family feel the same way you do right now. I can't turn back the clock, so my job is to try to stop the pain and suffering. And that means I have to ask questions during other people's worst moments. I wish it didn't have to be that way. At moments like this, I'd rather have any job other than the one I have."

Mrs. Sykes wiped her eyes and frowned. "Let me ask you something. It is a question I've been asking my husband for months. Where was God? Why wasn't He protecting her that night? Why did He desert my daughter?"

Barrister shrugged, "Mrs. Sykes, I ask that question a lot, and it seems no one can give me a satisfactory answer. It haunts me every time I view the body of a murder victim or have to visit with the family. In fact, I quit going to church, because I just couldn't come to grips with why so many good people end up like your Janet." Before continuing, the cop rubbed his forehead and sighed. "I want to make sure I stop this kind of evil so someone else doesn't have to deal with the question you just asked me; so someone else doesn't have the same doubts we both have. So, can you help me?"

"Thank you for being honest," she said. She took a breath, glanced over at a picture of her daughter on the table, and asked, "What do you need to know?"

"Where was Janet going the last night you saw her?"

"She left here to go to a party at the Roosevelt Hotel," Reverend Sykes explained. "I guess you already know she was a page at Galaxy Studios.

She'd won the chance to be at the Hollywood party because she was named employee of the month."

"She was excited," the woman added. "She bought a new royal blue dress with her own money. I fixed her hair and makeup. The studio sent a limo for her. I thought she looked like a movie star when she got into the back of that Packard. That car seemed to stretch forever."

As the woman's eyes filled with tears, Reverend Sykes picked up the story. "She called us from the hotel. She'd been invited to a smaller party at someone's home and wanted to let us know it would be after midnight when she got home. Even though she was still living at our house, she was nineteen, working, making her own way, so what could we say? We told her to have fun. That was the last time we talked to her."

"Do you know where the party was?" Barrister asked.

"No," Mrs. Sykes explained. "She was so excited, she didn't ever tell us. I know I was foolish not to ask. I've kicked myself a hundred times for not getting more information."

The cop continued to gently dig, "Who was hosting the party at the hotel?"

"Galaxy Studios," Reverend Sykes explained. "They were doing it to celebrate some kind of press awards. A few weeks after she turned up missing, Mr. Yates was nice enough to send us a picture that was taken of her at the party. Would you like to see it?"

As Barrister nodded, the woman got up, opened the door in an end table, pulled out a small photo album and opened it to the final page. "Here it is," she said as she handed it to her guest.

Janet Sykes, outfitted in a gown with a high neck, was smiling while standing beside Flynn Sparks. The movie star, a huge smile covering his face and a drink in his free hand, had his right arm wrapped around the young woman's shoulder as if pulling her close to his side. As Barrister continued to study the faces of those in the background, he posed another question.

"Did your daughter know Mr. Sparks before the party?"

"Oh yes," the preacher answered, "she constantly talked about the way he flirted with her at the studio. I think he made her feel like she was the only girl in the world. He sent flowers and a nice note after she turned up missing. He even called and talked to Judy a couple of times after that to check if there had been any progress made in the case."

Barrister took a final look at the photo before handing the album back to the woman. Putting his hands on his knees, he stood. "It's time for me to go. I'm so sorry I had to deliver such horrible news."

"Thank you," Mrs. Sykes softly said, "at least I

won't be constantly looking down the walk now. And I'm so glad that you were honest with me."

"I may have more questions down the road," Barrister advised the couple.

"We aren't moving," the preacher assured him.

"You two stay where you are," the cop proposed. "I can find my own way out."

"Thank you, again," Reverend Sykes said, almost choking on those three words.

Without saying anymore, Barrister hurried down the hall, out the door and to his car. While the last few moments had been some of the toughest in his life, he did leave with more information than he expected. Now there was another link to Sparks, but how could he break down the wall that had already been erected to protect Hollywood's greatest star?

26

June 21, 1936

Shelby relished observing her date squirm uncomfortably in the pew. This was even more fun than watching the actor in a movie. He was completely out of his element.

Dressed in a custom-tailored, dark brown suit, Flynn Sparks had likely never spent much time in a sanctuary, and having to keep his mouth shut for more than a few minutes was probably an even more foreign concept. He was a fish out of water. Everything that happened seemed unfamiliar to him. He sat when he was supposed to stand and stood when he was supposed to take a seat. Every eye in the church followed his every move. And, as the sermon was on fidelity, it likely hit the man right between the eyes. But the service was just round one. The second round took place at the Becketts' small home.

Sitting with the family around an unsteady, small wooden table and eating ham and pinto beans had to be a sharp contrast to the star's normal Sunday afternoon experience. Then as Shelby helped her mother with the dishes, Sparks, with no script in hand, struggled to find a line of conversation with John Beckett. Finally, Shelby, in an act of compassion, escorted her guest outside where they sat on the running board of his sporty blue Auburn speedster. For all practical purposes, he appeared like a man who'd just been released from a long stretch in prison.

"So this is your life?" he asked, his eyes fixed on the bungalow.

"Does it shock you that I am so backwoods? Have you ever eaten off metal plates and drunk tea from Mason jars?"

"Not recently," Sparks admitted. "In truth I never have. I just don't see how people live this way."

"Can't buy fun," she said.

"I seem to be able to," he argued. "And that preacher was crazy. Guilt is for losers. I think the poor and unknowns invented it, because they didn't have the means to find out how much fun temptation is."

"Interesting line of reasoning," she quipped. "Of course, those photographers who lined up outside the church as we came out were just there by chance. I'm sure you didn't alert them you were going to be there this morning. Or did you?"

"No," he laughed, "but Jacob Yates thought it'd be a nice touch after all the bad news from last weekend. He also made sure I was alone last night. I guess until the cops catch whoever killed that actress, I'm going to have to behave."

Shelby frowned. His words seemed cold and heartless. Didn't he have any feelings at all? "Flynn, you don't even remember the name of the actress who was murdered, do you?"

"Was it Lisa?"

"Leslie," she corrected him.

"Yeah, that's it. Let me be honest. When I was with her she didn't do anything memorable enough to make much of a mark. She was so boring. Trying to talk to her was like pulling teeth. In fact, kids' radio quiz shows are more entertaining."

"Doesn't it bother you that she died?" she asked.

"I'm not happy about it," he admitted. "This

whole thing has put me in a tough spot. But I learned a long time ago you can't worry about anyone but yourself. My job is to keep me alive, entertained, and happy. What happens to other people is not something I dwell on."

"So," she asked, "why are you here with me? Why did you do something today that seemingly offered no entertainment value and likely didn't have a prayer of making you happy?"

"It's the challenge," he proclaimed.

"The challenge?"

"You're locked in a world with no future and no fun," he explained. "My goal is to find a way to unlock that door and set you free. That preacher was trying to save my soul. Well, I am trying to show you that your soul would be a lot better off if it were enjoying the very things in life the church tries to keep you from seeing or doing."

After thinking about the man's explanation, Shelby pushed off the running board and walked over to her dad's dusty truck. Crossing her arms, she leaned against the back fender and closed her eyes. For a few seconds she enjoyed the warm sun splashing on her face and the wind blowing through her golden hair. She only looked back toward the actor when she posed a question that she likely had no right to ask.

"Dalton told me that Leslie Bryant was a really nice kid. She was innocent and fresh when she arrived in Los Angeles. Did you set Leslie Bryant free?"

He frowned, "If you're asking if I killed her, I can assure you I didn't. She was alive and well when I dropped her off at her apartment."

"That's not what I'm asking," she shot back. "I want to know if you stole her soul and broke her heart. I want to know if you left her broken and sad."

He pushed off the running board and quickly closed the distance between them, "Let's just say I took her places she'd never been."

As he leaned his face close to hers, she put her hand on his chest and challenged the actor. "But did she want to go there?"

"What difference does that make now?"

"Why did you do it?" Shelby demanded. "Why her? What was so important you had to lure her to your house and take what you wanted?"

He studied Shelby's huge blue eyes as his right hand traced her cheek. "For an innocent country girl, you sure talk about things most women don't even mention."

"You grow up fast," she explained, "when you're eighteen and already supporting your parents. You get a sharper picture of what's important when you are hungry and wondering where your next meal will come from. I had to grow up fast because when you're poor and good-looking, wolves are always howling at your door, and I had seen many others fall to their charms. I saw what happened when they gave in. It wasn't pretty; hearts were broken and lives were crushed."

He smiled, "Maybe you're viewpoint's wrong. Maybe you think the way you do because you're scared of giving in to your real emotions."

"Me, scared?" She mocked him.

"Scared and beautiful," he added. Taking her chin, he leaned close and whispered, "Do you know how we kiss in the movies?"

"Yes," she assured him, "with the lights on and cameras running. And as there is no director here to shout, 'Action,' why don't you back off?" As her sharp words hit home, she ducked under his arm and walked about ten feet toward the house.

"Millions of women would love to have the chance at what you just turned down," Sparks complained. "You ought to read my fan mail. It'd make you blush."

She whirled. "I don't blush easily, and no one takes me for a ride that I don't want to go on."

"You can be melted," he assured her, "and I'm the man who can—and will—do it."

"You aren't man enough for me," Shelby answered. "I met a lot of men back in Oklahoma, and I mean *real* men. You're just a spoiled kid who hasn't begun the first steps of maturing. You can't even begin to melt me until you become an adult. You see, I don't date children, I only baby-sit them."

If her words stung, he hid the pain well. "I could make you something special. People who are with me are viewed as being a step above other people—they are somebodies. Let me assure you it is better to hit that level once than live your whole life as a nobody. That actress who was strangled, she will always be remembered because she spent her last weekend with Flynn Sparks. She's immortal now. The folks in that church, they will never have their picture in the paper. No one will ever ask them for their autograph. When they die the world won't be talking about them. But because she was with me, Leslie Bryant is more famous than almost anyone on the planet."

She shook her head, "You might want to work on your self-esteem. It seems to be in a fragile state."

"Your preaching doesn't work on me," he taunted. "I live in a world where I make the rules and those who want to be with me play the game my way. Let me tell you a little secret. Even Jacob Yates, the head of the studio, does what I say."

Shelby wanted to hate the man, but she couldn't. In truth, she felt sorry for him. He was headed down a lonely road that few got to travel. If his star ever faded, and she figured it would, someday he'd be sitting in some big house by himself looking at scrapbooks reminding him of how life used to be. But there was no use trying to tell

Sparks that, so it was time to find a way to end this date on some kind of happy note.

"Flynn, speaking of the fact that you are Galaxy's biggest star, I was working on a gray suit for you on Friday. Guess you're starting another picture."

"Yeah," he laughed, "and my costar is your buddy Dalton Andrews."

"I'm sure it will be another winner for the studio," she replied. "What's it about?"

"I have no idea," he admitted. He glanced at his watch, "I have a tennis match with Gary Cooper at the club, so I need to be going."

"Flynn, thanks for taking me to church. I'll be there again next week if you want to join me."

"I don't think so," he assured her. "But, as you have done a lot of talking today and trying to put me in my place, let me tell you something."

"What's that?" she asked.

"There will come a time," he bragged, his brown eyes sparkling in the early afternoon sun, "that you'll beg me to take you up on the hill. In time, you'll realize the view you'll see there is more important than anything else in your life."

"Wanna bet?"

"Already have," he announced as he opened the door to his car. "Made it with Dalton."

She stood in the grass and watched as he switched on the V-12 and pulled away from the curb. She'd never met a man with so much gall.

He was selfish, arrogant, and immoral. And for reasons she didn't fully understand, she was drawn to him. Did she want to save him or did she—deep down inside—want to be like him?

27

June 22, 1936

Dalton Andrews, his arms folded across his chest, was dressed in a cheap blue suit, white shirt, red and yellow tie and scuffed brown shoes. It was just past nine on Monday morning, and he was leaning up against the desk in a police station that had been assembled on soundstage 6. He and the rest of the cast, as well as the extras and crew, were listening to director Vic Melton. Melton was the king of rapid-fire movie-making. If you needed a film done in a hurry, he was your man. And the mere fact Melton had been assigned this picture meant that things were about to be fast and furious.

"OK, folks," the redheaded, short, stout Melton began, "let me explain the rules. First of all, this set is closed. You will not grant interviews about what goes on behind these doors or when we go on location. You will not even talk to your friends or family about this movie. We are ripping this story from the headlines. The actors will be playing real people. We are not even changing the names. The script is being written on a day-by-day basis, so we will be shooting this story in order. This might be the only time you ever get to make a motion picture that starts with the first scene and ends with the last. Hopefully, it will also be the only time you are handed your scripts for that day first thing in the morning and will be expected to learn all of your dialogue right then. This is important . . . the script pages will not leave this lot. You can only study them here. After shooting the scenes, they will be burned. If you accidentally take them home, please destroy them. Don't let anyone else read them."

Melton sternly studied the 107 people surrounding him before asking, "Are there any questions?"

"You say it's taken from the headlines," Andrews called out, "but what headlines? We were assigned to this film and not even told what it was about."

"Your scripts will be here within the hour," Melton explained, "you will learn more about your characters then. But I can tell you this much, Dalton, you will be playing the city's top homicide cop—Bill Barrister." Some in the room chuckled forcing Melton to smile and admit, "I know, Barrister is short and fat, but for our sakes, he is going to be a bit better looking." The director's eyes scanned the room until they locked onto another familiar face. "Flynn, you will be Dalton's partner—Barry Jenkins. The movie starts with you two. The rest will find out your roles when the scripts arrive. Now, as I need to set up the shots with the crew, you all can grab a cup of coffee and a donut."

As the actors relaxed, the mystified crew gathered around the director. A curious Andrews observed the proceedings with interest. What could be so important that the studio was taking things to the top-secret level? As he turned the recent news stories over in his mind it hit him, there was only one case that was that hot right now. They must be shooting a movie about the murder of Leslie Bryant. Noting Flynn Sparks ambling up on his right, Andrews turned and smiled, "Interesting premise, the cops suspect you of doing in Leslie Bryant and, if I've guessed right about this film's focus, you're playing one of the cops trying to prove you killed Leslie. I just love ironic casting."

Sparks's face went red, "How did you know the cops talked to me?"

"How could they not?" Andrews quipped, "I mean, she spent the night at your place and then died. And, unless they have something else to go on that the papers don't know about, that means you are the likely target. You didn't kill her did you, Flynn?"

"You're just jealous that I won the bet," Sparks

shot back. "You miss that Packard. Did I see a Hudson parked in your spot this morning?"

"I wonder who'll play you in the movie?" Andrews cracked.

"If you're right about this being about her murder," Sparks quipped, "I won't be in this film. They only wanted to talk to me because they thought I might give them some leads. That's hardly worth mentioning in a script. But it will be interesting to see who they cast as Leslie."

"I'm not Leslie," a small blonde woman announced, causing both men to spin around and readjust their views, "but you are right on what this movie is all about. And I am playing the first victim. She must get killed on the beach because they've been having me trying on bathing suits since five this morning."

"I'm sure you look good in them," Sparks noted as his eyes slowly drifted from the woman's shapely legs to her face. "You can call me Flynn."

"I'm Agnes Sharp. All I've always been was an extra until Friday. Then my agent got a call for this picture."

Sparks grinned, "Miss Sharp, if you have any questions, please feel free to ask me. Maybe we can discuss things over dinner. I'd love giving you a more detailed view of the ins and outs of this business."

"Maybe we can," she smiled. She turned her

deep green eyes on the other man and said, "And you are Dalton Andrews."

"So I've been told."

"I hope this is my big break," she said wishfully. "Been treading water out here for a long time."

"Maybe that's why they cast you as a swimmer," Andrews wryly cracked. "Now if you will excuse me, I'm going to go over and grab a cup of coffee."

The actor left the hopeful actress and hopeless egotist to get to know each other, walked quickly across the stage to the exit and stepped out in the morning sunlight. As his eyes adjusted to the light, he noted a woman carrying a half dozen dresses over her arm.

"You going my way?" she asked.

"Where are you headed, Shelby?"

"Stage 10. These are for a tea party that's filming later this morning. I met the extras playing the parts on Friday. They're all over seventy and having the time of their lives. It seems they took this up when they retired from teaching grade school."

"They'll find the learning curve here much shorter," Andrews noted. "And if you let me carry those, I'll walk with you." After he took the costumes, they both headed south.

"Shelby, I wanted to apologize for the way I raved on the other night. I must have sounded like a real tried-and-true cynic."

"You didn't scare me," she replied, "if that's what you were wanting to know. Besides, even before the Depression almost every farmer in Oklahoma was likely a cynic unless he discovered oil on his land."

"Yeah, I guess so."

"Do you find it funny," she asked, "that you, Dalton Andrews, big-time cinema star, can't walk down a single street in this whole country without people stopping you, asking for your autograph, or gawking at your face, but here on the lot no one even notices you?"

"In truth, I like that. But, even on this lot, the men sure notice you."

"Oh, Dalton, quit it. Flynn's lines don't sound good coming from your mouth."

"They don't sound good on him either," he shrugged, "but they seem to work anyway. Have you seen today's newspapers?"

"I can't afford to read," Shelby explained with a grin, "don't have the time or the money."

"Well, your picture is all over them," he teased. "It seems the newspapers sent their photographers to catch Flynn going to church, and you were on his arm as he came out. Did you manage to introduce him to Jesus?"

She waited until a noisy truck filled with spotlights passed before noting, "Flynn's not on speaking terms with God. I'm not sure why anyone gives him the time of day."

164

"Well," the actor suggested, "you should come back to our soundstage and talk to a new actress who's hovering all around the guy right now." He waved at Sally Glenn as she rode by on a bicycle before continuing, "You don't bite on Flynn's tired lines because you aren't caught up in trying to be something you're not."

"I wouldn't be good at being anyone else," Shelby assured him. "I don't have enough tact to plunge into another role and make it convincing."

He nodded, "In a world filled with those pretending to be who they aren't, you are one of the rare ones who plays it straight. I like that."

"You should try it," she suggested, "though I guess you did at the diner the other night." She moved a few steps to her right to allow a group of Civil War soldiers to pass before sidling back up to her escort. "This is where I need to go. Why don't you hand me those dresses, and I'll take them in. And thanks for the help and the conversation."

"How about going out tonight?" he suggested as he passed the costumes to Shelby.

"No place fancy, I hope," she replied.

"How about a sandwich at Schwab's Drug Store, and then we can catch a movie?"

"One of your films?" she asked.

"Anything but that," he quipped. "I haven't had the chance to see *Mr. Deeds Goes to Town*."

"With Gary Cooper? That sounds like a winner.

I haven't been to a movie in years. That was another thing we cut out when the farm went bad. What time?"

"How about seven?"

"You remember where I live?"

"I dropped you off there last week," he assured her.

"OK, I've got to run, see you then." She smiled before adding, "and having music in my life is nice. But you shouldn't have."

He grinned and watched Shelby disappear through the soundstage door before happily spinning on his heels and studying the workings of Hollywood magic that surrounded him. Men were carrying everything from Revolutionary War muskets to machine guns, trucks rumbled by filled with extras dressed as medieval knights and ladies, and strolling down the streets of this massive lot were soldiers from the Great War, along with cowboys, Indians, and even English royalty. To his right, Abraham Lincoln was telling a joke to George Washington, and two women in form-fitting bathing suits were running their lines. In the distance, he could see New York City, or at least Hollywood's version of it, and to his right was Chinatown. As amazing and fascinating as it was, none of it was real. The buildings and even the people were all wearing false fronts that could be changed on a moment's notice. And he was a part of this illusion on a grand scale.

For the next few weeks, he'd be playing a cop looking for the murderer of a woman who thought her dreams had come true when she'd walked onto this lot and seen the things he was seeing right now. If Leslie Bryant had made a different choice, if she hadn't been at the wrong place at the wrong time, she would have likely had a career that would have lasted long enough for her to die a dozen times on film. She never got that chance because instead she died in real life. Now the actress who would play her in the film about her murder would likely be more famous than Leslie. He jammed his hands into his pockets and sadly shook his head; that was the paradox that defined Hollywood, and he owed his sorry existence to it. It seemed the only real thing on this lot was the poor girl from Oklahoma.

28

June 22, 1936

Back on the set Dalton Andrews went through the lines that were literally hot off the typewriter. After studying them for a few moments, he set them to one side and took a seat behind Bill Barrister's desk . . . or at least Hollywood's version of it. Leaning back in his chair he propped his feet up, crossed his arms, and pretended to be napping. A few seconds later, Vic Melton barked, "Action."

The overhead camera captured Flynn Sparks hurrying past a dozen desks and more than twenty uniformed cops and up to a door marked "Bill Barrister—Homicide." Sparks, playing Barry Jenkins, didn't bother knocking, and instead, just barged in. He paused at the door and studied his boss.

"You sleeping, Cap?" he asked.

Opening his eyes, Andrews casually evaluated his uninvited guest before pulling his feet from his desk, leaning forward in his chair and crossing his arms. "Have you ever heard of knocking?"

"I've got something hot," he explained. "They just found a dead girl and there's no doubt she's been murdered."

"Where is she?"

"Malibu, on the beach."

Andrews pushed out of his chair, strolled over to a coat rack, and pulled off his gray fedora hat. He dusted the top with his left hand before placing it on his head at a slight angle to the left. His fingers lingered on the brim before looking back to his partner and grittily speaking the hokey lines he'd been given by the writers.

"Barry, murder's a dirty game, especially when it involves a woman. Any man who'd sink so low as to take the life of a lady is the kind of scum that I hate. I live to take that kind of creep out of the world. I hope, when we find him, he puts up a fight because I'd love to save the state the cost of a trial and keep the hangman's rope stored in the closet on death row."

"I'm with you, partner."

Andrews smiled grimly and walked toward the open door, "Let's go. We have a dirty job to do." As the actors retraced the steps previously taken by Sparks, the camera followed.

Only when they'd exited the entry to the station set did Melton cry, "Cut!" After the two reappeared the director announced, "That was good, now let's reset the scene and catch it with a camera at ground level. After that, we'll shoot it once from Dalton's perspective and another time from Flynn's point of view."

It took just over an hour to complete all four shooting angles, and when Melton was finally satisfied, he gave the crew a ten-minute break. Andrews spent it at the desk that would serve as Barrister's for the next few weeks.

"I think they got the roles reversed," Sparks suggested as he took a seat in a hard wooden chair opposite his costar.

"What difference does it make?" Andrews asked. "I mean, they will probably find a way for your character to get the credit for bagging the killer. They always make sure you come out looking good in the end."

"That's in my contract," Sparks explained. "And I have to OK any script that has my character dying. I just couldn't break all those hearts."

Andrews looked into the overhead lights and bit his lip. He watched a man on a small catwalk adjust the angle of a spot before looking back at his costar. "Flynn, do you actually buy into what you say, or do you just spout out stuff that makes it appear you are the most egotistical jerk on the planet?"

"You're starting to sound like that tomato in wardrobe," Sparks jibed. "She's always trying to find something worth saving in me. But I can tell you this for sure, she's got it for me, she just won't admit it."

Andrews wryly smiled, "Did you drive the Packard to work today?"

"Of course," Sparks assured him. "I rather enjoy explaining how I won your car."

Andrews leaned forward and asked, "You think Shelby really does carry a torch for you?"

"No doubt."

"Do you believe that strongly enough to be sure she'd go out with you, if you asked?"

"Dalton, she owes me. I took her someplace she wanted to go, and now she will go where I ask her to go."

"And what makes you think that?"

"Because," Sparks explained, "that's the way those kind are. You take them to church and after that, they'll let you take them anywhere. You need to study my technique and learn."

Andrews shrugged, "Maybe I do. In fact, I might be up for some education right now. Shelby just walked in with some wardrobe." He pointed to a point by the outside wall, "She's right over there."

Sparks's head spun like a freshly wound top until he spotted the woman in question. "So you want me to land a date with her?"

"That's not specific enough; let's make it a bit more interesting."

"Dalton, now you're starting to sound like me."

"Flynn, I've a thousand dollars in my dressing room. My wager is this: I'll give you all ten one-hundred dollar bills if you can land a date with Shelby for tonight."

Sparks caught Shelby's attention and waved. She immediately smiled and waved back. "Can you imagine what she'd look like in an evening gown?" He turned back to the other actor, "Ah, the grand is all but in my pocket, but just in case things don't go my way, what happens?"

"I get my Packard back," he replied, as he stuck out his hand. After the two men shook, Andrews leaned back in his chair and watched Sparks saunter across the set. He got to the woman just before she walked out the door. Though he couldn't hear the conversation, Andrews had no problem imagining the dialogue as Sparks lightly touched Shelby's hair and then dropped the same hand down to her shoulder. Finally, using a technique he employed countless times on film, the actor leaned closely, saying something that caused the woman to shake her head, and then, based on the body language, popped the question. Andrews could read lips well enough to know that Shelby answered with a simple, "I'm sorry." That is when things started to really get amusing. Like a politician debating a bill, Sparks used his whole body to make his case. It did no good. Shelby just patted the man's cheek, turned, and walked out the door. Seemingly in shock, the defeated actor dug his hands into his pockets and dejectedly walked back toward the studio's version of Barrister's office.

"I take it that it didn't go as well as you would have liked," Andrews noted with a smile.

Sparks reached into his pocket, "Here are your keys," after tossing them across the desk, he added, "but it's not that she didn't want to go out with me, it's just that she had another date. Can you imagine that country bumpkin having . . ."As if a light had just been turned on, Sparks looked at Andrews, "Dalton, you already made a date with her. You conned me."

"Flynn, you suggested I start playing things your way, and I did."

Rather than get angry, Sparks laughed, "You took me in hook, line, and sinker. I never thought you had it in you. I'm kind of proud of you. Besides, that car of yours is really too heavy to drive hard. My Auburn's got a lot more kick."

"Glad you're taking it so well," Andrews chided, basking in the glory of finally beating Sparks at something.

"It's OK, Dalton, I haven't lost anything that I paid for. And I have no doubt I can convince that new actress . . . what was her name?"

"You mean the girl we met this morning?"

"Yeah."

"Agnes Sharp."

"I can convince Miss Sharp to go out with me. I can take her to a nice romantic dinner and then drive her up to my place."

"Sounds fine, Flynn, I just hope she has a car."

"Why?"

"Because you don't have a way to get home from the studio."

As Sparks's face deflated, Melton cried out, "OK, we need to move over to soundstage 13. We are going to film the beach scene next."

As he would not need a change in wardrobe, Andrews pushed away from the desk and stood. Grabbing the fedora, he waltzed toward the exit leaving the other actor in a state of shock. Knowing he had some time to kill, he strolled over to the parking area to the Packard convertible that was once again his. After running his hand along the fender, he glanced inside. Except for a newspaper, there was nothing in the front. His eyes moved to the large, cream-colored leather back seat, and he smiled. It was empty as well. It looked like Sparks had done a good job taking care of the car. Satisfied and relieved, he was about to leave when he noted something on the far side of the rear cushion. Quickly walking around the to the passenger side of the vehicle, Andrews opened the rear door. There was a dark stain about the size of a half dollar on the seat. Sparks must have spilled something. What was it? Leaning closer he dabbed it with his finger. It had been there for a while; it was dry. His eyes moved from the seat to the floor. All but hidden under the car's front seat was a handkerchief. Andrews retrieved it and held it up in the sunlight. In one corner, embroidered in light blue thread, were the initials L.B.

29

June 22, 1936

In truth, in spite of the tons of sand they'd brought in, the soundstage looked very little like the beach at Malibu or anywhere else. To Dalton Andrews it more closely resembled a sand box for a kid about the size of King Kong. But thanks to shooting angles, lighting, and some rear projection, those who gathered in theaters and watched this scene would likely be completely fooled. They'd hear the waves crashing, see some actual footage of the ocean dropped in, and actually believe the scene had been shot outdoors. When it came to deception, Washington D.C. had nothing on Hollywood.

Andrews, his coat unbuttoned and his hands in his pocket, looked down at Agnes Sharp. The young woman who, only this morning, had hoped this part would be her breakthrough role was laying on the sand in a blue bathing suit, her open eyes staring toward the point where the ocean should have been. The way her face was turned it was likely the audience would never see just how cute she was.

"You doing OK down there?" Andrews asked.

"I'm going to melt," Sharp announced, "if we don't start shooting soon. The lights are cooking me."

The actor leaned closer, "It has to look like the sun is shining. It could be worse, the woman might have been found in a swamp."

It was a bizarre experience to shoot scenes based on something that had really happened. The actress was playing a real woman who died. Vic Melton had allowed Andrews to read the police files over lunch, and seeing this woman's real name brought the crime into a new light. Maggie Reason was just twenty-three when someone dumped her on a beach. Unlike Sharp, the temperature didn't bother her. In fact, nothing bothered her now. She was a kid from Illinois who had dreams and then someone snuffed them out. And, rather than let her sad life just fade away, Andrews was a part of exploiting her sad demise. No one around him, not the director, the crew, or even the actress playing Maggie Reason cared enough to even offer a prayer. To them, she hadn't ever laughed or cried or even breathed.

As he imagined what the woman's life must have been like before she ended up alone and dead on a beach, Andrews fiddled with the handkerchief hidden in the left pocket of his pants. Just touching the small piece of cloth pushed his mind in a new direction. Now his thoughts were focused not on someone he didn't know, but on a person he'd met. Sparks had likely used the Packard to take Leslie Bryant home that last day of her life. So there were several logical explanations about how the small piece of embroidered cloth ended up in the car, but then there was that stain. Was it somehow tied to Leslie Bryant's disappearance? Was her first ride in the Packard also her last? And, if that was so, had his car been used as a hearse?

"You need anything, Mr. Andrews?"

The actor glanced to his left at Willard Mace. He was a funny kind of guy; a strong man with a mind that seemed to often run in slow motion. He tried so hard to get everyone to like him. Yet the big guy was such an odd egg and his social skills were so weak he just couldn't quite seem to find anyone who'd give him the time of day. Andrews often wondered how Mace had even managed to land a job at Galaxy. There had to be thousands of unemployed people much more qualified for the job. And yet, he was here and a part of a team selling escape to people whose lives were ordinary and boring.

"No, thanks, Willie," the actor answered. "I'm good."

"I could get you some water," the man offered. "It's kind of hot in here."

"If I need some," Andrews assured him, "I'll let you know."

Standing off to one side, his eyes fixed on a buxom script girl standing beside director Vic Melton, Flynn Sparks leaned against one of the light stands. If he was feeling any pain about losing the bet, he didn't show it. As Andrews studied the man who the studio painted in the press as "his best friend," the actor couldn't help but touch the handkerchief and run his index finger over the embroidered initials. What did Sparks do to Leslie? His mind slipped back to the notes he'd read in the police files. Were they right? Did the actor actually put his hands around Leslie's throat and squeeze the life from her? If he did, was he also the man who murdered this girl on the beach? And if so, how in the world could he be so cool while reliving it now?

"Is everyone ready?" Melton called out from

his chair just behind the lights and cameras.

The director's words pulled Andrews back from being an amateur detective to playing the part of a real one. Moving to his mark just to the right of the girl's head, he waited for Melton to get things moving.

"Let's see if we can get this in one take. And we are making a change from the notes I gave you earlier. I see no use in shooting this from more than two angles. We'll get it from Dalton's perspective first and then from Flynn's. Then we'll just grab a couple of establishing shots to close things out." He paused as Sparks walked across the sand to his mark and then added, "Miss Sharp, please don't move. Now, lights, camera . . . action."

"Strangled," Sparks noted.

"Not a good way to go," Andrews gruffly replied and then said it again for emphasis. "Not a good way to go at all. A man who does this wants to take his time and enjoy it. He has a lust to watch the life snuffed out of a body."

"So," Flynn playing Jenkins asked, "do you have any idea as to who we are looking for?"

Andrews pawed at the sand with his right foot, "In my thirty years on the force I have learned a few things. The first is never make guesses. But I can tell you this, and you need to hear it; the guy behind this murder is likely a madman." Andrews, now wondering if he wasn't spitting out dialogue to the person who might have committed this crime, was suddenly fueled with a real passion to make the lines written for him hit home. He wanted Sparks to hear them and understand the picture they painted. "This man is sick. He's more animal than human. He plays with souls and lives as if he thinks he is a god. He likes what he is doing and likely replays the moments of this woman's death over and over again."

"So," Sparks cracked, "we are looking for the Hollywood Madman."

Andrews paused. If the other actor knew that the lines were directed at him, he certainly didn't show it. Nodding and moving the scene forward, Andrews recited his next burst of dialogue. "Until we actually catch the guy, that is as good a name as any. Let's make sure the crime scene boys get a lot of photos. You never know what we might need when this case comes to trial."

Flynn's eyes went to the body, "She was a pretty gal."

"That makes it even tougher, Barry. A woman this beautiful had a future. She could have been an actress or a model, but the man who killed her cheated her out of all those things and more. I'll make him pay for that or my name's not Bill Barrister!"

With his jaw set, Andrews turned and moved off to the right. Flynn watched him and then turned his eyes back to the dead girl.

"Cut," the director called out, "and we can print that one. Now, let's move the camera to catch Flynn's view."

"Here's some water, Mr. Andrews."

After taking the glass, the actor responded politely, but with little emotion, "Thanks, Willie."

As Andrews took a sip, Mace popped a question, "What's Mr. Sparks doing?"

The actor looked back to the sand where he'd just been standing. A smiling Sparks was leaning over talking to the woman playing the body. "Willie, there is no doubt in my mind that Flynn is getting a date. That guy wears women on his arm like most of us wear wristwatches." He took another sip of the clear liquid before handing it back to Mace. "Thanks. Now it's time for me to get back to work."

Walking over to Melton, Andrews stood to one side and looked at the set. The director glanced his way and asked, "Something on your mind?"

"Do you know Bill Barrister?" the actor asked.

"I've met him a time or two but never talked to him."

"Well, Vic, I know the man. I sat behind him at the track and we visited. I can assure you of this . . . the lines they have written for me sound nothing like the man I know. Barrister is not vindictive, he's not trigger-happy, and he doesn't spit out lines that sound like they came out of a George Raft film. We aren't doing the man justice."

Melton smiled, "You're right, but he is also not good looking, thin and tall, so it is a wash. It's time we get the second shot, and then we'll move back to the station set for a couple of scenes setting up where they find the next body."

Andrews had made his point and lost. That was fine. At least he felt good about trying. Now it was time to go back to playing a part the way it was written and trying to forget his costar might also be a madman.

30

June 22, 1936

Shelby did a full turn in front of the mirror and grinned. This suit, made for a movie that wrapped three weeks ago, was the nicest thing she'd ever worn.

"It goes with your eyes," Betsy Minser noted. "Just the perfect blending of blue. And it fits your figure like it was tailored for you. Now we just need some stockings and pumps. What size shoes do you wear?"

"Seven."

"That will be easy," the woman assured her. "I'll get those and be right back."

"You look really nice!" Willard Mace exclaimed as he walked in through the door leading to the sewing factory. "Now, you really are the most beautiful woman on the lot."

Shelby pushed her honey blonde hair from her shoulders and studied her reflection more closely in the mirror. She couldn't believe the woman she saw. There was no hint of the Cordell, Oklahoma, farm girl showing right now.

"Why are you all dressed up?" Mace asked.

"It seems that my measurements are the same as Miss Foster's, and Betsy opted to have me try on one of the dresses from *Darkness Is Light*. I might become a human dress form. I guess Miss Foster is so busy, the studio is looking for a way to cut some corners and save her some time."

Mace's eyes locked on Shelby, "I remember that outfit. She never looked that good in it." He paused and giggled, "And I guess I know your measurements now too. I have memorized all the facts on the actresses." His tone and smile indicated he was very proud of that fact too.

Shelby turned and frowned at the man. She wasn't sure she wanted him or anyone knowing those details. Especially when it concerned her.

"Got the shoes and the stockings," Minser announced as she strolled back into the room. "This will complete the outfit."

The seamstress-turned-model shook her head, "I can understand wearing the shoes to check out the way it looks on the body, especially the hips, but why the stockings?"

"Because," Minser explained, "I'm rewarding you for your hard work, and also because having you being Miss Foster's size will save us a lot of overtime. And, as I understand you have a date tonight, the outfit and shoes are yours to keep."

Shelby's mouth dropped, "I couldn't." Though every fiber in her body assured her she needed to accept this generous gift.

"Actually," the woman corrected her, "you can. And as I make the rules in this part of the world, you will. But to really look good, we need to do something with your hair and makeup. Follow me."

"But I have work to do," Shelby argued, though her tone showed she wasn't going to put up much of a fight.

"You're days ahead on everything," Minser replied, "and it is quitting time, anyway. Now follow me."

31

June 22, 1936

A waiter dressed in a white shirt and black dinner jacket escorted Shelby and Dalton Andrews to a round booth about forty feet from the bar. After they were seated, the short man with the thin mustache asked, "Would you like something to drink? Might I suggest a martini?"

Shelby looked to her date and shook her head.

"Are you sure?" Andrews asked.

She studied her date, dressed in a dark blue, pinstriped suit and looking every bit as handsome as his studio portraits, before announcing, "I don't drink."

The words had barely come out of her mouth before the waiter frowned.

"Do you mean you don't drink or you haven't drunk?" Andrews asked.

"Both," she assured him.

"Would you like a Coke?" the actor inquired.

"As long as there's nothing in it."

"We'll have two Cokes," Andrews announced, "and don't worry, Cosmo, I'll tip you just as if we'd downed a bottle of your best champagne."

"Thank you, sir. And what about the meal?"

The actor glanced over to his date, "Do you see anything you like?"

"I'm overwhelmed," she replied. "What do you suggest?"

"Cosmo, bring us the Manhattan steaks, boiled potatoes, carrots, and, of course, your famous bread."

"How do you want the steaks?"

"Shelby, it is up to you."

"Medium."

Andrews flashed a smile, "The beautiful woman in blue wants hers medium, as do I."

"As you wish, sir."

After the waiter strolled off toward the kitchen, Andrews turned his attention back to his companion. "I meant to say something earlier, but words escaped me. It looks like you've been shopping, and that might be the most stunning suit I've ever seen."

"Actually," she corrected him, "you've seen the suit before. In fact, you actually kissed Betty Foster when she wore it in a scene you shot a few weeks ago."

"It didn't look that good on her," he shot back. "If it had, I'd have never been able to remember my lines."

"There you go sounding like Flynn Sparks again."

"No, seriously, I mean it. You really are the most beautiful woman on the lot, and this proves it. And the best part about it is that you're real."

Shelby grinned, "You put a lot of value on the 'real' element."

"It's rare around these parts," he explained.

"So how's the new movie?" she asked.

"I can't talk about it."

She raised her eyebrows, "It's that bad?"

"No, the whole thing is hush-hush, and I can't say anything about the script." He chuckled. "Here's an irony, I can't talk about it because what we are shooting is real. So in other words, I can talk about anything at Galaxy except the truth." His eyes scanned the restaurant. "Shelby, look over to your right. Now don't stare, just kind of glance over and tell me who you see."

"That's Cary Grant," she quickly answered.

"And Norma Shearer is in the next booth. With her is her husband, Irving Thalberg. Outside of the business, there are not many folks who know his name, but he's one of the most powerful men in Hollywood. The man eating with them is David O. Selznick. Folks often joke about him by saying, 'The son-in-law also rises' because he is married to Louis B. Mayer's daughter. Folks think the marriage gets him a lot of movies around town, but in truth, he's that good."

Andrews's eyes flashed to the other side of the room. "There's a guy sitting at the back booth who you may not know now, but you will. His name is Humphrey Bogart. Warner Brothers brought him out here after he garnered some success on Broadway. He can act better than any newcomer I've ever seen. If he can get just a small break, he'll be one of the best-known people in the world. He played Duke Mantee in the Bette Davis movie *The Petrified Forest*. He was amazing in that part!"

"A bit different from the folks sitting around us on our first date," she noted as she studied some of the other faces in Musso and Frank's Grill. Franchot Tone was sitting at a table with Joan Crawford, and Bette Davis was visiting with a man she didn't recognize. Near the front were

Joan Blondell and Dick Powell. And just five tables over was a star she'd actually met. "I see Flynn has a new date tonight."

Andrews frowned and craned his neck to the left. "That would be a bit player he met this morning. Her name is Agnes Sharp. This was her first day on the set, and he moved in on her faster than a vulture that had spotted a dead rabbit."

"The way she's fawning over him," Shelby noted, "I'm guessing she's enjoying herself. Back home we'd say she landed in high cotton."

"She's landed somewhere," he grumbled.

She sensed that Andrews was in no mood to be teased about Flynn Sparks. So rather than push it, she made a suggestion. "Let's change the subject."

"I would love to," he replied.

As his eyes returned to their table, she shyly grinned, "Thanks for the radio."

"What radio?" he asked.

"So we are going to play it that way?"

"Play what?"

Shelby placed her elbows on the table, clasped her hands, and rested her chin atop her fingers. "The radio that some unknown person sent to us has made our little home a lot happier. Mom's not as homesick or lonely now that she has something providing some background noise. She's already hooked on a couple of soap operas and quiz shows."

"Do you listen to it?" he asked, his eyes almost dancing as he waited for her response.

She nodded, "Mainly music. My range of knowledge in that area has increased tenfold. I think my favorite song this week is 'Robins and Roses.'"

"By Bing Crosby," Andrews chimed in. "I play golf with him from time to time, and we often go to the race track together. A nice guy, but I'm amazed a man whose ears are that big can generate the box office he does. He gets twice the mail I get."

"So," she teased, "we are going back to judging people on their appearance again?"

"And Shelby, if I were, you'd be the most beautiful woman in this room."

"You're starting to sound like Flynn," she warned.

The actor glanced away from Shelby and back to Flynn. "Let's remove him from this conversation."

"If you're worried about me going out with him," she explained, "I shot him down today. I think he's attractive and there's no doubt he and Gable are considered the hottest things in town, but it would be hard to take a man seriously who has already met the love of his life."

Andrews looked back at Shelby, his face spelling out his obvious confusion. "Well, it's not the blonde over there. So who is it?"

"Flynn loves Flynn, and there is no room in his world for him to love anyone else. Any woman who can't see that is either a fool or a person angling to use her connection to him to get a career boost. Any guesses on what tonight's date is after?"

"The latter," he quickly replied.

"And," she added, "I'm after neither. So don't waste your time trying to reuse old lines from your movies to make me believe I'm special. I know who I am."

"But you are beautiful," he argued.

"I can look in a mirror and see that," she agreed. "But roses are beautiful for a little while, and then they fade in the presence of newer, fresher flowers. But there is something you need to understand. I like you, I really do, but I'm not sophisticated enough to share quips with Claudette Colbert or swap stories with Carole Lombard. When it comes to the big picture, I'm not in it. But if you want a friend, someone you can pal around and be real with, then I'm your girl."

"Good a place as any to start," he reasoned, "but you underestimate yourself in a lot of different ways. I've been to those parties and the women pretty much talk about recipes, shopping, and music; that is, when they are not playing the Hollywood game."

"I could do the talking," she assured him, "but I'm not equipped to play the game."

"You might change your mind," he suggested.

"I hope not. Now, I think that's our dinner on the way. And even in this city of make-believe, I'll bet that steak's real."

32

June 22, 1936

Andrews walked Shelby to the door just after eleven. This time he didn't ask for a kiss, but just took one. It was a bit longer and less tentative than the last one. She stood on the porch watching him drive away before glancing up to the sky. Maybe it was because of the city lights, but there seemed to be only half as many stars in the California night as there had been in Oklahoma. As she searched for the Big Dipper, she unconsciously began humming a tune.

"I heard that on the radio today," her mother announced as she stepped out the door.

"I'm sorry, Mom," Shelby quickly answered. "I didn't mean to bother you."

Mary Beckett smiled, "Even in the moonlight I can tell that is a beautiful suit. And look at your hair. Are you playing Cinderella tonight?"

"Not really," she answered. "My boss gave me this outfit at work today. It was worn in a movie they finished a few weeks ago and the studio didn't need it anymore. And she did my makeup for me too."

"You father told me you had a date," the older woman explained. "I understand it was with that actor who took you out last week."

"Yes, but it is nothing serious, Mom."

"Why's that, child? Is he not a nice person?"

Shelby shook her head, "No, he's nice, respectful, and polite."

"But?"

"But I'm just a kid from Cordell. And no matter how someone fixes my hair or what clothes I wear, I'm still the girl who went to school in a place that was so poor the prom queen didn't get a crown and the young woman who worked in a dress shop that went out of business."

"Shelby," Mary gently prodded, "you've got to dream. Just have to. Don't settle, reach for the stars. If you come up short, you might at least grab a piece of the moon."

The young woman spun around. Her tone was measured, but firm. "Mom, you just don't understand. This place is different. The morality I was taught doesn't fly in Hollywood. At first, they might find my innocence charming, but in time even a man like Dalton Andrews is going to see it as childish. I can't let myself dream because for my dreams to come true I have to give up things you assured me were important. So I'm just going to live in the moment and not think beyond it."

Mary patted her daughter on the shoulder, "I guess I understand. But there are times when a person who hangs onto her principles lifts others up. You don't have to give in to get something special." She smiled, "I'm going in now. Are you coming? I'm sure we can find something on the radio to listen to."

"I'll be there in a minute or so," Shelby assured her, "but first I'm going to look at the stars for a bit longer."

"If you see one falling," her mother announced with a grin, "make a wish."

Shelby nodded. As her mother stepped back into the bungalow, the young woman turned her gaze back toward the sky. She understood why her mother was begging her not to give up on something big. After all, her mom had been forced to scrape by her whole life. Shelby had seen the woman sacrifice for as long as she could remember. She even listened to her mother weep when Shelby earned the honor of being valedictorian of her class. Her mother had cried not from happiness, but because she knew the family didn't have the money to hang onto their farm much less send their daughter to college. And while Shelby accepted that and moved on, her mother couldn't. It still haunted her. And now Mary Beckett was hoping and likely even praying that a man like Dalton Andrews would pave the way for the kid from Oklahoma to forever escape the Beckett family legacy of poverty and despair.

The almost silent sounds of footsteps on grass broke Shelby's connection from past disappointment and shifted her gaze from the sky to the street. For a moment, as she peered into the shadows between two shotgun-style frame homes, she thought she saw someone. She waited and watched for whomever it was to step out into the streetlamp's glow, but nothing changed. A cold nose on her hand pulled her attention to the ground. Rex, his mouth open and grinning, had somehow snuck up beside her.

She glanced back across the street and saw nothing. Patting the old dog's head, she whispered, "I think it's past our bedtime. Let's go inside and lock the door."

33

June 25, 1936

It had been a quiet week for Bill Barrister. Unable to dig for new information that might connect Flynn Sparks to Leslie Bryant's murder, he sifted through old evidence and tried to find something he'd missed. He'd come up as empty as most of the prospectors did in the Gold Rush of 1849. The ringing of his phone mercifully yanked him out of thoughts of self-pity.

"Barrister."

"Cap, this is Dick Titan, I work the beat by Canoga Park."

"What can I do for you, Dick?"

"About thirty minutes ago, I grabbed a burger, drove my car over to a quiet spot, got out, and sat down under a eucalyptus tree. A small mutt came up and, before I could react, he stole the sandwich right out of my hand."

Barrister chuckled, "Call the robbery division or animal control, this one is out of my line."

"Actually," the caller continued, "it is right up your alley. I chased the mutt down by the aqueduct and in the process ran right into a body someone had dumped there."

"Are you sure it's a murder?"

"Beautiful twenty-year-old girls don't usually drop dead in such out-of-the-way places."

Barrister drummed his fingers on the desk as he worked up the strength to ask a question he didn't want to have answered. "Dick, what do you think killed her?"

"Looks to me like she was strangled."

"I was afraid of that," the captain quickly replied.

There was a knock on Barrister's open office door followed by, "What's up, Cap?"

Barrister glanced toward the man who'd just stepped into his private lair. After covering the receiver, the homicide chief whispered, "I've got a patrolman on the wire. He's found another body.

This time it's located at Canoga Park. As soon as I give him a couple of orders, I'm going to put you on the phone and have you get the body's specific location. Once you've got that address, come meet me down at the car. I'm going to run by, notify the crime scene team to grab their stuff, and then get the car out of the garage. I'll meet you down front."

After uncovering the phone, Barrister turned his attention back to the caller. "Dick, I'm going to put my partner on the line in just a second. Give him the directions on how to get to your location and then I want you to go back and stay by the body. Don't let anybody touch it. Oh, and why didn't you use your radio to call it in?"

"I figured the newspapers and radio stations would be listening to the police band. I just guessed, based on the other strangulations we've had in the city, you want to keep this thing on the hush-hush."

"It's that kind of thinking that will get you promoted," the captain promised. "I'm going to hand the phone over to Barry, you give him the best route to where we need to be."

Barrister tossed the receiver to his partner and rushed from the office, down the steps to the first floor. Sticking his head into an office on the right, he yelled, "We've got a body in Canoga Park." After he was sure he had the quartet's attention, he lowered his voice and filled in the

195

details. "Looks like it might be related to the Bryant case as well as the women who've been strangled. Get your stuff together and have your wagon follow me to the location. I'm about to get my car out of the garage and pull it around front. Let's get moving!"

Jogging down the hall, Barrister pushed through a door leading to the garage, waved at the attendant and rushed by a half dozen patrol cars. As the old man in the blue uniform waved back, the captain hollered, "Pops, I need my car."

"It's in the shop," the man explained. "You needed new tires. You said it would be OK to put them on today."

Barrister snapped his fingers, "Well, I've got a murder, so I need something now. What have you got?"

Pops rubbed his hand through his closely cropped gray hair, "I have those patrol cars."

"No, I don't want to call that much attention to myself. I need something that doesn't scream cop. I don't want the press jumping on this yet. For the past few days, they've been following me and the chief wherever we go."

"You can have my Model A," he suggested. "It's dirty and kind of beat up, but it makes the city speed limits, and no one will follow you in that. Heck, my wife won't even ride in it."

The captain looked along the far wall to an old Ford Phaeton. The top was ragged, both front fenders dented, and the driver's side rear door was tied on. "You sure it will run?"

"Don't let looks fool you," Pops bragged, "she's got a lot of life left in her, and I just filled her up this morning."

"I'll take care of her for you," Barrister assured him.

"The keys are in it," the old man explained.

Strolling quickly over to the Ford, he pulled open the door and was greeted by the hideous screech of a rusty hinge and the site of a seat covered with an Indian blanket. Sliding in he quickly discovered the horsehair padding under the blanket was almost gone and at least two of the springs were broken. Frowning, he turned the old car on and hit the starter. The four-cylinder came immediately to life. So far, so good! Putting the car into first, he let out on the clutch, and the car stubbornly crawled from its parking spot.

"Give her some gas," Pops urged.

Bearing down on the accelerator, Barrister all but willed the car up a ramp and out onto the street. Rounding a corner, he pulled up in front of the crime scene wagon and to a waiting Barry Jenkins. As the car squealed to a stop, its mechanical brakes fighting to grab the pavement, the captain grumbled, "Get in, and don't ask any questions."

"Yes, sir."

As soon as his partner shut the Model A's

passenger door, Barrister let out the clutch and headed for the street. Glancing into a rearview mirror held in place with two strands of bailing wire, he watched in horror as the crime scene wagon disappeared in a cloud of blue smoke. Sadly, as long as he stayed on the force, he knew he would never hear the end of this.

34

June 25, 1936

She's over this way," a bemused and confused Dick Titan announced as Barrister shut off the coughing Model A, threw open the door, and stepped out onto a gravel drive. The uniformed cop took a final long look at the jalopy before pointing to a spot that apparently was just over the hill.

"Lead the way," the head of homicide suggested. "Is she in the water?"

Titan headed through a stand of weeds, "No, she's in the grass next to the edge."

"Good," Barrister grumbled. "I didn't want this to be a water adventure. Barry, you and the crime scene boys coming?"

"We're right behind you," Jenkins called out.

"Can I ask you something, Captain?" Titan asked as he led the way up the rise.

Barrister looked toward the young man and nodded.

"I know the economy is tough right now, but I can't believe the chief is making you drive a wreck like that."

"It's a step up from last week," the captain jibed.

"Really?"

"Yes," Barrister replied, "they had me in a 1914 Model T then. They assure me if I get this murder solved, I'm going to get a 1929 Moon."

Titan scratched his head, "Didn't that company go out of business?"

"Yep, and that's why the department can get them so cheap."

"Gee," the patrolman said, "I guess we regular cops are lucky. We never drive anything more than a couple of years old, and it's always made by one of the big companies."

Barrister nodded, "And never forget how lucky you are. Now son, where is this body?"

"Just a few more feet," Titan explained. "It's right at the bottom of the hill."

The captain, breathing hard from the energy it took to bring his two hundred and sixty pounds up the rise, stopped and looked down toward the aqueduct. Sprawled out beside the edge of the manmade waterway's concrete wall was a woman dressed in a pale blue, tea length dress. He glanced back to his crew, "There she is. Let's get a bunch of photos. I'll be down in a second." He paused and watched the quartet of men make their way carefully down the embankment before turning to his partner. "Barry, what do you see?"

The young man looked from the water to the body and back to his boss. "A woman's been killed and dumped."

"Yeah, and you can see the tracks our crew just made going down to her and those of Titan, but there is nothing else. There are no signs she was dragged. So how did the body get here?"

Jenkins scratched his head before offering a hunch, "On the water?"

"Has to have been brought in by boat," Barrister agreed. "It took some work getting to this point. But why here?"

"Cap, isn't that the same question we've asked at each scene?"

"It is," Barrister agreed, "and there has to be a motive behind it. So what are we missing?"

"Bill," one of the men called out, "we've got the scene photographed. You want to see her before she's moved?"

"Sure, on my way."

Barrister waddled more than climbed down the steep bank. As the others stepped back, he took a look at the woman. She was small, likely not more than five feet tall, had blonde hair done in a ponytail. She was blessed with what his wife would have described as the perfect hourglass figure and her dress was made to accentuate her curves. And, as Titan had pointed out on the phone, there was obvious bruising on her neck.

"Looks like the others," Jenkins noted. "There's a broken, unused kitchen match about two feet beyond her head sitting on the concrete wall. It was as if the murderer placed it there so it couldn't be missed."

"I see it," Barrister said. "Did you boys find a purse or any identification when you looked her over and shot the photos?"

"No, sir."

"OK, men, let's put her into the wagon, get her to the ME and let him have a look. Come on, Jenkins, let's get back in our car . . . if you can call it that."

After struggling back up the hill, Barrister, now reathing hard, worked his way over to the Model A and slid behind the wheel. He flipped the key on and stepped on the starter. The car kicked right off. After adjusting the spark, he looked across at his partner and asked, "What are the odds you think this thing will make it back to the station?"

"The wagon will beat us," the younger man suggested.

"No doubt," Barrister agreed while popping the clutch and hitting the gas. After the badly smoking vehicle made it up to twenty, the captain grimly smiled. "It could be worse."

"How's that?"

"We could be walking," Barrister explained.

"Now, Barry, when we get back to the office, you need to run down that gossip columnist."

"Ellen Rains?"

"Yeah. Have her come down to the morgue and view the body. Beyond the strangling, the pattern I now see emerging is a possible connection to the movie industry. Rains was able to identify one of the others, maybe she can peg this one as well."

35

June 25, 1936

It was just past seven when Jenkins found Rains and convinced her to come down to the station. Wearing a pink suit and matching shoes and hat, the woman finally walked through the door at eight. After meeting with Barrister, she followed him down to the medical examiner's place of business . . . the morgue.

"Will I be meeting with Mr. Forrest?" she asked.

"Not this time," the homicide cop explained. "Arnie's already gone home. But the body's on ice, so I'll pull out the drawer and let you take a look."

When they arrived at the door, Barrister pulled a key from his pocket and unlocked the door. After opening it, he stepped inside and felt around the wall for the switch. When found, he flipped on the lights and signaled for the woman to come in.

"She's in drawer sixteen," he explained as he

walked over to what looked like oversized file cabinets built into the back wall. There were two drawers stacked one on top of the other. The bottom drawer on the eighth stack was number sixteen. The lighting was eerie, the shadows caused by the overhead lights giving the place the atmospheric feel of a movie set from a horror film. With his face half bathed in light and the other side all but lost in shade, Barrister stopped and looked back to his guest. He waited for what probably seemed like an eternity to Rains before asking, "Are you ready?"

Her expression mocked the man's attempt at drama. As cool as a winter's night in Maine, Rains smiled, "If you'd have been here when I viewed the other body, you'd have learned I'm not squeamish. Just open it up and let me take a look."

He waited until she was beside him before stepping out in front of the drawer, grabbing a handle and pulling it toward the center of the room. When it was three feet out of the wall, he stopped, stepped opposite Rains, and folded a sheet back from the dead woman's face.

"This is our gal," Barrister sadly noted. "Have you ever seen her before?"

Rains took a close look and shook her head. "She must have been a pretty thing, but I don't know this woman. And, as I make my living remembering faces, and this gal had a nice one, you can take that to the bank."

"That's not the answer I was hoping for," the cop replied.

"What's that on her upper chest?" the gossip columnist asked.

"Looks like a birthmark or a scar," he replied as he leaned closer. "My guess is a birthmark."

"Maybe that will help you," Rains suggested. "Do you need anything else from me?"

"No, that's it. You are free to go."

The woman nodded, adjusted her hat and strolled quickly down the hall and out of the building. She walked quickly to a 1936 Lincoln K sedan parked at the curb. A man in a black uniform nodded and opened the door for Rains. After she slid in, he closed the door and hurried around to the driver's side of the long dark vehicle. After entering, he looked over his shoulder and asked, "Where to, ma'am? Would you like to go home?"

"No," she snapped, "back to the office. I've got a few things to look over, and I need to make a call or two. Because of what I saw in there, this night is just beginning."

"Yes, Miss Rains."

As the long car sped off toward her Sunset Boulevard office, the woman shook her head. Why another attack so soon? The others had been separated by months. Was the madman's lust for blood pushing him to kill more?

"We are here, ma'am," the driver announced.

An impatient Rains didn't wait for her chauffeur

to get out of the driver's seat, rush around, and open her door. For the first time in weeks, she pulled the handle herself, put her size eights on the running board, took a deep breath of the night air and stepped out in a world reflected in neon and street lights. Not pausing to take in the unique sights and sounds of a Hollywood evening, she raced across the walk and rushed into the building where she leased four rooms and employed a staff of five. Her girl Friday, Susan Chontos, met her at the door. Her face displayed her shock at seeing her boss.

"I thought you were going to the police station and then heading home?" The twenty-five year old brunette didn't have to wait long for the older woman's answer.

"I was," an obviously stressed Rains shot back, "but there is something I need to see or I won't sleep a wink." As she shuffled her legs, the gossip columnist seemed bent on setting a speed record to her lair, but that didn't keep her from firing out questions. "What happened to those pictures Jack shot last night outside Musso and Frank's?"

"You mean from that set you used to get the Cary Grant photo?" Chontos asked.

"Yes."

"I've got them in my office," the assistant quickly assured Rains. "But the photos are only fair at best. You picked about the only shot we could use."

Rains snapped, "I don't care about quality, just bring them to me. I need to look through them again. If I'm right, we have our hands on the biggest story this town's ever seen."

As Chontos turned and ran down the hall, Rains continued to her private office, opened the bar, grabbed a bottle of Scotch and a glass. After pouring, she briefly studied the liquid before downing it in one swallow. The woman's throat was still burning when her short, excited assistant strolled in with at least two dozen eight by tens.

"I'll take them," the woman barked, "You get back to work. And close the door behind you."

After setting them in the middle of her desk and turning on a brass lamp, the columnist hurried through the black and white images. Tossing shots of Bette Davis, Dalton Andrews, and Humphrey Bogart to the side, she stopped when she came to one that featured a smiling man and his petite companion. It didn't matter the shot was slightly out of focus and there was a shadow hiding a part of the man's face, the picture was dynamite. She dropped the shot on her desk, ran a finger over her lips and picked up her phone. She dialed a seven-digit number known only to a handful of people on the planet. She listened as it rang three times before a man answered.

"Jacob, we need to meet, and I don't mean tomorrow."

"Is this you, Ellen? And this better be good for you to bother me at home."

"It is not just good, it's the hottest rock you and I've ever played with, and what I've got to tell you can't wait until tomorrow. Where can we meet?"

"How about the all-night café on Ventura?" he suggested.

"The one that's about a mile east of the country club?"

"Yeah," he assured her. "I can meet you there at eleven. I have a party here and I have to at least stay long enough that it appears I care about our guest. After all, he is England's ambassador to the United States."

"I'll be there," she answered and hung up. Taking a final look at the photo, Rains got up from her desk, walked back to the cabinet, and poured herself another drink. Defusing this bomb was not going to be a job for amateurs.

36

June 25, 1936

Yates was waiting for Rains when her chauffeur dropped her off at Ralph's. The small, out-of-the-way eatery was not the sort of place that the woman usually frequented; it was too dingy and cheap, the food too common, but tonight it was just where she wanted to be. Unlike the nightclubs and top restaurants, those who rolled into Ralph's as it neared the bewitching hour would have no idea who she was, and it was the anonymity she needed at this moment.

The woman slid into a booth near the back of the dive. Across the table, Yates, dressed in a dinner jacket, was already working on a cup of coffee.

"How was your party?" she asked.

"Bland, boring, and costly," he grumbled. "Now, what's so important?"

Rains opened up her huge pink purse and retrieved a folder. Only after carefully studying the half dozen patrons and locating the waitress did she pull a photo from the oversized envelope and slide it across the tabletop to the movie mogul. He casually glanced at the image and shrugged.

"So what?"

"Who's in that picture?" she whispered.

"Give me a break," Yates hissed, "I'm not some hick on a quiz show, and I'm not blind either."

"Then who is it?" she shot back.

"OK, I'll play it your way. It's Flynn Sparks."

She shook her head, "I'm well aware of that." From the corner of her eye, she saw a young, skinny, gum-chewing woman heading their way. Reaching across the table, Rains grabbed the photo, turned it over and placed it on her lap.

"Can I get you something?" the waitress asked.

"I'll take a cup of coffee," Rains replied. "Make it black."

"That's the only color we offer, lady," the woman teased. "Anything else?"

"What kind of pie do you have?" Yates inquired.

"Cherry, peach, and chocolate."

"I'll take the chocolate."

"You got it."

As the waitress walked away, Rains slid the picture back toward the man.

He didn't bother looking at the shot before bellowing, "I told you it was Sparks."

Rains frowned, shook her head, and demanded, "Who's the dame?"

Yates nonchalantly glanced at the shot a second time before pushing it back to the woman. "It's some new girl we have under contract. Her name is Ann or Anita or something. I know it starts with an A. She is eye candy, nothing more. My directors tell us she has no talent. So you won't be writing about her."

"Actually," the woman cut in, "I will."

Rains didn't get a chance to explain what she meant before the waitress waltzed back to the table carrying the pie and coffee. After setting them down, she asked, "Anything else I can do for you?"

"That's it for now," Yates assured her. He was already chewing on his initial bite before the waitress sauntered back toward the main counter.

He smiled as the flavor filled his mouth, "You should try this, Ellen; this is good. It reminds me of that place just off Broadway. What was the name if it?"

"Use your napkin," she suggested, "you've got chocolate on your lip. And I thought we agreed we wouldn't talk about our days in New York."

As the man wiped his mouth, she again spoke in hushed tones. "Listen Jacob, the girl you're writing off as being nothing became something last night."

"How did she do that?" he asked as his fork cut another portion of the tasty dessert.

Rains eyes were almost as cold as her tone, "She was murdered."

Yates froze, halfway through his second bite. Realizing he couldn't answer with his mouth full, he forced the pie down his throat without chewing. "No!"

"Yeah," she assured him, "and the last person to see her alive was Sparks. Do you see a pattern developing? If you don't, I do."

He leaned over the table until their faces were just inches apart, "Do you know what you're suggesting?"

"I'm not suggesting anything," she answered as their eyes met. "I'm just pointing out the facts."

"So the cops know?" the suddenly rattled mogul asked.

"They showed me the body," she explained.

"They thought I'd be able to identify the girl."

"Ellen, did you tell them who she was?"

"No, how could I Jacob? I'd never met her. But as I looked at the body, I did remember seeing this picture in my office earlier in the day. My photographer was at Musso and Frank's shooting shots of the stars last night."

He nodded, "So the cops don't know who she is."

"Not yet," Rains assured him. "And the photo didn't run with my story; I didn't mention that Sparks was there, and I've already destroyed the negative. Things are covered on my end, but you will need to do some work on yours. You'd better put some space between the dead girl and Galaxy before Barrister finally figures out who she is and who she was with."

As Rains slipped the photo back into her purse, Yates drummed his fingers on the table. "OK, I'm remembering now. Sally Glenn brought the girl to my office."

"Ah," the woman solemnly jested, "nothing like a murder to clear the fog. So she was a friend of Glenn's?"

"No," Yates smiled, "she wasn't. But Sally spotted her at a movie theater, the girl was an usher, and thought she had the right look for film work. Sally does that all the time. She couldn't tell you the names of half the kids she's tried to help get into show business." He snapped his fingers, "Her name was Agnes Sharp. She just moved out here from the Midwest . . . I think it was Iowa or maybe Nebraska. I remember her telling me she came to California by herself."

"That works in our favor," Rains suggested. "It will take the cops a long time to trace her, if at all. If you spread a little money around, it might delay them even more."

Yates nodded, "I'll get my security people to find out where she lived and clean it out. If it takes it, we can pay the landlord off and a roommate, if she has one. We can make up a cover story about the girl needing to go back home."

"Now you're acting like the Jacob I know," Rains smiled. "Based on what you've told me, it won't take a very big broom to sweep this under the rug."

The studio mogul reached into his pocket and tossed a couple of dollars in change on the table. Without a word, he grabbed his hat off the bench, got up, and hurried outside to his car. Through the glass, Rains watched him speed away into the night.

"Your friend left in a hurry," the waitress noted as she wandered back to the table.

"He remembered some work he had to do," Rains explained. "Now, could you bring me a piece of that pie? I have suddenly found my appetite."

37

June 26, 1936

With a full hour to herself, Shelby opted to read rather than go with Minser and Mace to the commissary. Wandering out in the bright sunlight, she glanced in both directions before turning right. As nothing was being shot on New York Street that day, she strolled to the iconic set, grabbed a spot on an empty bench, and opened a copy of the just released-novel, *Gone with the Wind*. She was finishing the second chapter when she realized she was no longer alone.

"So you're reading it too?" Flynn Sparks noted.

Shelby pulled her nose from the book and frowned. What had been a good day had just taken a U-turn.

"It seems everyone is reading that novel," the actor suggested. "There's even talk of the studio buying the film rights to it."

Shelby bent the corner of a page to mark her spot before setting the book in her lap. She then watched her uninvited guest sit down on the curb.

"Of all the places on this huge lot," she snapped, "you had to pick the one corner I thought was my own."

"Don't flatter yourself," he shot back, "I wasn't looking for you. I was out taking a walk."

She frowned and glanced across the vacant street to a movie theater. Like everything else on this outdoor set, it was nothing more than a false front. In that way, it was pretty much like the man who'd just graced her with his presence. Sensing he wasn't going to leave, she opted to at least attempt conversation. She figured she should lead with something he loved to talk about . . . his life.

"Did you enjoy your date last night?" she quizzed.

"I know she did," he chuckled. "Nice girl. Had good taste too. She appreciates compliments and takes them to heart. You know, she spent a couple of hours just looking through scrapbooks in my living room."

"So nice for her," Shelby replied.

He turned his head and his eyes caught hers before landing his first verbal volley. "What about you, did you and Dalton light up the night? What am I saying, that guy doesn't have enough wattage to illuminate a closet. Well, at least this time he took you some place with style. But did he introduce you to any of the famous people who were there? I would have."

"We had a nice dinner, and then we went to a Gary Cooper movie."

"Your story and Dalton's match," Sparks noted.

"I forgot you two are working on the same movie," she admitted. "I'm guessing you trade war stories during breaks."

"We talk when we're forced to," he explained. "In truth, we don't have all that much in common. For starters, he's dull and I'm not. But why discuss him, when we can talk about me?"

She shook her head and sighed, "It's likely the only subject you know very much about."

Sparks stood, put his left foot on the bench beside her and rested his elbows on his knee. "There are a lot of places in this town you haven't seen. I can show them to you. So why don't you let me take you out to eat and dancing and then compare my charms to Dalton's."

"I'm not going out with you," Shelby flatly replied.

"But . . ."

"But nothing," she finished his thought for him. "I'm not dating you. There is an old saying back home about dogs and fleas. It seems if you hang around dogs too much, you end up with some things you don't want. Your reputation is something I don't want or need attached to me. When Flynn Sparks takes a woman out everyone always thinks the worst of her. I don't even know the blonde who admired your scrapbooks last night, but I'm already judging her. I don't want people to think of me the way I'm thinking of her right now."

He laughed, "You're missing the point. You think having people think those thoughts is a bad thing. It's not. They only point fingers because they want to be doing what you're doing but don't have the guts. I'm not taking advantage of the women who go out with me; I'm setting them free to really experience life." Sparks chuckled. "You're clinging to the old-fashioned concepts that are a part of Oklahoma. They will hold you back and ultimately fill you with regrets. Someday you will look to the past wishing you'd given in to your desires. The invitation stands: go out with me and see life the way it should be lived. And don't fool yourself, you'd like it."

Sparks pulled his foot from the bench and slowly ambled down the empty street toward the soundstages. Her eyes followed him until he rounded a corner and disappeared.

What if he was right? What if forty years from now she did look back at her life and wish for the things she hadn't tried and the things she hadn't done? She grimaced. He'd done it. He'd made her begin to doubt herself.

38

June 26, 1936

"I need you to do me a favor."

Shelby looked up from sewing lace onto a 1860s party dress and into the eyes of Betty Minser. Her normally relaxed boss seemed agitated.

"Just set that to one side," Minser advised as she held up a blue gown, "and run this to the hotel set on stage 6. At the last minute, they change the shooting order on a film and one of the actresses there will need this number for a couple of scenes today rather than tomorrow. Oh, and take this tuxedo as well. Some new actor is actually playing Flynn Sparks in the same scene."

"What?"

"Makes no sense to me either," Minser assured her. "It's just weird. Sparks is playing in the film, so he can't actually play himself. So Hunter Nelson is playing Flynn. At least he looks a bit like him."

"Why can't Willie take them?" Shelby asked.

"Because," Minster explained, "I don't know where he is. He took off about an hour ago on an errand and didn't come back."

"Betsy, it seems he does that a lot. Why do you put up with it?"

The older woman sighed, "Because I have to. Now hustle these over to the set."

With no further explanation, Shelby grabbed the two items and hurried out the door, down the street and to stage 6. A guard stopped her at the door and asked the reason for the visit before allowing her to pass. As she stepped toward the lighted staging area, she was amazed. It was as if she was walking into an actual hotel ballroom. Her mouth agape, she studied the detail in the three walls that had been created for the scene then turned her gaze to the furnishings and people filling the room. How was it possible for a crew to put this together so quickly? Just last week, this same stage had been a pirate ship. As she pondered the marvels of movie magic, she spotted a waving Willard Mace standing beside a camera on the far side.

As she hurried over to warn Mace to get back to work, a balding man in a suit stopped her and asked, "Are you the young woman who is working for Betsy?"

"Yes, sir," Shelby quickly replied.

"I've heard good things about you," he explained. "But Betsy failed to tell me how beautiful you were. Rather than carrying costumes you should be wearing them. And believe me I can make that happen."

She frowned before angrily saying, "Why is it that every man feels they have to use that line?

I'm not dreaming of being an actress. So I'm not buying what you're selling. Besides," she chided, "you're too old for me."

He chuckled, "Aren't you the fresh one?"

"No," she shot back, "I think you are. Now, if you will excuse me, I have a job to do."

"And I'm paying you to do it," he informed her.

"What?" Shelby's blue eyes were aflame. She'd had to put up with Flynn Sparks at lunch: she didn't need to go a second round with someone else.

"I'm Jacob Yates, the head of this studio."

Shelby's knees grew weak as the color drained from her face, "I'm sorry, it is just . . ."

"That everyone in this town comes on to beautiful girls," he said with a smile.

"That's still no excuse for my being rude," she announced. "My mama raised me better than that."

"I like fire and spunk, kid," Yates replied, "and I admire someone with some backbone and obvious morals. It's kind of rare and refreshing."

"Thank you. But I really need to get those costumes to the director. I believe you're about to shoot the scenes where they will be used."

"You do your job, kid," the mogul agreed. "We'll talk another time."

Shelby nodded before finishing her trek across the stage to where Mace stood.

"Betsy wants you back at work," the young

woman hissed. "She's hot enough to cook a steak."

"She'll be fine," Mace laughed. "I want to watch them film the next scene."

Shelby couldn't believe the man's attitude. What was he thinking? And why did Minser put up with this? She was still trying to figure things out when a script girl walked over from the lighted set.

"Are these the costumes we need for the scene?"

"Yes," Shelby replied, handing them to the tall, plain woman.

As she draped them over her arm, the thirtyish lady added, "He might seem nice at first, but don't trust him."

Shelby glanced back to Yates. She shuddered as she realized his eyes were still locked on her. Suddenly, she felt as though the man owned her body and soul, and for the second time in a few hours, she felt as though she was losing control of her life.

39

June 26, 1936

At about three-thirty, the wardrobe department experienced a sudden rush of costumes demanding repair work or alterations, so for the remainder of the afternoon, Shelby barely had time to look up. Afternoon became evening and by seven, she was regretting not eating lunch. By nine, when she finally finished cuffing a pair of pants needed by Hunter Nelson for the next day's shoot, she was both famished and exhausted. Shelby was also without a ride, as her father had left earlier so that he could take her mother to a movie.

The young woman noted it was a bit cloudy as she exited the door and stepped out onto the street, but it didn't appear that there would be any rain. But, with the temperature in the eighties, it was sticky. And as she would be walking the mile home, the heat and humidity were going to take their toll.

As she hurriedly strolled along streets that were now very familiar to her, she marveled at how different they seemed at night. In the daytime, the lot was almost like a circus filled with people and noise, it seemed there were parades everywhere, but now it was more like a ghost town. Her footsteps echoed off buildings and down alleys, and those unfamiliar sounds drove her to move even faster. At New York Street she took a right, thinking a shortcut to the front gate would be just the ticket she needed to escape a lonely and foreboding world where she suddenly felt very vulnerable. Yet, this outdoor stage with its tall facades and dark alleys opened up a whole new set of fears and insecurities. A sudden and earsplitting noise just to her right caused her to stop in her tracks. Quickly turning her gaze from the street to an alley, she noted a large cat sitting beside a turned-over tin trash can.

There is no reason to be scared, she told herself. The studio had guards, and no one could just walk in without the proper identification. So this empty lot was far safer than the streets outside those gates. But, if that were the case, why was her heart trying to beat through her chest and why were her knees shaking like two saplings standing up against a gale force wind?

As she tried to gather her wits, she realized she was near the same place where Flynn Sparks had interrupted her lunch and momentarily forced her to wonder about her own convictions. She studied the bench where she'd sat and felt a chill run down her spine. Rubbing her arms, she then remembered the way Jacob Yates had studied her. That wasn't a man looking at an employee; it was as if he was an animal sizing up a kill.

"Lord," she whispered, "I want to be in Oklahoma."

Her prayer wasn't answered. Her feet were still anchored to a street that seemed real but wasn't.

She glanced over to the movie theater. The marquee boldly proclaimed the film now showing as *The Black Death*. As dark as this night was, the movie could have been shot right on this street.

Her neck was now on a swivel as Shelby yanked her feet from the imagined glue holding them in place and moved quickly down the vacant street.

Why had she taken this shortcut? Why hadn't she just taken the normal route to the front gate? As she rushed quickly by buildings claiming to be a police station, a dry cleaners, and a drug store, she felt eyes on her. Were they real or were they in her imagination? Was there someone here or was this setting just reminding her of the way Yates had examined her on the set? Rounding the corner onto what the studio called New Orleans Street she found herself in a world void of streetlamps. It was as dark as the inside of a closet. She stopped and stared into the blackness for at least a minute. Should she retrace her steps or move forward?

"Calm down," she whispered rather than thought. "Three more blocks and you'll be outside the gates. You've just got to keep moving forward."

Back home in Oklahoma she'd relished being alone. She loved the nights when she was the only one on the farm. But at this moment, she longed to be with people, even those she couldn't trust, rather than be surrounded by dark and menacing shadows seeming void of life but ripe with terror.

On now unsteady legs, she moved past a Cajun mansion set next to a man-made swamp and by a series of two-story, French-style restaurants. Stepping under the canopy of a dress shop, she stopped to get her bearings. She believed the front gate was a block and a half to her left, but she wasn't sure. She had to trust her instincts and move forward.

Shelby took a deep breath and continued along the dark street until she came to another corner. She turned, stood on the corner, and surveyed her surroundings. She had arrived at the Western town set. She'd been told this street had stood in for everything from Dodge City to Deadwood. To her right, barely visible in the shadows, was Boot Hill.

She hurried by the cemetery before stepping up on the wooden sidewalk that took her past a newspaper office, a saloon and a jail. A sudden wind blew a large hunk of sagebrush along the street just before she stepped off the sidewalk and onto an alley paved with bricks. At the end of this outdoor set was a church. She'd seen it from a different angle as she'd entered the studio, so she was confident she was now almost to the lot's front gate. Taking a deep breath, she rushed past a hotel and general store then crossed another alley and moved quickly in front of a livery stable. A sudden noise, like the slamming of a door, caused her to stop and look cautiously over her shoulder. Though her mind was screaming someone was there, her eyes seemed to prove she was still completely alone.

"Got to move forward," she told herself. "You're only a block from the gate now. You can use some of the money you have to get a cab. No use walking home."

Just as she was about to step beyond the empty

stable, she sensed a presence. Too afraid to turn around, she dug her foot into the dirt street and was about to push off into a sprint when she felt hands around her neck. Instinctively, she launched an elbow into her attacker's gut and then flung her arms up. The move gave her the room she needed to break away from his grip and race across the street toward the church. Climbing the eight steps two at a time, she grabbed the doorknob and twisted. It didn't move. Why in heaven's name would they lock it? Before she could turn and race for the gate, the panic-stricken woman felt a hand on her shoulder. There was no time to think, only react. Whirling, she brought her left hand across her attacker's face.

"What are you doing?" the man demanded as she flattened against the door and readied for a second strike.

"Flynn?"

He was rubbing his cheek as he assured her, "Yeah, it's me."

"Where'd you come from?" she angrily asked.

"I was at the front gate," he explained. "I heard some noise coming from this way, looked up, saw something, and decided to check it out."

Shelby flew into a rage. "So pretending to choke me in front of the livery stable was your idea of fun? How long have you been following me? Did you watch me coming out of wardrobe or did you pick me up on New York Street? Maybe you were the person who scared the cat. This is not funny."

Even in the low light, Sparks appeared confused. "What are you yapping about?" he asked. "And for Pete's sake calm down, Shelby. You are trembling like a leaf. I saw someone from the front gate, just like I told you, and then I came down here to investigate."

"And," she demanded, "why were you at the gate at this time of night?"

"We just finished shooting," he explained. "I was going home when my car stalled out. I got out and Calvin, the night guard, and I were looking at it trying to figure out what was wrong. That's when he spotted you."

"I thought you said you spotted me."

"He saw you first," Sparks groaned. "Why is this suddenly a federal case? He was about to call an all-night garage to come look at my car, so I told him I'd find out who was trespassing. We figured it was some kind of weird fan. And what were you doing there?"

"I worked late too," she answered, "figured I'd cut across the outdoor sets and save a few blocks." She rubbed her neck with her right hand before asking, "But if you didn't put your fingers around my throat, then who did?"

"Maybe," he suggested, "your being alone on the lot has led to your imagination running away from you. After all, you are still shaking." He glanced up and laughed.

"What's so funny?" she bellowed.

"It seems the only time I get to actually be with you is at churches. Come on, I'm not going to bite. Let's walk back to the gate, so you can catch your ride home."

"I don't have a ride home, I was going to walk."

"OK," Sparks replied, "but, as you have been scared a bit, why don't you take a cab? I'll pay."

After the episode at lunch, she didn't want to have anything to do with the actor, but tonight was different. If his car had been working, she'd have even let him drive her home.

As he took her hand and led her toward the front gate, she glanced back over her shoulder. Was there someone there in the shadows waiting for her? Did she miss becoming the victim of the same person who killed Leslie Bryant? Or was it nothing more than her imagination?

40

June 27, 1936

Ellen Rains waved at the guard as she passed through the Galaxy Studio gates; he obviously knew better than to stop this woman and ask for credentials. Her chauffeur-driven Lincoln took her to the main office building where she got out of the car, walked up the steps and got into an elevator. A black man, dressed in a red uniform, sitting on a stool smiled and closed the mesh door.

"Are you on your way to see Mr. Yates?" he asked, "And that sure is a pretty blue dress. My wife would love it."

"I am going to see the big man, Oscar," she assured the elevator operator. "And, as I remember her, your wife is about my size. Next time I come to this studio, I'll bring this number and hat over in a bag and she can have it."

"Wow, that'd sure be nice. She'd be stepping high going to church in that getup."

"I might have a few others she'd like too," Rains added with a grin.

"Then this will be a nonstop ride to the third floor," he assured her. As the lift slowly climbed upward, Oscar then politely said, "Could I ask you a question, Miss Rains?"

"You may," she answered.

"I've been working on this lot since it opened. I was here long before pictures talked, and I've watched a lot of folks go in and out the gates."

She grinned, "I bet you have."

"I was just wondering if you thought there would ever be a time when colored folks actually had a chance to star in a picture?"

"The studio," she quickly replied, "makes a few films every year for Negro theaters."

"I know that," he softly answered, "but I was

just wondering if my people would ever get to be in a big-time film playing something other than a porter or maid. Do you think there's a chance?"

Rains shook her head, "I don't know, but I do sometimes wonder about things too."

"Like what?" Oscar answered.

"If a woman will ever run a studio."

He smiled, "My folks will likely be playing cowboy heroes and society dames before that happens. This is your floor," he announced as he pulled the door open.

"Thanks. Just keep on hoping, Oscar, just keep on hoping."

Without knocking, she walked into the studio mogul's outer office and waved toward Eve Walen. "Is he in?"

"Yes."

"Hold his calls and see that we are not disturbed," Rains ordered as she marched over to Yates's large, imposing door and opened it. He was sitting behind his pool table-sized desk, rubbing his head and frowning. She stopped, tilted her head to one side, and asked, "Do you have a headache, Jacob?"

"It just got worse," he noted as she closed the door. After moving to a chair, she dropped her robin's egg blue hat on his desk. Only after she appeared comfortable did Yates complain. "We have to meet in an out-of-the-way café one night so no one sees us together, and now, you're just letting everyone on the lot watch you waltz into my office. You are either crazy or the most forgetful person on this planet."

"I'm neither," she assured him while removing her blue gloves and looking at her freshly manicured nails. She held her hand up and asked, "What do you think of the color?"

"It's red," he grumbled.

"I mean," she quizzed, "is it a good red?"

His stare all but cut the woman in half, "I don't know and I don't care."

"Fine," Rains chirped. "You don't know anything about style anyway."

"Why are you here?" he demanded.

"I guess," she joked, "into everyone's life a little Rains must fall."

"You're anything but little," he pointed out. "Those days are way behind you."

"Ouch," she hissed. She then brushed off some lint from the bodice of her dress before saying, "I visit every studio head a couple of times a month. Check your schedule; this is my normal time to visit with you. And, Jacob, it is when I quit meeting with you, folks will start to talk."

"And last night?" he asked.

Her expression deadly, she spat, "There are things that can't be talked about on the phone, and after hours we don't need to be seen together. Not only would people wonder what we were doing, but Constance wouldn't like it at all."

"Leave my wife out of this. Now, what do you need?"

"How is our movie going?"

He shook his head, "Why do you think I have such a headache? I found out this morning that the girl who got strangled yesterday actually was in this film. She played the first victim of the Hollywood Madman."

"I will hand it to your director," Rains quipped, "that is typecasting at its best."

"I've seen footage," he replied. "You can't tell it's her. She doesn't say any lines and we never see her face."

"That's good," the woman said showing so little concern that Yates's jaw dropped.

"A woman's dead," he said. "In fact, several are."

"And," she added, "the body count mounting will be good for the box office."

"Ellen, I'm so happy you seem to find sunshine in everything. But let me assure you, there are a lot of clouds you are missing."

As she turned her attention once more to her nails, she muttered, "Give me the weather forecast, Jacob."

Leaning back in his chair, the mogul sadly reported, "Every scrap of evidence that is smuggled in from the police, in addition to all the stuff you and I know that Barrister doesn't, points the finger to my biggest star as being the real Hollywood Madman."

"Which," she jabbed snidely as she once more looked toward the man, "brings up the question of the day. Do you think he did it?"

"I don't know," Yates admitted. "I mean, the Flynn Sparks I know is a rounder, completely self-centered, and a professional jerk. I don't think he cares much about anything other than himself and his own desires. But I can't see him having what it takes to murder someone with his bare hands."

"Oh," she argued, "let me disagree. I think he's strong enough."

"I'm not arguing that," he agreed, "but he doesn't have what it takes in the gut. In other words, I don't see him having the stomach for it."

"But he treats women like dirt," she chimed in. "He uses them and throws them away. To him they are conquests, not real people. If women have no real value in his world, maybe he doesn't see anything wrong with killing them."

"So, Ellen, you believe he is the man the cops are looking for?"

"I didn't say that," she assured him. "But if I were a cop, I'd believe it. Our main job is to find out who did it before the cops do. Then we have to film that ending and get it out on the streets so that Barrister has to buy a ticket to make an arrest."

"Let me assure you of this," the mogul explained, "I've got my writers and researchers as well as three detectives working on it. And as they have a lot more to work with than Barrister, they should have the tactical advantage. Right now they're looking into everyone's background here at the studio . . ."

Rains raised her eyebrows, "Everyone?"

"Except me," he backtracked.

"That's a relief, because I know you have more skeletons in your closet than anyone, and a few of them lead back to me."

"Don't worry Ellen, we are safe. Right now two of my best men are trying to figure out who might have hated the girl that was murdered yesterday."

"That's good," she assured him, "but I'm more concerned about your wiping out her trail."

"Her landlord is all but blind and a drunk," Yates explained. "He obviously couldn't identify her if he was two feet from the body, but we paid him off anyway. She didn't have a roommate and hadn't been here long enough to make friends."

"What about people looking for her back home?" Rains asked as she pulled a compact from her purse and checked her makeup.

"Her dad took off when she was eight, and no one has heard from him in years. Her mother died right after Miss Sharp graduated from high school. She's an only kid. After her mom died, she moved to St. Louis and lived with her grandmother until the old woman passed away. Agnes took the inheritance and came out here. So no one is looking for her."

"We grabbed a break," Rains noted. "Did you see the information I passed along on the identity of the second victim?"

"That part is just about finished filming," Yates explained. "I watched the party scene yesterday. We borrowed a new gal from MGM to play the part. She did a nice job. I might try to buy her contract and use her down the road."

"Jacob, I have enough faith in you and your team to believe you can figure this out before the police do, but . . ."

"I don't like the way you stopped," Yates cut in.

"OK, here is what is bugging me," she added. "Last night after our meeting I got to thinking that we need to do some work on Flynn's image so the cops can't push the mayor and chief of police hard enough to have him arrested. And that could happen if Miss Sharp is identified."

"What kind of work?" the mogul quizzed the woman. "I mean, I've been trying to put a muzzle on him but . . ."

"But look what happened last night," she interrupted. "So that's why you need to create a safe girlfriend for him. Somebody who is squeaky clean and can fend off his advances. Then you use your publicity department to make it appear like she is the love of his life . . . the woman who will tame him."

"Most of the women on this lot," Yates pointed

out, "have problems just playing women of virtue. They're not going to fool anyone."

Rains reached down beside her chair and pulled out a photo. She tossed the eight by ten across the studio mogul's desk. "Who is that girl? She was at the church with Sparks, and I've seen her with Andrews as well. She is beautiful but wholesome. I've gone through every studio's actresses' portfolios and even studied the headshots agents have sent me of hopefuls, and I can't find her."

He glanced at the picture, "That's because she's not an actress. I don't know much about her other than she works for Betsy Minser."

"In costumes?"

"Yeah, Betsy says she's the best woman with a needle and thread she's ever seen. She already does all the work for key costumes. Betsy has even requested we give the gal a big raise."

Rains smiled and nodded. "Is the girl on the lot today?"

"It's Saturday, so I doubt it."

"What about Minser?"

"I saw her car as I drove up," Yates said, "so she's here. Beyond the studio, the woman doesn't really have a life."

"Then," Rains suggested, "let's go down to wardrobe. I need to know more about the only beautiful blonde in Los Angeles who doesn't want to be the next Jean Harlow. I mean, this girl sounds fascinating."

41

June 27, 1936

"My goodness!" Betsy Minser exclaimed as Yates and Rains entered her private lair. "To what do I owe the pleasure of having Hollywood royalty come to visit my humble place of work?"

Yates looked around what Minser called her finishing room. They appeared to be alone. Still, he figured it would be smart to ask. "You by yourself today?"

The woman nodded, "I am now. I had my new girl here for a few hours earlier. She did some work on a costume Queen Victoria will be needing early next week."

Rains smiled, "I seem to recall that Sally Glenn was cast in that role. I find that a rather interesting choice."

Yates shrugged, "It was the only way I could get Locklee to direct it. Rudolph is getting picky in his old age, but he's still the best! I'm sure he feels he can get Sally to drop her tomboy walk and fit into the role."

"I'd be shocked," Rains noted, "if he can just get to her quit smoking cigars on the set. That woman has the manners of a merchant marine."

"Well," Minser assured them, "at least Shelby will make her look the part."

The wardrobe supervisor bent over, grabbed a large heavy wooden box filled with fashion accessories and placed it on the table. As an impressed Rains looked on, Minser began searching through the various colored beads.

"How did you manage to pick that up?" the columnist asked. "That must weigh a ton."

"Probably about fifty pounds," Minser explained. "And when you work through thick fabric with needles and have to lift huge bolts of material, your back, arms, and shoulders get really strong."

"Wow," Rains said with awe. "The two men who work for me couldn't do that."

"Betsy," the studio mogul announced as he pulled himself up and sat on one of the wooden sewing tables and changed the course of the conversation. "I met Shelby yesterday. I was impressed. She's got spunk."

"And she's talented," Minser added. "But more than that, she has some other qualities that make her very rare in this town. In fact, I'd forgotten girls like her even existed."

Rains chuckled, "I thought we either had everything or could make anything in Hollywood. So what does she have that I couldn't find on any movie lot in the city?"

"Innocence," Minser explained, "charm, and compassion. She's fresh and wholesome. She looks for ways to be kind to people rather than use them. But don't confuse that for weakness. She has a strong backbone, and no one can walk on her." The woman paused and chuckled, "And she's about the only woman on this lot that doesn't have the mirror illness."

"Mirror illness?" Yates asked.

The wardrobe supervisor grinned, "Yes, half of the actresses can't walk by one without staring at themselves as if they were expecting the glass to scream out how beautiful they were. Those women worship their image. The other half can't help but look into every mirror they pass, because they see themselves aging and realize their days as a lead performer are numbered. So they are always putting on more makeup to try to cover what they really can't . . . the passing of time. In this strange world, nothing is to be feared more than that . . . especially if you are a woman."

"And this girl," Rains said, "what did you say her name was?"

"Shelby Beckett."

"She doesn't have that?"

"No, she is comfortable with her beauty but doesn't believe she should be judged by it. Mirrors don't really interest her much. She walks by the ones in here a hundred times a day and only occasionally glances into that unforgiving glass."

"She is a rarity," Rains agreed.

Minser, her face filled with pride, continued to

extol her employee's virtues. "Today she came in talking about the church on our Western set. She wanted to know why it was so big. I explained that it was not just a façade, but was made so that the inside could be used for filming as well. So, for all practical purposes it was a real church. And do you know what she asked me then?"

Yates shrugged. To him the church was nothing more than a prop. What other purpose could it serve?

"Shelby wanted to know," the wardrobe supervisor explained, "why the studio didn't hold services there on Sundays. She thought maybe the actors, crew, and even some tourists might want to worship in the church on the Western set. Is that not the craziest thing? She told me it reminded her a bit of her church back in Oklahoma."

"Does she live in an apartment with some other girls?" Rains quizzed.

"No," Minser explained, "her parents moved out here to try to start over. She lives with them. In fact, her dad works building props over in the woodworking shop."

Yates beamed, "It sounds like we have a winner. I'm so glad you have her, Betsy." He pushed off the table and turned to the columnist. "Now, Ellen, I think you wanted me to show you the set where Dalton Andrews is working as a cop."

"Yes," Rains replied, "you lead the way." As the two stepped out onto the road outside the building, she noted, "About half the traffic I'm used to seeing."

"We don't shoot that much stuff on Saturday," he explained as the pair walked back toward his office.

"She's perfect," Rains announced as she sidled up beside him. "I mean, this girl is an answered prayer."

"Who is?"

"The wardrobe girl—Shelby Beckett."

"No argument there," Yates agreed. "I wish I had a hundred like her. I might get more done around here."

"You only need one," Rains assured him. As they continued to walk, she put words to the ideas that were demanding to escape from her head. "Starting on Monday, you need to begin finding excuses to get photos of that girl and Sparks. Have her fixing his jacket or watching him as he films scenes. Get them eating together at the commissary and talking on the back lot. Use any excuse you can to get them together, and then get all the photographs you take to me. I'll build this into the romance of the century. I can already hear my copy singing. The wholesome girl from the heartland tries to convert Hollywood's number one playboy into a respected citizen." She laughed, "Let's see Barrister get the mayor or chief to allow him to go after Sparks with that kind of publicity working in the actor's favor."

Yates shrugged as he opened the door to the main building and casually noted, "It might buy us some time to pin the murders on someone else."

Rains, her eyes sparkling like diamonds, added, "And that church idea is brilliant. Fans and stars worshipping together."

"How's that going to work?" he asked. "I mean, that's about the stupidest thing I've ever heard."

Excitement now dripping from her every word, Rains all but shouted, "You get a real preacher and assign actors and actresses to go to church. In other words, they have to be there. Have some of your talent sing a special each week. And then, have drawings so fans can win tickets to worship with their favorite stars. It's not only a great public relations move, but it will keep the Hayes Commission off your back. And here's the kicker, have Flynn co-chair this effort with the wardrobe girl. Thus, you have another reason to put them together for photo opportunities."

Yates shook his head in disbelief, "You're serious."

"Jacob, I've never been more serious in my life. Now you need to get moving and moving fast. With all the bad stuff going on right now, we need to have services in that church a week from tomorrow."

"Ellen, do you know what you're asking?"

"Just what you do every day," she replied with a smile, "making the impossible possible and

241

making something that is not real appear real. Goodbye, Jacob."

He stood in the doorway and watched the woman happily skip out to her car. He could have sworn someone had just informed her she'd won the Irish Sweepstakes. She was absolutely giddy.

Shaking his head, he stepped into the office building and walked slowly to the elevator. The idea of actually having services each Sunday was completely crazy, but, he had to admit, it was also the best one he'd heard in years. Every denomination in the country would likely give him an award for this, and that was the kind of publicity he needed.

42

June 29, 1936

Bill Barrister solemnly opened the door to the morgue and reluctantly ambled in. His sad eyes surveyed the surroundings before looking toward the medical examiner's desk. Arnold Forrest was sitting in his chair eating a piece of chocolate cake. "It's good," he announced as icing dribbled from the corners of his mouth. "Would you like some?"

"I don't understand how you can eat in the same room," Barrister soberly replied while looking over to the dead body of a middle-aged woman resting on a table, "where you do this."

"You mean you don't eat at a crime scene?"

"No, Arnie, I don't. I tend to smoke like a chimney, but I never eat."

"Bill, we are just cut from a different piece of cloth." The ME glanced at the cop's bulging stomach and added, "You must make up for not eating at crime scenes somewhere. I think you're twenty pounds heavier than you were in January."

"Only fifteen," the frowning homicide cop assured him. "Now, did you call about our most recent strangulation victim? Have you figured out who she is?"

Forrest put his cake on a piece of typing paper and stood. After wiping his mouth with a handkerchief, he brushed some crumbs from his shirt and walked over to a file sitting next to the dead woman, picked it up, crossed the room, and handed it to the captain.

"Here's the deal," Forrest explained, "I don't know who the kid is you recently brought in, but I did identify the victim that we found recently. You know the one who'd been dead more than a year."

"So you were able to figure out who a bag of bones is, but not a beautiful young woman who was still breathing last week."

"It's a strange business," Forrest replied. "I have found that death moves at its own pace."

As Barrister took the file he glanced back over to the ME's current patient. "What about that woman?"

"She's forty, her name's Grace, she took her own life."

"Any idea why?"

"Bill, her family said she was almost always happy, but in the last few months she had incredible mood swings. It wasn't poverty as her husband is in advertising and owns a successful business. And it wasn't her family as she has three kids, two in college and another an honor student in high school. It wasn't her spiritual life, either. She was very active in church and sang with the choir two days before she took rat poison. In her note, she wrote of demons that haunted her dreams."

The cop sadly shook his head, "That doesn't make any sense."

"On the surface," Forrest explained, "it doesn't, but when you dig down to what you can't see, it does. I have discovered she had a brain tumor. No one knew about it, and it would have killed her within a year. You see, the brain is a delicate piece of machinery, and something growing inside it can affect everything from motor skills to emotions. If you damage just a small part of the brain, everything from personality to judgment can change. A normal person can become a madman. A woman with everything to live for can be frightened into taking her own life. In Grace's case, the damage to her brain caused her to see things that weren't there."

"Sad," Barrister said.

"Maybe not," the ME noted, "I mean, the family now understands why she did what she did. And what all of us want in life is for there to be a reason when something happens. If we know the why, it helps us accept the pain and move on. It is when we don't find answers that it eats at us like a hidden cancer."

"Guess you're right." The cop looked from the body back to his host. "What is this file going to tell me?"

"As best as I can tell, you might just have a new Victim #1 in your strangulation cases. This woman died before the others you have identified and has no connection to California, much less Hollywood. She left her eight-year-old son with a friend in Gary, Indiana, and came west. According to the missing persons report I read, the only thing she told a friend was that she'd be gone a couple of weeks and she'd be bringing lots of money back when she returned."

"Got a name?"

"Wanda McMillan, she was twenty-six when she died. She never married, so I guess her kid is illegitimate. I don't deserve too much credit on the ID. I was looking for a blonde, and she didn't line up with any of the missing people with that color hair. I did note that she had once had a broken right arm and leg. Missing persons brought me a report on a brunette with those injuries. I pulled the body back out and looked at the skull. Her hair had been dyed. The roots were brunette. I sent off for dental records and confirmed her identity this morning. Now, finding out why she was here and her life story is up to you."

"Anything else?" Barrister asked.

"I can give you what I think is the likely time of her death . . . May 13, 1935."

The cop's jaw dropped.

"Don't be too shocked," Forrest replied, "I'm good, but not that good. Don't forget the crime scene guys found a newspaper with the body. That was the date it was printed."

43

June 29, 1936

"Should I go?" Shelby asked her boss.

"Are you kidding?" Minser laughed. "Do you really have to ask that question? Of course you should go."

Shelby crossed her arms as she leaned up against one of the alteration tables. She got a faraway look in her blue eyes as she whimsically said, "But, and I know how this sounds, I have nothing to wear."

"Well," Minser quipped, "that would certainly make you the center of attention, but I believe I can remedy that issue. As you and Betty Foster are the same size, we'll just find you an evening gown from her old wardrobe. I remember making one in jade green that would be perfect on you."

"It's not just the dress," Shelby explained, "it's the fact I would be going to a party where the Who's Who of Hollywood will be."

"And you'll do fine," Minser assured her. "I have no doubt Dalton wouldn't have asked you to go with him if he wasn't sure you could handle yourself there. In fact, I believe the only one who has doubts about this is you. Now, we are ahead of schedule on everything, work can be put on hold, and we have got two hours until Dalton picks you up, so let's get rolling." She looked across the far side of the room where Mace was sorting clothes. "Willie, you know that green dress Betty Foster wore for the party scene in *Don't Take a Dive*?"

"Yes, ma'am," he hollered.

"It's in the storage room with the other clothes for that movie. Get the gown and the shoes."

As Mace rushed out, Minser looked back to Shelby, "Why can't he move that fast all the time? Now get back in the changing room and wash your hair. Then, put on a robe and we'll get started on your makeup. When we are finished with you, Joan Crawford will be spitting nails, and when you show up at the party, Miss Crawford will have more than just Jean Harlow stealing her thunder tonight."

44

June 29, 1936

As Dalton Andrews drove his Packard through the ornate twin metal gates and up the paved drive, Shelby nervously looked at the country club–like grounds and the huge stone mansion nestled in the middle of the circular drive. Surrounded by so much grandeur, she began to once more drown in her doubts. She feared she wouldn't actually blend in well enough not to embarrass her date and therefore make a fool of herself.

"Are you sure about this?" she asked the man behind the wheel of the long luxury convertible.

"Absolutely," he replied. "Just be yourself."

"That's not going to work," she warned. "Country bumpkins don't fit in at the home of Fitzgerald Standhoff. I mean, this guy is the greatest director of all time."

"That's the way he tells it," Andrews chuckled, "and he will talk about his legacy for hours if you let him."

As the car stopped, Andrews pushed the Packard into neutral, opened the door and stepped out onto the drive. Meanwhile, on the other side of the vehicle, a uniformed man opened Shelby's door and watched approvingly as she slid out of the car. When an admiring Andrews took her arm, he leaned close and whispered, "I think the servant likes your dress. He should be parking our car, but instead, he is still watching you."

"I think it's too tight," she noted fearfully.

"It highlights all your good qualities," he laughed, "but it's also high-necked and long, so you have nothing to worry about. You look classy, not cheap."

A butler opened the mansion's huge entry, and the pair stepped into a large foyer with polished stone floors, a twenty-five-foot ceiling, an enormous chandelier covered with so many lights it sparkled like diamonds and two twelve-foot-tall open walnut doors leading to a grand ballroom.

"Wow," she gasped.

"Fitz always was a bit understated," Andrews joked as he whisked her across the floor and through the doors to where the party was already in full swing.

The ballroom sported five more chandeliers, floor-to-ceiling mirrors on one side of the room, and thirty-foot-tall windows on the other. The floor was marble, the walls white with inlays of dark walnut and the furnishings looked like something out of a French castle. At least two hundred guests were either milling around a fifty-foot-long buffet table, standing beside a thirty-foot-bar, or dancing to a full orchestra positioned on a bandstand larger than most New York theater stages.

"Wait until you see the bathrooms," Andrews quipped.

Shelby's gloved hand clung to her date's arm as she studied a twelve-foot high fountain that seemed to be spouting out some kind of alcohol. Beside that was a round table supporting a white cake likely taller and definitely wider than she was. A four-foot wide, round gold bowl sat in the middle of the dance floor and from time to time someone would toss money into it.

As she marveled at the mysterious actions playing out around her, she leaned close to Andrews's ear and posed a question. "What is the purpose for this party?"

He smiled, "It's not a party, it's a social event. It is where our host spends tens of thousands of dollars in order to raise a few thousand for soup kitchens."

"But," she argued, "why not just give the money spent on the party to the kitchens? It would do so much more good."

"Because," he explained, "the real reason for the event is to have a good time and pretend it is for a good cause. That makes it appear far more noble that just throwing a party for the sake of having fun." After allowing that bit of illogic to settle in, he asked Shelby, "Would you like to dance?"

"Sure."

As the pair whirled around the floor, Shelby took inventory of the royalty that had gathered for the event. Crawford, Dunne, Harlow, Stanwyck, and Colbert were just a few of the actresses decorating the room while Gable, Cooper, Brent, Tracy, Cagney, and Grant were among more than fifty tuxedo-clad actors holding court there.

"Don't be too impressed," Andrews warned. "None of these people really want to be here. They'd much rather be at home. But it is expected they turn out for charity and for Standhoff."

"It's amazing," she sighed.

"Maybe," he groaned, "but to me it looks like Buckingham Palace collided with Barnum and Bailey and somehow created an over-the-top version of a high school prom."

To Shelby, there was so much to see and do that time flew by. Over the next two hours, she danced and made small talk with more than two-dozen actors. It seemed everyone wanted to dance with the wardrobe girl. She was still floating in the clouds when, at just past ten, Flynn Sparks cut in on William Warren. As he took Shelby into his arms, he flashed that perfect smile.

"Aren't you the belle of the ball?" the actor noted, as they glided across the floor.

"I'm just being me," she replied. "Who did you bring tonight?"

"Sally Glenn."

"I thought she was married," Shelby quickly noted.

"Her husband doesn't like parties," Sparks explained, "and the studio thought it would be far safer for me to have someone who wouldn't be tempted to come back to my place when this shindig concludes."

With no warning, a photographer, armed with a camera the size of a small suitcase, ran out onto the dance floor and yelled out, "Smile!" The flash that followed all but blinded Shelby.

"See," Sparks quipped, "you dance with the likes of Gable and Cooper, and no one notices. But when I take you in my arms, the press rushes out to record the moment for history."

"It will be little more than a footnote," she mocked, looking for a way out of his grip.

"You sell me short," he bragged. "The only person in this room who doesn't recognize who I am is you. And deep down, I think you know, but are scared to admit it."

As the song ended, Shelby pushed out of Sparks's arms and made a harsh suggestion. "I think it's time we both find our dates." She pointed across the room, "Yours is over there and looks lonely. Good-bye."

Standing alone for the first time in almost three

hours, she stood in the middle of the ballroom and studied the scene. Her gown, as tight as it was, was still one of the most modest at the party, and though she felt like a painted lady, she wore far less makeup than any other woman she saw. Almost everyone was either drinking or smoking or eating food she didn't recognize. Though she'd gotten caught up in the moment, she now recognized she was out of place. She didn't belong here and no longer wanted to be here. Why had she accepted the invitation?

Needing a breath of fresh air, she noted doors that were opened onto a huge patio. Walking slowly in that direction she weaved past a couple of dozen different people and overheard tidbits of nine or ten conversations. Just before she got to the door she stepped by Ellen Rains, outfitted in a yellow dress and matching hat, and made it out into the warm, evening air. Standing by a three-foot-high stone wall and looking out at the huge swimming pool was her date. She wasted no time joining him.

"Been a while since I've seen you," she said.

"I got tired of the small talk about nothing," he answered. "You want a drink? I'll be happy to get you one."

She shook her head, "I don't drink."

"Oh, I know that, but I just wanted to see if you'd changed any over the past few hours."

"Why would I?" she demanded.

He reached his hand to her chin and lifted it until their eyes met. He then explained, "Because you've been getting so much attention that it made Joan Crawford sick enough she had to go home. Since you walked in no man in this place has been able to take his eyes off you, and most of the women hate you for being so beautiful. And every woman I've known who has experienced that is never the same again."

"If you're asking," she replied, "if I am going to throw the past away, the answer is no. No matter what those ads in magazines and on radio say, a dress does not make a woman. And dancing with Clark Gable doesn't make me want to give up the morals my folks taught me and I heard preached about in church." She smiled and looked back through the doors to the ballroom, "Don't get me wrong, this is every little girl's dream, but it didn't turn my head or change my heart. If it had, then it would have only proven that my backbone and my mind are weak." She winked, "Someday I'll take you to an Oklahoma barn dance and show you what real fun is. Now, I'm ready to go home, if you are."

"I've been ready since before we got here," he admitted. "But for two reasons I'm glad I came. The first is that I got to see you in that gown. The second is knowing that there is at least one person in this world who still treasures being real."

45

June 30, 1936

Ellen Rains sat in her swanky office and studied the photograph that had just been developed and printed. The shot was sharp, crisp, and perfectly framed, and the subjects were simply beautiful. If she'd owned a magazine, it would have been cover material.

Satisfied the picture fit her needs, she glanced at her notes. The girl's eyes were Carolina blue and her hair honey blonde. She was five-four and blessed with a Miss America body. She moved with both power and grace. Her voice displayed her Oklahoma roots, but her tone projected a rare confidence. She embraced her faith and held herself to high virtues.

Rains moved her desk chair two feet until she sat in front of her typewriter. Picking up a sheet of paper, she rolled it into the machine and then placed her fingers on the keys. Within seconds, the room was alive with the song of a journalist at work. Ten minutes and three sheets of paper later, her story was finished. She read through it once before picking up her office phone and ordering her assistant to come in to see her.

Susan Chontos, dressed in a brown suit and

heels, knocked once before letting herself into the office. As Rains studied the photo for a last time, the ever-patient Chontos stood in front of the desk and waited.

"Susan, let's get this over to the *Times* for the afternoon edition. Tell them I want it played up big."

After taking the photograph and copy attached to it, Chontos scanned the story. "Miss Rains, you didn't mention the woman's name."

"I'm not going to yet," the columnist explained. "We are going to build this one up this whole week. I want to start the focus with Flynn Sparks finding a new gal who has beauty, brains, and morals. In the past, most of his dates have only had one of those qualities. I'll let you guess which one. Tomorrow, I'll drop in the name of the mystery woman and the fact she isn't an actress. I'll add more as the week goes on."

"Sounds like you have the stories already written," Chontos noted.

"If the people at Galaxy do their part," she admitted, "I do. Now hurry that over to the *Times* and tell them it needs to go out to every newspaper that runs my column. By tomorrow, I want fifty million people to have seen that photo. I want Flynn and this beautiful mystery woman to be the talk of the nation."

As her girl Friday left to run the errand, Rains eased back in her chair. For the next few days, she would be playing a very strange role. She'd be building up a big star rather than tearing one down. If her plan worked, by the following Sunday she'd recast Flynn Sparks as a former sinner turned saint and have created a hurdle so high that the cops would never be able to touch him for the murders.

46

June 30, 1936

Bill Barrister sat at his desk and studied the information he'd just received on Wanda McMillan. Her child was named Ron; he was a good student who, over the past year, had settled into life with Bertha Kemp. Kemp had worked with McMillan for just over a year when the woman was given the child to keep for a week or two. Now, for all practical purposes the boy, who would be nine tomorrow, was hers.

Regrettably, in their phone conversation, Kemp was able to give the cop just minimal information on McMillan. Wanda was a local girl, and her parents died a few years ago in a car wreck. She'd been a so-so student in high school and the word was that her morals were suspect. She was cute but not beautiful. She'd never married nor had she shared why it was so important for her to leave her son for a trip to Los Angeles.

"What do you have?" Barry Jenkins asked as he strolled into the office, tossed his hat on a table, and sat down in front of his boss.

"Very little," Barrister admitted. "The woman who is still taking care of McMillan's son tells me Wanda never mentioned knowing anyone on the West Coast. So who did she come to see?"

"The killer?" Jenkins suggested.

The captain shrugged, "Perhaps, but I've got another angle I need to work on. I called the Gary, Indiana, police to get me more information on McMillan's son. They are running down that information now. I'm hoping a call will soon give us something to go on." The words had no more than escaped his lips when the phone rang. The cop smiled and grabbed the receiver. "Barrister here."

"This is Jack Hurst in Gary. I've got the information you wanted, but I'm not sure what it means."

"Anything might help, so give it to me."

"I was expecting the son's birth certificate to not list a father."

Barrister nodded, "As was I."

"But she did list a name. It was William Hamilton."

"Do you have any information on him?"

"Barrister, before I called you I did some checking around. Drove over to the high school and looked at yearbooks. There was no William Hamilton that was in Wanda's class and none in the four classes above or below her. There are three other William Hamiltons who live in this area, and none of them knew Wanda. In fact, they are not even the right age to have run into her. It would take weeks to run down all the William Hamiltons in this part of the state as well as those in Illinois and Michigan. We just don't have the manpower to undertake a task like that."

"That's OK, Jack, I have more than I did before your call. Did you run down any more information on Wanda?"

"Based on the high school yearbook, she was attractive, but was not into very much. Her senior picture doesn't list many clubs or activities. She grabbed a series of jobs after graduating, and her record at Montgomery Ward, where she was a secretary, was solid. She lived in a rental with her son. When she didn't return from the trip, the man who owned the place waited a month, got rid of her stuff, and leased it to someone else. She didn't go to church and didn't have a crowd she ran with. She did date a lot of different men over the years, but never settled down with any of them. And that was all I was able to find out."

Barrister rubbed his head and looked toward his partner before posing one more question for the man who'd called. "Jack, are there any unsolved murders in your area that might have taken place in the past? They need to be cases where a woman or women were strangled."

"I've been on the force for twenty years," the Gary cop explained, "and I don't know of any in our city. There were a couple of society dames strangled in Chicago in the late twenties. Those murders were never solved."

"Interesting," Barrister replied, "I'll call the police there and get some more information on those cases. And Jack, could you send me a photo of Wanda from her high school yearbook?"

"Sure, it might take a few days."

"That's fine, and thanks for all your work. If you ever need anything from out our way, give us a call."

"You're more than welcome; hope you get the guy who did this."

Barrister set the phone back into the cradle and frowned. Picking up a pencil, he doodled on a piece of typing paper for a few moments before looking to his partner. "Barry, we need to find every William Hamilton in this part of the world and question them about Wanda McMillan. My guess is the father of the woman's son moved here and somehow made a lot of money. When she found out, she was coming to Los Angeles to cash in."

"Blackmail?"

The captain nodded, "If Hamilton is a successful businessman, if he has a family, if he is well-

260

known, then he would want to hide an old affair that produced a son. People have been murdered for less."

"But how does that tie in with the others? If this was a murder to avoid blackmail then what was the motive in the others? Those appear more like thrill killings."

Barrister leaned back in his chair and stared at the ceiling, "Barry, were you here when David Lane headed up homicide?"

"I met him once or twice when I was rookie."

"After a while," the captain explained, "the job got to him. It got to where he was carrying it home with him every night. One night he didn't go directly home. Instead, he stopped by a bar and had the first drink in his whole life. He went back again the next night and the night after that. Soon, he couldn't get through a day or a night without the booze. It cost him his job, his family and, one night, while out driving, his life."

"But," Jenkins cut in, "what does that have to do with our case?"

Barrister's gaze fell from the ceiling to his partner, "Maybe our murderer killed Wanda to keep her quiet and found out he liked it. After that, something deep down in the far reaches of his mind demanded that he experience that feeling again. Like Lane had to have a drink, this guy has to watch women die."

Jenkins scratched his head, "So does this mean

that we no longer have Flynn Sparks in our sights?"

"No," Barrister quickly replied, "Sparks is still someone I am keeping my eye on, but now we need to find William Hamilton and shake him down too. So let's get to work."

47

July 1, 1936

Dalton Andrews, dressed for his role of Bill Barrister, stood on the Galaxy back lot and watched director Vic Melton set up the next shot. Sitting in a chair a few feet away was Flynn Sparks. Though he'd not been required to say a single line so far today, he looked uncomfortable. For much of the morning, he'd watched Hunter Nelson play Flynn Sparks on a date with Leslie Bryant. Bryant was being played by Eilene Waters, who was on loan from MGM. She was a raven-haired beauty who could have been Bryant's sister. She was almost as good at being Bryant as Bryant was.

With cast and crew looking on, Nelson and Waters reenacted the nightclub dinner and then the evening spent at the set designed to stand in for Flynn Sparks's home. During these scenes, Andrews spent as much time watching the real Sparks as he did the pretend version. During most of the shooting, the real Sparks had not even been able to watch the action. Now it was time to play the scene where the two policemen study Leslie Bryant's body, and Sparks was as nervous as a cat that had been cornered by hungry hounds.

Melton was looking at a crime scene photo while instructing Waters how and where to lie down. Once he was satisfied he had the actress properly situated, he walked over to Sparks and signaled Andrews to join them.

"You should have memorized your lines by now," the director said, "right now the camera is getting close-ups of the body. We'll cut those in and out in the final edit." He glanced over to his crew who gave him the thumbs-up. "Let's see if we can do this quickly. I'd love to actually get the shooting finished early enough tonight to spend some time with my family."

As Andrews watched Sparks follow Melton over to the mocked-up crime scene, he reached inside his pocket and rubbed his fingers over the handkerchief he'd found in the back floorboard of his Packard. When the director positioned Sparks in place, Andrews pulled his hand from his pocket and strolled over to his own mark. As he did, Melton backed away.

"Action."

Assuming the role of Barrister, Andrews pushed his hat back on his head and stuffed his hands into his pants pockets. "I'm getting tired of this, Barry. I mean, it's getting old. There's a man out there taunting me. He's killing women just to prove to me he's my superior. This is personal."

Sparks looked from Andrews to the body, "I . . . I . . . " He waved, "I can't remember my line."

Melton called out from his chair, "You say, Bill, this guy is a madman. He has no morals. He kills for the pure joy of draining the life out of these girls."

Sparks nodded, "I got it. Let's try it again."

Andrews once more said his line, and once more Sparks blew his. It took five takes before Sparks, playing Jenkins, managed to get through the three short sentences, and even then, the delivery was anything but smooth. Still, even though it wasn't perfect, Melton kept the scene going.

The next line belonged to Andrews. "Barry, have you seen this morning's paper?"

"No, Captain, I haven't."

Andrews jerked the *Times* from his coat pocket, opened it up, and pointed to a photo. "This story, by Ellen Rains, shows Leslie Bryant with the actor Flynn Sparks. She even spent the night with him on Saturday night. She died sometime on Sunday, so do you know what that means?"

Sparks was supposed to verbally answer, but instead the actor just shook his head. When Melton didn't yell cut, Andrews kept going.

"That means Sparks is the first suspect we've

had. And it makes sense to me too. The guy has a laundry list of offenses over the years. He thinks he's above the law. And on top of that he's a playboy who has no respect for women."

Andrews looked from the body to Sparks, who was at the moment supposed to be playing Jenkins. The line that was supposed to come never did. Finally, after ten painful seconds Melton called, "Cut. What is wrong with you, Flynn? All you have to say is, 'Let's go get him.' "

"Let me see a script," Sparks mumbled. As a woman brought the pages to the actor, Andrews stepped over to Melton.

"Vic, I've read the police files, Barrister didn't have a newspaper with him at the scene. It was another cop who recognized the body as that of Leslie. Aren't we supposed to be shooting it as it really happened?"

"It would take too much time," the director explained, "so we are consolidating whenever we can." He leaned closer and whispered, "I know it's good box office to cast Flynn in this role, but do you think he can handle it? I mean, the press is being pretty brutal right now and having to spit out lines that paint him as Suspect Number One seems pretty cruel."

Andrews looked to Sparks, before softly asking, "Do you think he did it?"

"Flynn? Of course not."

"Then," Andrews suggested, "as long as the

scriptwriters prove the Hollywood Madman is someone else, things will be fine. And if they don't, then you and I will be a part of a movie that will live forever. So, as I see it, Vic, you can't lose."

Melton nodded, "You ready, Flynn?"

"Yeah, I think so."

"Then let's get back to work."

48

July 2, 1936

Shelby Beckett was bent over a table sewing intricate beadwork on a yellow gown when a man entered the finishing room and called out her name. She looked up and into the smiling face of Jacob Yates. Just behind him was a team of people, including Flynn Sparks.

"I need to borrow you for a while," the studio boss explained. "Where is Betsy?"

"I'm over here," Minser wryly noted. "You walked right past me when you came in."

"I guess I missed you," Yates answered. "Betsy, I need Shelby in a really nice work outfit. Something that we'd put one of our stars in if she were playing a professional woman. I have people here who will do her hair and makeup. When we get her all fixed up, I need some shots of her with Flynn. She can be pretending to fix a button on his coat and maybe mending his shirt or something. After that, I need her in a dress, and we'll get shots of them walking around the lot. Maybe Flynn could be carrying a load of costumes as if he was helping her take the stuff to a sound-stage. And, after that, she'll need a Sunday outfit so that we can take some pictures of them at our church on the Western set."

"Why do you need all this?" Minser demanded.

"Because," Yates announced, "I like that idea Shelby had on the church. And Flynn did too. So we are going to make the two of them the chair-men to making it happen. Right now, Ellen Rains is talking about the project on radio. Later today, we are announcing a contest for fans to win passes to attend worship services there next Sunday. Betty Foster is going to sing the special music, we are bringing in a choir, Cubby Wickins is going to play piano and Reverend Gerald Chance is coming out of retirement to give the message. Some of the top celebrities on our lot will be in the pews with the fans. After it's all over, we're catering a dinner on the ground for everyone. And, to top it all off, the Mutual Radio Network is going to broadcast it live! And this is just the start. We are going to do this every week. Galaxy Studios is going to be a beacon for morality and faith, a place where stars and fans come together as one to sing and pray."

"This doesn't sound like you," Minser noted.

"Maybe not the old me," he agreed as he walked quickly over to Shelby's side, "but thanks to this young woman, I've discovered a way for Galaxy to give back to America and promote the lessons on morality we often embrace in our films. Can I hear an 'Amen'?"

"Amen," Willard Mace answered weakly.

"OK," an enthusiastic Yates continued, "we have to be at the church by two, and I want those other shots finished by then. Most of the national media will be at the church this afternoon, and almost every star on our lot will be in the pews. This is going to be big!"

Minser looked to Shelby and shrugged. The young woman returned the gesture with a confused smile.

"Betsy," Yates announced, "I need to speak to you about Miss Beckett's clothes. Because she and Flynn will be the center of this 'Bringing Faith to Hollywood' movement, I need for you to get her outfits that will make her look beautiful and wholesome. Also, I will send a makeup and hair team down here each morning to have her all dolled up. After all, you never know who will be coming by for a visit. For all I know, the Pope might want a piece of this action."

Minser winced, "I think you might want to phrase that a bit differently."

"Come over here, Betsy," Yates suggested, "let's you and me have a private talk."

As the studio head outlined his plans to the wardrobe chief, Flynn crossed the room and pulled Shelby to one side. When he was sure Yates was not watching, he whispered, "I didn't do this. No matter how the studio spins it, this wasn't my idea. And I had nothing to do with that picture in the newspaper."

"What picture?" Shelby asked.

"The one in Ellen Rains's column," he explained. "It was taken at Standhoff's party. Her article indicates that you are the new love of my life."

"Really?" She all but spat, "and I don't get any say in this?"

"Shelby, I'm not sorry we are going to spend some time together, but I wish it was because you were entranced by my charms, not because Yates sees it as good publicity." He stopped, smiled, and finally added, "Did you know that every time I look into your eyes it's as if the dark blue sea was begging me to jump in?"

She frowned, "OK, what movie was that from?"

"*Lady Love*," he admitted. "It worked in the movie."

"Flynn," she hissed, "those hokey Hollywood lines don't work on me. Now, why is the studio really doing this?"

He took a deep breath, "Probably because they think I killed all those girls. The way this business

269

operates is that enough good publicity can erase any sin in the world."

Shelby didn't hesitate firing back, "Did you?"

"I can't believe you'd think that of me," he argued.

Before she had a chance to follow up, a quartet of people from the hair and makeup departments grabbed Shelby and whisked her back to a dressing room. She'd barely caught her breath when the transformation began.

49

July 2, 1936

True to his word, by two, every major news organization and most of the Galaxy stars were gathered inside the church to listen to Jacob Yates explain what he had planned for Sundays at the studio. As writers hovered on his every word and jotted down quote after quote, photographers took hundreds of photos of actors and actresses dressed in their Sunday best while sitting reverently in pews. In the very front were Flynn Sparks and Shelby.

After Yates finished, Dennis Moltry, the studio's musical director, led those gathered in an interesting rendition of "Amazing Grace." Once the unprepared actors put their hymnbooks down,

Flynn Sparks rose to recite the scripted remarks he'd been given to read.

"Church has always meant the world to me. I dearly love the old hymns and treasure the times of my youth spent in Bible study and prayer. When I came west, I forgot the faith of my youth and fell into things that the old Flynn would have never even considered. Who knows how long I would have continued along that path if I had not been asked to attend a church service by one of the women from our wardrobe department? Shelby Beckett is responsible for not only waking me up to the creature I'd become, but reminding me of who I should be. After all, we actors are role models; young people across the country and world look to us as heroes. We therefore have a responsibility to meet that challenge."

As Flynn's memorized words continued, Dalton Andrews leaned up from his spot on the second row and whispered into Shelby's ear, "I think I might be sick."

As Shelby smoothed her red and white suit, one that Minser had hurriedly found and altered for this event, she nodded at Andrews's comment and then studied those watching this hastily prepared attempt at goodwill. Like many in the building, she was wondering if this was going to be just another piece of Hollywood fantasy or did her idea have a chance at bringing something real to Galaxy Studios? As the mayor, chief of police, and more than a hundred reporters and photographers appeared to be hanging on Sparks's every word, it seemed like at least a few people were buying into Yates actually turning this building into a working church. But as his goal was likely saving a troubled actor's skin, would God buy into this supposed act of faith and find a way to use it? Turning her attention from the unusual congregation back to Sparks, she once more tuned in on his words.

"So, in closing, I just want to quote my favorite Scripture. 'For I was an hungred, and ye gave me meat: I was thirsty, and ye gave me drink: I was a stranger, and ye took me in: Naked, and ye clothed me: I was sick, and ye visited me: I was in prison, and ye came unto me. Then shall the righteous answer him, saying, Lord, when saw we thee an hungred, and fed *thee?* or thirsty, and gave *thee* drink? When saw we thee a stranger, and took *thee* in? or naked, and clothed *thee?* Or when saw we thee sick, or in prison, and came unto *thee?* And the King shall answer and say unto them, Verily I say unto you, Inasmuch as ye have done *it* unto one of the least of these my brethren, ye have done *it* unto me.' Thank you."

As Sparks stepped down from behind the pulpit, Yates rose and took the actor's place. After thanking his number-one-box-office draw, he looked to Shelby.

"This young woman, a simple but beautiful girl

from Oklahoma, is the inspiration behind taking this building and using it for something higher than just a setting for movie scenes. She gave birth to this idea. Now, I would like Miss Shelby Beckett to come to where I now stand and say a few words."

The invitation to speak caught Shelby completely off guard. Her heart caught in her throat as she stood on suddenly wobbly legs and walked up the three steps to the podium. As Yates stepped aside, she moved over and took a deep breath. Yet, rather than speak, she closed her eyes and silently prayed. As the impatient gathering looked on, she finally lifted her head and opened her mouth.

"When I told my supervisor, Betsy Minser, in wardrobe, that I thought it was a shame a building like this was not really used as a church, I had no idea she would share my thoughts with Mr. Yates." She paused and looked out on the crowd until her gaze locked onto Dalton Andrews. He smiled, as she continued, "A friend told me that everyone in Hollywood is just an illusion. All we do in the studios is pretend. My prayer is that on Sunday mornings in this building, we can transform a bit of movie magic into a place where real faith can live and grow."

As the camera snapped pictures and a few applauded, Shelby stepped away from the pulpit, walked down the steps and back to her pew. A few minutes later, after Reverend Gerald Chance, looking wise and distinguished in a three-piece dark blue suit, prayed, the doors opened, actors rushed back to their sets, reporters and photographers hurried off the lot, and Yates and his crew went back to their offices, leaving Shelby completely alone in the small building.

Looking to a painting of Jesus hanging on the church's back wall, she began to sing.

As along life's way you go,
Clouds may hide the light of day.
Have no fear for well you know,
Love will roll the clouds away.

When the road is rough and long,
And the world is cold and gray.
Lift your voice in happy song,
Love will roll the clouds away.

50

July 4, 1936

On Thursday, Shelby accepted a date to spend Independence Day on Catalina Island with Dalton Andrews. On Friday morning, Jacob Yates informed her the publicity generated by the announcement of church services on the studio lot was so overwhelming that she'd been invited to a holiday event sponsored by the city in Griffith Park. A few minutes later, she and Betsy Minser were assigned the task of making a red, white and blue outfit for Shelby to wear. At lunch, she informed Andrews that they would have to change their plans and enjoy the fireworks at the park. He was fine with that. But at three, when Yates came down to watch Shelby model the dress, he further informed her that Flynn Sparks would be escorting her to the city's celebration. Andrews did not take well to having their date broken. In fact, he stormed off without saying anything. Now it was Saturday afternoon, and what started as potentially the most wonderful July 4th she'd ever known had become a nightmare.

Sparks, dressed in a white shirt, red tie, and blue slacks, picked Shelby up at six. They drove to the park in silence. While both of them smiled and mingled with movie fans and the social elite at the gathering, neither really said much to each other until they got into Sparks's Auburn and headed back toward the city.

"You've been quiet," she noted as she glanced over as he drove.

"The heat's been turned up," he explained. "What do you know about the movie I'm filming right now?"

"Nothing too specific. I've heard that it is based on the murders of the actresses."

"It's the true story," he corrected her. "They are

pulling it from police files. And, I don't know if you realize this, but the cops actually believe I did it."

"Did what?" she asked.

He frowned, "Don't play dumb. You know what I mean."

"Do I?"

They rode in silence for a couple of blocks, during that time Shelby leaned her head against the edge of the convertible top and let the breeze coming through the open window blow through her hair. She was all but lost in the warm breeze when he finally broke the silence.

"It's all Leslie Bryant's fault. If she'd lived a couple of more days, they wouldn't be punishing me the way they are. I even think the cops are following me. I think they are watching my every move."

"Flynn, what makes you think that?"

"Everywhere I go I see people that look like policemen, and they seem to be watching me."

"You're a star," Shelby pointed out, "everyone knows you. So naturally when people see you, they stare."

As he guided the powerful car around a curve he shrugged, "Maybe, but even if you're right, Yates has me on a leash. He's not even letting me take women to my house. If he finds any girl there, he is going to fine me. I had to let my maid go and she is sixty!"

Shelby tried unsuccessfully to stifle a smile as she quipped, "I think you'll live."

"It's like being a priest," he complained. "And speaking of that, there is this church thing. Not only do I have to pose for pictures, give interviews, and memorize Bible verses that were supposedly my favorites as a child, but I have to be there not just this week, but every week."

"Yeah," she laughed, "that hour or two each Sunday is going to kill you."

"And then there is the media attention," he moaned, "Did you see this morning's paper?"

"No."

"There's one behind the seat, take a look. There are four pages of photographs of you and me together. The story makes us sound like we're about to get married. I mean, you're the only woman in the world who won't let me kiss you, and they have us practically engaged. What kind of a cruel joke is this? How can I get a woman interested in me when the press is printing this kind of garbage?"

She raised her eyebrows, "I thought you wanted to go out with me!"

"I did," he spat, "and I still do. But I am not interested in marrying you. And when folks think we are an item, it messes up my love life."

Shelby grabbed the copy of the *Times* and glanced through the text. She quickly discovered she was quoted in the story about how close she and Sparks had become. "My word," she moaned. "They have me as your spiritual guide, the love of your life, and the woman who has tamed the playboy! I never said those things."

"Now you know how things operate," he suggested. "The publicity department makes up whatever it takes to frame their stars in the best light possible."

"But," she complained, "I'm not a star."

"Yeah," he shot back, "try telling that to millions who see you as the woman who is causing Hollywood to look at its sins and back away from them. It won't be long before they'll tag you as Saint Shelby."

Sparks suddenly smiled, "This might work out all right. You can actually date me. People will see it as nothing more than a prayer session, and Yates will not care if you go to my place. I'll finally get to show you the view and, once you're there, you'll likely be wooed enough to enjoy at least some of my charms."

"Yeah," she cracked, "you just keep on dreaming."

He smiled, "We'll see."

The rest of the twenty-minute drive to her house was made in silence. As the car stopped out in front of the Becketts' bungalow, Sparks reached to the passenger side of the Auburn, wrapped his hand around Shelby's neck and roughly pulled her lips to his. She didn't have time to react.

When he finally released her and dropped his arm to his side, he grinned, "I'll see you in church."

Still stunned, Shelby opened the door and stepped out into the grass. Wide-eyed, she watched the Auburn's taillights as they disappeared into the night. In a matter of just four days, she'd lost complete control of her life.

51

July 4, 1936

Somewhere in the night, kids were shooting off firecrackers and a radio was playing patriotic tunes, but, as she stood motionless in the darkness, Shelby didn't hear any of it. She was still trying to comprehend what had just happened. As she turned the events of the night over in her head, a hand grabbed her shoulder and whirled her around.

"I thought you said this was Yates's idea."

Even in the dark it was apparent that Dalton Andrews's face was flushed, his expression angry, and his eyes on fire. His rage was made even more apparent by his digging his fingers into her shoulders so deeply it hurt.

"Dalton, what are you doing here?"

"Watching the show," he snarled. "And what a show it was."

"Are you talking about the kiss?"

"What else?"

"Flynn sprung that on me," she snapped. "We hadn't so much as held hands up until then."

Andrews dropped his hands from her shoulder and shook his head. "Great story. I read the papers. I saw all the pictures. I read what you said. When are you heading to Reno to get hitched?"

Shelby vigorously shook her head, as if that would help soothe the angry man, before pleading, "I didn't say any of those things in that article. I didn't even know about the story until Flynn showed it to me."

"How many autographs did you sign today?" he demanded.

"I don't remember," she admitted. "And I don't know why people asked me for them. I work in wardrobe."

He laughed, "Wake up, the studio is grooming you for two things. The first is as a tool to keep Sparks out of jail. The second is to create the ultimate story of a girl who sews dresses being discovered and transformed into Hollywood's new All-American girl. They have their hooks into you now. How long before you really become one of us? How long before you take your high and mighty ways and throw them in the trash?"

"Dalton, how can you even suggest that?"

"Because I've seen it happen a thousand times. Girls come out here with virtue and trade it for a shot at stardom. A few make it, but most wind up in either the gutter or the grave." His eyes flashed, "Look at Leslie Bryant, she was just like you. She could sing hymns and quote Scripture. She cherished her morality and clung to her values. Then I saw her sleeping in Flynn Sparks bed, and believe me, that's the gutter. And later that day, she bought her ticket to the grave. How long before you go down that same path?"

His words so stung that Shelby didn't stop to consider what she was doing. Pulling her hand back, she brought it hard against his face. The resulting noise was so loud it echoed off the street.

It only took a second for Andrews to react, reaching out with his hands and grabbing the woman by the throat. He left them there for a moment, but he never tightened his grip. A second later, he dropped his arms to his side, turned and slowly walked off into the night, leaving Shelby confused, hurt, and frightened.

52

July 5, 1936

Just like any other Galaxy production, the first service in the white church on the studio lot started on time, and each well-rehearsed element went off without a hitch. With Jacob Yates beaming from the back room and the Mutual Radio Network taking the service into millions of living rooms all across the nation, the choir sang "A Mighty Fortress Is Our God," the congregation, which included more than fifty actors and actresses, came together on four well-known and much-loved hymns, Flynn Sparks read Scripture from the book of Matthew, and Reverend Chance gave a moving message on the Sermon on the Mount. From her assigned seat on the first row next to Sparks, Shelby watched the fans that'd won tickets to the performance. Few seemed to pay much attention to anything but the stars that'd been assigned to fill pews.

The dinner on the ground was just as well organized. There were matching blankets, hundreds of pounds of fried chicken, and enough cherry pie to feed an army. Studio photographers roamed through the proceedings snapping shots of fans with their favorite stars. And autograph books outnumbered Bibles three to one.

Outfitted in a simple blue suit made by Betsy Minser, Shelby posed for a few photos before moving away from the picnic area and sitting on the church steps. As she watched the events from her perch, a short, heavy man in a dark suit approached.

"It was a nice service," he noted. "I guess you must be proud?"

"Are you a member of the press?" Shelby asked.

"No," he replied, "My name is Bill Barrister." He reached inside his coat pocket and produced his badge and credentials. "I'm a cop. Did you want to talk to the press?"

"No," she admitted, "but if you were press or one of the fans who won tickets to the big event, my answer would have had to have been much different to that question."

"And why's that?" he asked.

She looked into his round face and dark eyes, "I guess I would have told you how this was a dream come true and I hoped it was the first sign of a new day in Hollywood."

He smiled while putting his size eight shoe on the bottom step, "Well, that sounds good."

"But," she assured him, "it's not what Shelby Beckett would really say. Dalton Andrews is right; this place is already changing me. I'm already learning how to play a part."

"I don't think I'm following you," Barrister admitted.

"OK," she explained, "I was really disappointed in the service. It wasn't real. The songs had no passion, the prayers were nothing more than scripted words and the man reading the Scripture didn't even understand what he read. It was great theater, but it wasn't church. Oh, and those stars who shouted 'Amen,' they were doing so on cue."

"Does it matter?"

She shrugged, "I guess to those fans out there it doesn't. And maybe to those listening on the radio it doesn't either. But I've been in real churches and heard the songs of people who were hurting or lost. They might have not been on key, but they sang from their hearts. And the dinner on the ground wasn't catered."

Barrister nodded, "I get it. But you know, this is the first time I've been in church in more than a decade, and, let me assure you that I got something out of it. It kind of showed me something I'd been missing. So don't write this off too quickly. And something you need to remember, the first services in most new churches are pretty much scripted and polished. The spontaneity takes a while."

Shelby glanced back out at the picnic and noted her parents eating on a blanket with Sally Glenn and Simon Taylor. They seemed to be having the time of their lives.

"Miss Beckett." Shelby's attention turned once more to the policeman. "May I sit beside you for a moment? I need to ask a favor."

"Sure, the stair is open."

After he positioned himself to her right, Barrister looked toward the crowd. "Miss Beckett, I've read in the newspapers that you and Mr. Sparks are a couple."

She grimly smiled, "Don't believe what you read."

The cop looked stunned. "So you aren't dating him?"

"Only when the studio arranges it," she explained. "I hope this doesn't come off the wrong way, but I have higher standards than he offers."

"I see." Barrister scratched the bald spot on his head before continuing, "Is there any way I could get you to consider dating Mr. Sparks? It would be a great help to an investigation I'm conducting."

"I'd rather not," she firmly replied. "He's a chump."

"I think he might be a murderer," the cop sincerely shot back. "I was hoping you could help us find out. I need someone to get into his home and see if there is any evidence connecting him to six different murders."

"Six?" A suddenly shocked Shelby turned her shoulders to face the cop. "I thought you were looking at him because of what happened to Leslie Bryant."

Barrister nodded, "Besides, Miss Bryant, there have been five others, including an unknown girl who was strangled just a few days ago. And while we can only directly connect Sparks to two of the women right now, it is possible he might have known all of them. After all, they were young and beautiful, and that seems to be his type."

Shelby sat silently, her eyes focused on the

picnic as she considered Barrister's offer. As she thought, he continued.

"Miss Beckett, the murderer in these cases always takes the victim's identification and jewelry. I've talked to psychologists, and they've told me the man is likely keeping the stuff as some sort of bizarre souvenirs. He likely looks through them, maybe even plays with them, to relive the moment of the murder."

"That's just sick," Shelby observed.

"This guy likely appears normal," the cop continued. "He might seem like a nice person, but he is sick. And I think the murderer might just be Flynn Sparks. I want to stop this now, but the studio is so powerful, I can't get a search warrant. No matter the evidence we have against Sparks, I can't touch him. But I thought you might."

Shelby kept her eyes forward as she explained, "I'm not the kind of girl who goes to his house. Women who go there leave parts of themselves behind. What stays there can't be recovered."

"Some who go there might even die," he argued. "Do you want him to keep his free pass to murder?"

"No," she quickly answered, "but I don't believe he's your guy. I mean, he's consumed by his own desires and lusts, he is the most egotistical human I've ever met, but I can't see him killing a person."

"Then," Barrister suggested, "by helping us, you could prove me wrong."

Shelby stood and turned to face the cop, "I'm not going to give up my innocence to prove his. Now, if you will excuse me, I'm going to spend some time with my parents."

"Miss Beckett."

"Yes."

Barrister reached into his pocket and retrieved a card, "If you change your mind, please call me."

She grabbed the card, looking at the name and number written on the paper before pushing it into her Bible, tucking the book under her arm, and walking off.

53

July 6, 1936

This was the first time the cast and crew had traveled off the lot for a location shoot, and it took a dozen security guards to keep fans and the press away from the action. A bored Dalton Andrews stood beside a seemingly anxious Flynn Sparks as Vic Melton went over instructions with an eager young actress neither one of the actors had met.

As the director droned on, Andrews looked toward a barely moving stream and wryly noted, "It's so appropriate that we get our drinking water from an aqueduct. In Hollywood, even the rivers are manmade. Is nothing real here?"

Sparks shook his head, "I wear this same suit in every scene; don't cops ever change clothes?"

"Not on what they get paid," Andrews cracked. "You make more in a week than they do in a year." He glanced back to where Melton was explaining to the actress how to play dead before looking back to Sparks, "You weren't on the set this morning."

"No reason to be," he shot back. "I wasn't in any of the scenes."

"Actually," Andrews laughed, "you were. Well, at least Hunter Nelson was playing you in a restaurant scene. The actress playing your date looked a lot like the girl who played that scene in that bathing suit. You know, the first victim of the Hollywood Madman."

"That's such a stupid name," Sparks grumbled.

"What was that girl's name, you know the one you took to Musso and Frank's?"

"I take a lot of girls there," Sparks boasted. "You can't expect me to remember all of them."

Andrews rolled his eyes, "The name is on the tip of my tongue. Let me see . . . it was Sharp—Alison Sharp."

"Agnes," Sparks chimed in.

"So you do remember. Have you been out with her again?"

"No," he replied, "once was enough."

"Strange," Andrews noted, "I haven't seen her around the lot either. And now the girl playing our next victim looks like Agnes."

"This is Hollywood," Sparks cracked, "a lot of blondes look alike."

Andrews worked his way down the sloping ground to where Melton was finishing giving directions. He more closely inspected the woman in blue before turning his gaze up the hill. Sparks was on edge . . . why? Andrews looked back to the woman.

"I'm Dalton, and you are?"

"This is Rose Trebour," Melton explained, "She's new to the lot. Talent scout found her on Broadway."

"Nice to be working with you, Rose."

"I've been hoping to get the chance to work with you for years," she answered, a hint of Brooklyn in her voice.

The actor nodded before pulling Melton to the side and whispering, "What's up with Flynn? He's not himself today."

"What do you mean?"

"The Flynn Sparks we know would have already signed this girl up for a date. He hasn't even tried to meet her."

The director looked up to where Sparks was standing, "Maybe what they're writing in the papers is true. Perhaps that wardrobe girl has reformed him. If I were twenty years younger and single, I'd be going to church with her too."

Andrews frowned and glared at his costar. At this moment, there was nothing he wouldn't do to keep Shelby away from Flynn Sparks. Nothing!

54

July 7, 1936

The sun was just coming up as a sleepy Bill Barrister joined Barry Jenkins on a hillside just inside Griffith Park. As the crime scene crew waited for the light to get a bit brighter, the captain stuck his hands in the pockets of his gray slacks and looked toward a small pond.

"Barry, does anyone ever fish out here?"

"I don't know, is it legal?"

Barrister sadly nodded, "I haven't fished in years. When I was young, I even made my own flies. I used to wade into cold mountain streams and spend hours working the shallows. It didn't matter if I caught anything, just enjoyed being there. Now the only place I enjoy is home. It's like I close the door and hide. I don't even go out and talk to my neighbors anymore."

The captain kicked a small rock and watched it roll down the hill. "Barry, do you ever dream?"

"Sure Bill, doesn't everybody?"

"Are your dreams happy or sad?"

"Mostly happy, I guess," Jenkins answered. "I've never really thought much about it."

Barrister grimly frowned, "In my dreams, all I see are the faces of these dead women. Their lips keep moving like they are trying to tell me something, but I can't hear what they are saying." He nodded as he looked toward the sky, "Looks like we have enough light now to check things out."

The two solemnly walked back to where the crime scene crew was doing their job. Barrister leaned down to study the woman for a few seconds before inventorying the locale. Without looking back to the body he asked, "Who found her?"

"I guess you'd call him a ranger or something," Jenkins explained. "He's an old guy who looks after this part of the park. He picks up trash, gives people directions, and is trained to apply first aid in case someone falls and gets hurt."

"I'm guessing," Barrister groaned, "he didn't see anyone drop her off."

"No." Jenkins answered.

The captain turned around and took a second look at the body. He studied her for a few moments and then noted, "This one is not dressed up for a party. Those are the kind of clothes you'd go shopping in or wear around the house."

"Yeah," Jenkins added, "slacks and a cotton blouse. She has on flats too."

Barrister went down to one knee before saying, "She looks to be about five-feet tall. In fact, she could be the sister of the last victim. The size, the build, the hair color, the facial structure, it's uncanny."

"There's an unused, broken match beside her right hand," Collins pointed out. "I got a photo of it."

"Thanks." Barrister looked up at Jenkins, snapped his fingers, and whispered, "Blue. All these girls had on blue."

His partner quickly disagreed, "Not the bag of bones we found. She was wearing red."

The homicide head nodded, "But all the recent ones, starting with the bathing suit victim, have been outfitted in blue. The psychologist told me there had to be a trigger. He assured me if I kept looking, I would find it. It has to be blue. The color sets the murderer off somehow."

Barrister pushed off the ground and marched up the hill. Just as he topped the rise, he looked over his shoulder and yelled, "Let me know when you get her to Arnie. When she's there I'm going to get that gossip columnist to come over and take a look at this one. I'm betting dollars to donuts that this gal worked in the movie business."

55

July 7, 1936

A phone call started his day way earlier than he'd wanted. And now it was five, the sun hadn't even come up, and Jacob Yates was sitting in a downtown Beverly Hills diner working on a plate of scrambled eggs and toast. This was not the way to begin a Tuesday morning.

Yates glanced up in the long mirror hanging behind the counter and noted Ellen Rains push open the door. She was dressed in light green from her shoes to her hat. She anxiously glanced to both sides of the diner before spotting the mogul. Like a hog on the way to a trough, she rushed to his booth and slid in.

"We see each other way too much," he mockingly cracked.

"It's not something I plan," she assured him as she waved to a waiter. "Coffee, black, and a couple of donuts."

After taking a long sip of juice, Yates took a closer look at the woman who'd called him an hour before. Frowning he blurted out, "You look terrible!"

"I haven't been to bed," she explained. She waited for the waiter to drop off her order before glancing back toward the man. "There's been another one."

"If," he grumbled, "you mean another strangling, I don't want to hear about it."

"Actually," she assured him, "you do. What does the name Rose Trebour mean to you?"

So much color drained from his face he was whiter than a glass of milk. He gasped, "Someone murdered her?"

She sadly nodded, "They brought me in the morgue to look at the body last night. As you'd asked me to do an interview with Miss Trebour the day she first stepped on the lot, I couldn't lie on this one."

"It likely wouldn't have taken the cops long to have made the identification anyway," he noted.

"Does she have any kind of association with Flynn?" Rains asked.

"Yeah," he grimly answered, "they worked on a scene together yesterday. She actually played the blonde the cops haven't ID'd yet."

As the woman picked up a donut and took a bite, Yates pushed his plate away and sighed. His world was tumbling down around him, and there was apparently nothing he could do about it. As he glanced out onto the dark streets, he considered his options. For the first time in his life, none popped into his head.

"You'd think he'd be smart enough to actually stop for a while," he finally observed.

"You mean Flynn?"

"Ellen, who else could I be talking about? Our best bet might be just calling Barrister and turning Sparks over to the cops."

"Not yet," Rains argued. "You still have a movie to finish. And that movie might very well save your studio."

He shook his head, "These murders will bring it tumbling down around me. When this story breaks, the papers will jump all over us for protecting a madman. I might as well shoot myself now."

"Do your people have any proof," she asked, "that you know who the killer is?"

"Are you talking real, concrete proof?" he asked.

"Yes Jacob, the kind that could be presented in court and would convince a jury to vote to send Sparks to the gallows."

"No," he admitted, "I met with the writers and our detectives yesterday, and everything we have on Flynn is circumstantial."

"And," Rains pointed out, "you have more than the police do. So Barrister couldn't arrest him either."

"That's a real comfort," he sarcastically added.

"When you get any real evidence," she suggested, "turn him over to the cops. Until then you need to have your people watch him day and night. Follow his every move."

"I don't know," Yates said, "what if the cops turn up something before we do?"

"Odds are against that happening," Rains assured him. "You've got much more money invested in this than they do. Your team can pay bribes and put pressure on people to lie or even forget. The cops can't do that. Besides, if they do arrest Flynn, I have known what you were doing since day one. I can write stories that point out that you were so concerned about these girls you spent tens of thousands of dollars looking for the killer. I can make you and the studio look like you are pillars of justice."

"You might need to," he cracked.

She gulped down a mouthful of coffee and nodded, "But you have to promise that you'll call me if and when you find out if Flynn did it. I need to know first so I can break the story nationally even before you turn Flynn Sparks over to Barrister. That way I can paint you as a hero father rather than a mogul trying to protect one of his biggest assets."

"I'll make the call," he replied. "Shame about Rose Trebour; that girl had star quality. She was going to make the studio a chunk of change. I actually went to New York and watched her in a play on Broadway. She wasn't like the others this guy murdered; she could act."

"Make sure you send lots of flowers to her

funeral," Rains suggested. "Now, I have to get out of here."

Yates watched the woman take a last bite and then rush out into a city that was still sleeping. Sadly, even though he was living a nightmare, he was one of the few who were actually awake.

56

July 8, 1936

Shelby was sitting at her sewing table cutting out a pattern for a dress that would be needed next week for the film *The Pirate's Lure* when Betsy Minser strolled through the door carrying a man's suit coat. Across the room, Willard Mace looked up and shouted out a greeting. Minser ignored it.

"Shelby, do you have a little time?" the supervisor asked.

"In truth, this is the only thing I'm working on, so I have some time I can spare. Do you have a rush job?"

"This isn't even one we should be doing," Minser complained. "Somehow Flynn Sparks lost a couple of buttons on his coat last night. As it is his personal property, we shouldn't have to deal with it. He should hire someone or take it to the cleaners and have them do it, but, as he is the studio's pet, we will take the job."

"I can do it," Shelby assured her.

"Willie," Minser called out, "will you come over here?"

The big man moved quickly to Shelby's side and waited for instructions.

"You see the two buttons left on this jacket?"

"Yes, Miss Minser."

"There are some coats in storage that have the same buttons. Can you go grab one and bring it back to Shelby?"

"Are they in the men's vault at the far end of the hall?"

Minser nodded, "I think they are."

"I'll be back in a minute," he assured her.

As Shelby stood and stretched, Minser apologized, "I wish I didn't have to ask you to do this. I feel like I'm using you like Yates did last week."

"I work here," Shelby said, "it goes with the territory. I'm just glad to have a job. A lot of people aren't so lucky."

Minser crossed the room, picked up a dress from a table, checked the workmanship, and then hung it up. She let her fingers trace the light blue fabric before turning back. "I don't like this place."

"But you've given your life to it," Shelby argued. "You've been here since the day it opened."

"I know, but I just get tired of the way people are used. Even more, I'm just sick of how they sell themselves for a crack at fame. I mean, men like Flynn are jerks, but his type might be better than the women. So many of them do whatever it takes to land a part. It's just that in Hollywood everything and everyone is for sale, and it makes me sick to my stomach."

Shelby nodded, "That's true, I've seen it."

"Do you understand it?" Minser asked.

Shelby sat back down on her stool, "I guess so. Times are tough; a lot of folks back home go to bed hungry at night. I can't begin to tell you how many people I knew whose eyes looked dead. There was no life in them at all. They were good people, but I think they would have done any-thing . . . and I mean anything . . . to feed their hungry kids. When you want something really bad or you need something even worse, it's hard to say no."

Minser closed the distance between them until she stood across the table from the young woman. "My parents came over from Ireland." She sounded more like a woman confessing to a priest than a friend sharing a story. "I was born here a month after we arrived. My dad died in an accident a year later. Then, when I was three, my older brother and older sister died from influenza. After that, my mother and me lived in a tiny one-room apartment on the top floor of a five-story rooming house in New York City. Somehow, she always found a way to make enough to feed me and buy me nice clothes. She took me to the park and to church. We read books together and she taught me to sew. But several nights a week she left me at home alone. Our landlady watched out for me when my mother was gone. When I was eleven, I found out that Mom sold her body. Her street name was Blue. That's how we survived."

Shelby shook her head, "I'm sorry."

"As a teenager I wanted to die," Minser explained. "And when I got the chance I ran away. I ended up here. Ironic, now I help make the costumes for women who are involved in a more respectable form of selling themselves, and I work with men who use and abuse those women. My life has come full circle and I hate it."

"Not everyone is that way," Shelby assured her. "There are people who still cling to values. And besides, your mother did what she had to do, and she did it because she loved you."

"Shelby," Minser forcefully answered as tears rolled down her cheeks, "she took me to church and at the same time she was . . ."

"I've got a coat," Mace announced as he marched back into room. "I think the buttons match."

Shelby took the jacket and studied it for a moment, "These are perfect, Willie. I'll get right to work on it."

Minser wiped away her tears and stepped over to her desk. Sitting down, she opened and looked at the calendar before announcing, "I need to go out in our little factory and make sure the girls are going to get those European peasant gowns done today. I'll be back in a bit."

As her supervisor walked out, Shelby fell into her normal routine of dumping the coat's pockets onto the table—a matchbook, some change, and some keys fell out. She grabbed a sack, dropped the items into it, folded the top over and stapled it shut. She then wrote on the date and the name Flynn Sparks and pitched the sack onto the designated shelf before starting her work. Five minutes later, she finished and hung the coat on the rack behind the table. She was about to once more work on the dress when Dalton Andrews strolled in.

"I guess you didn't expect to see me," he said.

"It might be a big lot," she answered, "but I figured we'd run into each other at some point."

"I need to apologize," he added. "I was a real heel the other night. I let my emotions overrule my judgment."

"I told you the truth," she assured him. "The studio set up everything. I had no say in it. Just like you have no say in the movies you get."

"Can you forgive me?" he asked. "I'd like to try to make things right between us."

Shelby smiled, "Maybe a movie later in the week?"

"Sounds good," he agreed. "I'll be in touch." Andrews took another look at her before noting,

"That blue dress looks wonderful on you. The color perfectly matches your eyes."

As they were concluding their plans, Flynn Sparks strolled in through the outside door. He looked from the actor to the woman, grinned, and asked, "Is my coat ready?"

57

July 9, 1936

It was a crazy day at work. Shelby was called upon to repair four dresses ripped when a moving cart fell on soundstage 14, take four different sets of publicity photos promoting Galaxy's church services, help create a clown costume for a new scene written into a child's movie starring Mary Bright, and accepted a date with Dalton Andrews to attend a movie premiere on Friday night. Tired and hungry, all she wanted to do when she and her father got home was eat supper and listen to the radio. As it turned out, she didn't even get to go inside the house before a short, wide man in a suit was demanding her attention.

"Mr. Barrister," Shelby announced as she stepped out of the family truck. "What brings you to our house?"

"Can we talk?" the cop asked.

"Who is this man?" John Beckett protectively inquired.

"He's a policeman," Shelby explained. "You probably saw him at the studio church on Sunday."

"Is my daughter in some kind of trouble?" John asked.

"Not at all," Barrister assured the father. "There's a matter we talked about at church that I need to discuss a bit more today. Let me assure you if all of our city's residents were like your daughter, I'd be out looking for work."

"If it's nothing serious," John Beckett noted, "then I'll leave you two out here. I need to go inside and get cleaned up. It was mighty dusty in the shop today."

The cop watched the older man walk away and step into the house before looking back to the woman, "Your father carries the weight of the world well. I'm sure he's seen more than his share of troubles and yet he looks like a man at peace."

She mournfully shrugged, "He misses home. It breaks his heart he's not farming. But he hides it well. Right now, he just feels he's blessed because we have a place to stay, food to eat, and he has a job. A lot of our friends from back home don't have nearly as much as we do."

"I understand," Barrister assured her. "And compared to those whose loved ones have been murdered, I guess he is blessed. Miss Beckett, let's move over to my car. We can talk while sitting in the front seat."

"We can talk here," she suggested. "What's this all about?"

He folded his arms over his suit coat and posed a question, "Have you heard of a woman named Rose Trebour? She was an actress."

"I met her last week," Shelby quickly answered. "I spent a couple of hours with Miss Trebour when I created an outfit for her for a movie that was shooting on our lot. I love her laugh. It is infectious. And she is one of the nicest people I've met in Los Angeles. She even sent me a thank-you note for my work."

"Miss Beckett," Barrister continued, "do you happen to know if Flynn Sparks was in that film as well?"

"Yes, but what's this all about?"

"We haven't announced it to the newspapers yet," Barrister explained, "but Miss Trebour suffered the same fate as Leslie Bryant. That is now seven women who have been strangled and dumped. And about the only connecting factor we have is Flynn Sparks. We can tie him to three of them."

She took a deep breath and looked toward the house. "Miss Trebour cracked jokes for the couple of hours we were together and even laughed when I accidentally poked her with a pin. She was filled with so much life and excitement, it is hard to think of her being dead."

"Miss Beckett," the cop continued to probe, "I

still don't have the evidence to bring Sparks in. I can't get a search warrant. I need some help before someone else dies." Barrister paused, "Would he like to go out with you, or is the relationship with you nothing more than just publicity hype?"

"The studio forced me to go out with him last weekend," she explained. "I didn't want to."

The cop shot her a stern look and pushed harder, "I didn't ask you that."

"I know what you asked," Shelby admitted, "but I have no desire to be with him in any way, shape, or form."

Barrister shoved his hands into his pockets, "Are you scared or stubborn?"

She didn't immediately answer, instead she turned her head and watched two boys playing pitch and catch across the street. As she followed the ball from one kid to another and back, she tried to deal with the fact the cop had hit a sticking point. She was both scared and stubborn. But it was far more complicated than he could guess. She was not frightened Sparks would kill her, she was concerned he might cause her to say yes to something she'd always been taught to say no to. She also didn't like anyone pushing her to do something she didn't want to do. The harder someone pushed, the more she felt the need to push back. Finally, after sorting out the reasons she didn't want to get near Sparks, she spoke.

"I'm not scared for the reasons you think I am. I don't believe Flynn killed those women. I don't think he would physically hurt me. But I don't want to be used by him or you."

Barrister moved closer, "Would you rather someone else died?"

"You can be sure," she turned to the cop and forcefully said, "I don't want anyone to die."

"Miss Beckett, all I need for you to do is get into his house and see if there is any evidence linking him to the crimes. If he's the guy that killed these women, I'll bet there are souvenirs there."

Still not looking at the cop, she shook her head asked, "What do you mean by souvenirs?"

"I think the killer," Barrister explained, "keeps things that he takes from his victims."

She turned to face him, "I won't do it."

"Fine," he said with a shrug, "when the next girl dies, I hope that you can sleep at night."

Barrister adjusted his hat, walked back to the street, and opened the door to his car. Just as he was sliding into the seat, she turned his way. "All you need me to do is get in his house and look around?"

He pulled his bulky form from the car and nodded.

Walking quickly to Barrister, Shelby set some conditions. "I'm not going to sleep with him. If this requires sex, I'm out."

"I wouldn't want you to do that," he assured her.

"And I need to explain what I'm doing to a man I've been seeing."

"Who?"

"Dalton Andrews."

The cop shook his head, "You can't tell anyone."

"But," she argued, "if I don't it will ruin any chance I have with Dalton. He hates it when he sees me with Flynn. I've just convinced him that I didn't want to have anything to do with Flynn. If he sees me go back on that, how can he ever have any faith me again?"

"Sorry," Barrister explained, "if you told Andrews then Sparks would likely find out. That would compromise everything."

"But . . ."

"Sorry, ma'am, this has to appear to be on the level. After all, this isn't some movie, this is real life and people are dying. And when they die, they don't get back up."

Shelby pushed her hand through her hair. Just when she got things fixed this had to come up. It just wasn't fair. But what kind of person would she be if she said no? How would she feel if another girl died? And, as she believed Flynn was innocent, shouldn't she at least want to prove that the jerk couldn't be this horrible madman?

"I'll play by your rules," she grudgingly gave in. "But you have to promise me something."

"What's that?" he asked while placing his arms on the top of his car.

"When this is all over," she said, as her eyes caught his, "you explain everything to Dalton."

"I'll do that," he guaranteed. "Now, you've got my card; just call me when you can to give me updates. And there is one other thing."

"What's that?"

"Don't wear blue."

"Why?"

"We think that the color blue somehow sets the killer off," he warned. "Each of the victims has been dressed in some shade of blue."

"OK," she replied, "I'll take that to heart."

"I appreciate this more than you know." Barrister soberly offered his thanks. "Your studio church might save a few souls, and the mission you just accepted will likely save some lives."

"I've got one more question," Shelby announced·

"What's that?"

"How are you going to feel if Flynn is the murderer and kills me?"

Barrister looked from the woman to the ground before whispering, "I hope I don't have to find out." He then got into his car and started the engine.

As Shelby watched Barrister drive off she wondered what in the world she'd gotten herself into. She would be dating a man she couldn't stand and betraying a man she might be able to love. In the process, she could be putting her own life on the line. No, she wouldn't. There is no way that Flynn Sparks could be a murderer.

58

July 10, 1936

As Vic Melton went over his wishes for the office scene, a smiling Flynn Sparks walked by the cameras, past a script girl, and over to Dalton Andrews. Rather than actors playing cops, the two eyed each other much like boxers sizing each other up before a title fight.

"You're in a better mood than when I last saw you," Andrews noted.

"Why shouldn't I be," Sparks shot back, "Shelby just accepted a date with me for tonight."

Andrews tensed, "What?"

The reply was smug. "You heard me. But if you want I'll say it loud enough for the whole world to hear." Sparks chuckled, "Go ask her, she's at the back of the stage organizing today's wardrobe."

His face red, the actor shoved past Sparks and, with his shoulders thrown back, marched to the opposite side of the set. He was halfway there when the director shouted out a warning.

"Hey, we're about to shoot a scene with you. Where are you going?"

"I'll be back in a second," Andrews barked, "cool your heels."

"We've got to stay on schedule," Melton warned.

"What I've got to say won't take long," Andrews promised.

Pushing by several technicians, he walked over to the back door where Shelby was arranging a number of men's suits on a rolling rack. He fumed for a few seconds before lashing out.

"I can't believe you're going out with him."

The shocked woman turned to face the angry actor. It almost seemed there were tears in her blue eyes.

"Shelby," Andrews raged, "I gave you more credit. You told me you saw him for what he is. And now he tells me you are going out with him tonight."

"You don't own me," she whispered.

"Who would want to own you?" he snapped back cruelly.

"That was low," she argued. "What I do with my life is my business."

He grabbed her roughly by the shoulders, "Do you know what happens to women who date Flynn? They die. Someone literally squeezes the life from their bodies and then throws them away like trash."

She shook her head, but said nothing.

"That's what this movie we are filming is all about. I'm playing the guy looking for the madman who is killing these women. There's a man named Barrister running the case, and I'm playing him. But I have an advantage; you see, I know the identities of one of the victims that he has not identified. I have the stuff the studio has dug up, and I have access to the police case files too. I can assure you that we are miles ahead of Barrister and his crew. I can guarantee that what you're doing is suicide."

He pulled his hands from her shoulders and shoved them into his pockets. "You know that girl you saw with Flynn at Musso and Frank's? Well, she's dead." He pulled his right hand from his pocket and pushed something her way. "What does this look like?"

"A handkerchief," she whispered.

"Look at the initials," he demanded. "This was Leslie Bryant's; I found it in my car after I won it back from Sparks. It was in the back floorboard. I wonder how it got there?"

"I don't know," she softly answered. After taking a second look at the handkerchief, she continued. "Why don't you call the cops on him? Why don't you give them what you know?"

"Because I want to expose him on this movie," the still livid Andrews explained. "I want to hang him out to dry on film and let the whole world see him for what he is."

Shelby, her eyes open wide, asked, "And you think you have what it takes to do that?"

"Not enough to convict him in court," Andrews admitted, "but I know something the cops don't. And when that plays out, it'll tie the noose around his neck."

A script girl came running up to the actor, "They need you now."

He waved, "I'm coming. I've got no more to prove here."

Andrews set his jaw, spun, and walked back to the set.

59

July 11, 1936

As she observed the coconut trees that were used for decoration in the Hollywood hot spot, Shelby Beckett, in a dress the studio had given her, did her best to act pleased as punch to be out with Flynn Sparks. In truth, after her blistering encounter with Dalton Andrews, she was nervous as a cat in a dog kennel. She was simply no longer sure that Sparks was innocent. Even as she pretended to flirt with the handsome actor, she watched the clock praying that time would fly by. It didn't.

"So what do you think of the band?" he asked, during a break in the music.

"They are great," she assured him. To keep the conversation going she asked, "How often do acts like Benny Goodman play at the Grove?"

"Quite a bit," Sparks explained, "and even when the name bands aren't here the local combos still light it up." As the strains of a new tune sounded, he turned his attention back to the stage. "Oh, this is one of their new ones."

"I think I've heard it," she chimed in.

Sparks nodded, "It's called, 'The Glory of Love.' If you would like to dance to it, I'd love to take you out for a spin."

"Sure," she answered apprehensively. At least if they were in public she was safe. But, until she got into his house, she would also have to keep seeing him.

Sparks pulled her chair back and Shelby got up, smoothed her pink evening gown and led the way to the dance floor. As he took her in his arms and spun her around the floor, she listened to the female vocalist sing the number's upbeat lyrics.

Tonight, the words about the give-and-take of love just didn't ring true. She was giving a great deal and not wanting anything back, except for her date to do something that might give the police what they needed to toss him on death row. The other thing she was sure of was, this wasn't the story of love. At least none she'd heard about.

As the song ended and the pair and forty other couples made their way back to their tables, she leaned close to Sparks and, in the most seductive voice she could muster, suggested, "Why don't we go someplace quieter?"

"Don't you like the club?" he asked.

"It's wonderful," she admitted, "but I deal with loud sewing machines and people barking out orders all day at the studio. I'm tired of yelling just to be heard."

He stopped and looked sadly into her eyes, "There are places I'd love to take you where we could be alone. I'd like nothing better than that, but Jacob Yates has me on a leash. If I'm with a woman, it has to be in a public place. And, if I take a girl back to my home, I have to write a check for five grand. So we better stay here and enjoy the music."

Disappointed, Shelby took a seat and mournfully observed the merriment that filled the club. It was going to take more than one date to get inside Sparks's mind and maybe even longer to get to his lair.

60

July 12, 1936

Shelby's second night out with Flynn Sparks proved even less exciting than the first. The actor drove her to Wrigley Field in South Los Angeles to watch the Angels take on the Portland Beavers in a Pacific Coast minor league baseball game. Supper consisted of hot dogs and peanuts, and most of the conversation centered on John Bottarini and if he had a chance to make it to the major leagues. Sparks was even nice enough to buy her an Angels cap. She was disappointed it didn't have a halo.

As they drove back to her parents' home, the actor put the top down and sang along with the radio. It didn't take the woman long to figure out he would never be a threat to take Dick Powell's place in musicals. His off-key concert, which likely woke up half the city, only ended when he turned the blue Auburn into the drive by their bungalow.

"It's been a great night," he said with a smile. "This is the most relaxed I've been in weeks."

She turned sideways and put her back against the door. "I've heard there has been some tension on the set."

"You mean between me and Dalton?"

"That's been the gossip around the studio," she said, trying to push him a bit.

"There's not much to it," he laughed. "I always get the girl and he doesn't. You know, it's been that way in all our movies too."

"I've heard the script is kind of touchy too," she pushed harder.

"We're not supposed to talk about it," he explained. "That's another of those things that could get me fined."

She shrugged, "You forget I've been on the set. I know it's all about the series of murders that are rocking the city right now."

"It's strange," he admitted. "There is another guy playing me, as I play a cop. You know what's really weird?"

"What?" she thought she might have finally struck pay dirt.

Sparks looked at her and grinned, "He's got me down pat. The lines he's using on women are my lines, and every time I hear them I'm embarrassed."

What was up? For a man whose guilt was being questioned in a script, at a police station, and in the media, Sparks was sure playing it cool. Why wasn't he worried?

"The parts I've watched filmed," a now curious Shelby pointed out, "make it seem like the cops are after you."

He smiled, "That's the way movies are written. They set the audience up to suspect the obvious and then pull something out of a hat at the last minute to shock them. But I've been thinking how funny it would be if my character of Jenkins had to arrest the guy playing me in the movie. That would be a big chuckle."

"Flynn," Shelby's voice was now assertive, "don't you get the fact that the cops believe you killed Leslie Bryant and the others?"

"Of course I get it," he replied, "but I also get this. If they had the goods on me, then I'd be in jail. Here's something you need to understand. Jacob Yates has a building filled with the best legal minds in the state, and they are all working around the clock to make sure I never spend a day in jail."

"But," she argued, "what if the cops find something that directly links you to one of the murders?"

"They won't," he explained, "if there was anything like that, the studio would have destroyed it. Someone will get hung for this thing, but it won't be me."

"You sound pretty sure of yourself," she said.

"When you're Flynn Sparks, you've got nothing in the world to worry about except paying fines." He checked his watch. "And I have curfew. If one of Yates's flunkies doesn't see me drive into my house by eleven, it will cost me a thousand."

"When are we going to see each other again?" she asked.

"I guess next Saturday."

"That long?"

"The studio has me booked the next few nights at charity events. I'll be signing autographs, posing for pictures, and dancing with a few fans." His face grew suddenly serious, "And by the way, I kind of enjoyed church this morning."

"You did?"

Sparks grinned, "I didn't know preachers talked about second chances. I kind of related to that. I think golfers call them mulligans. And I'm all for them. After all, we blow lines all the time on the set, and we just get to start over and do them again." He leaned across and gently kissed her, "Sleep tight. I'm sure we'll see each other at the studio."

It was a confused Shelby who walked to her front door. Either Flynn Sparks was a much better actor than she thought possible or Barrister was barking up the wrong tree.

61

July 14, 1936

After work on Tuesday, Shelby walked to a corner drug store about a block from the studio's main gate and slid into a back booth. Ten minutes later, when she was already half finished with her Coke, Bill Barrister joined her.

"What have you got for me?"

"Nothing really," she admitted. "I've pushed and prodded, but either he has nothing to hide or is giving nothing away. I keep suggesting we go to a place so we can be alone, and he always shies away. He keeps telling me he'll get fined if he takes any girl to his house."

The cop nodded, "That means the studio has the same suspicions we do and are babysitting their bad boy. When are you going out with him again?"

"Not until Saturday." She then sipped on her straw as Barrister rubbed both his chins.

"Well," he sighed, "the good news is we have found no more bodies. So you being with him has kept him from killing anyone. But it's also kept us from getting him behind bars. You're going to have to push harder on your next date. You've got to get in that house."

"Let me explain something again," Shelby shot back. "If he takes a woman to his house, Galaxy will fine him five thousand dollars. Even in his world that is a lot of money."

Barrister set his jaw, "Then you've got to make it worth five grand."

"Now wait just a minute," her words spitting out like bullets, "I didn't sign up for that."

He held his hands up, "I'm not asking you to do that, I'm just asking you to make Sparks believe you would be willing to do that."

Her anger showed in her cheeks as she set out to verbally abuse the cop. "So the man that thinks it was so noble of me to get the church started now wants me to play the role of a harlot. I might not be old and wise, but unlike most of the actresses I've met in this town, I know that you can't have it both ways. There is no such thing as a kind of good girl. You are either good or you are bad."

"So," he grumbled, "You're not going to do what it takes to nab a killer. Your pride is worth more to you than the lives of other women. Is that because you think you're better than them? Is that what this is all about? At least one of those young women who were strangled was a preacher's daughter. She was just an innocent kid who won a contest and ended up spending the evening with Flynn Sparks. So don't put yourself above her or any of the rest of those girls who died because a studio felt that protecting their prize property was more important than letting us arrest a perverted human being. I mean, this guy is going to continue to get away with murder for who knows how long. Isn't that important to you?"

Shelby crossed her arms and pushed her back against the booth. She didn't need to be lectured. "Who else knows about this?" she demanded.

"Just me and you," he quickly replied.

"So you haven't told anyone at the station?"

"No," he assured her. "I didn't want anyone to talk about you or think you were something you weren't."

Her eyes aflame she quipped, "You mean that something you're asking me to be."

He shook his head, "I'm not asking you to be that way. I'm asking you to act that way."

"And that's the problem," she explained, "This whole town is filled with people who act. They act so much they forget who they are. I didn't come to Hollywood to lose myself."

"And I respect that," he admitted. "But I also have to protect women who don't have your grit and convictions. I have to protect them from a monster that is lurking out there and waiting to get them alone. Because let's face it, most girls your age couldn't resist a Cary Grant, Clark Gable, or Flynn Sparks."

"OK," she sighed, "I give up. I'll keep trying to get to the house. But, I ask you again, how are you going to feel if I'm the next victim?"

Barrister went mute as he looked out the window and studied the traffic. A nearby radio played almost all of "Melody From the Sky" by the Jan Garber Orchestra before the cop finally turned back to face his unwilling accomplice. His eyes caught hers for just a moment before he reached into his coat and pulled out a .38 revolver.

"Keep this in your purse. I hope you never have to use it. But if he attacks you, pull the trigger as many times as it takes until he stops breathing. Then call me."

She tentatively reached out and took the gun. As her fingers wrapped around it, she looked back at the cop as he sadly nodded. After she placed the deadly gift into her bag, he tossed a dime on the table, pushed away, and walked out the door.

62

July 16, 1936

It was already past six, and the crew had been working since seven this morning. Everyone was tired and on edge. The fact the two lead actors weren't speaking to each other off the set wasn't helping matters. Likely due to the strained atmosphere coupled with the tight shooting schedule, Vic Melton had already exploded in rage three times during the day, and his red face indicated another volcanic eruption was on the way. Meanwhile, Dalton Andrews, his face placid and his manner relaxed, sat on the edge of his character's desk and waited for instructions.

"OK, people," Melton barked, "Barrister has seen the ME, and he finally knows the identity of the first victim. He's now back at his desk and the phone rings. We only hear him talk, not the party at the other end. Toward the end of the call, his partner walks in." The director looked over to Sparks, "Have you read this part of the script?"

"Only the part I'm involved in," he replied. "I didn't bother looking at anything that he says other than enough to recognize my cues. I mean, how hard is it? I'm playing a second banana who's boring, dry, and clueless."

"Perfect casting," Andrews chimed in.

"Why you . . ."Only Melton stepping between the two men saved a fistfight from breaking out.

"Whatever it is you two have going on, save it for after hours. Flynn, get out of the shot until I signal for you to come in." He waited for the actor to move off the office set and then looked back to Andrews. "Dalton, you need to be behind the desk in the chair."

As the actor took his place, the director returned to his seat and signaled for action. A second later the desk phone rang, and Andrews, now immersed in his role as Barrister, picked up the receiver.

"Barrister, homicide." He pretended to listen

for a short period of time before saying, "OK, what can you tell me about her background?" He waited again, "I see. And what do you know about the son?" As he paused again, Sparks, now in character as Barry Jenkins, casually entered the office. "OK, wait just a minute, I need to write that down." Andrews picked up a pen and a notepad and scribbled on the paper. "Thanks. Along with what you told me this morning, this is good stuff. I appreciate it. If you ever need anything from me, don't hesitate to call."

Slamming the receiver down, Andrews leapt from his chair. "Barry, we got a break."

"Who was that?" Sparks now in his role as Jenkins asked.

"It was the police in Indiana."

"What do they have to do with anything?"

"That's right," Andrews cut in, "you weren't in the building this morning. Those bones we found in the section of brush, Arnie traced them to a missing woman from the Hoosier state. She was out here looking for a big payoff of some kind. My best guess is that it had to do with her son. You see, she's never been married. But there's a name of the father on the birth certificate. I figure she was coming out here to see him. He's probably some successful guy who couldn't afford to have his reputation ruined, so he killed her."

"Bill, if that's the case, then how does it tie in with the others? Where's the link?"

"Maybe," Andrews continued to recite his lines, "the guy discovered he liked the power that strangling a woman gave him. Perhaps like the drunk who has to have another drink, this guy now has to continue to get a fix through murder."

Sparks, playing his part of the dull-witted cop, asked, "What makes you think the father's out here?"

Andrews, showing the appropriate amount of excitement in his manner, explained, "Because I found out she doesn't have any relatives or friends in California. She came out here looking for the father and expecting a payoff. That's the only thing that makes sense."

Andrews had just rattled off his lines when a light bulb popped and showered glass down on the set.

"Cut." Melton yelled. "And get that cleaned up and the light replaced." He looked toward the two actors, "When we get this fixed, we can pick it up from where we left off. You both know the rest of your lines?"

"I got mine down," Andrews assured him.

"I don't have any more," Sparks noted. "When Dalton finished his epic speech I was supposed to pull out a pad and pencil, pretend to write something down, and run out."

"Do you remember where you were?" the director asked.

"We haven't moved," Andrews answered.

"Glass is off the floor and the light is working again," a crewman called out.

"Let's do it," Melton suggested, as he hurriedly moved back to his chair. "Is everyone ready? Action."

"Barry, get out your pencil, I've got a name to give you. I don't care how long it takes, I don't care if it means interviewing a thousand men; we are going to find that child's father."

Andrews paused for dramatic effect before saying, "William Hamilton."

Andrews watched as Sparks froze. Rather than pretend to write down the name on the pad, he went ashen white. Confused, but still wanting to save the scene, Andrews ad-libbed, "You better write that name down, Barry. I think he might be the Hollywood Madman."

As if he'd been pinched, Sparks woke up, jotted down the name, turned, and rushed from the office. When he was out of the camera view, Melton yelled, "Cut." The actor didn't stop. He continued off the set and through the stage door leading to the main street.

As Andrews eased down on the corner of the desk, Melton strolled over to him. "What was that all about?"

The actor slipped his hat back on his head, "I don't know. But something sure spooked him. Did anyone walk into the room that would have upset Flynn?"

"No one came into the room at all," Melton replied. He then looked back at the stunned crew, "That's it for today; we start in the morning at eight. I need the actors here at seven for makeup and wardrobe."

63

July 18, 1936

Flynn Sparks was almost an hour late picking Shelby up for their date. Rather than coming to the door, he'd simply blown his horn as he drove up. As she opened her door and slid in, he forced a smile, backed the Auburn out of the drive, and pulled out into the street. She was shocked the normally fastidious man's face was unshaven, pale and emotionless, and his dinner jacket wrinkled. Also surprising was that, other than when he ordered his meal at the Brown Derby, he remained as mute as a statue.

As they waited for their order, Shelby looked around the room and made several observations. "I just spotted Barbara Stanwyck. Looks like Robert Taylor is at her table as well. Gable is here. I can't understand what he sees in his wife. She's much too old for him." When Sparks failed to respond, she added, "This is the nicest outfit the studio had made for me, and you haven't said a word about it."

"You look good in it," he offered.

"Close your eyes," she demanded. "What color is it?"

"Green," he answered.

"It's burgundy," she corrected him. "What's going on?"

"It's complicated," he replied. "I'm not feeling well, and I haven't slept much."

"Have you been drinking?" she asked.

"A little." He held his thumb and finger just about a half-inch apart.

"When did you start?" Shelby demanded.

"Last night," he admitted. "I had a few at the charity gig at the race track and have been sipping the stuff in tiny doses since then. Errol Flynn swears this is good for whatever ails you. He and I swapped hard-luck stories for about three hours last night. That's been the highlight of my week."

"Did your pity party make you feel better?" she asked.

"He felt better," Sparks admitted. "It didn't help me much."

Shelby looked around until she saw their waiter and signaled for him to come over to their table. "Mr. Sparks is not feeling well. Does he have an account here?"

"Yes, he does."

"Put the bill on his tab. I'm going to get him

out to his car." She looked over at her date. "Don't argue with me. You and I are walking out of the restaurant, and I'm taking you home."

"We can't do that," he explained, "I'll have to pay a big fine."

"I'll explain to Mr. Yates," Shelby countered, "that this was a humanitarian mission. I think he'll let you off."

Though the actor walked steady and straight, he didn't seem to be able to focus. When they got to the car, Shelby escorted him around to the passenger side, fished into his pocket for the keys, and then pushed him in. By the time she got to the driver's side and had adjusted the seat, Sparks was sound asleep. He stayed that way as she wandered around the city streets until finally discovering the road leading up to Hollywood's most famous bachelor pad. As she drove through the gate, she waved at a man sitting in a three-year-old Ford. He didn't wave back. Once in the drive, she shut off the motor, set the brake, woke up her date, and pulled him of the car.

"Which key?" she asked as she held the ring in front of his face.

He pointed to the second one.

She left him standing by the Auburn as she climbed four steps up to the front door. After slipping the key in, she opened it and glanced back toward Sparks. "Come on, you've always wanted me to see the view."

Seemingly a bit more alert, he walked up to the front door and stepped in. Sparks then turned around, looked at his guest and said, "Welcome to my lair. Let me take your hand, and I will give you the tour."

After pushing by him, she found a switch and brought a bit of light to the situation. With him following along behind, she went room to room until every lamp in the place was burning.

"Let's stay in here," Sparks suggested. "My bed is really comfortable."

"Then," Shelby suggested, "why don't you go lie down on it, and I will join you later? I want to see the view first."

"Will do." He announced with a salute.

She then watched as he yanked off his coat and fell face first onto the wine-colored bedspread. She stood at the door and watched him for a minute, but he never moved. Sensing she had some time, she decided in the moment to start doing some police work.

The home was impressive, the furnishings dark and ornate, and Sparks seemed to have a thing for mounted wild animal heads. They were every-where. The art hanging on his walls and sitting on tables and dressers consisted of photos of himself from his various films. Except for some soured milk and three eggs, there was nothing in the refrigerator. The cabinets contained a lot more bottles of booze than cans or boxes of food. The place was void of fresh vegetables or fruit. There were also no surprises in his drawers or closets other than stacks of scrapbooks all filled with press clippings and articles on the home's owner. He even kept the bad reviews.

A mantle clock, with brass lion heads on both ends, announced the hour of nine. She'd spent an hour and a half searching and found nothing linking the star to the dead women. Now the only room left to search was where Sparks was sleeping.

Throwing her purse over her shoulder, she crept down the hall to the master bedroom. The man, his eyes closed, was now lying on his back. He breathing was steady.

"Flynn," she whispered.

He didn't move.

Sensing she was safe if she worked quietly, she moved over to his walk-in closet. Lined with cherry wood, it was a dozen feet deep. It took only a few minutes to find there was nothing out of the ordinary there. So, she stepped back out in the room. Sparks had not moved.

Moving past the walnut bed, she walked over to a huge chest. There were nine drawers. The first contained underwear. The second socks. The third was ties. The next one was filled with under-shirts. The fifth contained sweaters. The sixth was home to hundreds of fan letters. The seventh was filled with matchbooks from hundreds of different clubs and restaurants. None of them were alike. She looked back toward the bed to assure herself that the man was still sleeping before she pulled open the eighth drawer.

Jackpot! Barrister would like this. A beaded purse sat on top of a stack of women's lingerie and five handkerchiefs. Each of the hankies was monogrammed, and none of the initials were the same. Sensing the handbag was the big prize, Shelby pulled out the small purse and undid the clasp. Reaching in, she retrieved a wallet. She slowly opened it. The driver's license read, "Leslie Bryant."

"Did you find what you were looking for?"

64

July 18, 1936

Shelby dropped the purse back into the drawer and slowly rose to her feet. After standing, she looked into the mirror and noted Flynn Sparks standing behind her.

"It's not what you think," she explained.

"Oh," he quipped, "let me guess, you are really a thief. I saw this in a William Powell movie once. You came up here to rob me. It's what you do. You seduce actors and then, as we sleep, you turn into a master criminal. Have you found the good silver yet?"

She slowly turned to face him. As their eyes met, she shrugged, and said, "You caught me."

"Actually," he replied, "I didn't. You're not a thief, and I haven't been drunk. In fact, I haven't had a thing to drink this whole week."

"You set me up?"

"I haven't been asleep," he admitted, "I figured out that you were trying too hard to get to my house. You really didn't want to be with me, you just wanted me to believe that. I'm not stupid enough to think you'd suddenly changed that much. You need to give me more credit."

"Maybe I have changed," she suggested. "I mean, you are a good-looking man. There are a lot of good girls who'd go bad for you."

He looked toward the door, "You're here. You might as well see the view. Let's go."

His tone indicated it was not a request, but an order. She glanced to the hall and took a deep breath. Finally, she asked, "Do I lead the way?"

"You've been all through this house," he quipped, "you likely know it better than I do. Of course, you're going to lead the way."

Shelby nodded, stepped past the man, walked down the hall, through the living room and to the double French doors. After snapping the lock, she pushed the entry open and strolled out on he stone patio. He followed.

The view was all he'd advertised it to be. She felt like she could see forever. The fact there was no moon made the city lights and twinkling stars seem that much brighter. She only got to study them for a second before he grabbed her arm and pulled her over to the stone wall separating the patio and the dropoff.

"Take a look down," he suggested. "You can't see it at night, but there are rocks at the bottom of the hill. They tell me the drop is about two hundred feet." He pushed her closer to the edge. "I got this place cheap. You know why?"

As his right hand kept pressure on the middle of her back, her legs pressed into the wall. Taking a deep breath to slow her heart, she asked, "Why was it such a bargain?"

He laughed coldly, "Because the two previous owners jumped to their deaths. People now believe this place is haunted. They tell me it's hard to sell a haunted house."

He let his hand slide from her back and stepped beside her. "On dark nights like tonight, no one can ever see us. It's as if we are invisible." He took a deep breath before demanding, "Are you working for Yates? Is he paying you to get the goods on me?"

"No," she quietly assured him. "No one is paying me anything."

"Then why search my house?" he growled.

"I'm curious," she replied.

"Curiosity killed the cat," he jibed.

Shelby nodded, "I've also heard that cats have nine lives. I believe that means I still have eight more to go."

"I don't know what your game is," he admitted, "but you now know about my souvenirs. I can't let you tell others about them. They would think things I can't afford to have them think."

Shelby nodded and slowly slipped her right hand down to her purse and undid the clasp. As it was so dark, she was banking on him not being able to see her actions. When her fingers felt the cold steel, she pushed her hand around it, took a deep breath and yanked the gun out. Before he could move, she aimed the short barrel at his gut.

"You came prepared," he noted, a hint of admiration in his tone. "Is it real, or did you borrow it from the prop department?"

"I can assure you it's real." Her hand was shaking even more than her knees as she waited for his next move.

He stared into her face rather than at the gun. "You left the keys to the Auburn on the table next to the front door. You can drive yourself home. I'll pick it up the next time I'm at the studio."

"Don't you want to tell me anything else?" she asked.

"No," he replied. "Now just get out of here before anything else happens."

Shelby backed across the patio until she felt the back of the door with her hand. Slipping through it, she ran down the hall, only stopping long enough to pick up the keys. Racing out the front door and down the steps, she hopped into the car, jammed the keys into the ignition, and flipped the switch. When the V-12 roared to life, she pushed the vehicle into first and made a U-turn in the wide drive. She didn't breathe easy until she was home with the door locked.

65

July 18, 1936

After watching Shelby drive away in his car, Flynn Sparks slowly wandered back to the bedroom to look at the final drawer the woman opened. Pulling it out, he returned to the living room and dumped its contents on the couch. He stood and despondently studied the collection for several minutes. Finally reaching down, he picked up a lace handkerchief and traced the initials S.R. before tossing it in the fireplace. He repeated that act until all that was left was Leslie Bryant's purse.

Sitting down on the couch he spent almost a half hour examining everything in the small, beaded handbag. He looked through her photographs, opened her lipstick, and even counted the money in her wallet. Finally, after taking a deep breath, he put everything back into the purse and pitched it into the fireplace with his other souvenirs.

Pushing off the couch, he wandered into the kitchen and opened a drawer beside the stove. Grabbing a four-inch long box, he retraced his steps to the fireplace. After opening the flue, he slid the box open, pulled out a kitchen match, and closed the box. Just to his right was a copy of today's *Times*. He retrieved it from the coffee table, glanced at the photo of Shelby and him that Ellen Rains had used in her column, before striking the match against the box. He looked momentarily at the flame before holding the match to the newspaper. When the paper caught fire, he stuck it in the fireplace and set the cache of collectibles aflame. Sensing that he would need more fuel to accomplish his mission, he grabbed several magazines and added them to what would soon become a small blaze. Moving back to an overstuffed chair, he watched the fire until it finally burned out.

Getting up, Sparks grabbed the shovel and broom from his fireplace tools and began the clean up. After dumping all that was left into an ash can, he slowly walked out onto his patio and over to the wall. He took in the view as he turned the can over and let the slight breeze spread the ashes all over the canyon below. When the job was finished, he returned to the living room, closed the flue, and took the matches back to the kitchen. After turning out the lights and locking the door, the actor marched resolutely back to his bedroom. Within fifteen minutes, he was asleep.

66

July 19, 1936

Shelby didn't wait for her parents to get ready for the Galaxy Studio church services. Wanting to rid herself of the last vestige of her encounter with Flynn Sparks, the young woman quickly dressed, jumped into the actor's Auburn Speedster, and drove to the studio. Once there she parked the car in the place reserved for the actor's car and, without turning back, quickly walked away.

Through it was still a half an hour before the services were to start, a crowd was gathering. Excited fans stood in the churchyard eagerly watching for the arrival of the stars Galaxy had assigned for church duty. Ignoring them, Shelby marched up the steps and into the building. What she wanted more than anything else was to sit on a pew and spend a few minutes gathering her thoughts.

Grabbing a spot next to the aisle on the second row, the woman set her purse beside her and placed her Bible in her lap. She was just pulling down the hem on her light blue dress when she sensed a presence. Slowly turning to the right, she found herself looking into the face of Flynn Sparks.

"You probably didn't expect to see me here," he announced, his voice calm and even. If he was the least bit agitated, he didn't show it.

She tried to speak, but with thoughts of looking at the canyon once more filling her head, she could only manage a shake of her head. Moving her gaze to the front of the church, she prayed someone else would enter, but no one did.

"I've got something to tell you, Shelby," Sparks said. "Yes, Leslie Bryant did spend the night at my house, but nothing happened. I didn't know she'd never had anything to drink, and the booze made her sick. I let her sleep in my bed, and I spent the night in one of the other rooms."

She balled her hands on top of her Bible and whispered, "How is that supposed to make me feel better? She's still dead."

"And I wish she wasn't," Sparks assured her. "I'd do anything to bring her back. That is beyond my power. But let me assure you of this, I understand why you did what you did last night. I realize you had to know if you could trust me. I got to thinking after you left that, if I had been in your shoes, I'd have probably done the same thing."

Shelby was still looking at the cross hanging on the back wall of the church as the man slowly walked back down the aisle and to the door. She heard it open and close before turning back. He was gone, but for reasons she didn't fully understand, she still didn't feel safe.

67

July 19, 1936

Bill Barrister watched the services from the back pew, but it was only after the dinner on the ground was in full swing that he strolled over to where Shelby sat. After she related the events of the previous night, the cop swung into action. He first interrupted the district attorney during a round of golf. Next came a district judge. By three, Barrister had the search warrant he needed to finally get the goods on Flynn Sparks. Thirty minutes later, the captain and seven cops knocked on the star's door.

"May I help you?" Sparks asked as he pulled the entry open.

Barrister studied his host. Dressed in tennis clothes and holding a racket, the actor seemed confident and unconcerned by the fact three police cars were parked in his drive.

"Mr. Sparks," the captain began, "I'm Bill Barrister of the Los Angeles homicide squad." He stopped to flash his badge. "We have a warrant to search your home and property in connection with the murder of Leslie Bryant. Here is the warrant if you would like to read it."

"Just set it on the kitchen table," Sparks calmly suggested. "Gentlemen, I have a tennis match at the country club. If you need me for any reason, you can find me there. As far as my home, feel free to look anywhere and everywhere. If you get thirsty, I have some Cokes cooling in the refrigerator. I bought them this morning. And if you could, lock the door when you leave."

The stunned cop watched as Sparks strolled by him and over to his car. After a few seconds to gather his wits, Barrister glanced over to Barry Jenkins. "You get in one of our cars and follow him. I don't want him trying to skip out."

"Captain Barrister," the actor yelled from his Auburn. "I've been in a lot of police movies. I assume you just told one of your men to tail me."

Barrister nodded.

"There's no reason to do that," Sparks assured him. "I have plenty of room in my car. He can just ride along. When you finish, you can come by and pick him up."

"What do you think?" a uniformed cop asked.

Barrister wasn't sure what to think. Why was Sparks being so cooperative? What game was he playing? Or was he just reconciled to the fact the chase was about to end?

"Mr. Sparks," the captain announced, "one of my men, Sergeant Barry Jenkins, will be happy to ride with you."

"Jenkins," the actor laughed, "I feel like I know him already."

As his team went to work, Barrister stood on the steps until the Auburn was well down the hill. Still puzzled, the cop then made an initial walk-through, stopping in the bedroom and moving to the chest of drawers. He opened the eighth one and looked inside. It was empty. He frowned, even though Miss Beckett had not told the actor she was working for the police, Sparks somehow must have figured it out.

"Cap."

Barrister turned toward a uniformed officer named Sims. "You got something?"

"I found these typed pages in a kitchen trash can. They look like they are part of a script."

"So?"

"You're name is here, as is Jenkins, and it also has the name of one of the victims."

Barrister moved quickly to the bedroom entry. He grabbed the three pages and began to read. It took only one sentence for him to realize what was going on. He glanced at the top of the page and noted a date . . . July 14, 1936. Reading the remainder of the pages proved something else. Whoever was writing this script had access to information directly from police files. But what was more troubling was the studio seemed to have uncovered things his investigation hadn't.

"Sims, I want everyone in the living room now. Gather up the team. I have some very specific instructions for them."

As the officer assembled the six other officers at the meeting point, Barrister reread the three pages of the script. Without his knowledge, Galaxy was making a movie about this case. Someone was playing him like a bass drum. Who was it? How did the studio have this information?

Moving through the door, down the hall, and back to the living room, he looked at his men. "OK, he's onto us. And that's just the beginning of our problems. I want you to go over this place with a fine-tooth comb. Look under, over, and behind everything. But, put everything back just as you found it. This place needs to look just as neat now as it did when we arrived. And, Sims, put these pages back where you got them too."

As the crew went back to work, Barrister sat down on the couch and considered his options. After a few seconds to assemble his thoughts, he pulled an address book from his pocket and searched for a number. He then picked up the phone and made a call.

68

July 19, 1936

It was just past seven when Bill Barrister knocked on the door of the palatial, fifteen-room home on Beverly Glenn and waited for a response. A formally dressed butler answered.

"May I help you, sir?"

"You can't," the cop bluntly answered, "but Miss Rains can. And don't bother announcing me; she knows I'm coming. Just guide me to the right room."

The elderly man stepped back and allowed Barrister to enter. He then pointed a long bony finger toward a door on the right. The captain moved quickly across the tile floor to the ten-foot-high slab of wood, grabbed the knob, twisted it, and walked in.

"Have you ever heard of knocking?" Rains asked.

She was dressed in rose red from her slippers clear up to her hat. She even wore matching lipstick. She was reclining on a dark blue couch; beside her appeared to be a glass of iced lemonade.

"I'm tired of knocking," Barrister grumbled. "I'm also tired of being used and kicked around.

And this time I'm going to grill you even more deeply than you do the stars you interview."

"There's no reason for being pushy," she suggested. "I've always done my bit to help the police."

"You've also done your bit to sell us out," he snapped.

"If you're going to roar," she said, "then do it while sitting down."

"I'll stand," Barrister quickly replied. "There's a cop in records, his name is Tim Thomas. I think you know him."

She smiled, "It doesn't ring a bell."

Barrister unbuttoned his suit coat and shoved his hands into his pockets. "Let me remind you. Whenever a star is arrested, Thomas calls you with the tip."

"Oh," she grinned, "is that his name? I do wish you would sit down. The way you move when you talk, I feel like I'm watching a tennis match."

"Miss Rains, you can make light of this if you want, but you're in some trouble here. Thomas also passed along files that concern the murder of several young women in this town."

"Why would I want those?" she asked. "I make my living writing about entertainment, not homicide."

Barrister growled, "Let me pass along some information that Thomas was going to give you but never got the chance. My team searched Flynn

Sparks's house today. We found three pages of a script in which I appear to be the lead character. The movie is about the homicides I just mentioned. There is only one way that Galaxy Studios could have gotten the information, and that was from our police files. And Thomas has admitted passing copies of all our materials from the case on the strangler to you."

Rains set her glass down, ran her manicured fingers across her chin and sighed. "Do I need to call my lawyer?"

"That depends upon what you tell me right now."

"Would you please sit down?" she asked. "Take that chair across from me." After the cop was seated, she swung around into a proper sitting posture and continued, "Thomas and I have an arrangement. He always gets me the information first, so that I can beat the other columnists. When the murder case came in, he called and informed me there were some studio links. I offered him a bit extra to get me all the information you all collected."

"But," Barrister noted, "you haven't been writing about it."

"No," she admitted, "I don't have the files here. When new information came in, I passed it, by messenger, directly to the studio. They gave it to their scriptwriters and have been filming a movie about the strangler for several weeks now. You might be interested in knowing that Dalton Andrews is playing you."

The cop considered the irony of a tall, good-looking man filling his shoes, then looked back to his host. "Miss Rains. There was information in the pages of that script I read that I didn't have. Are they making stuff up?"

"Bill, if you're asking me if they are taking liberties with the facts, the answer is no. Jacob Yates has a team of investigators working it as well. The scriptwriters combined the stuff Galaxy uncovers with what you have dug up."

It was now starting to make sense. The studio was therefore well ahead of his department too.

Fearing the answer, Barrister asked, "Do they know who the strangler actually is?"

"If Yates knows," she quickly explained, "he hasn't told me. But I would bet they are close. My sources indicate it will wrap this week. Now, what kind of trouble am I in?"

"That depends," Barrister replied. "If you get me on the movie set when they present the evidence as to who the strangler is, I might forget a lot of things I know."

"I'll talk to Yates," she assured him.

Barrister stood and moved toward the door. Just before he exited, he turned back to Rains. "Would the studio frame someone in order to protect one of their own?"

"No," she assured him. "Because that would

make them look foolish when the movie was released and you guys solved the crime arresting the real killer." She paused, as if thinking, "But, if Yates saw things working against what he wanted, he'd scrap the project and burn the film."

The cop pointed his finger into the woman's face, "Don't tell Yates I know anything about this. I want to spring that on him myself."

"I thought you wanted to be on the set when they filmed the finale?"

"Miss Rains, I do, but as I think about things now, I realize I'm the one in the position of power. I don't think I'll have any problem being on the set when this whodunit wraps up. I do have a word of warning for you."

She nodded, "What's that?"

"Don't tell anyone that I know what is going on. If you do, I'll make sure we find a way to toss you in jail for a while."

He smiled, tipped his hat, turned, and walked out.

69

July 20, 1936

"You're up early today," Victor Melton noted from his office on the second floor of Galaxy's administrative building.

Jacob Yates, donut in one hand and a cup of coffee in the other, marched in and took a seat beside the director's desk. As he took a bite of his breakfast, he glanced around the seemingly disorganized twelve-by-fifteen-foot room. Scripts were stacked in every corner, ash trays overflowed with cigarette butts, an Academy Award on a shelf was all but hidden by four empty Coca-Cola bottles, and a half dozen suit jackets had been taken off and just tossed on the floor.

"How can you find anything in here?" the mogul asked.

Melton smiled, "You could ask me where my copy of a script to *Destiny or Die* is, and I could find it in just a second. What appears chaotic to you is actually my filing system. I know where everything is, and I take great pains in leaving it there."

A perplexed Yates, his eyes still on what seemed to be nothing but random piles of stuff, addressed the reason for his visit. "I got a note saying we were wrapping this thing up on Wednesday."

The small, redheaded man smiled, "*The Hollywood Madman* will be behind us by Wednesday night. That is except for editing, music, and possibly a couple of retakes. But the principle filming will be finished."

Yates turned away from the mess and to the director. "Isn't that awfully fast?"

"Jacob, what is your favorite MGM whodunit?"

The mogul didn't have to think before ticking off, "*The Thin Man.*"

"And that movie was shot in two weeks," Melton explained. "Columbia shot *It Happened One Night* almost as quickly, and it won all the major categories at the Academy Awards. The sets in this film were easy, we only had to go off the lot for one location shot, and the scriptwriters did a great job supplying lines that were crisp, clean, and easy to learn."

"But do we know who did it?" Yates asked.

"That is where the problem comes in," Melton admitted. "Evidence found right here on the lot proves who it has to be, but you might not like the person our detectives have fingered for the crimes."

The studio head frowned, "I take it he is one of our own."

"Do you want to know who?" the director asked.

"Not really," Yates admitted. "But right now,

I sure would like to strangle Ellen Rains."

Yates got up and moved over to a window looking out on the lot. He studied the scene for a few moments before speaking. "We've known each other a long time. You and I have always been honest. So I want to admit I'm scared. I am afraid that I'm losing control of what I built. I have nightmares about an earthquake opening a crevice so large that it swallows everything on the Galaxy lot. And I'm wondering if these murders and this film will be what causes my nightmare to become a reality."

"If you're worried about the murders," Melton chimed in, his voice solemn, but his tone positive, "no studio has ever been taken down by a scandal. Fatty Arbuckle killed that girl, and Paramount survived. That same studio didn't miss a beat when William Desmond Taylor was murdered. And you've always told me that anything that actually puts a studio in the news is good for business."

"Maybe," the mogul replied sadly, "but this project is different, and it scares me. This is the only behind-closed-doors movie we have ever done. No one outside of the cast and crew know about it. Right now that works to our advantage. But what might hang us is that we used real people and events in the script, so at the last moment, we can't turn it into a fictional movie. It won't fly past legal that way."

The director walked over and stood beside his boss, "Jacob, we could scrap it."

Yates grimly smiled, "I've thought about that. All weekend long I was playing around with that thought. For the sake of the studio's image, it is the only way to go. After all, we are an industry that protects our stars. We magically erase all their sins and keep them from paying for their wrongs."

Melton nodded, "It might be time to pull out that old code and use it again. I'm going to be honest, I'd hate to see this picture die—I really would—because everything about it is first-rate. There is no doubt in my mind it will be the best crime film Galaxy has ever made. But I'm a company man, and I will go along with what you tell me to do."

"Thanks for that," the mogul softly replied. "But I need to ask you a question. It is one I've been battling all week long."

"Shoot."

"Vic, is killing *The Hollywood Madman* the moral thing to do?"

"What kind of question is that?" the director asked. "Frank Capra doesn't work here. We've never worried about what was right or wrong, or if we inspired people or just entertained them. Our job was chasing the money."

"But," Yates argued, "we have passed on certain projects in the past that we deemed too hot to handle. Has this become one of those?"

Melton shrugged, "What do you think?"

"I made a mistake," the mogul explained. "I let Ellen Rains convince me this project could make us a lot of money. And that's why I jumped on it. But I forgot one important thing."

"What's that, Jacob?"

"Vic, we are in the business of making fantasy seem real. Doing that is safe because we control everything from beginning to end. We give stars new names and write up biographies for them that repaint their whole past. We build streets that are nothing more than facades. We have sound-stages that take us all over the world without leaving Los Angeles. I mean, think of this . . . everything we do is just a series of magical lies, and this studio works wonderfully as long as we check reality at the front gate. I messed up and brought reality onto the lot, and now I realize we have no control over it in this world. Truth eats lies for breakfast and comes back hungry for lunch."

"So," Melton chimed in, "we kill the film."

Yates took a deep breath, pulled a newspaper from his jacket pocket and tossed it on the director's cluttered desk. "Ellen Rains wrote a long feature in today's *Times* that pats this studio on the back for having the courage to film the true story of the Hollywood Madman. She put a crown on our head for finally ridding this city of the man who has killed all these young women.

In other words, in making me look like a saint, she has painted us into a corner."

"Why did she do that?" Melton asked.

"Because, Vic, she owns a piece of the film. This is her way of making sure it is finished and released. You might want to read the story; you get cited for being a director who shows grit, determination, and courage." Yates shook his head, "I hate being *forced* to do the right thing."

As the mogul headed for the door the director called after him, "You going to be on the set on Wednesday?"

Yates stopped and turned, "I wouldn't miss it. But until then, I'm going to try to pretend that the film is just another movie."

70

July 20, 1936

Betsy Minser was going over a long, handwritten list when Shelby walked into the finishing room. The young woman paused, looked toward her boss, and asked, "What outfit am I supposed to wear today?"

"The red suit," Minser replied, "though the church gimmick is going so well in the media there are no publicity photos scheduled for today. Still, you never know when a reporter will come on the lot and request to meet you. The church has been such big news that it is being talked about all over the world. MGM and Warners are even considering following in our footsteps. And, because of all the ink it has generated, it has pushed the murders of the young women to the back pages." The woman stopped and noted, "You feeling all right? You look kind of pale."

"I didn't get much sleep," she explained. "Been a really strange weekend. Once I get changed, what do you need for me to do?"

"They are wrapping up that secretive movie they've been working on the past couple of weeks. This is a list of all the stuff they will need for the last two days of shooting. We have a few things to mend, a few others to clean, and a lot of things to move over to the soundstage."

"What about the pirate film?" Shelby asked.

"Oh, we have to finish those costumes and get a few things ready for the turn-of-the-century musical on stage 22. I've got all the factory girls alerted that they'll be staying late, and Willie is supposed to be getting the material we need from the warehouse. So just plan on a long day."

"That's OK. Working keeps my mind occupied. And the longer the day, the better."

Minser studied her worker more closely, "I take it you don't have a date tonight."

"Betsy, I'm not sure I'll ever have a date again."

"What happened?"

"Where do you want this stuff?" Mace asked as he ambled into the room with four bolts of fabric.

"Just set it on the middle worktable," Minser ordered. Turning her attention back to Shelby she asked, "What do you mean you will never date again?"

The young woman frowned, "The last couple of weeks have revealed some things that have soured me on men right now."

"You mean Flynn?"

"And Dalton too," Shelby added. "Flynn is scary."

"What do you mean scary?" Minser asked.

"I can't tell you any more right now," Shelby admitted, "but Dalton is not what he seems either."

"I found," the older woman explained, "that men are users. They look at women as possessions, but most of them don't really value us. Their world revolves around their desires. That's why I've never married."

From the corner, Mace gently suggested, "I don't think all men are that way."

"You're right, Willie," Shelby agreed, "My father isn't. Now I need to get changed so we can go to work."

71

July 21, 1936

It was just past ten in the morning when Eve
Walen escorted Bill Barrister into Jacob Yates's
office. The mogul was behind his desk studying
a script. His expression was neither welcoming
nor disdainful. Tossing the script to one side, he
waited until the cop was seated and had removed
his hat before speaking.

"I've been expecting you."

"I thought about coming yesterday," Barrister
admitted, "but I decided to make you sweat
for twenty-four hours before I graced your
chambers."

Yates rested his arms on his desk, "If you came
to ask me who did it, I can honestly tell you, I
don't know. And I will happily go before a grand
jury and swear to that as well."

The cop set his jaw, "If I were in your place, I
wouldn't want to know either. I'd be kind of like
the kid who covers up his head with a blanket to
make the monsters in his bedroom go away."

The mogul glanced at a painting on the far wall
and, after studying it for a moment, announced,
"I know you came here for a reason. If you are
going to arrest me, let's get it over with."

"Let's put that off for a few days. I actually came here to ask a favor."

A seemingly relieved Yates turned to face his guest, "And which one of my people do you want to question now?"

"None of them," Barrister assured him.

"Well," the mogul replied, "that simplifies things. Perhaps you would like a tour of the studio. I would be happy to conduct it."

"No," came the quick answer. "Let me get straight to my point. I understand that you're filming the final scenes in your little movie tomorrow."

"Ah, what movie is that? We have a dozen different pictures shooting at this very moment."

Barrister grinned, "I think you are calling it *The Hollywood Madman*."

"It's a B picture," Yates assured him, "it's not the best way to really get a feel for what we do. I think you'd enjoy the pirate film more."

"Let's quit playing games," the captain suggested. "The cat is out of the bag, and Rains told me that tomorrow is the day. Now, I want to be there with a couple of my men when you announce the man who is behind the murders."

"What happens if I refuse?" the mogul asked.

"Then I guess I'd have to shut you down and begin questioning everyone who is associated with the film. That also means I'd have to lock down the studio so that none of your thousands of employees got to go home until I found out the truth and arrested the person responsible. And then I would have a grand jury decide how many of your people would be charged with obstructing justice, hiding a fugitive, and likely, a dozen other charges. And I bet those charges would stick and there would be a lot of your folks serving some time."

"It is so tempting to let you do that," Yates admitted. He ran his hands over his head as he pushed the air from his lungs. "I get the idea there's something else you want too."

Barrister smiled, "The files you received from us were illegally obtained. I have been able to determine how each new bit of evidence came to your office first. That means that you accepted delivery. I can arrest you right now if you like."

"Or you can do what?"

"I want it played this way," the cop explained. "Give us credit for sharing the files. Tell the world that, because these crimes were so horrible and our resources were somewhat limited, we approached you asking for your help. You then employed a number of the nation's top investigators to work with us. This unique marriage produced a way for us to fully develop the case and save many other women from being killed by this madman. I expect everything to read just that way in the press releases and in the film credits."

Yates smiled, "I'm guessing that this little lie

will keep my people from being investigated or arrested?"

"It will," Barrister countered, "if you follow through on the final part of my request."

"Lay it out," the seemingly exhausted mogul said.

"Fifty percent of the profits are split among the families of the victims, and the rest go to the police widows and orphans fund."

"That's highway robbery," Yates complained. "That means Galaxy gets nothing."

"Actually," the cop explained, "what I'm suggesting is doing nothing more than living out what the pastor preached in your studio church two days ago. I was there and heard it. I think I saw you there as well."

"OK, fine," the mogul replied. "I give you my word."

"That's good," Barrister quipped, "but it is not enough. I know better than to trust the man who stole my files. You have your legal team put the agreement in writing and send it to the chief's desk by three this afternoon. Now what time do I need to be here tomorrow?"

"Meet me in this office around eight," Yates said. "We'll walk over to the soundstage from here."

Barrister stood, put on his hat, stared sternly into his host's face and gloated, "First time the cops have ever beaten a studio. If those girls hadn't

lost their lives making this possible, I would
enjoy this moment. And one more thing . . . if
you don't deliver the right man tomorrow, I'll
personally make you pay. Until tomorrow, Mr.
Yates."

72

July 22, 1936

As her father had to be at work an hour early to
build a collapsing table for the pirate movie,
Shelby was the first employee to arrive in the
wardrobe department on this bright and sunny
Wednesday. Grabbing a dress that would be used
next week in a period piece set in London during
the days of Queen Victoria, she began finishing
the beadwork around the bodice. She'd been at it
for fifteen minutes when Willard Mace arrived.

"Hello, Shelby. That's a pretty blue dress you
have on today."

Startled, Shelby apprehensively looked up.
When she saw it was Mace, she relaxed and
smiled, "Just another number the studio dreamed
up for the church publicity. It's doing so well
now, I think my days of getting free clothes and
doing publicity are about over. And I don't mind
a bit."

The man moved over and sat on a stool on the

opposite side of the worktable. "You've seemed kind of jumpy this week. Does it have anything to do with the girls getting strangled?"

She nodded and admitted, "I'm not really going to be relaxed until the guy who did it is locked up."

"Do you think they'll ever get him?" Mace asked.

"I think they know who he is," she explained, "but I'm not sure they have the evidence they need."

"How do you know that?" the man quizzed.

"Just what I've heard," she explained before adding. "You know, Willie, I have about decided it's not good to get what you wish for. Everything around us is just make-believe, and you and I are a part of it. And because of that, I got to wishing for a life where things were real and people didn't put on masks. After getting a taste of what is going on in the actual world, I've decided this world might be best. I mean, look at it this way, on our lot people get murdered every day, but they always get back up."

Mace tilted his head, looked into Shelby's blue eyes, and asked, "Do you ever miss where you used to live?"

"I've missed it a lot this week," she explained as she looked back down and continued her work. "Oh, don't get me wrong, the dresses I've worn and the things I've experienced and seen are wonderful. I'd be lying if I didn't admit it was really nice feeling like Cinderella. But there's a boy from back home I miss. He was sweet and kind of shy, and Calvin didn't know any of the lines men use out here. You know he even asked me for a kiss rather than just expected it. He couldn't act like anyone but who he was. I'd kind of like to go to a barn dance with him or maybe sit in church and just hold his hand. But that's not going to happen."

Mace smiled and nodded. In his own simple way, it looked as though he understood what she meant. As he picked a piece of lint from a coat sitting on the table, he quietly posed another question. "Shelby, did you really go to Flynn's house?"

As she thought about that night, a shiver raced up her spine. She looked from the dress to the man as she tried to explain, "That's a loaded question. Yes, I was there. And I discovered I didn't belong there. It wasn't a place for someone like me. And maybe that's why I've been thinking about Oklahoma. I'm wondering if I need to be in a world like Hollywood."

"That's a nice speech," Betsy Minser announced from the back corner of the room.

"I didn't hear you come in," Shelby said.

"I learned how to walk from cats," the woman explained. "I can sneak up behind anyone, and they never know I'm there. Now, on what you said, quit thinking about Oklahoma and concentrate on the moment. Today, you are going to be on soundstage 6. They are wrapping up the film starring Andrews and Sparks, and you have to be on hand to sew up anything that might get torn on the set."

"Couldn't you do it?" Shelby begged.

"I probably could," Minser assured her, "but I actually have a fitting to do today, and I also have to meet with a couple of designers the studio might start using."

"When do I need to be there?" the young woman groaned.

"About nine. And I doubt if you will do anything but watch, but you still need to be there just in case. Take one of the big sewing kits with you. Now I am off to meet with Wendy Storm."

"Are you serious?" Shelby asked.

"Not only am I serious," Minser replied, "but that's her real name. The studio found her in Kansas. Willie, get off the stool and get those dresses on the far rack to the pirate set. They'll be using them later in a big dance number."

As Minser and Mace headed in different directions, Shelby tried to focus on finishing the dress. Yet, even as she did the beadwork, she couldn't shake thoughts of Saturday night. Why was Flynn Sparks still on the lot? Why hadn't Captain Barrister arrested him?

73

July 22, 1936

Bill Barrister eased back into a director's chair beside Jacob Yates and shook his head. "So this is what my police station looks like when constructed at your studio."

"Did we get close?" Yates asked.

"It's not bad," the visitor noted, "but my office is a bit smaller and we have a ceiling and all four walls. But that guy playing me . . . Dalton Andrews . . . you nailed me there. He's a dead ringer!"

Yates smiled as he looked toward the door that led to the street. Pointing with a tilt of his head, he announced, "Look who's joining us."

Barrister watched Ellen Rains saunter into the room. Today must have been orange Wednesday because that was the color of her suit, hat, shoes, purse, and even lipstick. The mogul leaned close to the cop and warned, "Never trust that woman."

The captain whispered, "I never trust anyone, especially you."

"Ellen, my dear," Yates said, with an obviously fake smile, "so good to see you on our lot. Have you met Captain Barrister of the Homicide Department?"

Rains extended her plump hand toward the policeman. As he took it, she cracked, "Bill, I'm guessing you're here to investigate Jacob's impending death. Word on the street is this picture is going to kill him."

"If it does," the mogul grumbled, "you'll be the one pulling the trigger. Why don't you take the chair on the other side of Captain Barrister? That is, if you can get into it."

She flashed a huge grin. "I'll get in that chair a lot easier than you'll get out of this mess."

Yates nervously laughed, "Ellen, remind me to thank you for the story you wrote in yesterday's paper. You know it made this whole day possible."

Barrister climbed back into his chair, his body somewhat shielding Yates and Rains from each other's sight line, and studied the stage. Dalton Andrews was sitting behind the desk, and Flynn Sparks was leaning against the back wall, his arms folded over his chest. Another actor the cop didn't know was sitting in a chair just in front of the desk.

"Yates," the cop asked, "I know Andrews and Sparks, but who's the other guy?"

"His name is Hunter Nelson. He's actually playing the role of Flynn Sparks."

"Then who is Sparks playing?"

The mogul pointed to one of the two cops in the back of the room, "That guy who came in with you."

"Barry Jenkins?"

"Yeah, that's it."

"But why not have Sparks play Sparks and Nelson play my partner?"

Yates shrugged, "This is Hollywood, the top actors get the big roles. The Jenkins role is a large part, and the Sparks role is kind of a background bit. And Flynn gets the Jenkins part because it is really the one where we can better use his charms and charisma. No offense, but you are kind of dull."

"Really?" Barrister noted. "It still makes no sense to have a guy not playing himself."

"Maybe," Yates agreed. "But I have to say this. The guy who is playing Sparks does a better job in that role than Flynn does in real life."

Trying to come to grips on what seemed like upside-down casting, Barrister continued to study the rest of the set. Not far from his men, he noted Shelby Beckett sitting in a chair beside a water cooler. She looked both beautiful and very nervous. As he noted her innocence, he was now almost sorry he'd put her through the experience of dating Sparks. But in a world where the studios controlled police investigations, it was his only way of beating the system. And it almost worked.

As he continued to study Shelby, the cop leaned close to Yates and asked, "How long before we begin?"

"Vic Melton's not here yet, so it will be a few minutes."

"Good, I'll be right back. I think I'll walk over and get a glass of water."

Barrister, being careful not to trip over any wires or cords, casually made his way to the cooler. He grabbed a paper cup, took a long drink, and then finally greeted Shelby.

"I hope you are feeling well."

"I'm not here because I want to be," she assured him. "Why haven't you arrested him? That would make me feel a lot better."

"Because he got rid of the stuff you saw before I could get a warrant."

Shelby reached into her purse and pulled out the gun, "You might want this back."

After making sure no one was looking his way, Barrister took the weapon and slipped it into his pocket. With his eyes fixed on Sparks, he said, "Miss Beckett, I'm sorry it didn't work out, but I do appreciate what you did. It took a lot of courage. And no one else has died recently. You can take some pride in that."

"I just want it over," she bluntly replied. "Is this movie really going to produce the evidence to get him?"

"I've been assured it will," the cop replied. "Now, I need to get back to my chair. I want to be as close to this as possible when it all breaks."

As Barrister ambled back through the set, Vic Melton strolled in. Behind him was a girl holding four folders in her arms.

74

July 22, 1936

From his place just off the set, Barrister watched Melton walk out into the middle of the large room and clap his hands. Once everyone was silent he took charge.

"Ladies and gentlemen and those of you who are neither, we are about to create film history. The writers have identified the person who is the Hollywood Madman. The scene we are about to shoot will reveal his identity. Deborah is passing out the scripts at this time." Melton looked back to the police office as each of the actors took a folder and opened it.

"Vic," Andrews announced with a wave, "this only has my lines."

The director nodded, "That's true. I wanted this to have the feel of shock and surprise. I wanted the actors to be reacting just as people would in real life. Therefore, no one knows what the other one is saying." Melton turned back to the trio of thespians now studying their dialogue, "Each actor is given the cue word that calls them to action, but that is all they have. Also gentlemen, I want you to move and react as needed, and it will be the cameramen's jobs to follow you. I'm going to give you five minutes, and then we'll get started."

Barrister leaned over to Yates, "Is this normal?"

The mogul shrugged, "We stepped out of the range of normal the moment Ellen convinced me to do this project. But no, I've never seen this before. Melton is a genius, so this will likely be great theater, and it will likely leave me in tears."

"You will cry all the way to the bank," Rains pointed out. "The pain you experience will be temporary, but this will likely make your legend one that will live forever. In fact, it might just forever change how we do business."

"I hope not," Yates soberly responded, "I kind of like the old way. And Louis B. Mayer and Jack Warner do too."

As the mogul finished his thoughts, Barrister looked over to an apprehensive Shelby and then to his two officers who seemed more than ready to move in and take the killer into custody. This was not a perfect way to make an arrest, but it seemed foolproof and that was the bottom line. And if something did go wrong, the captain was also comforted in knowing that all the doors to the building were being covered by at least two armed policemen. If the murderer was in this room, there would be no escape.

"Are you Captain Barrister?"

Turning, the cop looked into the smiling face of Vic Melton.

"I am."

"May I ask you a favor?"

Barrister nodded.

"There will be a few lines that will need to be said after we announce the name of the murderer. I need for those to play out. I need for my guys to make the arrest and cuff the guy. After I yell 'Cut,' your people can move in."

"We can do it that way," Barrister agreed, "but I need to ask you something."

"Yes, sir."

"Andrews and Sparks are likely carrying weapons. Have they been checked? Do they have any live rounds in their guns?"

"I personally looked at each weapon before they were passed out," Melton assured him. "As this scene requires no gunplay, they don't even have blanks in them."

"Good," the cop assured him, "and my men won't move until I signal."

"Thank you," Melton answered. As the director moved back toward the office set, he yelled out, "Do you guys know your lines?"

The three nodded.

"OK, Deborah, collect the scripts, actors take your places, and let's do this."

Barrister studied the three actors. Andrews, sitting behind the desk, appeared relaxed; Nelson, slumped in the chair, seemed eager; and Sparks, leaning on the edge of the desk, was nervously playing with his suit coat.

"Action." Melton called out.

As the scene started, Andrews looked to Nelson, "It's been a long time coming, but I think we've got you."

"What makes you so sure it's me?" Nelson shot back.

Barrister was amazed. The actor had perfectly captured Sparks's cocky attitude.

Andrews continued, "You made a mistake, and it was a critical one."

"Cap," Sparks playing Jenkins cut in, "I've seen the evidence, and unless you have something new, we can't tie him to anything."

"Ah," Andrews announced, "I do have something new." The actor pulled a photograph from a desk drawer and then continued with his dialogue. "Here is a picture of you and Rose Trebour. A fan snapped it when you stopped to give a Miss Molly Riddle your autograph. You will note that it was taken when you left the studio with Miss Trebour at your side."

"So we had a date," Nelson shot back. "It proves nothing."

"That jacket you're wearing proves a lot," Andrews explained as he got up and moved toward Nelson. "The next morning, you brought this same jacket into wardrobe to have a torn place repaired in the coat. After it was fixed, it was then returned to the set. When you put it on that night after a day of shooting, four witnesses saw something drop out onto the ground. You were in such a hurry, you didn't notice. Those four were Deborah Rawlings, a script girl; Emma Nance, a maid; Jeff Weiss, who was an extra; and your costar Dalton Andrews."

"I don't know what you're talking about," Nelson snapped.

A pale Sparks leaned closer, "What was it that fell out, Cap?"

"In the photo," Andrews explained, "Miss Trebour was wearing a bracelet with her initials inscribed on a heart. Now study this picture of the woman at the crime scene. There is no bracelet." Andrews took a long look at Sparks playing Jenkins. He appeared almost paralyzed. Before delivering the next line, he looked back to Nelson. "But the witnesses saw that bracelet fall out of your pocket. The only thing that could have happened is that it must have fallen off in the struggle between you and Miss Trebour the night you killed her, and somehow it dropped into your coat. That is what will hang you, Flynn Sparks."

"No! That's not right!"

Along with everyone else, Barrister looked off the set and to the side of the stage. Rushing with purpose toward the actors was Shelby Beckett. As she moved into the view of the camera, an angry Melton screamed, "Cut!"

75

July 22, 1936

Shelby was now standing between Andrews and Nelson, with Sparks about six feet in front of her. Her blues eyes were on fire, and she was pointing the index finger of her right hand right at Andrews, who up until the stop in the action had been playing Barrister.

From his seat just off the set, the real Bill Barrister observed the strange scene playing out before him with interest. What was this all about? What was the girl doing? Except for Shelby, it appeared everyone else was all but frozen.

"I'm betting this wasn't in the script," Ellen Rains whispered to no one.

Meanwhile, his face now as red as his hair, Vic Melton yanked himself from a trance, jumped from his chair, tossed his copy of the script down on the floor, and exploded like a volcano.

"What in the name of all that is and has ever been are you doing?" the director screamed. "You ruined what was shaping up to be an incredible scene." Rushing up to the woman, he stood inches from her, his hands balled into fists, and yelled, "Don't you know you can't just rush on a set? How stupid are you? I don't care what you do or where you work, you are fired. Get off this lot now!"

Andrews stepped out from behind the desk and shoved the director back into a dolly. "Can it Vic, or I'll take you out. And I can do it too."

"And," Sparks added, "If Dalton can't do the job, I can."

"What kind of madhouse is this?" Melton demanded. "Someone tell me who's in charge here?"

Yates pushed off his chair, stepped onto the set, and quietly announced, "I'm in charge. And, Vic, you can't fire the girl."

Rains leaned over to Barrister, "This should be in the script. It's a shame the cameras aren't rolling right now."

Barrister watched as Melton frowned and walked back over to his chair. After he was seated, the studio mogul looked toward Shelby. "What is this all about?"

"The script's wrong," she suggested. "And I can prove it."

Yates leaned over to the girl and whispered something. She then softly spoke her answer into his ear. After nodding, he looked back to Melton.

"Vic, let's pick it up with the last line Dalton says, then let's have Shelby run in through the office door and say 'no.' At that point, Dalton can ad-lib his questions to her. If things run as smoothly as I think they will, we will just keep it going until the actors don't have anything left in their bag of tricks. Then we can determine what we've got."

"You're serious?" Melton asked.

"Dead serious. If what Shelby told me is right, then our script might be wrong." Yates paused, "And Ellen, let's you and I stand over here. This thing might take a turn where we need to walk through that door and add our two cents' worth."

"I'm game," the columnist announced as she pushed from her chair. "I've always thought the studios missed out not signing me as an actress. Move over Marie Dressler, here I come."

Barrister looked at her, "I thought Dressler was dead."

"She is," Rains said with a grin as she walked toward the set, "Marie died in thirty-four, but I'm ready to fill her shoes."

"Nelson," a still-dazed Melton called out, "please remember you are playing the role of Sparks. And Flynn, if you need to disagree with anything that Nelson is saying, try to figure out a way to do it and keep in the character of Barry Jenkins." He stopped and pointed to Shelby, "And you, get outside the room and please cry out 'No, that's not right' with the same conviction you did a few minutes ago. Let's get set."

The director watched everyone get in place before he shrugged and admitted, "I have no idea what I'm doing." He looked at his camera operators, "This time use all three. Doug, you do close work; Ron, follow the action with medium shots; and Ray, you keep the whole office in your view." He pointed once more to Shelby, "What's your name?"

"Shelby."

"Are you ready?"

"Yes."

"Dalton, are you ready to go with your last series of lines?"

"I'm ready."

Melton shook his head, "I still have no idea what I'm doing. Let's get ready. Cameras. Action."

Andrews began, "In the photo Miss Trebour was wearing a bracelet with her initials inscribed on a heart. Now look at this photo of the woman at the crime scene. There is no bracelet. The only thing that could have happened is that it must have fallen off in the struggle between you and Miss Trebour the night you killed her, and somehow it dropped into your coat. That is what will hang you, Flynn Sparks."

Shelby charged in and screamed, "No, it couldn't have happened that way."

Acting shocked, Andrews looked to the woman standing in the doorway and demanded, "Who are you?"

With scores of fascinated eyes looking on, the young woman continued into the office.

"I'm Shelby Beckett. I work in the studio's

wardrobe department. The morning after the murder of Miss Trebour, Flynn Sparks brought his jacket into our department to fix. He'd lost two buttons."

Andrews, now once more immersed in his role as Barrister and working on instinct only, demanded, "What does that have to do with anything?"

"We have a policy," Shelby announced. "We search every pocket and take out every item before we do any work on the clothing. I took everything out of the pocket of Flynn Sparks's coat that morning and put them in a small sack. There was no bracelet in the jacket."

"Are you sure you checked all the pockets?" Andrews asked.

"Yes," she assured him. "I always look through things twice. I had double-checking drilled into my head by my high school math teacher."

Barrister watched as the actor playing him rubbed his mouth and eased back onto the corner of his desk. As the cameras rolled, Andrews then studied the man playing Sparks for a moment before picking up his line of questioning.

"Miss Beckett, what did you do with the coat when you finished?"

"I hung it up on a rack just behind my work station."

"And how did Mr. Sparks get it back?"

"He came by a few hours later," she explained.

"In fact, there was another actor in wardrobe when Flynn walked in."

"Who was that actor?"

"Dalton Andrews."

The actor playing Barrister stopped, as if remembering a certain moment, then plunged on. "When the jacket was in your department, who had access to it, besides you?"

Shelby paused before saying, "Betsy Minser, my supervisor, and Willard Mace."

A completely fascinated Barrister moved his gaze from the action to where Yates and Rains were standing just out of the cameras' viewpoints. The studio head seemed as though he'd just received the best news of his life, while Rains's reaction was just the opposite. Her face had turned ashen gray.

Andrews, depending upon his own devices, looked toward the real Flynn Sparks. "Barry, if what she says is true, then someone might be trying to set Sparks up."

"So it would appear," came the quick reply.

Andrews reached back and picked up the desk phone. After dialing a zero, he barked into the receiver, "Get down to Galaxy Studios and bring Betsy Minser and Willard Mace to this station. I need to question both of them."

After the actor placed the phone back into the cradle, Melton called out, "Cut."

76

July 22, 1936

During the twenty-minute break, Yates strolled back to Barrister and shrugged. "I didn't expect this. I thought it would be open and shut. I thought our writers had everything figured out. Does this ever happen with police work?"

"If you're asking if we ever think we have a ribbon tied around a case and then watch it come undone, the answer is yes. In fact, what I'm seeing now is pretty realistic. And that guy you have playing me is asking all the right questions. I might just want to hire him when this is over. Unless, of course, he's the actual murderer."

Barrister turned back to look at Andrews still sitting behind the desk. The man seemed to be lost in thought. It was as if he'd become an actual homicide investigator and was plotting his next move. He only looked up when two uniformed policemen brought Betsy Minser into the room.

"Are those real cops?" Melton asked.

"They are two of my guys," Barrister admitted.

"Betsy," the director explained, "Dalton is going to question you as if he is a real cop. Film will be rolling. Just answer him as you would if you were at a real police station." Melton looked up, "Nelson, move back to the couch against the office wall. When the officers bring Betsy in, put her in the chair where Nelson has been sitting. By the way, where is Willard Mace?"

One of the cops looked past the director to Barrister, "We couldn't find him. He was taking clothes to some studio and wasn't in wardrobe. We've got a couple of guys looking for him and two more waiting in the wardrobe building."

Barrister nodded.

"OK," Melton barked, "we'll go with Betsy and bring Willard in later. Let's get things set up. Dalton you take the lead again. I want all three cameras rolling just like last time." He paused and looked around, "Action."

Andrews sat on the corner of this desk and studied the latest addition to the scene. After folding his arms he asked, "Miss Minser, Miss Beckett has informed us that when clothing is brought in to wardrobe to be mended that everything is removed from the pockets. Is that correct?"

"It is," she quickly replied. "It is put in paper sacks, and we write on the outside the date, time, and name of the actor or actress whose outfit we are working on."

"What happens to those sacks?"

"We fold them over a couple of times and put a staple in them. Then we set them aside."

"So," Andrews noted, "you don't put those items back in the clothing."

"No, sir," Minser explained, "there are times when, after mending the clothing, it needs to be washed or cleaned. We keep the sacks in our department until the people whose possessions are in those sacks come by and pick them up."

"Did Mr. Sparks come by and pick up the items that Miss Beckett took from his jacket before she repaired it?"

"No," Minser replied. "I actually have that sack with me now." She reached into her purse, pulled out the small paper bag, and handed it to Andrews, still playing Barrister.

Andrews held it for a moment before looking back to Nelson. "Mr. Sparks, do you mind if I open this and look at the contents?" Both Nelson and the real Flynn Sparks nodded approvingly.

Andrews opened the bag and dumped it on his desk. He looked at what fell out before noting, "Nothing unusual here." He then turned his attention back to Minser, "Did you place a bracelet in Mr. Flynn's coat after it was mended?"

"No, sir. In fact, I actually looked through the coat soon after Shelby worked on it. You see, Mr. Sparks called and asked if he'd left a lucky rabbit's foot in the jacket. First, I looked through the sack, and, when it wasn't there, I went through every pocket. There was nothing in the coat."

Andrews looked to Nelson and then moved his gaze to Sparks. "Barry, I remember Dalton Andrews telling me he saw Sparks put the jacket on when he picked it up and take it off when he returned to the set. Do you remember where our suspect set the coat after removing it?"

"It was on a table, just to the right of where the set ended. It was kind of out of the way and to the back."

"Could anyone have had access to the jacket while it was there?"

"I don't know," Sparks replied, "but there is a man who could tell us for sure."

"Who's that?" Andrews asked.

"The director, Vic Melton. And he is waiting outside in the main part of the station. He came in because he felt Miss Minser needed a friend with her."

Barrister looked over at a shocked Melton. This was getting better by the second.

Andrews ordered Sparks, "Go get him and bring him in here."

Sparks, now seemingly enjoying his role as Jenkins, rushed out the door, behind the camera and to Melton's side. The director shrugged and followed the cop back onto the set. A few seconds later, he made his first on-screen appearance.

"Are you Vic Melton?" Andrews asked.

"I am," the director assured him. "And Mr. Jenkins brought me up to speed on the information you need. I was watching the whole time, and no one crossed the set to the place where the jacket was sitting. I would have seen it if they had."

"So," Andrews said, "that means the bracelet could have only been dropped into the jacket when it was in wardrobe." He looked back to Minser, "What does Willard Mace do?"

"Mainly our heavy work," she explained. "He picks up bolts of fabric and takes racks of clothes to various soundstages. He also sorts things for me."

"How long has he been working for you?"

"Just over eleven months."

"Why did you hire him?" Andrews asked. "Was he the best man for the job?"

"No," she admitted, "there were a dozen applicants who would have been better. I wanted someone who also possessed some basic sewing skills, and several of our applicants had those skills."

"Then," Andrews asked, "why did you give him the job over the others?"

"Because Mr. Jacob Yates told me to."

Beyond the set, the mogul quickly glanced over to Rains. She was looking at the floor and didn't return his worried stare.

Andrews looked from face to face in the room before turning back to the woman, "The head of the studio demanded that you hire Mace?"

"Yes, sir."

Seemingly relishing his role, Andrews looked back to Sparks, "Find out if our people have tracked down Mace." Sparks hurried through the door and looked toward Barrister. The cop shook his head. Retracing his steps, the actor once more stepped into the camera's view and through the office door.

"No sign of Mace yet."

"Then get me the head of the studio . . . Jacob Yates. I want him in my office as soon as possible! And if we don't find Willard Mace soon, I'm going to fire someone!"

77

July 22, 1936

Barrister watched, his arms folded, as chaos seemingly broke out on the set. The most interesting action was taking place about six feet to his right with Yates who was facing off with Melton.

"I'm not going to let that actor interview me," the mogul yelled. "There is a limit to what can be done here."

"Oh," the director shot back, "I seem to remember you were the one who tossed the scripts away and opened things up. It seems to me that Andrews is running the show now. Go talk to him. Tell him you won't be interviewed."

Barrister slowly pushed out of his chair and ambled over to the two squabbling men. "Mr.

Yates, your man playing me has opened up a new avenue of evidence in this case. You can either talk to him as the cameras roll, or I will take you down to the real station where you can visit with me in my real office. In truth, even as good a job as your actor is doing playing me, in real life I'm a lot tougher."

"Fine," Yates fumed. "But I'm not doing this alone."

Barrister followed the mogul's eyes across the stage. He appeared to be staring holes through Ellen Rains's orange dress. What did she have to do with Mace? As the cop was continuing to try to figure out the body language between the mogul and the columnist, Dalton Andrews left the set and approached the cop.

"Can I talk to you?" the actor asked.

"Sure," Barrister answered.

"Let's go over by the back door where no one can overhear us," Andrews suggested. "I need a bit of advice."

The cop followed his acting counterpart back to the corner. Once out of earshot of the rest of the cast and crew, Andrews spoke in hushed tones.

"I know a couple of other things that need to be addressed. One involves the first murder of the woman from Gary, Indiana. The other centers on something I found out about the Leslie Bryant strangulation. But right now what I know on those murders doesn't seem to fit with the others. Now I have to admit, when Shelby dropped that bombshell, it pretty much blew what I was sure was true and turned it all upside down."

"That happens more than you could guess," Barrister said. "The fact is, most murder cases are not cut and dried. And, remember this, murder doesn't make sense. Sane people don't murder people. Unless you're crazy, you have to be motivated by greed, self-preservation, or hate. It can also be a combination of all three with a bit of insanity tossed in."

"But," Andrews noted, "I'm acting on instincts. I don't know what I'm doing."

"Actually," Barrister assured him, "you are doing just what I'd be doing right now. You are following the trail. Just keep going down it, and when you get a chance and the time is right to toss in your new information, then do so." The cop looked back to the set. "It appears that Melton has Yates convinced to get some camera time too. So this is the moment for you to go back to work. I can't wait to watch."

78

July 22, 1936

After the director called for action, Andrews stood at the side of his office and studied those present. Seated on the couch against the wall were Shelby, Minser, and Nelson. Sitting on the far corner of his desk was Sparks. Directly in front of his desk were Jacob Yates and Ellen Rains, and he was fully aware both of them had the power to end his career in Hollywood. This was anything but an ideal situation. As he gathered the strength to get back into character, he wondered if he was playing the last scene of his last role. Folding his arms over his chest, he cleared his throat and jumped headfirst into the lion's den.

"Mr. Yates, Betsy Minser told me that you insisted she hire Willard Mace in spite of the fact that several other applicants were better qualified. Is that true?"

Yates expression was cold and his look stern, "It is."

"I want to know why."

"I did it as a favor," came the quick reply.

"A favor to whom?"

"Ellen Rains."

As he moved to the desk chair and took a seat,

Andrews looked from Yates to Rains and back. The mogul was obviously angry, but the woman was displaying an emotion he'd never seen in her face . . . fear. Rather than her normal calm, collected self, the gossip queen looked as though she were sitting on a tack—a very hot one.

"Mr. Yates, since when does Miss Rains have the power to make employment decisions on your lot?"

Yates frowned, "Ellen is the kind of woman who knows every skeleton in every closet. As long as she is treated the way she demands to be treated, those skeletons stay in the closet. She threatened to trot out an old set of bones if I didn't hire Willard Mace. As the job did not require much in the way of skills, I agreed to give the man the position. I also agreed not to fire him, no matter how poorly he did his job."

Andrews shifted his gaze to the antsy woman. After studying Rains for a few moments, he glanced over to Sparks. "Barry, bring those uniformed cops back in here. I have a question."

Sparks walked out the door and a couple of moments later returned with two of the city's finest. Both men seemed more than happy to once more be in the middle of the action.

"Any news on Mace? Do we know where he is?"

One cop looked to the other, before the larger one answered. "We can't find him. More than twenty policemen are looking for him now. We have people on the way to his apartment. We're guessing he somehow got off the lot."

"Thank you," Andrews said, "you're dismissed." As the real cops left, the actor turned his attention to the columnist. "Miss Rains, why was it so important for Galaxy to give Willard Mace a job?"

"He needed a break," she answered.

Andrews smiled, "Ellen Rains doesn't just give away breaks. She trades for them. So what was this man holding over you that forced you to demand a favor from Jacob Yates?"

The woman balled up her hands in her lap and looked over to the studio mogul as if begging for help. He gave her none. The writer who spun out thousands of words a day now seemed to be struggling to find just one.

Andrews pushed, "I'm waiting, Miss Rains."

"What's the use in hiding the past?" she said as her eyes focused on the floor. "It's likely poetic justice, maybe it is even God laughing at me, but after all the years of digging up dirt on everyone else, now I'm going to reveal my own little secrets." She paused and looked over to Yates before continuing her story. "Mace is not Willard's last name. In fact, Mace was his grandfather's last name. I told him to use his middle name when I got him the job here. You see, he'd just spent several years in a sanitarium. He'd made a lot of progress there, and the doctors thought he was ready to live life on the outside of those walls. When he was released, I got him a place of his own, some new clothes, and even a car."

She stopped, smiled, and looked up toward the office ceiling that wasn't really there. "Except when he'd have his spells, he was always a good boy. And he isn't really slow. He can read, write, and manage things like spending money and finding his way around. He is a good driver too. And I thought the studio was a good place for him. It was a safe world, and I knew that Betsy would have the patience to put up with his little idiosyncrasies."

"Miss Rains," Andrews cut in. "You haven't answered my question about why you felt the need to help this man."

"I've been trying not to," she admitted. "Anyway, here goes. Thirty years ago, I lived in New York and was going to college. There was a boy I really liked, and things happened. He moved away and never knew that I was pregnant. About eight months later, Willard was born in a charity hospital. My mom raised him, and I landed a job at a newspaper. Within a year, I was covering the entertainment scene. Things were going pretty well for me. Then twenty years ago, my mother died, and the owner of the newspaper discovered that Willard was my child rather than being my brother. Because of a morals clause in my contract, I lost my job. When that happened, I figured I needed to start over somewhere else. The movie business was just taking off out here, so I moved west. I landed a job at the *Times* and kind of righted my ship. Then one night I was in a car accident, and Willard was seriously injured. After that, my bright little boy was never the same."

Andrews leaned forward in his chair and rested his elbows on the desk as Rains dabbed tears from her eyes. He was about to suggest she continue when she did so without prompting.

"I first noticed something might be wrong when I bought him a kitten. He loved that cat until it took a shine to a neighbor's child. He reacted so violently to the cat's playing with the little girl that he strangled the cat. She was dead before I could pull her away from him. A few months later, he did the same thing to a puppy. He'd be fine for months and then something would set him off, and he'd just go crazy. When he was twelve, he attacked a little girl in his school, and that is when I decided it would be best if I put him away for a while. I didn't just leave him there; I'd check him out of there from time to time, but every once in a while he'd act up again, and I'd have to put him back behind those walls."

As she took a breath, Andrews thought about the notes Barrister had written in his evidence files. As he went over the various entries, something jumped out.

"Miss Rains, the neighbor that was playing with the cat, what color clothing was the girl wearing?"

"Blue . . . she had on blue pants and a blue shirt."

"Was there any blue color associated with the attack on the puppy?"

Rains paused before nodding, "Yes, the dog had taken a blue spread off the bed and was playing with it."

"And the girl at school?"

"My word, she was also wearing blue."

It was time for Andrews to take a huge leap, "What color was the car that hit you when your son was injured?"

"The car that ran into us was a light blue. The car I was driving was a darker shade of blue. And now that I think about it, the times he got violent at home after I would check him out of the sanitarium, I was always wearing blue. You know how I always wear the same color from shoes to hat. I don't wear blue much, but when I did . . ."

Andrews looked from the woman to Sparks, "Are the men who are looking for Mace all uniformed policemen?"

"I don't know."

Andrews shook his head, "We have to make sure that we pull off all uniformed men from the search and use only those wearing regular clothing."

"I'll get the word out," Sparks, seemingly now

loving his role as Jenkins, announced as he left the room.

"Blue by itself can't be all that sets him off," Rains suggested. "There were many times I wore blue and nothing happened."

Andrews thought back to something Barrister had told him earlier. Murderers were motivated by greed, self-preservation, or hate. The cop had left out another key motivation for killing . . . jealousy.

Possibly because he hadn't gotten to say any line in a long time, Nelson called out, "Now that all of this has come to light, can I go home?"

Andrews shook his head, "No." He turned and looked back at the woman. "Miss Rains, you said that Willard was released from the sanitarium about a year ago?"

"Yes." Rains took a deep breath before dropping her final bombshell. "He got out May 27, 1935. I remember that because I'd gone to a movie premiere on the twenty-sixth. And there is one other thing you might want to know about Willard."

"What's that?" Andrews asked.

Rains, her expression suddenly hard and cold, announced, "His father is Jacob Yates. If he didn't give Willard the job, I was going to drop that bit of news to his wife."

79

July 22, 1936

As a completely fascinated Barrister watched, Melton signaled his cameramen to keep the film rolling. After glancing over at Jenkins, the cop sat back in his chair and studied the scene in the studio's version of his office. Sparks, who had just come back through the door, appeared strangely at ease, Andrews confused, Rains on the verge of a nervous breakdown, and Yates in a state of complete shock. As a tense crew looked on, Andrews glanced at each person in the room before finally landing his gaze on the studio mogul and breaking more than a minute of awkward silence.

"Did you know that you were Willard Mace's father?"

"No," Yates quickly assured him. "I knew Ellen back when we were both in college. And then I saw her again not long after she moved out here from the east. At that time, she told me her son was the product of a failed marriage."

Andrews looked back to Rains, "Is that correct?"

She nodded, "Jacob was married. He had a new life, was just starting his studio; I didn't want to complicate things for him. What purpose would it have served? If I wrecked his family, he wouldn't have married me, anyway."

Andrews stood, moved to the corner of his desk, sat down, and crossed his arms. With Barrister carefully observing his every move, the pretend cop aimed another pointed question at Yates. "Did you know that Mace had spent years in a mental institution?"

The mogul nodded.

"Then, if you were aware of that and you didn't know Mace was your child, why hire him? What does Rains have on you that could make you do that?"

Rains cut in before Yates had a chance to answer, "He was driving the car that hit us the night Willard was hurt. And he was drunk. We covered it up so well there wasn't even an accident report filed. To keep things quiet, he's paid for all the treatments and care since that night."

"OK," Andrews said as he brought his hand to his jaw, "it would seem that Mace had the best motive for most of the murders. But, until we can track him down and get his story, I can't be sure of that. But there is one thing that I know, as he was still in the asylum, there is one murder he couldn't have committed. And this is the one we have labeled as the first murder. Not long ago, our medical examiner discovered that victim's name."

Andrews picked up a copy of the official police

files and opened it. He studied the report for a moment before announcing, "Does the name Wanda McMillan mean anything to anyone here?"

Andrews looked toward the far wall, Yates shook his head, and Rains pulled a handkerchief from her purse and dabbed at her eyes. When no one volunteered any information, the actor pointed to Nelson, "Would you mind stepping out for a bit? I have a few things I would like to speak to my assistant about."

Nelson nodded, pushed off the couch, and walked through the door. When he was gone, Andrews turned his attention to Sparks, still in his role as Barry Jenkins.

"Barry, you questioned Flynn Sparks a great deal. Would it be an exaggeration to say you know him better than anyone in this room?"

Sparks stood, faced the other actor, and announced, "I think I know him better than anyone in the world."

Barrister was amazed the actors could continue to stay in character. In all this craziness, they were still playing their parts. Like everyone else in the room, the cop was sitting on the edge of his seat in anticipation of finding out information that had so far eluded his own investigation.

Andrews, his eyes locked onto Sparks, asked, "What does the name Wanda McMillan mean to him?"

"It was the name of a woman he dated for a

while in Gary, Indiana, before he came to Hollywood."

Andrews nodded, "What was Mr. Sparks's name when he lived in Gary?"

"Bill Hamilton. Or to put it another way, Bill Hamilton died when Flynn Sparks was born."

"Barry, Wanda McMillan's friends in Indiana told the police she came to Los Angeles in search of big money. I'm guessing she was trying to blackmail the father of her child. Is Flynn Sparks the father of her child?"

The actor playing Jenkins resolutely shook his head, "No. She tried to shake him down, but he couldn't have been the father, and he didn't bite. He took her out to eat and even paid for her to have a special beauty treatment, but he refused to budge on the blackmail. After a couple of meetings, he wished her well and gave her enough money to get back home."

"She came to me as well," Rains freely admitted. "She told me her sad story and wanted to know what'd I pay for an exclusive. She was a pretty girl, and I felt a bit sorry for her, so I sent her to the man with the most to lose, figuring he might spring for some cash."

"Who was that?" Andrews asked.

"Jacob Yates."

The mogul shook his head, "She called, but I never met with her. So I actually never saw her."

"That's a lie," Rains shot back.

"How dare you call me a liar!"

"Wait a minute," Andrews said as he held up his hand. "Yates, I know you pretty well; you're telling me that as protective as you are of Flynn Sparks, with the money you've laid out over the years to protect him, you never met with the woman?" He allowed the words to settle in before sticking the knife in a bit deeper. "Your secretary keeps a log of who comes in and out of your office. It won't be any problem for us to look at it and find out if you are telling the truth."

"Jacob, tell him the truth," Rains demanded. When the mogul remained mute, she filled in the blanks. "Jacob, you told me you offered her ten grand. And, because she told you she'd seen me, you also gave me that much to keep the story quiet. What you didn't realize was that I wasn't going to use it. So the ten thousand was for nothing."

Yates looked as though he'd been kicked in the stomach. Grabbing the woman by her shoulders, he yelled, "You took me?"

"I've taken you scores of times," she taunted. "It is easy to take advantage of a man who wants to cover up all the bad-tasting truth. My house was paid for by chumps like you."

"OK," Yates announced as he let the woman go. She was still brushing the wrinkles from her sleeves as he explained. "I met the little blonde at a café. She was smart and crafty. She had just enough evidence to convince me the kid was Flynn's. We haggled for a while, and I paid her off. That was the last I saw of her."

"Wait a second," Sparks again assuming his role as Jenkins said, "when Wanda met with me . . . rather with Flynn Sparks . . . she was a brunette. When Sparks met her for lunch at Gilbert's Restaurant, there was a waiter who talked about how beautiful her hair was. I know he'll remember her and can confirm that, if we need corroborating testimony."

Rains chimed in next, "After she left my office, I had my man follow her that day too. He took a photo of Flynn with her at Gilbert's."

Andrews pointed a finger at the woman, "So you were interested in her story."

"I thought she was lying," Rains admitted, "but I'm not always right. I decided to follow her trail and see if Flynn was scared. My guy tailed Flynn for a week, but after that lunch at Gilbert's, they never met. So I don't think he could have paid her off or killed her."

"Do you have the date," Sparks asked, "of the last time Sparks met with Wanda McMillan?"

"Not off the top of my head," the woman said, "but if you let me make a call to my office, I can ask Benny. He was the one tailing Flynn, and he keeps incredible records in a log book."

"Don't use this phone," Andrews suggested. "Go out into the main office. I don't want to tie this one up in case we capture Willard Mace."

Barrister grinned. The actor realized the desk phone was just a prop and had made up a story to cover that fact. As the cast and crew watched, Rains hurried through the office door and off the set. At the back of the room was a wall phone, and she went right to it. As she made her call, Andrews looked back to Sparks.

"Did the actor give you any more details about that last meeting?"

"Yeah, he said Jean Harlow walked in just as they were leaving. He introduced Wanda to the actress and said she loved the way Harlow's hair looked. That was when she asked for and he gave her money to go to a beauty shop. McMillan must have dyed her hair blonde right after that."

Yates shook his head and muttered, "This is a big waste of everyone's time."

The mogul had just finished complaining when Rains returned. "The date was May 13, 1935."

"And that was the date of the newspaper that was found under her body," Sparks noted.

Rains walked over and took her seat. She glared at Yates for a few moments before announcing, "I had my assistant check the notes in my journal too. On May 21, 1935, I asked Jacob about the woman with the son who was trying to blackmail Sparks. He assured me she wasn't a problem anymore, that he had paid her off. When I asked how he could be sure she wouldn't come back asking for more, he replied she was now as silent as Valentino. There's only one way someone becomes that silent."

"You've got nothing," the mogul bragged. "There is nothing connecting me to that girl."

"We will see," Andrews said. "The mere fact you knew she was a blonde means you had to be one of the last people to see her alive." He glanced at the police file before adding, "And the fact her watch stopped at fourteen minutes after six narrows our window a great deal. I hope you can prove where you were at that time. If you can't, then the stain of possible guilt will follow you the rest of your life."

Barrister grinned. Andrews was doing this just like he would have. In the cop's mind, there was no doubt that this guy was the best actor in the world.

As everyone looked at a completely deflated Yates, two real cops walked onto the set and directly into the fake office. One of them announced, "We can't find Mace, but we have searched his apartment. There is evidence linking him to all but two of the strangulation cases, and in the kitchen, we found matches that are the same as the ones left with the bodies. We even found more than a dozen photos of Flynn Sparks that had been mutilated."

"Which two cases did you not find anything on?" Andrews asked.

"The one from May of last year," the cop replied.

"I think," Andrews said with a satisfied smile, "we've solved that one. We know Mace couldn't have killed Wanda McMillan. He had not been released from the asylum yet."

The uniformed cop nodded, "And the other is the murder of Leslie Bryant. For some reason, there was nothing of hers at Mace's home."

80

July 22, 1936

Andrews looked to Rains, "Any idea where your son might be?"

"No," she admitted. "When he was a kid playing hide-and-seek no one could ever find him. They told me when he was locked up in the asylum that he once stayed out of sight for four days, and he never left the grounds. They had people looking all over the state for him then."

Andrews glanced off the set toward Barrister. The cop shrugged. The actor was hoping for more help than that. Yet, with the real cops looking for the man responsible for all but two of the strangulation murders, he figured the best thing to do was keep the film rolling and solve the killing of Leslie Bryant. With that in mind, he glanced to the couch where Shelby Beckett was sitting with her boss.

"Miss Beckett," Andrews asked, once more falling back into character while opening the file and turning to the sections devoted to the Bryant murder. He scanned the latest notes until he came upon a section involving Shelby's trip to Sparks's home. He then looked back to the woman. "You had a chance to search Flynn Sparks's home last Saturday night. What did you uncover?"

"I found a man who was a compulsive collector," Shelby explained. "He had scrapbooks that contained every clipping from every story ever done on him. He had a drawer filled with matchbooks from what looked like every restaurant and nightclub he has ever visited. It seemed he had every piece of fan mail ever sent his way too."

"OK," Andrews cut in, "you've established he had amassed a lot of things concerning his career and travels. But there was something you found in another drawer that was tied to this case. And, as that drawer was empty by the time police got a warrant, maybe you can tell me what you saw."

"In his bedroom," Shelby explained, "was a drawer filled with personal items taken from women. On the very top was a purse. Inside that handbag, I found identification that proved it belonged to Leslie Bryant."

As Sparks watched, Andrews once more looked

at the file. He scanned Barrister's notes before again turning his attention to the woman. "Miss Beckett, as I said, the next day when we searched the home those items were gone. As you did not take them and the man watching the place for the studio told me no one visited Sparks from the time you left until we arrived the next afternoon, I have to believe that the home's owner destroyed them."

Andrews looked to Sparks. "Barry, did you ask Mr. Sparks what happened to the items?"

"I burned them," came the straightforward response.

"Cut!" Melton screamed. "Flynn you are playing Sergeant Barry Jenkins, not yourself. Please stay in character. Camera one, give me a close up on Flynn, and Sparks, you give me that answer in the third person please." He waited until everyone was back in place before saying, "Action."

Everyone looked to Sparks, "He told me he burned them because he knew they would point the finger of suspicion at him for the murders. Cap, I'm guessing without that evidence there is no case."

"Except for one thing, you would be right," Andrews explained as he reached into his pocket. Retrieving a handkerchief with the initials L.B., the actor tossed it on his desk.

"Where did you get that?" a now apprehensive Sparks asked.

Andrews grimly explained, "Dalton Andrews found it in his Packard, the one that Flynn Sparks used when he took Leslie Bryant on a date and then later home. There was also a stain on the backseat that the lab can analyze. Taken together with the testimony of Miss Beckett, the guard, and the numerous people who saw him with Miss Bryant on those nights, it might just be enough to convict him for the crime."

Sparks frowned, rubbed his brow, and nervously and slowly walked around the room. He carefully studied each of those present before speaking. As Andrews watched the actor pace, it reminded him of a tiger in a cage at the zoo. There could not be an escape for Sparks now. The noose was tightening around his neck as each second ticked by.

"I know," Sparks cautiously acknowledged, "how the handkerchief got into the back floorboard of the car, and I can explain why the purse was where it was also."

"We're waiting," Andrews announced as he returned to his chair and sat down.

"Captain," Sparks said, "when she was taken home, Leslie Bryant was sick. The liquor she'd been served the night before did not sit well with her. At one point, the actor even had to stop the car so she could get out and vomit. After she was feeling a bit better, she got a handkerchief from her pocket and wiped her mouth. She then decided to get into the car's backseat and lie down. She did throw up one more time during the trip. Sparks later cleaned that place on the seat as best he could. He likely didn't notice the handkerchief was on the floor."

Sparks, playing Jenkins, took a deep breath before he continued. "When Sparks finally got Bryant home, he escorted her up to her apartment. Later, after playing tennis with Clark Gable and having dinner, he noticed that she'd left her purse in the Packard. It had fallen between the seat and the passenger door. The actor took it inside and had planned on returning it to her at the studio, but when he found out she'd died, he tossed it in the drawer."

Andrews dug a bit deeper, "What was all the other stuff in the drawer?"

"Just like the scrapbooks and matches, they were keepsakes . . . something from all the women who have been to the house."

"It's a good story," Andrews said, "but as there are no witnesses to prove what Flynn Sparks said, it is nothing more than a story. And until proven differently, Sparks was the last person to see Leslie Bryant alive, and that makes him the most likely murder suspect. After all, the mere fact that there was nothing from Miss Bryant in Willard Mace's collection seems to indicate he didn't do it."

Sparks anxiously moved over to where Andrews

stood beside the desk and almost pleaded, "Captain, do you have a photo from the murder scene?"

Andrews opened the folder and pulled out one that included the body and the area around it. Sparks studied the shot before handing it back. He looked to Shelby as he announced, "Flynn Sparks had never heard of the other murders. He knew nothing of the other crime scenes. If he had murdered Leslie Bryant, he would not have known to drop the unused, broken kitchen match at the scene." He turned back to Andrews, "The reason Willard Mace has no souvenirs from Bryant's killing is because the woman left her purse and the handkerchief in the Packard. So, the only thing he could take from the woman was her bracelet, and he couldn't keep that; he had to use it to frame Flynn. Mace must have been watching the whole time and grabbed the woman as soon as Sparks got her home."

Staying in character, Andrews looked over to Sparks and nodded. "Barry, I will actually admit that makes sense. And I think, thanks to what you just said, I finally figured out why the match was left at each scene." Andrews took a deep breath, centered his thoughts, and continued, "Of course, we heard about two things triggering Mace's rage. One was the color blue and the other was jealousy. I think we will find that Sparks took out each one of the dead women and, while Mace might have had some mental issues, he was still pretty bright. He likely knew Sparks could take him out in a fair fight. So what was the best way to make him pay for stealing the women Mace wanted? It was to leave a clue pointing us to the actor. And when struck, a match sparks. It was almost the perfect frame."

Andrews got up from the chair and stuck his hand out towards the other actor, "Congratulations, Barry, you helped figure out the last element in this case. Why don't you go find Flynn Sparks and inform him he is no longer a suspect?"

After shaking hands, a smiling Sparks announced, "I will do that right now."

"And Jenkins, send in some cops to haul Jacob Yates downtown." Andrews folded his arms and nodded, "Now all we have to do is find Willard Mace."

Five seconds later, from somewhere off the set, Melton yelled, "Cut."

As the cameras stopped, Barrister stood and looked at Jenkins. "Now it's time to make an arrest. And, like my film counterpart said, it is also time we found Mace. With every cop in town looking for him, he can't run far."

81

July 22, 1936

With the avalanche of information that had just landed on the soundstage, Shelby was still reeling. In the course of the morning's filming, almost everything she thought and believed had been proven false. The man she was sure was guilty was not, a citywide search was going for her co-worker—the man who really was the Hollywood Madman, and the owner of Galaxy Studios was being led away in handcuffs. It seemed that when reality hit a studio, it struck with a knockout punch!

"I guess we need to get back to work," Betsy Minser noted. "With or without Yates, I figure we will still be making movies. And we've got to finish the gowns they need for the country club dance that is being shot next week on sound-stage 14."

Rising from the couch, a still numb Shelby walked slowly off the set. She was just about to the outside door when Bill Barrister put his hand gently on her shoulder and stopped her.

"I want to thank you," the cop said. "You did some great work."

"But," the woman argued, "he was not guilty."

"And," Barrister replied, "that's just as important as finding someone who is guilty. And don't worry; we'll track down Willard Mace."

"I'm not worried," Shelby assured him. "What concerns me is that I thought of people as things they weren't."

The cop smiled, "Miss Beckett, you work in a world where nothing is as it really is. Even a cop like me has problems telling the difference between the reality and fantasy in a place like this. Now, I have a job to do. I hope you will excuse me."

After stepping out the door, Shelby made the two-block walk back to the wardrobe department. Her mind was still so overwhelmed she failed to notice anything during that short trek. Once inside the finishing room, she sat down at her worktable and glanced up at the clock. How could it be only a quarter past eleven?

A somehow energetic Minser was already in full work mode as she pitched a pattern package to Shelby and rushed over to her own desk to look through the weekly work checklist. "OK, there are some dresses that Willie was supposed to have already taken over to the Western movie. I can see them on the other side of the room. I guess I'll run them over for the saloon scene. They shoot that later this afternoon. I should be back before lunch. Maybe we can eat together."

"That sounds good," she agreed. "Betsy, I never

thought it was Willie. How can you work with someone and not know?"

"He is sick," Minser explained. "Something inside him was just not right. You know, I realized the matches at the scene were meant to frame Flynn, but when I heard about the fact that they were broken in two, it made me think of something else."

"What's that?"

"Well, Shelby, each time Mace killed someone, he snapped, just like those matches."

"And," Shelby sadly noted, "none of it had to happen. It was the accident that did it."

"Consider the irony," Minser suggested. "The man who built this studio and became rich doing it was brought down by driving drunk twenty years ago. And the person who Yates injured back then was the son he didn't know he had."

"And," Shelby sadly replied, "it is all because so many different people—including Yates, Rains, and Flynn—were trying to hide from what was real by creating fantasy, not just on this studio lot, but even in their own lives. And it all built into a storm of deception that took the lives of all those poor women."

"Almost sounds like a biblical story," the supervisor noted. "Now, I need to get these costumes delivered."

Shelby watched her supervisor push a rolling rack of clothes through the door leading outside to the street. As soon as it closed, the young woman pulled the pattern from the envelope and started to lay it out. She didn't bother looking up when she heard the door open again.

"Did you forget something?" Shelby asked as she picked up a piece of material to begin the dress.

There was no response.

She was holding the fabric while looking from the pattern to the design sketch when instinct finally kicked in. She hesitantly lifted her eyes from her work and found herself staring into the face of Willard Mace. Her suddenly racing heart jumped up into her throat. He was less than five feet from her.

Mace looked confused and upset. His eyes were wild, his clothes dirty and stained. As he stood just on the other side of her table, he rocked from side to side and slowly opened and closed his hands.

Finding a sliver of courage, Shelby gently asked, "Are you all right? We've been worried about you. We didn't know where you were."

He didn't answer as his eyes went to her suit. Those almost deranged eyes lingered there as if memorizing every detail and, as the seconds ticked by, Mace's face twisted into something that somehow mirrored pain, rage, and humor all at the same time. And then she remembered Barrister's warnings about wearing blue. That was the trigger. Her mouth dried, she swallowed hard, and she silently prayed for a miracle while looking for someplace to run and hide.

"I loved you," he whispered as he took a small step to his left. While still closing and opening his hands, inch by inch, he continued to work his way around the table coming closer and closer to where she stood.

"Where did you hide?" she asked while taking a step back.

"I know places," he assured her. "I know lots of places. I'll show them to you. We can hide there too. They'll never find us."

It would be at least ten minutes before Minser returned. No one was due for an alteration. If she was going to survive, it was going to be up to her. Never taking her eyes off Mace, Shelby took four more backward steps.

"Willie," she suggested calmly as she moved, "we need to talk."

"About what?" he asked. He was moving, too, even faster than she was, and now was just three feet away; so close his hands could almost reach her throat.

"You need to get some help," she said as she took another step backward. There would be no more steps; the wall was now against her back.

He grinned, "I don't want to go back there. The only thing that was good there was the garden." He got a faraway look in his eyes before adding,

"I worked with the flowers and the rose bushes. Whenever a flower or rose was damaged, they taught me to get rid of it." Mace took two more steps. He was now close enough that she could feel his breath. "Flynn Sparks damaged you just like he did those others. You were beautiful until you went home with him."

So that was it. Mace saw Sparks as a parasite that destroyed women just as an insect might damage a flower, and he pruned the damaged women just like he'd once pruned the damaged plants. How paradoxical was it that the very place he was sent to get help accidentally gave him the motive and justification to kill? And, in his mind, she was the next damaged flower he must get rid of. What could she do or say to prove to Mace that she was still pure?

"Flynn never touched me," Shelby announced, her voice shaking as she pushed out the words.

"I saw him kiss you," he shot back. "I was hiding by your house, and I saw him put his lips on yours. I watched you a lot. I used to hide and watch as you came home."

So that was who was in the shadows. Those were the eyes she felt in the darkness.

"Why did you let him kiss you?"

Shelby was trying to think of a response when Mace lunged forward. For a big man, he was quick. Somehow ducking under his arms, she managed to escape and dash around her table toward the outside door. Moving like a wildcat, Mace leapt up on the workstation, knocking the pattern, a bolt of material, and needles and thread in all directions. Then using the table as a launching pad, he bounded at her like a lion would an antelope. As he landed on top of Shelby, his powerful hands grabbed her shoulders and took her to the ground. Her face pinned against the floor, she sensed the end was near. With his knees pinning her body to the floor, she couldn't breathe and had no chance of moving. Then he did some-thing unexpected and bizarre. Rather than place his powerful hands around her neck, he moved his legs until he straddled Shelby, grabbed her arms and roughly turned her over.

His face was just inches from hers as, with lightning quickness, his hands jumped from her arms to her neck. He then moved his legs just enough to pin her back to the ground. She lashed out with her hands, trying to get to his face and tear at his eyes—those eyes that now wouldn't release their grip on hers—but his hulking shoulders fended off her wild swinging. She then felt his thumbs push on her throat, and as he began to apply pressure, Mace nodded and smiled.

"Shelby." He whispered as he squeezed harder. "Just relax, it will all be over very soon. And then you'll be perfect again. You'll be just like you were before Flynn Sparks ruined you."

"No!"

A man's voice coming from the back of the room caused Mace to relax just enough for the woman to grab his wrists and dig her sharp fingernails into his flesh. The unexpected pain caused him to rise up off the ground just enough for her to roll over and scramble under his arms and away from his grip. As she pushed off the floor, she saw a shocked Flynn Sparks standing just two feet inside the doorway. Mace, responding now like a cornered animal, rushed the intruder, catching him with a shoulder in the chest and driving him into the wall. Sparks's head struck a shelf holding hundreds of hats. Scores of the bonnets, fedoras, and Stetsons crashed to the floor along with the actor. Not fully unconscious but obviously stunned, Sparks's eyes rolled back in his head, and he struggled to stand. Like a boxer who'd just taken a right to the jaw, he rose to one knee and then, when Mace delivered a hook, the actor collapsed.

With Sparks taken care of, a now even more enraged Mace turned back to Shelby. He studied her momentarily before racing forward. A frantic Shelby glanced to a seemingly helpless Sparks before turning and running back toward her workstation. When she arrived at her workstation she did the unthinkable and turned to face her attacker.

"Don't come any closer," she warned.

Mace, likely stunned by her boldness, stopped. He stood there panting like a wild beast as his eyes locked once more onto hers, then with no warning, he leapt forward. Reaching back to the table, she grabbed her cutting shears in her right hand and pushed them forward. Her attacker's hands were just inches from her neck when Shelby drove the large, sharp scissors into her attacker's stomach. Stepping quickly to her left, she watched him stagger for a moment and then fall to his knees. Running over to the phone, she called the switchboard. As soon as the operator answered, a breathless Shelby screamed into the receiver, "Willard Mace, the man the police are looking for, is in the finishing room in the wardrobe department. Send the cops and also the studio doctor."

Sparks, his senses now beginning to return, pushed off the floor and wobbled more than walked to her side. "Are you OK?" he asked.

"Yes," she replied, "your timing was perfect."

After rubbing his head, Sparks looked down at Mace, now face down on the floor, and noted, "I guess this case is a wrap."

"I prayed for a hero," she announced as her hand went to his shoulder.

"And you got a heel," he quickly acknowledged. "In truth, it looks like you saved me."

She nodded, "Seems like you've been saved a couple of times this morning. About the only thing left to save is your soul. Maybe we can save that another time."

The outside door burst open, and Barrister and Jenkins, guns drawn, marched in. The pair rushed over to Mace, rolled the man onto his back and carefully studied the strangler that Shelby had somehow taken down.

"He's alive," the captain announced.

"Good," Shelby replied, relief obvious in her tone.

"Good?" Sparks shot back. "He's killed a half dozen or more women, and you're glad that he's not dead?"

"He's not all there," she explained. "His mind is injured, and he can't always reason."

"But he kills people," Sparks argued.

Shelby shrugged, "In his mind, he is just getting rid of those who are damaged to make room for those who are perfect."

Barrister looked up from where he knelt beside Mace. "But no one is perfect."

"And that's Willie's problem. In his mind some are, but when they fall from grace, he gives them no second chances."

"I sense a sermon coming on," Sparks complained.

She smiled and looked at the actor, "Flynn, I forgive you for being a jerk and a host of other things. And I think God is willing to do that too." Her eyes turned back to the madman she'd stopped, "And I forgive him too. He simply did not have the ability to realize what he was doing."

Her eyes went from Mace back to Sparks, "Now, why did you come down here today?"

"To apologize," he admitted. "But don't confuse this one act as a sign of a complete change of character. Besides, I have a date with a script girl. I got to talking to her after we wrapped today, and she finds me a flawed but interesting character."

Shelby smiled, reached up, and kissed Sparks on the cheek.

"Excuse me," he announced, "that's no way to say thanks to the guy who walked in, tried, and miserably failed to save your life." Pulling her mouth to his, he gave her what many would call a movie kiss. Just as they were about to break their embrace, Dalton Andrews strolled in, followed by the studio doctor. As the physician moved to treat Mace, Andrews looked at Shelby, shook his head, turned, and stormed out.

"Whoops," Sparks said.

82

July 22, 1936

Shelby finished work at seven. As her father had already gone home and as she was going to have to call a cab, she opted to spend a bit of time by herself trying to put things into perspective. So, with time on her hands, she strolled over to New York Street, down the New Orleans set, and through Western town. At the end of the block, she walked up to the church and tried the door. Surprisingly, it was open. She made her way inside, stopped, looked at the cross hanging on the wall, and then took a seat in the back pew. She was lost somewhere between prayer and sleep when the door opened and Dalton Andrews walked in.

He undid the button on his suit coat, pushed his hands into his pockets, and looked at the floor. She watched him fidget for a few moments before she finally broke the silence.

"Have you ever wondered," she asked, "why the back pew is closest to the church's front door? And did you ever stop to consider that the front of the sanctuary is actually the most distant point from the front door? I wonder what the logic behind that is?"

"I don't know," he admitted. "In fact, I'm not sure I know much of anything anymore. I mean, this morning I was sure Flynn was a killer, and now I realize he's just a jerk."

"Maybe a bit less of one," Shelby suggested, "than he was yesterday."

Andrews took a deep breath and said, "You might be right. I mean it was Flynn who told me what that kiss was all about. I just assumed . . ."

She cut him off, "Never assume anything on a studio lot. In fact, I think you were the one who first told me that. Everything is fake, and nothing is as it seems."

Andrews looked up and smiled, "You've had quite an effect on Flynn. He actually told me the truth for a change. And not just about the kiss. He admitted that you actually had to save his life."

"And," she added, "he actually came into the finishing room to apologize to me. That's another big step for him. We might reform him yet."

"It will be a lifelong project," the actor laughed. As his eyes caught hers, his expression grew more serious. "Shelby, I was wondering if you were going to sign up to try to change Flynn? I mean, he does have his charms, and if you are, I could understand."

"I'm not signing up for anything," she assured him. "Right now I'm just thankful to be alive. What about you? What's in your future?"

He chuckled, "You're never going to believe

this. Barrister thinks I need to become a cop."

"You did good work," Shelby admitted. "But it would mean a huge pay cut."

"Yeah, and I don't think I'm ready for that. Besides, playing people in the movies is one thing, playing with people's lives for real is another."

An awkward silence once more descended into the room. As it dragged on, Andrews picked up a hymnal and looked through the pages. Shelby studied the handsome man for a few moments before finally opening up her heart.

"Dalton, I have a confession to make. Until I found that stuff in Flynn's house, I thought you might be the murderer. The way you acted that night at my house, the fact you seemed to hate your sister, and she died while wearing blue, it all kind of fell into place to where I doubted you."

He nodded, "Speaking like my character, I can understand that."

She nodded, "What's going to happen to the studio? I mean it looks like the guy who runs it is gone."

"It will survive," Andrews assured her. "The studio is more than Yates. Someone else will buy it and come in and run it. Times aren't easy out there in the real world, and people still need to escape their dismal lives sometimes. What better way to do that than a movie? And the movie we will finish when we film that last scene where you take down Mace will likely be the biggest motion picture in the history of Galaxy Studios." He paused and looked deeply into her blue eyes. "But I didn't come up here to talk about the studio. I came here to find out what is going to happen to us. Now that we've been through what we have been through, can we try again?"

Shelby shook her head sadly, "You're not Jasper anymore, and I'm not that kid who came here six weeks ago from Oklahoma. We can't live in the past. We can't pretend we are not here in Los Angeles, and we can't ignore what has happened to us. I'm a different person. I almost died today. And before that I met people who did die. I'm not sure I can trust anyone besides my parents right now." She took a deep breath, "Especially someone from the studio. I want my world to be real."

"Shelby," Andrews suggested, "maybe we can't be who we were, but could you ever love who I really am?"

Rather than answer, she shrugged.

A disappointed Andrews looked toward the pulpit. He studied it for a moment before asking, "What about that song you sang? You know, the old gospel hymn."

" 'Love Will Roll the Clouds Away,' " she said.

He turned his face toward hers and asked, "Does love really roll the clouds away, or are gospel songs and hymns like the movie business?

Are they ways to escape reality rather than being things to cling to?"

Shelby stood and walked over to the man. She wrapped her arm around his, leaned her head into his shoulder, and whispered, "I don't know if I love you, and I can't know until I deal with what has happened today. There has been too much senseless death and too much fantasy covering up the truth. You need to give me some time. Why don't you call me in a few weeks, and maybe we can go out then?"

"To a movie?" he asked.

"Anything but a movie," she replied.

"I'll wait," he assured her as he leaned down and kissed her forehead. "Just let me know when."

Andrews turned and walked down the aisle and out of the building. She followed behind him to the church door and watched him slowly make his way down the steps to the lonely street. He was almost to the livery stable when a voice deep inside her demanded she take a leap of faith. Rushing down the steps two at time, she cried out, "Dalton, wait a minute! I just realized I need a ride home."

Group Discussion Guide

1. The Great Depression saw hundreds of thousands of people move from the heartland to California. One of the best-selling books in American history, *The Grapes of Wrath*, dealt with these refugees' struggles. Why did most head to California rather than go east or north?

2. Shelby is obviously levelheaded and mature beyond her twenty-one years. What do you feel caused her to grow up so fast?

3. Rather than discipline Flynn Sparks, Jacob Yates sought ways to cover up the star's moral failings. Why would he do this, and where do you see examples of this in your own life?

4. How did their lives before stardom shape Flynn Sparks and Dalton Andrews? How did it affect the way they viewed what fame and fortune could bring them?

5. Rev. and Mrs. Sykes tried to put off having Barrister actually give them the news of their daughter's death. Do you think this was a natural response, and why do you feel they didn't want to actually hear the truth?

6. Sparks won Andrews's Packard automobile on a bet. Why do you think it was so important for him to get the actor's car? And how did the Auburn Speedster better reflect Sparks's personality than the Packard?

7. Barrister feels pressure to avoid direct dealings with the major film studios. Why do the mayor and police chief fear alienating those in the movie business?

8. Ellen Rains is just a reporter, so why does she have so much power? Why are people so scared of her? And do you see her as a positive or negative force in Hollywood?

9. Why do you think movies in the 1930s were largely dialogue-driven rather than action-driven as they are today?

10. In the 1930s, racism was a largely accepted part of society. How was this obvious in the motion picture business?

11. Shelby quickly discovers that in Hollywood the studios rewrite people's pasts to fit the kind of people they want to sell to the public. What do you think that did to an actress's or actor's identity away from the cameras? Would it make it harder for them to remember values taught to them in the past?

12. Would using a studio church building really offer any opportunity for real worship? Could the fact that the structure was built for "show" keep it from being a place where spiritual lessons could be taught and learned? Why or why not?

13. What ironies did you note in having a lavish party raise money for the poor? Do you know of any cases where this still happens today?

14. What was Jacob Yates's real motive in making the movie about the strangulations?

15. Do you feel, as Shelby seems to, that poverty often makes it easier to give in to temptations that compromise a person's values? Why?

16. How did her mother's actions affect Minser's view of men? Do you feel this is what is meant by "the sins of the parents shall be visited upon their children"?

17. Barrister pushed Shelby hard. Why do you think this seemingly protective father was so intent on putting Shelby into a dangerous situation? What were his motives, and do you feel they were justified?

18. Shelby stands up for the man who seems most guilty. What in her background do you believe gave her the courage to speak up during the filming of a key scene in the movie?

19. What significance does the message found in Shelby's favorite gospel song have to Andrews?

20. Why did Shelby go back to the studio church at the end of the story? What do you think she was hoping to find there?

Be sure to visit Ace online!

www.acecollins.com

Center Point Large Print
600 Brooks Road / PO Box 1
Thorndike, ME 04986-0001 USA

(207) 568-3717

US & Canada:
1 800 929-9108
www.centerpointlargeprint.com